North Carolina

North Carolina

Three Novels of Romance
Nestled in the Heart
of the Tar Heel State

Terry Fowler

BARBOUR
PUBLISHING

Carolina Pride © 2002 by Terry Fowler
Look to the Heart © 2005 by Terry Fowler
A Sense of Belonging © 1998 by Barbour Publishing, Inc.

ISBN 1-59789-109-6

Cover art by GettyOne

Published by Barbour Publishing, Inc., P.O. Box 719, Uhrichsville, Ohio 44683, www.barbourbooks.com

Our mission is to publish and distribute inspirational products offering exceptional value and biblical encouragement to the masses.

Printed in the United States of America.
5 4 3 2

Dear Reader,

I love calling North Carolina home. For me, *A Sense of Belonging, Carolina Pride*, and *Look to the Heart* reflect the heart and soul of North Carolina—home and family.

Always an avid reader, I dreamed of becoming a librarian, but circumstances prevailed and I work full time in an office.

After losing my parents in 1991 and having my own medical crises in 1992, I accepted I couldn't do it alone. I gave my life to God.

God had plans to use my love of books in a different way. My greatest joy is to witness for my beloved Savior in my writing.

I'm the second oldest in a family of five and share a home with my sister. She's also my best friend. I also enjoy working in my church, gardening, home decorating, and genealogical research. Please visit my webpage at www.terryfowler.net.

Yours in Christ,
Terry Fowler

Carolina Pride

Chapter 1

Okay, God, here's another fine mess I've gotten myself into. Liza Stephens stood defeated in the latest battle of her life—that of a seventy-pound puppy and a five-pound cat. Listening to them growl and hiss at each other throughout the ten-mile drive should have clued her in that she was heading for trouble. Instead, she'd ignored the situation.

After parking at the vet's office, she'd grabbed Barney, her Saint Bernard puppy, under one arm and Fluff, her mother's cat, under the other. It was then that Barney took offense to Fluff's presence, and his fight to reach the cat resulted in Liza's current dilemma.

Mama always said God looked out for fools and children. Right now, Liza certainly felt she belonged in the first category. Why did doing good deeds always seem to backfire on her?

Liza eyed her purse on the roof of the car, just out of reach. She could let go of either of the animals to retrieve it, but Barney was an obedience school dropout; Liza doubted her mother would appreciate her allowing Fluff to take off for the woods, probably with Barney hot on her trail.

It wouldn't work anyway. Her oversized shirt was caught in the car door, effectively pinning her to the side of the car. Liza leaned back to wait. Hopefully someone would soon leave the vet's office, and she could further embarrass herself by asking for help.

"Stop it, Barney," she snapped when the dog made a move for Fluff. She tried shifting the cat away, only to be jerked back by her shirttail. She was well and truly stuck.

Dropping the keys into her bag probably hadn't been the smartest thing she'd ever done. A new thought entered her head. What if a thief took advantage of her predicament?

Leave it to her—and all because she tried to be a good daughter. It wasn't enough to spend half the night working with her dad on his books. Her mother shook her awake at the crack of dawn on a Saturday morning with a request to take Barney and Fluff to the vet.

"Not together," she objected. "They'll kill each other."

"I'll ask your dad to do it later."

"No. I'll take them."

After all, Barney was her pet. Maybe she should just let him go for help.

9

Another bad idea. He definitely did not understand the premise of being a rescue animal. Letting go of Barney would probably mean neither she nor Fluff would survive. She was already caught between the two of them. There was no need to get teeth and claws involved.

"You'd think you two could get along after six months," she muttered.

Barney's response was a low growl in his throat and a renewed fight for freedom.

"Shut up, idiot."

"Excuse me?"

Liza looked straight into the eyes of the most handsome man she'd seen in a long time. He stood tall and confident, his hair a sun-streaked brown, his face a mixture of jutting cheekbones, strong nose, arrogant chin, and the most penetrating blue eyes she'd ever encountered.

"No. No. . .not you," Liza stammered. "The dog. I seem to have gotten myself into a predicament." Shifting the animals, she said, "My shirt's caught in the car door."

He chuckled, and Liza felt a telltale blush trailing its way over her face. She hated situations like this—feeling out of control. "Could you get my keys? They're in my bag."

He lifted the purse and flipped the flap back, glancing at her. "May I?"

"Please do."

Watching him remove item after item, Liza grew even more embarrassed. One of these days, she was going to clean that thing out. She'd put it on her schedule, right after the next time she took these two animals anywhere ever again.

She released a relieved sigh at the welcome jingle of her key ring. The audible click of the locks disengaging when he hit the remote button was a beautiful sound. She tried to shift to open the door and grimaced when the shirt jerked her back again.

"Maybe I should open it from inside."

He went around to the passenger side, and seconds later when the door popped open, she was freed. "Thank You, God," Liza murmured.

He came back around the car and asked, "How did you manage that?"

Everything had happened so fast. While struggling to keep the animals separated, she'd backed up against the door to close it, planning to grab her purse. "It seemed awfully easy at the time. I can't tell you how much I appreciate your help. I figured I'd be caught in the midst of a fur fight any moment."

He chuckled again and held out his hand. "Hi. I'm Lee Hayden."

Liza glanced at the animals and shrugged, lifting Fluff higher to extend her little finger. "Liza Stephens."

Lee grinned and shook her pinkie. "Why don't I lock up the car and help you get your furry friends inside?"

"Thanks again."

"No problem." He pushed the items back into her purse, along with her keys. He tucked it under his arm. "Lead the way."

Lee pulled open the office door and waited for her to go first. She stopped at the chest-high desk and stared at the clipboard. "Hi, Sheila. Could you sign us in?"

"Liza, my goodness. You look great."

"Thanks," she murmured self-consciously. "Barney and Fluff need their shots."

"Have a seat. We'll be with you soon."

Two other Saturday-morning patients waited with their owners in the small waiting area. Liza chose a chair in the corner and sat. Another dilemma arose when she tried to figure out a way to free her hold on the animals. She glanced up as her rescuer spoke to Sheila.

"Could you tell Dr. Wilson that Legrande Hayden is here to see him, please? It's a personal call."

"Certainly, sir. Have a seat."

Lee took the chair next to Liza. "Does he bite?" he asked, indicating Barney.

"He never has before, but today I make no promises."

"I'll hold onto him if you'd like."

"No, I couldn't," Liza said.

"It's no problem."

She considered her dilemma and relented. "If you're sure you don't mind. Just put him on the floor. You don't want dog hair all over your clothes."

Lee shifted Barney to sit by his leg and petted his head. "He's a big fellow."

"He's going to get bigger. Daddy says he doesn't know who eats more—Barney or my horse."

"Unless it's a very small pony, I'd say the horse." The phone rang, and when Sheila answered, Lee glanced at her and back at Liza. "Why did she act so surprised just now?"

Startled by his question, Liza's head jerked up. Leaning back in the yellow plastic chair, she hugged Fluff closer and rubbed a hand over the tabby fur. "My metamorphosis. You could say they knew me when."

"When what?" he persisted.

People's reaction to her changed outer appearance had been startling. Inwardly she was the same, but they rarely looked that deep. "I've lost weight. My changed exterior shocks people." Liza rubbed her neck self-consciously at his intent examination.

"I'm intrigued."

Eager to change the subject, she said, "You've got an interesting name. Legrande. I've never heard it before."

"Lee, please. I try not to use Legrande any more than necessary. I was named after my father and grandfather."

She nodded, a smile touching the corners of her mouth. "Family name. I can identify with that. I'm a heaven-only-knows-what-generation Sarah Elizabeth. The name has been given to the oldest daughter of the oldest daughter in my mother's family for years. I have a grandmother named Elizabeth, a mother named Sarah, and until recently I had a great-grandmother named Beth."

"And you're Liza." Her name slipped easily from his tongue.

Another pet and owner came through the door. After signing in, the man chose a seat farther away from them. The boxer promptly obeyed his command to sit.

"Be quiet," Liza demanded when Barney growled in his throat.

Lee grinned. "He's a brave fellow."

"Not sure if he's brave or stupid. That dog could eat him for lunch. Barney, stop it," she repeated, pulling the dog's head toward her. "You're going to start a fight."

Disdain marked the boxer's owner's face as he looked at Barney. "You need to show that animal who's boss."

"He's just a puppy," Liza defended.

"Who will grow into an unmanageable dog unless you gain control now."

Liza hid her grin in Fluff's fur when the boxer growled at Barney. The man's stern command quieted the animal, but the danger of the situation made her a bit nervous. Maybe she should take Barney out until it was time for the vet to see them.

Sheila noticed the commotion. "Bring them on back, Liza."

Only then did it occur to Liza that she hadn't thought to bring a leash. Seeing her dilemma, Lee caught hold of Barney's collar. "I've got him."

"No, you've done so much already," she protested.

The boxer's owner spoke sharply to his dog when he responded to Barney's growl.

Feeling totally out of her depth, Liza said, "I suppose you think I'm an irresponsible pet owner, too?"

Lee walked between the Saint Bernard and the other dog, pulling up tighter on Barney's collar when he attempted to free himself.

"Dr. Wilson will see you now, sir."

"Actually I think you're the perfect pet owner. It's been my pleasure, Liza."

Lee lifted Barney onto the table in the exam room and said good-bye before following the assistant out into the hallway.

The men's affectionate greeting made Liza wonder about their connection. Fluff jerked her attention back to the animals when Barney made a dive for her, and the cat buried her claws in Liza's side.

❧

"So this knight in shining armor came to your rescue?" her best friend, Kitty Berenson, prompted.

"He freed me from my prison." Liza propped the phone between her ear and shoulder, then stuck the brush into the polish bottle and slid it over her nail. "I hate to think what he thought when he saw me standing there with my arms full of animals and my shirt caught in the car door."

"Tell me about him," Kitty's cheery voice demanded.

Liza shared all she knew. "I wonder what he's doing here?"

"How long did you say you were you with this guy?"

"Fifteen, twenty minutes."

"And you didn't get his life history? I'm shocked."

No doubt she was. In that amount of time, Kitty would have discovered everything from Lee's date of birth to his current financial status.

"Not all of us have your ability, Kit."

"It is a gift," she boasted playfully, bursting into laughter.

Liza laughed. "Sheila made a big deal out of my appearance, and he asked why."

"Hmm. I think he's interested. Maybe you'll see him again soon."

"I doubt that."

"Too bad. Sounds like a nice guy. Gotta run. Dave's picking me up soon."

"Don't forget our duet in the morning."

"Why don't you just sing a solo? You sing better anyway."

Liza leaned forward. "Kitty, you promised."

"Okay, don't tie yourself in knots. I'll be there."

Her tense muscles relaxed. "You think tonight's the night?"

"I don't know what Dave's thinking. I'm sure he'll get around to popping the question one of these days."

"He'd better do it soon if you want that June wedding."

Kitty sighed loudly. "Too late for a June wedding now. I'd never get it planned in time."

"You've been planning this wedding since you were seven. You're going to get married down by the pond."

"Tastes change," Kitty said. "When I say 'I do' to David Evans, it's going to be a wedding this town won't forget anytime soon. Take care."

Liza replaced the phone and leaned back against her pillows, fanning her hands to dry the clear polish. Thoughts of Kitty and Dave's romance were soon replaced with fantasies of finding her own Prince Charming.

Every day she prayed that the Lord would send her life partner soon, but the situation seemed more and more hopeless. Not only was there a shortage of men in their small country town, but those she knew treated her more like their kid sister than an eligible female.

She had to agree with Kit on one matter: It was too bad Lee Hayden wouldn't be around. She could easily see him in the role of knight.

Chapter 2

Struggling to get her key into the lock, Liza juggled her briefcase and the mail, frowning when the old door opened easily. Mr. Wilson must have come in early again. After laying the mail on her desk, she went into the kitchenette to put on the coffee. It had become part of her routine since the day she'd found her boss disastrously close to poisoning himself and their clients with his own unpalatable brew.

While it perked, Liza opened the mail and pulled files, humming the song she and Kit had sung at church the previous day. Sometimes she found it difficult to believe she was actually standing before the congregation and singing.

What a difference the years had made! In high school, she'd suffered from terminal shyness. Even the thought of a simple oral book report caused nightmares. But that was before she figured out the miracles God was capable of when He said, "You can."

Lifting the stack of files, she stopped off to pour coffee in her boss's favorite mug. Liza pushed his office door open and was rendered speechless.

With the exception of a tattered hat sporting fishing lures of all descriptions, the desktop was clear. Her workaholic boss leaned dangerously far back in his chair, his feet propped on the corner of the desk. Clothes that had seen better days replaced his usual conservative suit.

Liza chuckled. "You forget to change this morning?"

His feet dropped to the floor. "Morning, Liza. I just came by to tell you I'm taking your advice and going on vacation and to make the introductions."

Liza set the coffee cup on his desk. "Introductions?" she repeated curiously.

John Wilson sipped the coffee and said, "I couldn't expect you to take on the office single-handedly."

"You could have," Liza mumbled. It wasn't as if she'd be idle. She had cases to research, tons of filing, and a phone that never stopped ringing.

"What was that?" he asked absently, missing her remark when a fluorescent orange lure on the hat caught his attention.

"Nothing." More than a little confused, Liza concentrated on spreading the files across the desktop. John Wilson wasn't usually a spur-of-the-moment man. Why now?

"We have a new attorney joining us."

"New attorney?" Liza parroted. What had changed? Mr. Wilson had always maintained they could do the work of six normal people. Why hadn't he mentioned his plans before?

"Should be arriving anytime now." The tan hat flopped back and forth with his efforts to release the fishhook. "First-class lawyer. Glad to get him," he rambled on. "Feels he needs to get out of Charlotte. Thinks this is a good opportunity to see another side of law."

"Sounds fascinating," Liza muttered.

"I hope I am."

Liza spun about to find Lee Hayden propped against the doorjamb. His look was one of faint amusement; his penetrating gaze fixed on her. "Leave your furry friends home today?"

She'd imagined meeting the handsome stranger again, but not like this. Surely he wasn't the new attorney? Mr. Wilson confirmed her suspicions by moving from behind the desk and hurrying to greet him.

"Glad to have you with us. Any problem locating the office?"

Lee straightened and grasped the man's hand. "None at all. You give excellent directions."

"Good. Good," he said, patting Lee on the shoulder. "Did you find a place to stay? There's always room at the house."

"I'm at the hotel."

Needing time to compose herself, Liza turned to leave.

"Oh yes," Mr. Wilson said, catching her arm when she started past him. "I want to introduce you to my secretary. Elizabeth Stephens, this is my nephew, Legrande Hayden."

His secretary? He hadn't called her that since she'd received her paralegal degree. Sure, she still did the typing and filing, but she was more than clerical help.

"We've met, sir," Liza acknowledged. "He came to my rescue Saturday at Dr. Wilson's office. Nice to see you again, Mr. Hayden. Welcome to the firm."

"Good. Good." Mr. Wilson gathered his hat from the desk, downed the coffee, and handed Liza the cup. "Teach him everything I've taught you. I'll see you both in a couple of weeks."

"But you have appointments," she said, totally baffled by his strange behavior.

"Lee can handle them. Help him."

Mr. Wilson chuckled at her surprised expression, tapping her chin to tip her mouth closed before he walked toward the door. His cheerful whistle filled the room.

"Lee," he said, "we'll discuss those plans for the future when I get back."

"Have a good vacation, Uncle John. Don't worry about the office."

Liza's gaze moved from Mr. Wilson's back to the desk. Lee had already slipped into his uncle's chair and lifted a folder from the desk. *Make yourself at home,* she thought grimly. The phone rang, and as she reached for it, their hands collided. "I'm the secretary, remember? John Wilson, Attorney-at-Law. May I help you?"

She propped the phone on her shoulder, setting the cup on the desk as she moved the files, hunting for the one she needed. "No, sir. Not yet."

The stream of crude words being shouted into her ear made Liza wish she had the nerve to hang up on the man. "I know you want it now. The papers just arrived in this morning's mail. I can. . ." She frowned. "Okay, if that's what you want. If you can't wait, you'll have to see Mr. Hayden. Mr. Wilson's out of the office. Fine. I'll call you back with a date and time. Yes, I'll make sure it's this week."

The receiver bounced when she replaced it in the cradle. First, Mr. Wilson didn't even think he owed it to her to share his plans, and now the clients wanted someone else when she could help. She looked up, meeting Lee's gaze.

"You want to tell me what's wrong?"

"Nothing."

"Your face is too expressive."

She didn't like that he could read her so easily. "Don't mind me. Nobody tells me anything, but I'm expected to know everything," she announced in a fit of pique.

"You're upset about me," Lee guessed.

The fight left Liza, her voice growing soft as she said, "I'm sorry. I shouldn't take my frustrations out on you."

His look grew even more serious. "You don't have to apologize. I'm sorry, too. Uncle John shouldn't have sprung this on you. He values you highly. In fact, he feels you have a lot of potential going to waste in this one-lawyer office."

Her boss had voiced his sentiments on the matter numerous times. "Some people do better behind the scenes than in the spotlight. I like being a paralegal just fine."

"Don't sell yourself short," Lee warned. "Uncle John knows the law and how capable you are."

"Thanks, but I'll stay where I am."

"I'm glad to have you here. Did you get Barney and Fluff home unscathed?"

What a way to be remembered. "Dr. Wilson loaned me a cardboard carrier for Fluff. That's the last time I take those two anywhere together."

"I imagine Uncle Dennis took it all in stride."

Everything clicked into place. Dr. Dennis Wilson, the town's vet and Mr. Wilson's brother, was Lee's other uncle. There was a sister who had left town years before. She must be his mom.

"Thanks again for coming to my rescue."

"Rescuing a lovely lady is always a pleasure." He indicated the desktop. "Are you ready to tackle this? You mentioned appointments?"

Liza pulled a chair up to the desk. She'd thought about Lee Hayden several times over the weekend, but not even in her wildest imagination had she thought they'd be working together.

And work they did. Never before had Liza labored so long and hard. Used to Mr. Wilson's more laid-back "we'll get it done tomorrow" attitude, she found herself struggling to keep up with Lee's driving demands. He examined every client file with great care and capably handled a number of situations that arose.

Although Liza felt certain Lee asked no more of her than he felt she was capable of performing, she found herself stretching to reach heights never before attained. She even changed her working style to match his and stayed late to complete the work he assigned, all the time thinking his momentum couldn't last.

The Friday signaling the end of the first week proved to be one of those irritating days when no matter how hard she tried, Liza accomplished nothing. She typed until her arms and shoulders ached, all the while dealing with constant interruptions. The telephone seemed to ring every minute and unscheduled clients dropped by, hoping to take care of business while in town.

When she finished the page, Liza took a break, working out the kinks in her neck as she ran the spell-checker. Involved with the legal jargon, she didn't hear Lee enter her office.

"Did you finish the Johnson brief yet?"

"Can't it wait?" Liza asked, dreading the thought of starting another lengthy document.

"You need to finish it before you go." At her disappointed look, his brow lifted, and he asked, "Can't you keep up?"

Resentful that he would criticize her competence, Liza snapped to attention. "If I couldn't, I can assure you I wouldn't be here, Mr. Hayden."

Lee waved a hand over her jumbled desk. "Then I can assume you plan to finish this tonight?"

Take it easy, Liza cautioned, forcing herself to take a deep breath. The downward sweep of long lashes dropped shutters over her hazel eyes. "Of course. It'll be on your desk within the hour."

After he left, she wasted precious seconds slamming folders around in her hunt for the right one. She knew her job. She'd been in this office for ten years, and he might be in charge now, but he wouldn't be in that role forever. Once Mr. Wilson got back, things would return to normal.

Liza laid the completed work on his desk exactly within the allotted hour.

"Good job," Lee complimented, signing his name with a flourish.

"Is that all?" she asked coolly.

He leaned back in the executive chair. "You're upset again. Why?"

Like he doesn't know the answer to that question. Liza permitted herself the luxury of a withering stare, lifted the stack of files, and marched from the room.

The file cabinet trembled when she jerked the drawer open. Determined not to leave one paper out of place, Liza quickly inserted the folders into the proper slots.

Lee followed, propping his hip on the edge of her desk. "What did I do?"

"I don't much care for being pushed," she snapped.

"I wasn't pushing."

"Right," came her sarcastic reply. She whirled about to face him. "I don't like having my ability questioned either. I don't work eighty-hour weeks. This is a small country town. We don't have hundreds of thousands of people, and those we do have aren't in as much of an all-fired hurry as you seem to think. Besides that, the Johnson trial isn't on the docket until next month. Monday wouldn't have made one bit of difference."

"I need to familiarize myself with the case."

In the course of her work, she had met a number of men but never one who exuded so much self-confidence. At times she was intimidated by his confident behavior, but not now. "Mr. Wilson will be back long before then. He knows the case inside out."

"I need to know it the same way."

His needs were beginning to get on her nerves. "Well, I need to go home and catch up on the chores I haven't been able to do this week."

"But I thought we would. . ."

Pushed to breaking point, Liza said, "I've done two people's work all week. I won't do it again. If that's the way you work, find yourself a new secretary."

She grabbed her purse from the drawer and started toward the door. Tears stung her eyes, blinding her.

"Liza, wait."

As Liza fumbled with the doorknob, Lee moved closer. He lifted her chin to look into her eyes and rubbed away the tears with his thumb. The wild flutter of her pulse when he smiled didn't surprise her.

"I'm sorry. Forgive me?"

"Sure." She felt embarrassed by her outburst. She would have never reacted to Mr. Wilson's requests in such a manner.

"Why are you conscience-stricken whenever you take a stand?"

"Because I feel guilty for treating you badly. My behavior just now was totally uncalled for."

"Your friends aren't going to stop liking you because you stand up for yourself. They aren't friends if they do."

18

Powerful relief filled her. "And are you a friend?"

"I'd like to be. Have dinner with me tonight."

It was more of a command than a request. When she hesitated, he prompted, "Say yes. This cruel boss wants to make amends to his hardworking assistant, and this man wants to see the beautiful woman he rescued last week."

The invitation was so tempting. "I can't," she admitted reluctantly. "I really do have chores waiting at home."

Lee frowned. "Don't you have hired help?"

"I wish. Right now, Daddy's in the field from dawn to dusk, and I'm helping by feeding the livestock. Mom usually does that chore, but she hasn't been feeling well this week."

"And thanks to me, the animals have been getting their evening feed quite a bit later than usual. When do you finish?"

"It takes about an hour."

"A late dinner sounds fine. Meet me at the restaurant next to my hotel at nine o'clock."

Liza examined Lee's face closely. Was he sincere, or was it a ploy to keep her sweet so he could work her even harder next week? Her men-judging skills were rusty, to say the least. Should she go? Why not take a chance? She nodded. "Okay."

He was obviously pleased. "See you then."

After leaving the office parking lot, her red sports car flew along the country roads. Anticipation had replaced her exhaustion, and she arrived in record time, somehow without managing to break the speed limit.

"Mom," she called when she entered the house.

Sarah Stephens came to stand in the archway to the living room.

"I'm going into town after I feed up and change. I'll eat there. Oh," she cried, stopping on the bottom stair, "what about you and Daddy? You aren't up to fixing supper."

"Go on. We're going to your grandmother's in a few minutes. I feel much better. Just a spring cold."

"Are you sure?"

"We'll be fine."

Liza changed into jeans before rushing out to feed the animals. "There, Barney," she said, pouring food into his bowl. The dog barked, blocking her way when she tried to move back to the barn. She brushed him aside. "I don't have time to play now."

Every chore seemed to take twice as long as usual. After feeding the livestock, Liza raced back inside to shower and change. Glancing at the clock, she reached for the blow-dryer. She should have known better than to wash her hair. It took forever to dry.

Liza decided on a dressy pantsuit. After slipping her feet into sandals, she picked up a pair of earrings and tried to get them into her lobes while running down the stairs.

Doing a slow pirouette for her parents' inspection, she asked, "How do I look?"

"You look beautiful, honey," her father said, barely giving her a glance over his newspaper.

"Daddy," she groaned, leaning to kiss his weathered cheek. "I could be dressed in a clown suit, for all you know."

He dropped the paper and teased, "Seen you in one of those, too. You were pretty cute."

Liza grinned.

"Besides, I think you're beautiful no matter what you wear."

"Partial, I guess," she said, giving her mother a wink as she returned his hug.

"Tell Granny hello, and don't you overdo," she warned her mother. "See you later."

⁂

Lee found himself wondering if Liza was going to show up. He checked his watch and found it was still a few minutes before she was due.

Her reaction to his badgering had been a revelation. Miss Stephens might appear meek and mild, but when she got upset, she had quite a temper. He'd felt well and truly put in his place when she finished with him earlier.

Lee knew she was right. He had pushed her too far. He doubted Uncle John kept hours much beyond eight in the morning to five or six in the afternoon. She'd dealt with her normal workload as well as his requests for client files and research requests.

He hoped she'd understand that he was looking at the possibility of being in charge of his own destiny. The idea of being his own boss appealed immensely. Of course, his success depended on several factors.

Most importantly, he had to prove himself capable to his uncle. Family ties were strong, but Uncle John wasn't about to turn his clients over to an incompetent. Protecting his reputation was vital enough to make that his number one priority.

The hostess escorted Liza through the dimly lit room to his table. Lee admired Liza's understated elegance. Tonight she wore slacks and a blouse with appropriate jewelry—all very modest, but something was different.

Her hair, he realized. Since he'd first been attracted to girls, long hair drew his attention. Tonight Liza wore hers in a fantastic rippling cascade of dark curls.

He smiled his greeting and stood to pull out her chair, fighting back the urge to touch her hair. "You look great. You should wear your hair down like this more often. It's beautiful."

"Thank you."

"Did you get everything finished at home?"

"Yes," she said, shaking out the mauve napkin.

"How's your mother?"

He could tell she was nervous by the way she sipped ice water and then glanced around, paying a great deal of attention to the decor.

"Better. She says it's a summer cold."

"Hope you don't catch one. Summer colds are really difficult to get rid of. Liza," he said softly, "what's wrong?"

She glanced down at the table. "It's me. I don't know what to expect."

"Why do you have to expect anything?"

"I just do."

Reaching for her hand, he squeezed gently. "All right. What do you say to an amicable working relationship and an enjoyable evening?"

"I'd like that. I'm just not sure. . . ."

"Don't analyze everything to death. Tonight we're friends. Coworkers from nine to five. Or eight to whenever," he joked. "I'm really sorry about this week. Blame it on my personality."

Lee worked hard at making her feel comfortable. They sipped ice water and studied their menus, discussing the various entrées. They had just placed their order when a couple stopped by to say hello to Liza.

She introduced them as her best friends, Kitty Berenson and Dave Evans. "Lee's working at the office," she told them, adding, "He's my rescuer from last Saturday."

When her friend smiled and nodded, he knew the women had discussed him at some point.

"Kit, our table's ready," Dave said, slipping his arm about her waist.

"You're dining late," Liza said.

"Dave couldn't get away. He's promised to take me riding tomorrow to make it up to me. Say, why don't you join us? I'm sure Majesty could use the exercise. You should come, too, Mr. Hayden."

"The name's Lee, and I don't have a horse."

"I'm sure my brother would love it if you rode his. Sir doesn't get much exercise now that Jason's working all of the time."

"Name the time and place."

They made the arrangements, and after the other couple went to their table, Lee said, "So I get to see this horse that eats less than your dog?"

Liza laughed. "He's a pretty big fellow, too."

"And how does he feel about Fluff?"

"They tolerate each other."

"But you can't carry him underneath your arm." Reminded of Saturday's escapade, they laughed together.

"I'll be sure to tuck in my shirttail this time."

"I haven't ridden in a long time. Hopefully I won't make a fool of myself."

"You'd have to go a long way to look more idiotic than I did," she pointed out. "Besides, this will give you a chance to see some of the countryside. It's particularly beautiful this time of year."

"So tell me about being a farmer's daughter," Lee invited, pushing the appetizer tray in her direction.

Liza indicated she didn't care for any. "How 'bout I show you tomorrow?"

"Think this city slicker is up to the experience?" Lee gave her a wide grin.

"It might give you an entirely different outlook on life."

He shrugged. "I'm pretty open to new experiences, but after this week, is it safe to put myself in your hands?"

"Nothing safer."

"Then it's a deal." Lee offered his hand over the table.

When Liza slipped her hand into his, Lee felt a tingle of anticipation at the thought of spending a day away from work with her.

Chapter 3

After stuffing clothes into the washer, Liza reached into the cabinet for the detergent bottle.

"Can you run me into town?" her mother called from the kitchen.

The cup overflowed, and the liquid ran over Liza's hand. "Mom, I don't have time. Can't it wait?"

"Not if you want Sunday dinner."

"Did you ask Daddy?"

"Forget it."

Liza heard her mother mumbling as she went into the pantry to dig around in the freezer. Her car would be in the shop today, of all days. If only Mom would drive hers, but the woman refused to drive the sports car. Liza pushed back the twinge of guilt and shrugged. Daddy would take her. He had said something at breakfast about picking up a tractor part.

Still, Liza couldn't help feeling guilty. She'd never finish if she took time to go into town. Her bedroom was in shambles, and the outside chores needed to be done. Maybe her laundry and ironing could wait until one night next week. Why hadn't Kitty suggested riding earlier in the week? Better yet, why hadn't she suggested a Sunday afternoon ride?

A couple of hours later, Liza stood under the shower spray, trying to restore enough energy to get her through the afternoon. Everything was done, including the grocery shopping.

In the bedroom, Liza looked at the clothes that lay on her bed. Jeans and a plaid cotton shirt might not be high fashion, but they were comfortable and appropriate. She dressed and dug a pair of worn boots from the closet.

Braiding her hair, Liza recalled Lee's compliment and thought only briefly about leaving it down. Streaming in the wind, it was a nuisance when it whipped across her face and eyes.

Liza walked into the barn to get a bridle and came back to lean against the gate. She watched Majesty run in the paddock, his movements as fascinating as they had been the first time she saw him. The idea of having a show horse had intrigued her, but life got in the way of that venture; instead, she'd found he was a good horse for riding. She loved his graceful, perfectly coordinated steps.

Liza whistled, smiling when he came immediately. "You know we're going riding, don't you, boy?" she asked, rubbing his neck. Majesty nuzzled her shirt pocket in return. "Rascal." She fed him the horse candy, slipped the bridle in place, then led him through the gate and into the barn so she could finish saddling him.

The powerful roar of Lee's car engine could be heard coming up the road. Liza forced herself to linger in the barn. It wouldn't do for him to see how eager she was.

When the car door slammed and he called her name, she walked to the door and gestured him inside.

Lee hesitated when Barney raced toward him. "Are you sure he doesn't bite?"

"Only salesmen and city lawyers," she teased.

"Call him off."

Liza laughed. "Come on, Lee. He's gentle as a kitten."

"Yeah, Fluff would attest to that."

"Come here, Barney." Liza wasn't surprised when the dog failed to follow her command. She crossed the yard and buried her fingers in his thick coat to grab his collar.

Lee moved to her other side, giving the dog plenty of distance. He never seemed to be in a rush, even when he was in a hurry, yet she knew he was a dynamo rolled up into one neat package. For a second, she envied him his self-confidence, then she sighed. She couldn't have everything.

"Where's this fantastic horse?"

She indicated the hitching post by the barn. "Over here."

Lee followed, whistling low. "Beautiful animal."

"I knew Majesty was the one for me the minute I saw him," Liza admitted, petting the nose he thrust over her shoulder.

"Looks like he feels the same way," Lee said.

"He knows the good life, don't you, boy?" The horse whinnied in return. "Ready?"

Lee nodded, coming over to stroke Majesty's silky mane. He spoke softly to the animal before lifting his foot to the stirrup and swinging into the saddle. Gripping the reins securely, he held the horse still for Liza to mount.

"Not back there. Come up front so we can talk," Lee insisted.

"You'll be uncomfortable," she argued.

"Get up here."

"Okay," she murmured, "just remember whose idea it was."

"What's that?" he asked, indicating the plastic bag she held.

Liza pulled it to her. "A surprise."

"You'll spook the horse with that rattling."

"Majesty's not easily spooked."

He looked doubtful. "At least tell me what's in there."

"You'll see."

The bag held a kite, the old-fashioned kind, brilliantly colored in reds and yellow. She made the impulse purchase earlier in the week after she'd seen a child flying one. She wasn't even sure she'd ever get it off the ground. At least there was a breeze today.

Once on the horse, Liza sat stiffly, her muscles screaming for release. When she could fight it no longer, she let go and leaned her shoulders against Lee's chest.

"That's not so bad, is it?" he asked, his breath warming her ear.

"No," she agreed shyly.

As they rode along the meandering dirt track, Liza pointed out landmarks: an old house that had once housed tenant farmers, and the huge spreading oak she and Kitty had climbed as children. Lee asked about properties, and Liza indicated where one tract ended and the next began with the wooded area on the Berensons' place. "That's Kitty's house over there."

In the yard, he jumped down and reached for Liza, his hands firmly gripping her waist to swing her to the ground.

"Liz. Lee," Kitty called, hurrying across the yard. "Glad you could make it. Dave's saddling Sir now."

"Thanks for making it possible. Excuse me, ladies. I'll see if he needs help."

Both women watched his trek to the barn.

"Looked like you were enjoying yourself," Kitty commented.

"I was."

"Want me to tell him Sir's out of commission?"

Liza laughed, taking Kitty's arm and pulling her along. "You have the craziest ideas."

Dave and Lee were chatting like old friends when they led the horse from the barn. Dave greeted Liza, but she doubted he heard a word she said when Kitty struck up a conversation with Lee.

David Evans was a neighbor, another member of their terrible foursome. Of course, now that everyone was older and worked harder than they played, the good times were more memory than anything else.

The Evanses were farmers also, although on a grander scale than the rest of the neighborhood. They were considered pretty well-to-do, but their financial status had never made any difference in their friendship.

The fourth member of their group, Kitty's brother Jason, was married with a family of his own. Liza knew it was only a matter of time before Kitty and Dave married. They had been sweet on each other for as long as Liza could remember. Sooner or later, he would ask Kitty. Knowing Dave, he was trying to come up with the grandest proposal possible.

After mounting, the other couple rode on ahead, leaving Liza to follow with Lee.

"Where did you learn to ride?" she asked, reining Majesty in to ride alongside Sir.

"My grandparents kept a horse for me. Thought every self-respecting—"

Both were surprised when the horse started. Lee pulled up the reins, and Sir reared, unseating him.

Liza jumped down and ran to where he lay on the thick green grass. "Lee?" She grew frightened when he didn't respond immediately.

He groaned and said, "I warned you about that bag."

Relieved, she breathed deeply. "Kitty took the bag. There was a rabbit. I thought you saw it. Are you hurt?"

"Nothing seems to be broken." He moved his arms and his legs cautiously. "The fall knocked the breath out of me."

"Here, rest your head in my lap." She dropped to the ground. "Are you sure you're okay?" she asked again, concerned that he might be hurt worse than he realized. Liza stroked his hair in a comforting manner.

"I think so," he murmured, his tone growing strangely anxious. "Liza, I'm seeing double."

"What are we going to do?" she cried, looking about for help.

Moving closer, she missed the mischievous glint in his blue eyes. Liza jerked back when he kissed her. Her movement dislodged Lee, and he hit the ground with the unexpected movement. "Don't ever do that again, Lee Hayden," she ordered sternly, anger replacing her fright. "If you do, I'll. . .I'll. . . ," she began, only to find herself at a loss for words.

Lee reached to massage his head before leaning back on propped elbows. "Sorry. I couldn't resist."

"You scared me."

Her anger abated beneath the warm glow of his smile. "I won't do it again."

"See that you don't." Standing, she reached down to help him up. Lee took hold of her hand, pulling her off balance once more. She was barely able to keep the laughter from her voice as she broke away and got to her feet. "Stop playing. The others are waiting."

"Let them wait. I'm sorry I frightened you. Forgive me?"

She wasn't experienced in the ways of men, but this was one of the most mystifying she'd ever met.

"Sure. You take Majesty," Liza directed, avoiding his gaze. "I'll take Sir. And be careful. You could really get hurt next time."

"I'll keep Sir, if it's all the same to you."

Liza knew he was determined not to be defeated by the horse. She climbed into the saddle and looked down at him. "Are you sure you're okay? We can go back."

Lee patted her knee. "I'm sure. Let's find the others."

He captured Sir and mounted, riding off in the direction the others had gone. Liza guided Majesty into a running walk, gliding past them. In the spirit of competition, Lee urged his horse on and soon caught up with her. Minutes later, the pond came into sight and they reined their horses, dismounted, and walked to where the other couple sat.

Their childhood haunt had changed little over the years. The earth had revitalized itself in the green foliage and lush green grass. A strategic rope dangled from the huge shade tree near the pollen-coated pond, a tire swing in the lower branches.

Liza dropped Majesty's reins to the ground. The well-trained animal remained where he stood. "You'd better tie Sir," she suggested when Lee attempted the same. "He's not likely to stand around long if you don't."

After checking for spiders and testing the rope, Liza maneuvered her legs through the tire and leaned back, her feet touching the ground briefly before she kicked them into the air. The increasing momentum raised her high into the sky, giving her the sense of freedom she recollected from childhood. "I'm glad this is still here."

"Compliments of Mom and Dad," Dave said. "They ordered me to get the place ready for the grandchildren this summer."

Liza nodded, twisting in circles as she said, "Mickey's kids are just the right age to enjoy this place." She let go. The rope unwound itself, and she climbed out, dizzy.

Kitty slipped out of her jeans and shirt to reveal a one-piece swimsuit. She stretched out on the blanket to work on her tan. "What took you so long?" she asked when Liza's shadow blocked the sun. "Dave and I thought maybe you decided to go elsewhere."

"Majesty's been rowdy today."

"You probably need to ride him more often."

Liza nodded, glancing at Lee.

"Thanks," he whispered. "You saved my pride."

"I should have told on you."

"But you wouldn't, would you, sweetheart?"

"I still can," she warned. "Where's my bag, Kit?"

The woman pointed to the bottom of the blanket.

She looked up at the clouds scudding across the Carolina blue sky. "Perfect day for kite flying. Sure you don't want to help?"

"No, thanks."

Liza found herself a sunny spot and sat down. She laid the kite on the ground, then took out the string and tail.

Lee followed and sat down across from her. "This is the big secret?"

She nodded, stripped off the cellophane wrap, and unrolled the kite. Laying

27

the sticks aside, she read the instructions, finding they made little sense to her mechanically challenged mind.

A pity Jason wasn't here. He'd always been in charge of their kite construction.

"Well, that's that," she said, giving up. "I should have gotten one of those preassembled jobs."

"May I?"

Liza hugged her knees. "Help yourself."

The instructions remained where she'd tossed them. Lee never glanced at the paper as he put the kite together and tied the string and tail in record time. "Want to run with it?"

Liza jumped to her feet and ran with the wind, frowning when the kite drifted to the ground each time she let go. "One more time," she called, lifting it over her head. She let out a whoop of joy when the wind carried the kite into the sky, taking it higher and higher on the string Lee unwound.

Liza's gaze touched on the bright colors that danced in the sky. There was something about flying a kite. But she wasn't really flying it. "Lee, can I. . ."

The hole that caught her foot was unseen. She fell face first on the ground and lay stunned, fighting to get her breath back.

"Liza?"

"Watch that last step. It's a doozy," she said, laughing at his shocked expression.

He stuck out a hand and pulled her to her feet. "Can we get on with this kite flying, or do you plan to lie around on your face the rest of the day?"

Liza wrinkled her nose at him.

The wind played with the kite, taking it higher. It soared and dipped, sometimes precariously close to the ground before the wind caught and carried it back. Shielding their eyes from the sun, they watched its antics.

"Why a kite?"

Her mouth curved in an unconscious smile. "It struck me as a fun thing to do."

"I think I was ten the last time I did this."

"Why so long?" she asked.

"It didn't fit in with everything else. I was too busy having a good time, and when I started work, I was too busy trying to make an impression."

"On whom?"

He concentrated on unwinding more string. "Nobody important. I realized there's more to life than making a name for yourself any way you can."

"I don't understand."

"Let's just say I didn't like the man I was becoming."

"So you've left that life behind you?" She trailed after him.

Lee handed her the string, flexing his arms. "I'll never go back to the way it was before. That much I know. Look out," he called when the kite caught a downdraft and crashed.

"Too late," Liza said, rolling the string into a ball as she walked over to where the kite lay.

"Want to try to fly it again?"

She knelt and examined the broken stick, a skeptical smile touching her lips. "This one is ready for wherever it is injured kites go."

"A little tape works wonders."

"You happen to have a little tape on you?"

Lee lifted his hands and shook his head.

Liza picked up the kite and walked toward the pond. "I'll leave it under the tree. We wouldn't want to spook Sir again," she teased with a cheeky grin.

"Just you wait until I get some tape," he threatened. "I'll make you run with the kite. Think your face can take it?"

Liza chuckled. At this rate, there was no way she'd ever impress him with her gracefulness. "I'd better not chance it."

Settling by the pond, she absently tossed pebbles, watching the ripples they made. Lee soon joined in, and they vied to see who could skip rocks the farthest. Liza conceded defeat when he outdistanced her time and time again. The sun bore down on them full force, and Liza slipped off her shirt to reveal the tank top underneath.

In the distance, she could hear Kitty's high-pitched demands that Dave stop tickling her feet.

"Where's your suit?" Lee asked.

"Home. I thought we were riding today."

Dave scooped Kitty into his arms and walked toward the pond. "Dave Evans, don't you dare," Kitty ordered. "I'll never speak to you again."

He feinted the drop, laughing when he swung the screaming woman to her feet at his side. Livid, Kitty stomped back to the blanket.

Stifling a grin, Liza glanced at Lee. "Dave just made a major mistake. Kit's serious about her sunbathing."

"Too serious," Dave agreed, dropping down beside Liza on the grass. "When does your father finish planting?"

"Monday or Tuesday." Her thoughts went to her dad and how busy he was. "He's been in the fields all week."

"Except for Sundays, this is the first time I've left the farm during the day in weeks." He glanced at Kitty. "I need to be home working now, but she'd kill me if I told her."

Liza sympathized, thinking of the amount of work there was to do on a farm the size of the Evanses'. The slightest delay could cost them. It wasn't only today he couldn't spare time. They would be extremely busy over the months ahead, as would every farmer in the county, including her father.

"Speaking to me yet, Kit?" Dave called when she sat up and looked at them.

"No," she snapped, lying back on the blanket.

He stood and walked toward her, his tone cajoling, "Come on, Kit. You know you want to."

Liza watched for a few minutes as Dave attempted to tease Kitty back into good humor. She was making him pay, but Dave was a charmer. He'd have Kitty saying she was sorry, if she didn't watch her step.

"Sounds like Dave has a fight on his hands," Lee commented.

"Kitty loves Dave. She has to accept his responsibilities."

Lee plucked a long blade of grass, examining it before he spoke. "What is it about farming that makes them keep at it? Why continue to work so hard and fight such a losing battle? What do they get out of it?"

Liza slanted her head to one side and studied him closely. "Farming's not only a business. It's a way of life. Daddy is the eternal optimist. He's willing to take the risks involved. He has so much faith in God's ability to grow that little seed that he's willing to make it his livelihood. A finished crop gives him a sense of satisfaction equal to, say—" she broke off, searching for the right way to make him understand. "To what you feel when you win a case you've worked particularly hard on. No matter how tough the winter, there's always promise of new growth in the spring."

"How can you work all day and go home to chores?"

"Most days, I get everything done, including taking care of Majesty, who is my responsibility anyway. I like to spend time with Daddy. After all, I'm the son he never had. He's taught me to do lots around the farm, and I let him because he doesn't have anyone else to pass it on to. He already tells me the farm is mine when he's gone."

"That throws a lot of responsibility on your shoulders. What happens when you decide to marry? Do you choose a farmer, or what?"

Liza laughed aloud, lifted her braid, and tossed it over her shoulder. She whistled for Majesty and climbed into the saddle. "That one's simple, Lee. No matter what his profession, I marry the man I love."

She urged Majesty into a run as the unusual restlessness pushed her. It was as if the animal understood her needs. Woman and horse raced along the farm road, churning up a cloud of dust. When she realized how far they'd come, Liza turned around. Reins in hand, she walked over to the edge of the pond where the others were gathering their stuff. "Are we leaving?"

"We thought you'd already gone," Kitty said. "Why did you take off like that? What were you two talking about anyway? I heard you say something about the man you loved."

"We were just getting to know each other."

"Lee has business in town. Dave's going to help with the horses."

"I'll take care of them," Liza volunteered. "I'm sure you and Dave could use some time alone."

Kitty giggled and suggested, "Take Sir home first, and then you take Lee back to your house to get his car."

"I could probably handle that," Liza said. Majesty tossed his head over her shoulder and nosed her shirt pocket. "No more treats for you today." She started to move, as surprised as the horse when in his determination Majesty gave one final nudge and landed her in the pond.

Liza splashed about wildly, gulping a mouthful of water before her sense of balance reasserted itself and she kicked out of her panic. "Ooh, you," she yelled, blinking away the water that streamed into her eyes. Majesty raced off toward home, heedless of her repeated whistles.

Grabbing hold of a nearby plant, she placed her feet against the embankment in an effort to gain leverage to pull herself out. The plant was a puny specimen at best, and when the roots pulled out of the muddy bank, she landed with yet another gigantic splash. "Help," she implored, holding out a hand to Lee.

He pulled her from the pond, her feet slipping and sliding along the muddy wall. She was thankful to have both feet on the ground again.

"You're green."

The pollen gathered on the water clung to her skin. The absurdity of her appearance struck Liza, and she began to laugh. The more she thought about what had happened, the harder she laughed; soon she doubled over at the waist.

"Liza, are you okay?"

She forced herself upright, her chest aching. "I'm fine. I can't believe all this stuff is happening to me."

"How will you get home?" Dave asked.

"Walk. If you see Majesty, bring him back. Although I'm sure he's well on his way to the stable at home. Based on the way he was running, he's probably standing by the door already. Guess he's not used to me in green."

"You can't walk that far," Kitty objected.

"You want me hanging onto you? I'm a slime monster." At her friend's hesitation, Liza said, "I wouldn't inflict myself on any of you."

Lee spoke up. "Your shirt's over there on the grass, and you can wrap Kitty's blanket about your legs." A grin developed at their surprised looks. "Ever ride sidesaddle?"

"There's a first for everything, I suppose." Dropping to the ground, she pulled off her boots and dumped out the water. She tied the strings together and passed them to Lee. Liza pulled on the shirt and wrapped the blanket about her hips, complaining, "I feel like a mummy."

"At least you get to ride back with Lee," Kitty offered in a soft aside. "I couldn't have arranged it better myself."

Liza shook her head at her friend's logic. She tried to figure out how she was supposed to get from the ground to the horse. The blanket became a definite liability as she tried to hold on to it and lift one foot into the stirrup. She overbalanced, falling back onto the soft cushion of grass.

"I don't play fairy princess as much as I used to."

Lee's grin deepened into laughter. "Dave, we could use a hand."

Dave lifted her into Lee's arms.

"I'll bring Sir back later," Liza promised.

"No problem," Kitty said. "Glad you could make it, Lee. Liza, take care. See you at church in the morning." She paused and asked, "Have you found a church home yet, Lee?"

He shook his head, not expanding on the subject.

"We'd love to have you attend ours, wouldn't we, Liza?"

"I'll think about it. I've been too busy for church."

Too busy? His excuse raised a warning flag for Liza. She had heard many similar excuses over the years.

They waved good-bye and rode off across the field.

Moisture from her clothes soon saturated the blanket. "I'm so sorry about this. I know you weren't expecting to ride home with a half-drowned female."

He shrugged. "Things happen. It's not your fault."

Minutes later, Lee stopped Sir in her yard. He flashed Barney a warning frown when he came running, his bark as spectacular as his bulk. "That animal is going to have us on the ground."

"Barney, hush," she ordered when the horse moved restlessly. "I said, be quiet," she repeated sternly.

"I don't trust him," Lee said when the dog ceased barking and sat down, his large brown eyes fixed on them.

Lee glanced at Barney once more before dismounting.

"Why?" she asked, slipping into his waiting arms. "He's just a big baby."

"Who's capable of taking a pretty big hunk out of anyone with whom he takes exception."

Dropping the blanket, Liza patted Barney's head. "Well, you'll have to see that you don't get on his bad side. I'm going to change clothes. Tie Sir over there."

Liza shed her jeans and caught sight of herself in the bathroom mirror. She grimaced and lifted her sodden braid. Using a washcloth and soap, she wiped as much of the pollen from her face and arms as possible and grabbed a towel. In her bedroom, she wiped the towel over her hair and hurriedly dressed in dry clothes, aware Lee and the horses waited outside.

As expected, Majesty waited at the barn door. He whinnied at the sight of her, and Liza rubbed a hand along his neck. "I guess it wasn't your fault," she allowed, removing the saddle.

"How long is this going to take?" Lee took it from her hands and moved toward the barn.

She followed with the horses. "I'll do it. You have to get back to town."

"I can't leave you with all the work," Lee objected.

"I'm used to work. You can help next time."

"I really hate doing this."

"I understand," Liza said with a forgiving smile. "I'm glad you could come with us."

"I enjoyed myself."

"Everything?" she teased.

"Everything. See you at work on Monday."

She followed him to the barn door and waved good-bye as he opened his car.

Work, Liza thought, snapping her fingers. "Lee, wait. I forgot to tell you. . . ," she said, breathless after her run across the yard. "I have to be off Monday and Tuesday. Daddy needs me here."

"You can't."

"I have to," she insisted.

"We have a full calendar next week. The week after. . ."

"Won't work," she said before walking away. Did he think the crops could be put on hold until the office allowed her to be off? "Mr. Wilson approved my request before he left," she called back to him. "There's a temp coming in. If you can't survive, get a replacement. Fire me if you want. I don't care."

"Liza." He laid his hand on her shoulder. "I understand you feel you have to—"

"No, you don't," she interrupted. "If you did, we wouldn't be having this argument."

Barney growled, coming to his feet when Lee's expression grew angry. "If you'd just let me finish a sentence."

"Who's stopping you?"

"Be quiet," Lee snapped at Barney when he growled menacingly. His hand swept through his hair, exasperation lighting his eyes. "I can see I'm wasting my time talking to you. If you don't have any more concern for the office than that, take two days, three, a week, the rest of the summer."

"I'll be glad when Mr. Wilson gets back," she called after him.

His car churned up clouds of dust as he raced down the driveway. He didn't understand. Maybe he couldn't. She didn't know. All she knew was, there was work to be done and she had to help.

⚬§⚬

By the time he reached the main road, Lee was convinced he had to be the biggest idiot in the state of North Carolina. What was he thinking?

Sure, he needed her help to keep the office going, but Liza was entitled to her approved vacation days. He'd always looked forward to R & R days. Though he couldn't see rest or relaxation in Liza's plan. Helping her father around the farm had to be exhausting.

What if she didn't return for the remainder of the summer? He wouldn't stand a chance. She had no idea how crucial she was to his success in the venture. In Charlotte, he was a little fish in a big pond, but here he hoped to be the prize catch.

From the first days Lee had worked with Liza, he knew they were a good team. Her knowledge level was invaluable. To her, the clients were her friends and acquaintances. As one of them, Liza understood their likes and dislikes, the diverse needs of farmers and business people alike.

For him to throw loyalty in her face was ridiculous. What had he done to deserve her allegiance?

In their one week as coworkers, her advice had kept him from antagonizing people. . .at least everyone but her. His foot rested on the brake momentarily. Should he go back and apologize? Somehow he doubted she was ready to hear it. Besides, he really did have to get back into town.

Lee depressed the accelerator and drove on. He'd ruined a wonderful afternoon with his behavior. He'd give her time to calm down, then he'd call later.

Chapter 4

Liza turned the page on her desk calendar and was jolted by the realization that Mr. Wilson had been away for almost four weeks. She could hardly believe it when Mr. Wilson called and lengthened his vacation by another two weeks.

The time had been spent getting to know Lee and experiencing his pleasure and displeasure at her responses to his demands. Her suspicion he wasn't a churchgoer had been confirmed when she mentioned her church again, only to have him tell her he didn't have time for that kind of thing. It certainly shed a new light on his behavior.

She struggled with the understanding and her growing attraction to Lee Hayden. The situation required plenty of knee time.

Beyond his call to apologize, Lee had not mentioned their argument again, but Liza had a gut feeling he felt she'd let him down.

At the time, she'd worried that Lee's reaction would be the same each time she requested a day off, but her dad hadn't needed her help again. She attributed that to the mention of Lee's negative reaction to her request. No doubt, he didn't want to cause her any problems at work.

Mr. Wilson was definitely coming back on Monday. He understood life in a small farming community. Lee had no idea what these people faced. Liza wondered why she even worried about how he felt and realized she wanted him to fit in. After that first week, she'd hoped they were becoming friends, but their differences would always serve as a wedge to separate them.

Liza finished straightening her desk, her thoughts on her plans for the weekend. She called good night to Lee and locked the door behind herself.

Her parents were visiting relatives while work on the farm permitted, and Kitty had invited herself over for the weekend. Liza almost laughed at the thought of Kitty promising to help with the chores if Liza went to the Evanses' cookout with her. She planned to go anyway, but Kitty's help was sure to make the work more interesting.

She glanced at the courthouse, appreciating its impressive dignity and historic significance. It sat on its island in the center of the traffic circle, with entrances to the building from all four directions.

Waving to some of the other people who worked in the area as they drove off, Liza hit the LOCK button on her remote and reached for the door handle.

When the door didn't open, she glanced down and let out a horrified scream. Who could have done something like this?

She looked around to find herself alone in the parking lot. Running back to the office, Liza yelled Lee's name as she opened the door.

He charged from his office. "What's wrong?" When she didn't say anything, he grabbed her shoulders and demanded, "Liza, what's wrong?"

"My car," she whimpered, tears stinging her eyes. "Someone bashed in the driver's side. The door's jammed."

"Did they leave a note?"

"I don't know."

Lee pulled her over to the sofa. "Sit down. I'll check."

Liza couldn't sit still and trailed after him. Lee stooped beside the car, examining the damage.

"No note," he said when she bent down beside him.

"What do I do?"

"Wait until the police get here and have the car towed." He pointed to the worst damage. "You can't drive it with the fender on the tire like that."

Standing, she slammed a hand against the car hood. "Why? How could someone do this?"

Lee placed an arm about her shoulder. "Come on, Liza. I'll take you home after you give your report to the police."

Back in the office, she waited while Lee phoned the station. "They're dispatching a squad car. We need to wait outside."

The anticipation of the weekend was lost in the wave of emotion that overwhelmed her. A fresh wave of tears choked her every time she looked at the damage to her new car. Would it ever be the same again? No one could do that much damage and claim not to know.

It took a few minutes for the patrol car to arrive. "When did you find it, Liza?"

"Around five. After work. It wasn't like this at lunch. Do you think you'll find out who did it?"

"Hard to say." The officer concentrated on a streak of dark blue paint along the door. "We'll ask around to see if anyone witnessed the act. More than likely, not."

Liza's teeth clenched, feeling even more furious that the offender would probably get off. "Why?"

"People who park here in the circle recognize your vehicle. If they'd seen the incident, they would have called you or the police."

"It makes me sick."

"Calm down, Liza," Lee urged. "It's just a car."

She eyed him. "My new car, Lee."

He hugged her close. "I know, but there's no sense in worrying now. The damage is done."

"It'll never be the same again."

"The body shop will make it as good as new. Let me take you home."

"We'll let you know if we hear anything," the officer said after checking to make sure the report was complete. "Where do you want it towed?"

Liza named the dealership where she had recently purchased the vehicle. Lee took hold of her arm and guided her to his car.

"Wait here. I'll lock up the office."

As they rode along, she had the strongest feeling of a child deprived of her favorite toy. She didn't want to pout but couldn't help herself.

For years, she'd driven her mother's old car. A breakdown had placed her in the dealership waiting area. The flashy red sports car spoke to her the moment she laid eyes on it. Though it was too expensive and more car than she'd needed, Liza had signed over a portion of her savings and received a fat payment book in return for the joy of driving her dream car.

The car had been another of her life changes. Everyone speculated on what had gotten into her, trading a paid-for compact that was good on gas for a fancy sports car. Now it was just another wrecked car.

"Liza? We're here." Lee parked in the yard.

She managed a weak smile. "Thanks for your help."

"Looks like Kitty's waiting."

"She's spending the weekend." Liza climbed out of the car.

"I'm glad you won't be alone."

She frowned. "I'm ticked off, not suicidal."

"I didn't mean it like that. Are you going to the Evanses' barbecue?"

"I don't feel like it."

"You need to get your mind off the car. With any luck, they'll find whoever did it."

Hope leaped in her. "You think so?"

He quickly averted his gaze, and she knew Lee was only trying to make her feel better. "Maybe. I don't know. But it's already happened. Don't let it spoil your weekend. See you at the Evanses'?"

She could hardly lift her voice above a whisper to answer him. Why did she feel this way? Was she too attached to a material possession? Probably.

Kitty came over to speak to Lee.

"You're kidding!" she exclaimed when Liza explained why she was late. "A hit-and-run accident at the courthouse, and no one saw it? There were a million cars up there today. Surely someone saw something."

"Yeah," Liza agreed. "The person who dragged his car alongside mine saw plenty."

In the kitchen, she opened the refrigerator and dug around until she found a chocolate layer cake.

"Liza, you don't want that."

The knife slipped through the cake, and Liza lifted the wedge onto a plate. "Don't tell me what I want. I'll eat the whole thing if the mood strikes me."

Kitty propped her hands against her hips and said, "Don't take this out on me, Liza Stephens. I didn't hit your precious car."

Liza shoved the plate away, dropping the fork with a clatter. Kitty was right. She didn't want the cake, and she shouldn't take her bad mood out on her friends. "I'm sorry. I'm just so angry."

"Of course you are." Kitty paused for a second. "Want me to call my dad and ask who he recommends for the bodywork?"

"I had them tow it to the dealership. Daddy will be back Sunday. I can ask him. I need to call Jason."

"He'll be at the cookout. You can tell him then."

Liza sighed. "Looks like I'll be thumbing for a few days."

"Kitty's taxi at your disposal—for the right price, of course."

Liza laughed. "The only thing I'm paying you is no attention. I seem to recall a certain crumpled fender that put you in Liza's taxi for a few days."

"That sounds like a pretty reasonable price," Kitty agreed.

Later, as they changed for the cookout, Liza considered her attitude. It was hard to smile, but she had to fight the depression.

"Lord, forgive me," she whispered. "I know I shouldn't feel this way about a car, but I can't help myself. Lift up my spirits and help me forgive the person who did this."

Going to the closet, she pulled out a white-and-lilac-striped sundress and slipped it on. She brushed her hair and left it hanging down her back.

The party was in full swing when they arrived, people milling around as they waited for the hamburgers, steaks, and ribs to cook. The scents were mouthwatering.

Liza spotted Jason across the yard and waved.

Jason Berenson was Kitty's brother. Older than the two of them by barely a year, he was married and the father of an adorable six-month-old baby girl.

"Looking for someone in particular?" she teased when Kitty eyed the crowds.

"Not particularly."

"You don't fool me. I know Dave's around somewhere and the minute he lays eyes on you, you'll be his for the night."

Kitty waggled her left hand. "He hasn't put a ring on my finger yet."

"It's just a matter of time, and you know it."

"Well, time has a way of changing things."

Sure does, Liza thought as she followed Kitty over to where Jason stood. Kitty patted her brother's stomach, the extra pounds revealed by the sport shirt he wore. "Time to start working out, Jace."

"Good to see you, too, Kit."

"Well, brother, you're a young man, but if you want to let yourself go. . ."

"I start working out tomorrow, thank you," he growled.

"Glad to hear it. Guess we'd better track down our host and hostess and say hello. By the way, Liza needs to report an automobile accident."

Kitty's words focused Jason's attention on Liza. His company insured all of the Stephenses' family vehicles. "Were you hurt?"

Liza shook her head. "Hit-and-run."

"That stinks. Don't worry. We'll make it good as new."

"Thanks, Jason. I'll be in touch Monday. Talk to you again later."

A mixture of successful business people and farmers filled the room. Some chatted in small groups while others danced to the music that blasted. Another group played basketball at a goal attached to the outside building. Others took advantage of the pool, and Liza wished she'd thought to bring her suit.

Dave came over and demanded, "What took you so long? I was beginning to think you'd decided not to come."

"Liza didn't get home till late," Kitty said. "Someone hit her car in the parking lot."

He looked at Liza for the first time. "Did you get his name and insurance company?"

"No such luck." She explained the situation as she looked around for Lee.

Dave let out a soft whistle. "Sorry, Liza. You haven't had that car long, have you?"

"Four months."

"Let's change the subject," Kitty suggested.

"Come say hello to Mom and Dad," Dave said. Allowing him to lead the way across the yard, they chatted for a while before Dave and Kitty went off to dance. Liza left them to wander around the yard on her own. She caught sight of Lee among the group playing basketball and stopped to watch.

"Time out," Lee called when he spotted her on the sidelines. He grabbed a towel and wiped his face.

"Good game?"

He nodded and gave her a one-armed hug. "Feeling better?"

Liza felt her chest tighten in anticipation. Maybe he did understand after all. "I wanted to apologize for acting like a baby."

He smoothed a strand of her hair before allowing his fingers to glide down the length of her face. His gentle touch was almost an embrace. "You acted normal, given the circumstances."

"Come on, Lee," the other players called, but he lingered for a second longer, reassuring her once more that the car could be repaired.

"Lee, you're holding up the game," the others cried in protest.

"Later," he promised with a wink before jumping back into the action. Liza watched him snatch the ball and fly upward, pushing it into the basket.

Be thankful he stopped to speak, she told herself glumly. Sinking onto the end of a nearby bench, she watched Lee. What was it about him that made her want his attention?

A scream left her lips as Liza found herself on the ground, the other end of her bench becoming airborne.

"I'm sorry," her seat partner exclaimed. Liza allowed him to pull her to her feet and jumped away just in time to avoid being hit by the unattached plank. It tumbled to the ground at her feet.

Smoothing her dress over her hips, she sneaked a peek around, seeing the looks of concern and then amusement on everyone's faces. Heat filled her face. "Hope you enjoyed the entertainment," she muttered.

"Are you okay?" the guy asked.

For the first time, Liza took a better look at him. Something very familiar about his face tugged at her memory. His obvious concern made her feel better. She nodded and said, "Now that I have two feet under me."

"Dad's going to demand a reimbursement of my college tuition for engineering such flimsy seating."

Liza glanced at the cinder blocks that held the board. No doubt, when he stood, he broke the seesawlike balance, leaving her end to hit the ground.

Dad... That was what he'd said. Surely it couldn't be. Not after all these years. "Rick?"

Recognition brought a smile to his face. He gathered her in a hug. "I'd recognize that blush anywhere. Hello, Liza."

"I can't believe it," she said, throwing her arms about his neck. If possible, he was even more handsome, his boyish charm more refined. "It's been forever."

Her companion regarded her with amusement, his arms supporting her waist.

"Only fourteen years," he protested. "Are you happy to see your old flame?"

"Old flame?" Liza scoffed. "I wasn't even allowed boyfriends."

"Well, you had one, and it was me. How could I forget? You and Kitty followed me everywhere. Not even Dave and Jason could tempt you and Kitty away. You had this same long black curly hair," he said, tugging one of her curls, "and those beautiful braces on your teeth."

"At least the braces are gone," Liza said, flashing him the straight white teeth her parents had worked so hard to pay for. "Not to mention a few of those pounds you were polite enough not to mention."

He stepped back and took a look. "I like what I see."

"Oh, Rick," she faltered.

"I always loved that," he said. "You blushed at the least little thing."

"And you were always doing something to make me blush," she accused. "Who'd have ever thought you'd look like this?" she mused, laughing at his taken-aback expression.

"Thanks loads," he said, tweaking one of her long curls.

Rick had never cared much for having his picture taken, and it had been difficult to tell what he looked like since most of the photos she'd seen over the years involved a hard hat and a foreign locale. His mother declared the only time she got to see his face was when she traveled to wherever he was to visit him.

"Think nothing of it," Liza said, taking his hand and leading him through the crowd. "Come with me. I want to surprise Kit." Her laughter floated as he quizzed her on the past, dwelling on her devotion to him. "I'm sure I never did anything like that," she denied when he accused her of threatening to follow him to college. "Kit, look who's here. Why didn't you tell me Rick was home?"

Kit lifted her shoulders in defeat, shaking her head. "I didn't know. No one said a word."

"They didn't know I was coming," he said. "I surprised them all when I called to be picked up from the airport."

Kitty hugged him exuberantly. "How long has it been?"

"Liza and I agreed on fourteen years," he said, glancing at her for confirmation. "She fell all over herself welcoming me."

"He dumped me on the ground. Some men will do anything to pick up a woman."

His laughter sounded rich, warm, and deep. "Our Liza's grown up."

"We both have," Kitty said, slipping her arm about his. "Tell us what you've been doing all this time."

"Seeing the world. Using my engineering degree to take the jobs I wanted."

"So we heard," Liza said. "No thanks to you. Why didn't you write?"

"I was too busy," Rick said. "I remember how you two reacted to my news. You were shocked that I'd consider leaving the country life behind."

"And us," Kitty defended. "We didn't understand why you wanted to become an engineer when you had the farm here waiting for you."

"Dad was a pretty self-sufficient guy. Besides, my heart was never in farming. Not like Dave's. This way we both do what makes us happy."

"And now?"

His gaze stopped on Liza as the question popped out, his lazy smile warming her heart. "I'm between jobs and home for a long-overdue visit. All these guys had better watch out." He wrapped his arms about their shoulders and hugged them to him. "I'm going to stake my claim on my girls."

"I still can't believe it," Kitty said with a laugh. "Just wait until I see David Matthew Evans."

"Don't be too tough," Rick kidded. "He remembers how you acted when I was around. Probably thought you'd go tearing off to find me."

"I would not have," Kitty denied hastily.

Liza smiled, shaking her head. "No good, Kit. He remembers how we used to chase after him, called us perfect little fiends."

"Did he now?" Kitty demanded playfully.

"Never. I'd be happy to take you two anywhere."

"Who wouldn't?" a familiar voice questioned.

Rick turned to look at Lee. "I don't know. If they're still like I remember, it could be trouble with a capital T. Do you remember the night I said you girls couldn't come on my date? She was pretty angry when you popped up from behind the seat and told her I took you everywhere."

"Ladies, you didn't?"

"Well, she wasn't good enough for him," Kitty defended.

"I seem to recall she was homecoming queen and the bank president's daughter."

"We never could figure out why you preferred her to us," Kitty teased. Without so much as a blink of an eye, she flashed Rick her irresistible smile and rested her red-tipped fingers against the tanned muscles of his arm.

Watching her is an education, Liza thought. Kit flirted outrageously, spinning her web while she stood by, wondering at her friend's feminine wiles. *Just once, I wish I could attract men like Kitty does.*

"Rick shouldn't tell everything he knows," Kitty said in a silky voice. She winked at Liza. "We could tell a few stories of our own."

"No, you couldn't." Rick placed a hand over her mouth.

"Old friends?" Lee inquired.

"I'm sorry," Liza said. "Rick Evans, Lee Hayden. Rick is Dave's older brother. Lee is Mr. Wilson's nephew."

"Nice to meet you." Lee reached out to shake hands.

"My pleasure," Rick said.

"I'm going to steal Liza away." Lee tugged on her arm. "There are a couple of burgers over there with our names on them."

Too startled by his suggestion to offer any objection, Liza went along. "Don't let him get away, Kitty," she called over her shoulder.

"I'm going to throttle Dave for not telling us Rick came home."

Her gaze followed them to the middle of the crowd. Kitty's hands wrapped about Dave's neck, and he was offering an earnest explanation while Kitty nodded doubtfully.

"How long have you known Rick?" Lee asked.

"A very long time. We grew up together."

"Together?" Lee repeated with raised brows. "He's what? Thirty-five? Thirty-six?"

"Only thirty-two," she corrected. "Kitty and I adored him. He chauffeured us to the beach, took us riding—taught us to ride, for that matter. He did just about everything we wanted. Of course, we harassed him into a lot of it."

"That was mighty agreeable of him," Lee said.

"He's a mighty agreeable person. Kit and I cried for days when Rick went off to college."

"How long is he home for?"

His seemingly casual question struck her as odd. "I don't know. Why?"

"Perhaps I don't want him stealing my assistant away."

Leave it to Lee. His curiosity only extended to her capacity to do her job. "That's an idea. I always wanted to travel."

"Don't even think about it." Lee's gaze fixed on her face. "We need you far too much for you to go off gallivanting around the world."

Liza concentrated on picking up a Styrofoam plate, not wanting Lee to see how hurt she felt.

"Okay, what's wrong? What did I say this time?"

Liza hated being so transparent. "It bothers me when you decide the good of the office is more important than my happiness."

"I was joking." His defensive words struck home.

"Call it what you like," Liza said. "Everything's work to you. Your life revolves around the office."

Lee took her hand and pulled her over to a private corner of the yard. "I don't know what's going on in your head right now, but I don't care more about the office than you."

"You do." Raw nerves made her far too emotional to get into this with him now. Her wayward tongue refused to be silenced. "Every time I make a decision you feel doesn't work for the 'good' of the office, you retreat behind a wall. I'm glad Mr. Wilson is coming back on Monday."

"Well, Miss Liza, I've got a news flash for you: Uncle John might be coming back, but not long term. He's talking retirement and looking for someone to take over. I'm his man."

His words hit her hard. Didn't all the years she'd invested in the office entitle her to know what her boss was planning? Unable to speak, she turned and walked away. She didn't care if she ever saw Lee again. He had taken too much pleasure in dropping the bomb on her, and it hurt, terribly.

"Liza, wait!"

Even now, he sounded exasperated. What did he expect? Did he think she would leap with joy at the prospect of having him as her employer? She blundered into Rick's arms. "Liza? What's wrong?"

"We seem to keep bumping into each other," she said with forced gaiety, her overly bright laughter bordering on hysteria.

"What happened?" he demanded, shaking her gently.

She saw Lee standing over by the shrubbery, watching them. In that moment, she knew her feelings for him were far stronger than she cared to admit. But it was senseless. She was part of the office machinery—a necessary evil.

"I shouldn't be here. Take me home, Rick. Please."

"What about Kitty?"

"She'll come later. She drove," she explained, sniffing as she knuckled away tears. "Rick," she exclaimed. "I'm sorry. It's your party. You can't leave. I'll catch a ride with someone else."

"No, wait for me in Dave's car. I'll get his keys and tell Kitty we're leaving."

"Thanks, Rick." She flashed him a tremulous smile.

"It's okay, baby," he comforted and offered a consoling hug.

Being there reminded Liza of the times she'd been hurt as a child and he'd done the same, and somehow it made a difference. "You called me that when I was little," she reminisced.

"I did, didn't I?" he said, wiping tears from her cheek. "Old habits are hard to break. I'll meet you at the car."

He disappeared around the corner of the house, and she walked toward the car.

"Liza, don't run away," Lee said. "Let's talk this out."

Anger seemed to grow, mainly at herself for not having seen this coming. She should have recognized her need to impress him for what it was—attraction. The simultaneous excitement and fear she felt when she was near Lee was so obvious. How could she have been so stupid?

"Stay away from me, Lee Hayden," she cried, breaking into a run. "I never want to see you again. Do you hear me?"

Inside Dave's car, she rested her head in her hands and moaned, "I can't stand it."

Rick shut his door quietly, turning the key in the ignition. "Can't stand what?"

She sat up in the seat and declared, "The way people take advantage of me." Her eyes drifted shut for a minute. "That's rich. You should be angry with me." Liza sniffed. "I drag you away from your cookout and then have the colossal nerve to talk about people using me."

Rick concentrated his attention on getting past the vehicles parked in the yard. "You obviously needed to get away. Want to talk about it?"

Liza shook her head and huddled miserably in the passenger seat. Rick tried to start a conversation, then gave up when she failed to participate. Liza chastised herself for her behavior, but she couldn't respond—not until she figured out how to deal with the situation.

He turned onto the driveway leading to her house.

"I'm sorry, Rick. It's been an awful day. I never should have gone tonight."

She couldn't tell him she was falling in love with Lee. She couldn't tell anyone that out of all the men who were looking for a woman to love and cherish, she had to fall for the one who considered her no more than an office fixture.

"When you're ready to talk, I'll be here."

The corners of her mouth lifted in a grateful smile. Thank God he wasn't angry with her. She didn't think she could bear much more. "You always were a good friend."

Liza glanced toward the house and saw the uniformed patrolman pounding on their back door. "They found the person who hit my car!" She jumped from the car almost before it stopped completely. Maybe, just maybe, something in this horrible day was going to go right for her.

Chapter 5

L iza, wait."

Ignoring his caution, she dashed across the yard to where the patrolman, a young officer she recognized from court, stood. "Did you find him, Bill?" she quizzed, her breath coming in deep, uneven gasps.

"Find who?" he asked.

When Rick joined them, she quickly became aware of the look the two men shared—the officer's almost apprehensive, Rick's curious.

"The man who hit my car," she wailed.

"I don't know anything about your car. They asked us to contact you. . . ."

A flicker of apprehension coursed through her at his expression. Fear drove her urgent demand. "Why are you here?" The volume of her voice increased to a near shout.

"Your parents were in a car accident. Your daddy had a heart attack."

She gasped, whispering a quick prayer that they were okay. "Is he. . . ?" she asked brokenly, unable to finish the sentence. Vaguely aware of Rick's comforting arms about her, Liza asked almost incomprehensibly, "Mama?"

"She managed to get help. From what we can tell, Mr. Stephens was driving when it happened. They hit the ditch going pretty fast, and she was thrown out of the truck."

Bugs charged against the yellowing glare of the porch light. Crickets chirped in unison while Barney barked in the background and Majesty whinnied in his stall. *It can't be true,* Liza thought. Soon Rick would go home, she'd go to bed, and tomorrow would be a better day.

"Liza?" Rick shook her out of her withdrawn state.

"How badly were they hurt?"

The man's distaste for his duty was evident in the way he carried out the task. "I don't know. I'll take you to the hospital so you can talk to the doctor. He'll be able to tell you more."

"Which hospital?" Rick asked.

"The one here in town. They were almost home."

Goose bumps popped up on her arms. "Home?" She looked at Rick. "They weren't due back until Sunday."

"Whenever you're ready," the patrolman said.

More than a little tempted to grab her bag and go, Liza refused. "I appreciate the offer, but I'll need transportation later."

"Are you okay to drive? I know this was a shock for you."

"Go ahead," Rick told the patrolman. "I'll stay with her."

Still he hesitated, his eyes speaking his concern. "I'm sorry I had to be the one to bring you bad news, Liza. Call if you need anything?"

"Yes, of course," she assured, managing a smile. "And Bill, pray for them."

Rick took the house key from her shaking fingers and unlocked the door. He steered her toward the stairs. "Change and call Kitty. I'll do a quick check outside."

Feeling numb as the reaction began to set in, she agreed.

It was nice having Rick to rely on. After replacing her dress with jeans and a shirt, she dialed the Evanses' house and got their answering machine. No doubt they were all outside. She left a quick message, hoping someone would let Kit know. Liza turned the lights off and found Rick coming out of the barn.

"Ready?"

Liza could barely lift her voice above a whisper. "I couldn't reach Kitty. Maybe I should pack a bag? They'll need some things."

"The hospital will provide what they need for now. They're going to be okay," he reassured, dropping his arm about Liza's shoulders and pulling her close.

Trusting eyes met his as she whispered, "They just have to be."

He nodded, helping Liza into the car. His regard felt gentle and comforting, as did the hand that squeezed hers. Liza prayed throughout the long, nerve-racking journey.

"I'm Liza Stephens," she told the nurse at the emergency room desk. "My parents, Paul and Sarah Stephens, are here."

"Wait over there. I'll tell the doctor you've arrived."

Dr. Mayes came out shortly and gestured her over to a door just inside the waiting area.

"I came as soon as I heard. How are they?" She found his calm maddening as she waited for an answer.

"Settle down," he said with a reassuring pat on her shoulder. "Your father suffered a heart attack and fractured his leg. We'll know more about the severity of his heart attack in a few days."

"And Mama?"

"She was thrown from the truck on impact. Sarah managed to get help before blacking out. We're waiting for her to regain consciousness. She has some superficial face cuts and a couple of cracked ribs. We'll know more when she wakes."

"Can I see them?"

"Your father. For a few minutes. Reassure him about your mother if you can. Worrying won't help him."

Liza tried, but her father felt convinced his wife was worse than they were telling him. His agitated state did more harm than good, so the doctor finally ordered a sedative.

"Pray for her, Daddy," Liza whispered, squeezing his hand.

The nurse asked Liza to step out of the room.

Liza didn't know how to reassure him. Her own worry kept her from thinking clearly. Wearied by her indecision, Liza leaned against the wall in the hallway. She swiped away a tear just as the nurse exited the room.

She recognized Mrs. Timmons from church. The woman patted Liza's shoulder reassuringly and said, "He'll be fine. You can go back in."

Familiar brown eyes pierced the distance between them. "Honey, you'd tell me if anything was wrong, wouldn't you?"

The medication began to take effect, and he calmed down, almost falling asleep. "Yes, Daddy."

This was the first time she'd ever seen her father this low. She needed his strength, but right now it seemed she had to be strong enough for her parents.

The nurse returned to check on him and allowed Liza to remain by the bed until he dozed off.

In the waiting area, she found Rick and explained what she knew.

"I got a message to Kit. They wanted to come, but I told them not to. Dave promised to run over and check the farm tomorrow."

She nodded absently, pacing the small waiting area. Her head throbbed from the worry about her mother and the added stresses of the day. Would Mom recover? Being unconscious like this couldn't be a good thing.

"You've got to sit down. You're wearing yourself out."

Liza massaged her forehead in an attempt to rub away the agonizing pain. "That's exactly what I want," she confessed. "To be so tired I can't think about anything."

"You can't," Rick reasoned. "You have to remain clearheaded enough to make any decisions that have to be made. Come here." He reached for her.

Liza placed her hand in his, trusting him completely.

"Sit here and rest your head on my shoulder. Try to catch a few minutes' sleep. I'll wake you the minute I hear anything."

"I don't think I can."

"Try."

Even though she considered it impossible, Liza soon fell into an uneasy sleep, troubled by nightmares of her parents and Lee.

"Liza, wake up." Rick shook her lightly. Surprised, she lifted her drowsy gaze to his face.

"Your mom regained consciousness."

She looked to Dr. Mayes for reassurance. He nodded and smiled. "She's still in guarded condition. She has a slight concussion, but everything looks good."

"Thank You, God," Liza breathed. "Does Daddy know?"

"No. He's still asleep. They moved him to coronary care about two hours ago."

Two hours. Liza looked at the clock on the wall, not believing she had slept so long. "Can I see Mom?" She needed to reassure herself.

The doctor nodded. "She's been asking for you. I don't think she believes me when I say your dad is okay. My patients will hate me, but I might as well make rounds while I'm here."

Rick grinned, watching the old doctor disappear down the hallway. "He hasn't changed."

"Not a bit," Liza agreed. "Want to come with me?"

"I'll wait until she's better." Rick chuckled and explained, "Seeing me after so long might be an even greater shock."

"She'd be delighted. You always held a special place in her heart."

"Not today. Go ahead, and I'll take you home afterwards."

Through the window at the end of the hall, Liza could see the sun coming up. The activity in the emergency area had lessened little overnight. The constant stream of sickness and injury kept the staff busy and the waiting room chairs full.

"Thank You, Lord," she whispered again, taking a second longer to pin on a bright smile before pushing the cubicle's curtain aside. Liza fought to regain her fragile control at the sight of her mother's pain-filled eyes. "Mom," she whispered, her throat tightening. *Superficial?* Those cuts looked terrible, and her face was black-and-blue.

"Liza," she called anxiously, "is your dad okay?"

"Daddy's fine. What were you two up to this time?" Liza asked, her voice growing stronger. She teased her parents often, saying they reminded her of a couple of teenagers with some of their antics. They were still so much in love.

"Paul wasn't feeling well, so we decided to come home early. It was terrible, honey," her mother said as she suppressed a shudder. "He grabbed his chest and slumped over the wheel. It happened so fast."

"It's okay," Liza comforted, resting her hand gently on her mother's shoulder for fear that she would hurt her further. Tears at the thought of almost losing them caught in her throat. "I've talked to Daddy. He's doing fine."

The woman tried to rise up on the bed, gasping with the pain that hit her. "Is he really? Please, tell me."

"They gave him a sedative, and he's resting," Liza answered easily. "He's worried about you, of course."

"How bad is he?"

There was no way to sugarcoat the harsh reality of what had happened. Her mother expected the truth. "He had a heart attack. The doctor doesn't know how severe yet. His leg's broken, too."

The woman's eyelids fluttered shut. "Mom, I'm going to leave so you can rest," Liza said softly. "Do you need something for pain?" At her mother's refusal, she said, "Get some rest. I'll be back later today."

"Are you okay?" she asked, warming Liza's heart with her motherly instinct. "I'm sure the news frightened you."

Liza dared not mention the emotional rollercoaster she'd been on before hearing the news. "Yes. God is in control. He's taking care of things. You concentrate on getting better."

Her mother's hold tightened. "Get Kitty to stay with you until we come home."

Liza leaned over to kiss her forehead. "I will. I've got a lot of people looking out for me. Oh, and guess who's home?"

"No idea," she countered weakly.

"Rick," Liza said. "He's with me now. I was at the Evanses' cookout, and he brought me home. Isn't that wonderful news?"

"I'm so happy for his family. His mother's been worried about him for some time. We pray for him every week."

"He looks really good."

"I'm sure you noticed," her mother commented, managing a feeble chuckle.

"Mother!"

There was an underlying teasing in her pain-filled gaze. "Tell him he must come see me."

"I will," Liza promised, kissing her cheek. "Love you," she called as she started out the door.

"I love you, too, baby," she responded tearfully. "Go home and get some rest. Your dad and I will be fine."

Her mother's words of welcome delighted Rick, and he ushered Liza home without giving her the opportunity to change her mind.

"Rest," he ordered, placing a light kiss on her cheek after he opened the front door.

She smiled gratefully. "I plan to. Thanks, Rick. I don't know what I'd have done without you."

"My pleasure."

No doubt he felt as exhausted as she did. "Be careful driving home."

As much as sleep appealed, Liza knew top priority was the number of telephone calls that had to be made.

"No, Granny, that was all he said," Liza told her mother's mother a second time. "They were both resting when I left the hospital. I'm going to do some things around here and go back later."

"Will you come stay with me?"

"I think it's better if I stay here. I'll get Kit to come over. Will you be all right?"

She listened as the woman went on for a few more minutes about her parents and her being alone in the house.

"I'm perfectly okay. I'll see you at the hospital later. Sure you don't want me to pick you up? Okay then, give Gramps my love."

Kitty said she would call later to see what time she wanted her to come over and made Liza promise to call the moment she needed anything.

"I'll have Mom call the pastor for you," Kitty added. "I'll be sure they activate the prayer chain."

"Thanks, Kit," she said, reaching up to push several strands of hair out of her face. "I'll talk to you later."

One more call. She dialed her boss's home number, deciding it might be the last opportunity she had over the weekend. He was very sympathetic and told her to take as long as she needed to get her parents situated. "Give them my regards."

"I will, sir."

"Liza, call if you need anything."

"Thanks, Mr. Wilson."

Relieved, she hung up the phone and fixed herself a sandwich and cup of cocoa. Upstairs, she slid into her nightgown and fell into bed, exhausted.

At first light the next morning, Lee drove up the road to Liza's house with no idea of what he hoped to find once he arrived. Maybe she had been there all night, ignoring the million or so messages he'd left.

Her reaction last evening before she drove off with Rick Evans frightened him. All night long Lee tried to reach her, only to have the phone ring the requisite number of times before her voice came on to recite the answering machine message.

And all because he'd opened his big mouth too soon. Or maybe too late. When he and Uncle John discussed the situation, they agreed to wait until Lee made a final decision. His uncle urged him to carefully consider whether he would be happy in a smaller town.

He knew full well Liza wasn't happy about her boss's choice to invite him into the firm in the first place. That fact led him to believe Uncle John's failure to bring her up to date on what they planned hurt her even more.

He felt very guilty for throwing the news in her face like that. Her pained expression along with the words that she never wanted to see him again cut deep into Lee's heart. He needed her now more than ever, and he knew it had little to do with the office.

Seeing her with Rick last night scared him. She seemed so comfortable around her old friend, certainly more at ease than with him.

Lee parked, and Barney greeted him. He hesitated, not sure he wanted to test Liza's theory about the dog's gentleness, but the need to know forced him from the car. He paused long enough to pat Barney's head, and the dog rewarded him by tagging along, woofing excitedly now and again. When the doorbell failed to get a response, Lee pounded on the door and called Liza's name. After several unsuccessful tries, he gave up and started to leave.

The door jerked wide, and Liza stood there, her long, sleep-tousled hair falling about her shoulders as she tied the belt of her robe.

He pushed past her without invitation, demanding, "Where did you go?"

Something very like relief touched her face before Liza yawned and asked, "Why do you care?"

"Why?" he repeated in disbelief. "You ran away last evening acting like some kind of crazy woman. I spent half the night trying to find you."

"It wasn't work hours."

Lee grabbed her shoulders. "Stop it, Liza. I was worried." Exasperation tinged his voice. "Were you with Evans?"

She jerked away. "Who appointed you my keeper?"

Each assessed the other's antagonism. "You need one."

"Get out."

Lee remained where he stood. "Not until you tell me where you were."

"Like I said before, it's not your concern." She pointed to the door. "Good-bye."

"If you don't tell me, I'll contact Evans. He'll enlighten me."

A smile touched her face. "I doubt he'd tell you anything."

"Liza, I'm warning you," Lee muttered. "I'll turn you over my knee like your parents should have done."

"Don't come into my parents' home, criticizing the way they raised me. Yours didn't do such a great job either, Lee Hayden."

Unable to look at her, he glanced at the plaque hanging on the entry-hall wall. " 'Be ye angry, and sin not: let not the sun go down upon your wrath,' " he read, and was filled with remorse. He knew they both spoke out of emotion, neither giving much thought to their retaliatory verbal warfare. "I'm sorry."

"Me, too," she admitted.

"I owe you an apology. I shouldn't have sprung the news on you like that. I called last night, and when I didn't get an answer, I thought you might do something you'd regret."

"You didn't push me into doing anything disastrous. I did spend the night with Rick. . . . But it's not what you think," she explained hurriedly. "My parents were involved in a serious accident. He took me to the hospital."

"Liza, I'm sorry. Are they okay?"

"The doctor said everything looked good early this morning. I've talked with both of them. Daddy had a heart attack. Mama only regained consciousness shortly before I left. Now, if you'll excuse me, I have lots to do before I go back to the hospital."

"Can I drive you to the hospital?"

"It would be simpler if I drove myself."

"In what?" he asked, reminding her of the damage to her vehicle.

"Mom's car is here. They drove Daddy's truck."

"You're tired. Let me take you," Lee requested. "What else can I do to help out?"

"Dave and Rick will be over later to take care of things," she said. "That's how neighbors are here in the country."

"How long before you're ready to go?"

"Around eight."

"I'll be back." She nodded and closed the door. Lee kept walking but patted Barney's head when the animal tried to engage him in play. He opened the car door and sat down, all the while considering the shock Liza must have experienced last night when she learned of her parents' accident. That news coming on top of the damage to her car and the bomb he'd dropped on her must have been devastating.

Starting the car, Lee vowed to be a better friend. She probably wasn't going to be receptive to his efforts to help, but help he would. He owed her that much.

❧

Liza's thoughts ran rampant with Lee's behavior and her feelings for him. How could she be hurt and angry one moment, and forgiving the next? "Don't be stupid; you'd forgive him anything."

The bell rang. He showed up right on time. She came down the stairs slowly. Opening the door, Liza invited him inside. She picked up her purse from the table and checked for her house keys, jumping when the phone rang. "Rick," she exclaimed. "I thought the hospital might be calling."

Lee stood nearby, listening to the one-sided conversation. Outwardly he showed no reaction, but he made no effort to give her any privacy.

She turned her back, lowering her voice. "Sure, why not? No, that won't be necessary. Lee came by and offered to drive me in. No, it'll be okay. See you later. Thanks, Rick. Bye." She replaced the receiver.

"Evans?"

"Yes, he's meeting me at the hospital later so he can visit with Mom and Dad, and then he's taking me out to dinner."

"Would you rather he picked you up now?"

Liza's head snapped up. He almost sounded jealous. "I told him you were taking me. If you've changed your mind, I'll drive myself."

"I want to do this for you," he said, taking the small bag she had packed for her parents.

In the car, Lee questioned her about the extent of her parents' injuries. He surprised her further by parking in the lot rather than pulling up at the door. "I thought I'd come in and say hello if you think it's okay?"

"What's your mom's favorite flower?" he asked as they neared the gift shop. "I'd like to do something to cheer her up."

"I suppose it's the least you can do for that comment about my upbringing," Liza told him.

He was back within minutes, carrying a vase of fresh-cut flowers and a single rose, which he handed to Liza. "Once more, I apologize for allowing my mouth to get out of control."

Lee escorted Liza to her mother's room. If possible, her mother's bruising seemed even more vivid today. Several times, Liza saw her wince when she moved the slightest bit.

After a few minutes of watching Lee charm the woman, Liza checked her watch. "I'm going up to see Daddy. Any messages?"

"Give him my love. I talked to him on the phone earlier."

Her father seemed happy to see her, even though he was clearly despondent. "I'd offer you a seat, but they aren't too keen on visitors here. Figure they can keep people from visiting too long by making them stand."

"The short visiting periods are for your benefit, Daddy."

"Liza, what will I do about the crops?"

She laid her hand on his. "We'll manage," she soothed. "Just don't worry about it now. Mom sends her love."

"They won't let me see her. Dr. Mayes said maybe after a couple of days. I'm so tired of this place. I wish they'd leave me alone."

"I bet," Liza countered. "Then you'd be grumbling about the service."

"For what they're charging, I'd be entitled."

His skewed logic brought a grin to her face. "I knew Mom spoiled you, but I had no idea how much until now."

"You're an ungrateful child." He laughed when she started to giggle.

"I'll have you know this ungrateful child called her boss this morning to tell him she'll be out of work indefinitely."

"Are you sure?"

Liza fidgeted beneath the intensity of his stare. "I think it's best. Any idea on what they plan next?"

"They won't say. They're monitoring me with all of this equipment, and the doctor says six weeks, maybe longer, with my leg. The timing couldn't be worse."

Irregular rhythms crossed the monitor screen. "Settle down, Daddy. You know they're trying to determine how severe your attack was."

"I know, but Dr. Mayes won't promise me anything. Said it could be weeks."

"Thank God you've got weeks," Liza whispered when the nurse came over to the bed to check on him and indicated she should go. "See you later." She kissed his cheek and slipped out of the curtained area.

Back in her mother's room, she described the situation and what she had said. "He's not going to settle down until he's reassured that things will work out. When I think about what could have happened to you both, nothing else matters."

Her mother's eyes drifted shut for a moment. "I'll remind him he's aggravating the condition when they let me talk to him again."

"Good idea. Why don't I ask the nurse if she can arrange a phone call? You tell him I fully intend to do the best job I can," Liza said.

"That's all he can ask for."

"I'm sorry this had to happen," Lee said. "I'll be happy to help in every way possible."

Sarah Stephens smiled at him. "Thanks. It's good to know you're there if we need you. Liza has been blessed with a wonderful employer."

He seemed surprised by her mother's comment. "I've got to go. Take care of yourself, Mrs. Stephens. Walk me out, Liza?"

Outside the room, Lee touched her arm. "Call if you need me?"

"Sure," she agreed. "And Lee, I'm sorry for the way I've acted. Forgive me."

"Of course. I should have recognized that you were operating on emotion. Maybe I'll be able to get a good night's sleep tonight. I'd stay longer, but I have plans for this afternoon."

Liza said good-bye and hesitated a moment longer, watching him walk away. "Lee," she called when he was halfway down the hall. "Thanks again for all you did today. It helps Mom and Dad to know I have people I can depend on."

He regarded her for a few seconds. "No problem. Take care."

His kindness played on Liza's mind. She was so confused by his ability to turn his emotions on and off at will. Perhaps being a lawyer made him cold and untouchable at times. That coldness, and the way he could shut her out, hurt more than anything else did. She was saddened even more by the fact that their comfortable friendship might be destroyed because of her growing attraction.

He stopped and turned back. "Liza? Did you really call Uncle John this morning?"

She nodded.

"Why didn't you call me?"

"Because I didn't think you'd understand what I had to do."

He took a few steps forward. "How could you think that? I know you have to be with your parents."

"It's not just for now, Lee," she explained. "I may have to resign. At best, I probably won't be back to work until the fall."

Liza gave him full marks for restraining himself as obviously genuine astonishment changed his expression.

"Let me know how things are going with you. I do care, you know."

Liza prayed he did.

Chapter 6

Rick arrived shortly after Lee's departure, giving Liza no time to worry about Lee's lack of reaction to her plans. Her mother and Rick caught up on the news, and Mom told him he should visit his family more often. At seven, she insisted they go meet Kitty and Dave for dinner.

Liza hesitated, but she knew there wasn't much she could do for her mother or father.

They went to a local pizza restaurant. Red dominated the room, from the countertops to the checkered tablecloths. Candle containers vied with red pepper flakes and Parmesan cheese in shaker bottles, table ads, and menus in small jackets.

Kitty and Dave shared a booth and seemed oblivious to their arrival.

"Cut it out, you two lovebirds." Rick grinned at Liza when they jumped apart.

"Liza!" Kitty cried, slipping from the booth to hug her. "How are your parents? I'm so sorry."

"Better. Daddy's not enjoying his stay. Mom will be better when they let her see him for herself. Her mothering instincts seem unaffected. She just felt well enough to tell Rick he should visit more often."

"Must be a mother thing," Rick said. "Mom tells me that all the time."

Everyone laughed, and Rick indicated Liza should slip into the booth. Kitty slid back in beside Dave.

"It was so frightening," Kitty said.

"You're telling me. I thought the officer came to tell me about my car."

"This hasn't been your weekend. The news shocked everyone."

"I called Mr. Wilson to let him know I'll be out awhile."

"Does Lee know?"

Kitty knew about Lee's reaction to her last request for time off. Neither understood his strong reaction.

"Yes," Liza said, not really wanting to get into it with Rick and Dave looking on.

"And?"

Liza glanced at the men, then back at Kitty. Reaching for the tea pitcher, she filled Rick's glass and then her own. "He didn't have a lot to say. Tell me about the party. What happened after I left?"

Smiles wreathed all three faces. "Well, there was some big to-do when a certain man got down on bended knee and asked a certain woman to marry him," Kitty said.

Puzzlement soon gave way to understanding as Liza realized they were the mystery couple. "Oh, I missed your proposal? What did he do?" She looked from one to the other and demanded, "Did you really ask her in front of everyone?"

"He did," Kitty said. "I was so shocked. He brought me a bowl of homemade strawberry ice cream, and the first thing I saw was this sparkling in the center." She held out her hand to show her new diamond.

"She never did eat that ice cream," Dave said. "Perfectly good waste of some of the best ice cream ever made."

Kitty tapped his arm. "Then he bravely knelt and asked me to marry him."

Dave sat a little taller in his seat at Kitty's mention of bravery as the waitress slid two piping hot pizzas onto the table.

"We ordered," Kitty explained, passing around the plates. "Dave thought you might be hungry."

"We certainly ate here enough in the past for you to know what I like."

The feeling of being watched was strong. Liza glanced up to find Lee near the doorway. She waved at him, and he returned the greeting. He looked tired. A wave of guilt coursed through Liza.

Kitty spotted him at the same time. "There's Lee. Let's invite him to join us."

"I don't know. Liza might. . . ," Rick began.

"It's okay," she said softly. "I'll ask."

Rick stood, and she scooted past him, unaware of the curious looks her friends shared. Liza walked over to the little corner table where Lee sat. "Hi. We thought you might like to join us."

He smiled at her. "No thanks. I don't want to interrupt your date."

"It's not a date, just old friends having dinner together. Kit and Dave are talking about their engagement."

"I didn't realize they got engaged."

Liza traced one finger about the checkerboard pattern of the cloth. "Last night. It sounds like we missed some production."

He pushed back the wooden chair. "I'll walk over with you and congratulate them."

She was very aware of his hand resting in the small of her back as they walked over to the booth. Rick stood, and Liza slipped into her seat.

"Pull up a chair," Kitty invited.

Lee shook his head. "I won't crash your party. Liza just told me the news. I wanted to congratulate you both."

"Nonsense," Dave said. "The more the merrier. Sit down."

They kept insisting, so Lee finally borrowed a chair from a nearby table and sat down. The waitress took his order for a soft drink and Kitty's request for another plate.

Kitty grabbed his hand. "Let's say grace. Our pizzas are getting cold."

He appeared surprised by her action but accepted Rick's hand and bowed his head as she prayed. Kit took on the job of serving the food, and soon everyone had a couple of slices.

The conversation was as varied as the table's occupants until Kitty started talking about planning a fall wedding. "It's the only time I'll be able to get my future husband out of town for a honeymoon. I want you to be my maid of honor," she told Liza. "And Rick will be Dave's best man."

"You should ask Dad," Rick said.

"I did. He said he'd rather you did it," Dave said. "You know how he hates to wear a tux."

Rick grimaced playfully. "I hoped you'd choose bib overalls and caps."

Liza giggled at Kitty's expression.

"No way."

"You are asking a bit much of a country boy. I felt sure you were planning the nature thing down by the pond—shorts, bare feet, and daisies in your hair."

"Stop joking. We're having a lovely wedding with everyone beautifully dressed."

"If you plan this shindig soon enough, I should be able to attend before my next job starts up."

"Believe me, she's already checking your itinerary for this visit," Dave told his brother.

Kitty looked at Lee. "And, of course, you have a standing invitation."

"Thanks."

Liza dropped the pizza crust onto her plate. "I'd have given a nickel to see Dave on bended knee."

"What happened to you anyway?" Kit asked. "I looked all over. I wanted to show you my ring."

"I went home." Liza refused to look in Lee's direction.

"Wow, good thing you went. You must have had a feeling something wasn't right."

The something not right had started at the party and worsened by the time she got home. Tears dampened Liza's eyes. "The news took years off my life."

She glanced up when Rick gently squeezed her fingers and caught Lee's gaze on them. "Don't worry," he comforted. "God is in control."

"There's no other way I could make it through this."

Kitty changed the subject. Rick brought them up to date on what he'd been doing, telling them about London.

"I'd love to go there one day," Kitty said wistfully.

"It's very different from here," Rick said.

The evening passed quickly. All too soon, it was time to say good night.

"This has been fun, but I need to get home. Ready, Liza?"

"She can ride with us," Kit said. "I'm spending the night at her place anyway."

"I'd be happy to take Liza home," Lee offered.

Everyone looked to her for a decision. "I can ride with Lee. We need to talk anyway. Thanks for everything, Rick."

He kissed her cheek and slipped from the booth. "I'll be in touch."

"I appreciate the help. Once we know what's going on with Daddy, I'll know better what to do."

"Take care. I'll check with you tomorrow."

Liza nodded. Emotion clogged her throat as the obvious love of her friends surrounded her. She wasn't alone. Not only was God with her every step of the way, He had sent these wonderful people to help carry her load.

Lee insisted on picking up the check for their celebratory dinner, and after he paid, they walked out to the parking lot.

"I'll meet you at the house before too late," Kitty promised. "My clothes are in the car."

Liza hugged her friend. "Thanks, Kit." Lee opened the car door and waited for her to get in. "Thanks for taking me home. I wanted to talk to you about this morning."

Lee didn't start the car right away. He turned to face her, resting one arm on the steering wheel. "My behavior was totally uncalled for. I had no right to strike out at you like that."

Liza felt the urge to take the conversation further and discuss the information he'd sprung on her, but now wasn't the time. Her emotions were still pretty raw. It hurt to think that Mr. Wilson hadn't shared the news himself.

"Let's forget it happened," she suggested.

❧

Lee wanted nothing more than to forget, but he knew he owed Liza an explanation.

"Don't blame Uncle John. I'm the reason we didn't tell you."

"When did he start thinking about retirement? Mr. Wilson's not that old, and he's never mentioned it before."

"He and Aunt Clara want to travel. I suppose he plans to maintain a certain degree of control, but I'd be responsible for day-to-day operations."

"I see."

Did she? He wasn't so sure Liza was convinced. "He wants me to be certain I want to live here before I commit to taking over. I'm beginning to feel at home. I like the people. Can't promise I'll lose all my big-city ways at once, though."

When she nodded, not saying anything else, Lee wondered about Liza's reaction. "Friends?"

"Sure."

Lee found the conversation less stilted on the way home. When Lee drove into the yard, Barney greeted them by barking as he jumped up on the side of the car.

Horrified, Liza reached through the window and pushed the dog away. "Barney, get down. Bad dog."

Lee smiled when she started digging in her purse for the house key. How she got so much stuff in that small bag intrigued him. The keys jangled as she pulled them out. "Thanks again, Lee."

"Let me walk you to the door."

"That's okay. Barney's right here. I doubt there's anyone waiting in the shadows with him running around, barking like that."

Lee eyed the dog. "True. Liza," he began hesitantly. "I hope you understand I only want what's best for you." He understood she was on an emotional tightrope when it took her a few seconds to manage more than a nod.

"I don't know what I'd do without my friends. The Lord has truly blessed me."

Taken aback, Lee wondered why she didn't feel angry at God for all that had happened to her this weekend. "You believe that, don't you? Despite the fact that your parents are both in the hospital, you feel blessed?"

"I only have to look for blessings to find them," Liza said. "My parents could have died in that crash. For that matter, Daddy could have died out there, in a field by himself, because we didn't know he had a heart problem. I could be alone, not knowing where to turn next. Instead, I have wonderful friends and neighbors who are pulling together and helping me do what needs to be done. Yes, I feel wonderfully blessed. I have many reasons to praise the Lord today and every day."

Lee hoped the car's interior light didn't illuminate his discomfort as Liza continued to speak of her faith.

"I'm never alone. God is with me always and has been since the day I asked Him into my heart. Most of all, I'm amazed that He loves me despite my failings. And believe me, I have plenty. His grace is worth more than anything to me."

"You'd better get inside. Tomorrow's another busy day."

"I hope we can talk about this more in the future, Lee."

Resigned that she saw through his delaying tactic, he said, "I'm sure we will."

꧁꧂

A couple of hours later, Liza and Kit sat at the kitchen table, drinking cocoa and discussing how their lives had changed in one weekend.

"And to think you were saying he didn't have a ring on your finger just minutes before the party," Liza teased after examining the round diamond more closely. "This thing is huge." She grinned as she pretended Kit's hand weighed a ton.

Kit's laughter was pure joy. "I know. The truth is, I've wanted him to ask me forever. I guess I used false bravado to cover my fear that he wouldn't."

"I never doubted he'd ask. Dave has loved you forever. You realize what you've agreed to, don't you?"

Kit shrugged. "Sharing my life with the man I love?"

"And sharing his life," Liza reminded. "Have you considered what that means?"

"It'll take some adjusting, but we'll work things out."

"Dave is a farmer, Kit. He doesn't have nine-to-five hours. Granted, you'll see more of him once you're living in the same house, but the land places all sorts of demands on those who choose to care for it."

A smile touched her friend's lips. "I'll be the one thing I said I'd never be—a farmer's wife. Goes to show the mind can't control the heart when it comes to love."

Amen, Liza thought. How could she possibly be in love with a man who couldn't understand her choices? "Mama always says, 'Never say never.'"

"What about Lee? What really happened last night?"

Reconciled to the truth of the matter, Liza admitted, "Mostly I made an idiot of myself."

Kit set the mug on the table. "How?"

"I was feeling flattered when he showed me a bit of attention." Embarrassed, she forced herself to continue. "I took offense to something he said. We argued, then he dropped this bomb on me about how Mr. Wilson is talking about retirement and he's going to take over. I was devastated. He explained that Mr. Wilson is waiting on his decision. It hurts, though. After all the years I've given that office, I expected a certain amount of loyalty. They should have at least told me what they're planning. It changes everything."

"In what way?"

"Mr. Wilson and I understand each other. His working style is nothing like Lee's."

"Understandable. Younger man. Has more to prove. Would you leave the firm?"

Would she? Liza didn't know. She'd never considered not working for Mr. Wilson. Could she work with Lee, given their problems? "I honestly don't know."

"How do you feel about Lee?"

"I'm so confused by his behavior. Most of the time, I feel like an office fixture."

"So you think Lee doesn't see you as a woman?" Kitty asked.

Liza shrugged as she stood and took their cups over to the sink. She rinsed them quickly and placed them in the dishwasher. "I don't know what to think. Lee's like the weather. Wait a moment, and he changes. I thought we were becoming friends, but now I feel like a body who keeps the office running efficiently."

"That bothers you?"

"A lot," Liza admitted, almost reluctantly. "I don't want to be attracted to him. He doesn't understand me at all. He doesn't attend church, and I've never met anyone more focused on himself."

"But you've developed a short circuit between your heart and your brain?"

Liza laughed out loud at Kit's analogy. "System overload. That's me."

"What are you going to do?"

"Nothing. Well, actually I'm dropping the load right into God's hands. He's more capable of sorting this out than I am."

"Good idea. There's a reason you came into Lee's life, and only time will bring an answer."

"A lot of prayer won't go amiss either," Liza said pointedly.

"We'll pray without ceasing," Kit vowed, smiling at her friend as they started up the stairs.

Chapter 7

The pattern for the remainder of her summer fell into place over the next few days. By Friday, they knew nothing less than bypass surgery could correct her father's heart problem, and it was scheduled for early Monday morning.

Liza felt even more frightened when the doctor outlined the procedure, which involved opening his chest from top to bottom and stripping veins from his good leg to use to repair the damaged vessels.

The doctors allowed Liza's mother to accompany her to the CCU when they gave Dad the diagnosis. He didn't take the news well, but Liza suspected he controlled his outrage in her mother's presence. As always, his wife's influence soothed him, and he relegated his health to secondary importance when he saw her.

A cold knot of fear formed in her stomach as Liza watched them, considering the impact of the responsibility the situation placed upon her shoulders.

An efficient nurse whisked her mother away at the first sign of tiredness, leaving her father's attention focused on his present problem. When the nurse came in with more medication, he demanded they stop drugging him so he could talk to his daughter.

"No manager for the farm," he declared.

Liza sat still, her arms stiffening as she pressed her hands against her knees to fortify herself. "But, Daddy—"

"You can do just as good a job, better in my opinion," he said before she could finish the sentence.

She prayed her despair wasn't obvious to him. He didn't need the added worry of an incompetent being responsible for his livelihood. "I hope I don't let you down."

"Liza, baby, I'll be as close as the house, and all our friends are willing to help. The pastor came by this afternoon. He said they're putting together a schedule to help."

But wanting and doing are different things, Liza thought. All those good intentions wouldn't be much help if the people didn't carry through. What would happen when they got caught up in the demands of their own farms? And given how busy every farmer got this time of year, they would be borrowing from Peter to pay Paul. She grimaced at the pun.

"Besides, your mother will be home soon."

"Lot of good she'll be with you sick," Liza countered with a knowing smile.

"I have enough confidence in you for the both of us," he told her without so much as a blink of an eye.

Let's hope it's justified, Liza thought as she agreed to take on the farm.

❧

Even the worst days at the office didn't compare with the juggling act Liza endured over the next three weeks.

Released on the day of her husband's surgery, Sarah Stephens insisted on going straight to the waiting area. Nothing Liza said could convince her otherwise. Her mother remained at the hospital after her father moved from the CCU to a room. Liza drove back and forth to check on them and bring her mother fresh clothes until they released him on Thursday.

Ecstatic over having him home, Liza thought they were through the worst of things. . .until he developed complications from a cold that resulted in his returning to the hospital for another brief stay.

Liza listened carefully when seasoned farmers took her under their wings and taught her how to deal with the situations that arose. The major surgery left her father in a weakened state, and she dared not say anything that would add to his stress.

Exhausted both emotionally and physically, Liza refused to look beyond each day. Rick helped all he could, and Mr. Wilson called to check on her parents and reassure her that they would make do until her return. She disliked the idea of leaving them in a bind, but the options were limited.

❧

On Thursday night Lee came by to bring what was left of a formerly gorgeous fern. "We tried," he said with a shrug. "Evidently neither of us has your green thumb."

Liza took the hanger, grimacing as she fondled the brown-tipped fronds. "Didn't you water it, or talk to it, or anything?"

Lee laughed. "We watered it. Actually it got so much water, I'm surprised it didn't learn to swim. As for talking, I doubt the clients would approve."

"Poor, lonely, drowned plant," Liza crooned, setting it on the corner of the porch. "Other than this, how are things going?"

"Don't ask." Lee adjusted his pantleg as he sat and made himself comfortable beside her in the swing. "The files and your desk are in shambles. Everything is stacked to the ceiling, and of course every folder I need is in the stack to be filed. It takes forever to find something."

"And it never occurred to you to file them?"

He ignored her question. "When are you coming back?"

She stirred uneasily. "I have no idea."

Lee's gaze narrowed, a heavy frown weighing down his face. "What kind of answer is that?"

His query destroyed their earlier ease. The tension grew as he sat, glaring and waiting.

"The only one I can give you," she said with quiet emphasis, glancing toward the house. "I'm needed here."

"I need you at the office, too. I can't do this alone."

"I can't help you right now. You'll do just fine."

"You don't understand. All my life I've been an overachiever. The highest grades, the highest SAT scores, the finest college.

"Please don't think I'm bragging, but I was recruited by a number of prestigious firms. I missed home and jumped at the chance to join a larger firm in Charlotte. I was certain I'd make partner in record time."

"What happened?"

"I realized I'm not a team player. At first, I tried to do whatever it took to assure I was in line for advancement. But my integrity is too important to me. I took on some pro bono cases they assigned, then I found out they didn't plan on me giving the same attention to detail to those clients as I did the ones with billable hours. It wasn't like they were bankrupting themselves by giving away a few hours of legal service. I refused to give the cases less than they deserved. The senior partners weren't very happy with me. I can't go back to that kind of law again."

Lee knew he wasn't being fair to Liza, but he needed her desperately.

"You won't have to," she pointed out. "Evidently Mr. Wilson is comfortable enough with you being there to go off on extended vacations."

"What about your priorities, Liza? You love your job far more than you do this farm."

"And I love my parents far more than either my job or the farm. I have other obligations, more important priorities right now. My parents and their livelihood come before my own needs. Why did you come here tonight? You knew my decision."

Lee all but jumped from the swing. "I thought you'd be back once you got things under control. Obviously I was wrong."

"Obviously."

He walked away without another word, Barney's barking echoing his departure.

❧

Lee's comment about her priorities made Liza realize the need to update Mr. Wilson on her plans. She wished she could make Lee understand: While she preferred the security of the office to the strangeness of the farm, she had no choice. If only she could turn back the clock.

She set aside the following morning to see Mr. Wilson. She could take care of it while her parents went for their follow-up visits with the doctor.

Family responsibility wasn't an alien concept to Mr. Wilson, Liza told herself the next morning as she unlocked the office door and stepped inside. The office was exactly as Lee described—a disaster area as well as very empty. The answering machine blinked repeatedly with a number of messages awaiting return calls.

Liza set her purse on the desktop and reached for the phone. She called the temp who usually filled in for her to ask if she was available for an indefinite time. The woman seemed eager, and Liza told her she'd be back in touch as soon as she got approval from Mr. Wilson.

While she waited, Liza slipped into the routine of her job. She wrote out message slips, opened several days' mail, checked folders, and filed those she could. She made notes on others, then stacked them in orderly piles on Lee's and Mr. Wilson's desks. It seemed she'd been away for only a day or so as she read the notes both men had left for her. 'Do this.' 'Remind me.' A despondent smile crossed her face as she updated the appointments on the computer. She would miss her job.

The bong of the grandfather clock in the corner confirmed the hour. Liza grabbed her purse and glanced around one last time. Just as she reached the door, Mr. Wilson pushed it wide, the warmth of his smile echoing in his voice as he welcomed her. "Liza, are you back with us?"

She shook her head regretfully. "Afraid not. I needed to talk to you. I did a bit of work while I waited."

He nodded approvingly. "As efficient as ever. Come into my office."

Liza followed, taking the seat across from his desk. She answered his questions concerning her parents and blinked back hot tears. "It looks like I'm going to have to request an indefinite leave of absence, sir. Daddy will be out of commission for the rest of the summer. . .maybe longer."

In the manner Liza expected, John Wilson sat, silently analyzing her words. He smiled at her as if she were a small child, his kindly words bringing relief to her troubled emotions. "I'm sure it's the only way. Of course, we hate to lose you for any length of time."

"I hate to go," she admitted, "but Daddy's not content with anyone else supervising."

"You'll have to be patient and understanding," he advised. "This is hard for all of you, but it's particularly difficult for Paul."

"The surgery left him weak as a kitten, and his leg is giving him a great deal of pain."

Mr. Wilson rose and came around the desk to pass her a tissue. "I'm sure it'll work itself out. How long do you need?"

Her forehead creased. "I'm not sure. Right now I'm thinking three months, until Daddy's back on his feet."

"Your job will still be here after that time, and longer if need be. We can hire someone on a temporary basis."

"Thank you, sir," Liza said. "You don't know what a load off my shoulders this is. Lee's upset that I haven't made the office my priority lately."

"Lee doesn't understand," his uncle explained. "I doubt he's ever experienced what you're going through now. Things would certainly be different if he were facing similar circumstances."

"I pray he never has to," Liza said.

"Amen to that. I'm going to continue your salary, Liza."

"You don't have to do that," she protested.

"Consider it a bonus. You've been my right hand for years."

They discussed her plan to get the temp in, and he asked Liza to handle a few tasks for him before she left. She sorted out the minor details before leaving the office.

As she walked across the parking lot, Liza relaxed for the first time in days. Her parents were going to be okay. Mr. Wilson had accepted her decision, and with everything else falling in place, the thought of managing the farm didn't frighten her as much.

The day seemed perfect—the warmth, the blueness of the sky, and the smiling faces of the people she met. She returned the greetings, carefully noting the messages people asked her to deliver to her folks.

She didn't see Lee until he walked up beside her. "What brings you to our part of town?"

Liza jerked around. "I was talking to Mr. Wilson. You told me to get my priorities in order."

"True, but I'd hoped you would choose us."

"I don't have a choice here," she protested, almost pleading with him to understand. "I've prayed about this, and I'm led to do what needs to be done. These are my parents."

"And where do you come into all this?"

"Everywhere. Nowhere. I don't know," Liza said. "It's all so confusing."

"And unfair," Lee added.

"I suppose it is unfair that an active man has to be sick during one of the busiest times of the year. Do you think that's what Daddy wants?"

"But what about you? How can you be so self-sacrificing?"

How could she make him understand? "It's not sacrifice to help those you love."

"What about your life? What you love? You don't want to farm. If you did, you'd never have dedicated the time to becoming a paralegal. You did that for you."

"What is this really about, Lee? Why are you so convinced I'm giving. . ." Her words trailed off as another realization hit her. "You know, I thought your objections had to do with me leaving the office in a bind, but there's something else.

Something I can't quite put my finger on."

His expression attempted to belie her words. "Why would you say that?"

"You're a 'me' type person, Lee. I'm not saying it's a bad thing, but there's a time when self ceases to be important. Tell me you wouldn't do the same if this involved your parents."

"They understand I have a career."

Liza's eyes widened. "You'd put career before the people who brought you into the world?"

"Not exactly. But they wouldn't ask. My parents are very self-sufficient. They've never asked anything of me."

"Mine didn't ask either. I made the decision. And just maybe your parents should ask something of you. It might help you understand what I've got to do."

"I'm not going to argue with you. I think they're wrong to let you throw your life away with both hands."

"Maybe you're wrong, Lee. Have you considered that? I've got to go. Mom and Dad are waiting at the doctor's office. Bye."

Liza was trembling when she settled in the car and pulled the door closed. She had never realized the depth of Lee's self-absorption until this moment. Surely he knew what the Bible said about honoring your parents. This went beyond honor for her. It was love for the people who had given her life and breath. It had nothing to do with guilt, but everything to do with her saying thank you. If Lee didn't understand, too bad. She wasn't going to let him change her mind.

It's a battle I'm not going to win, Lee thought as he closed the office door behind him. Liza's conviction outweighed his arguments every time. In his heart, Lee knew she had no choice. It did bug him that she wouldn't be around to help him. Instead, he'd have to muddle along on his own.

He stuck his head into his uncle's office to let him know he was back from the courthouse.

"Got a minute?"

Lee crossed the expanse of the expensive Oriental rug and sprawled in one of the chairs across from the desk. "What's up?"

"Liza came by."

"I saw her out in the parking lot. Looks like she's prioritized us right out of her life."

John Wilson kicked back in his burgundy leather chair and eyed Lee. "What other choice does she have?"

"Surely her dad could get someone to help out," Lee said. "It's not fair to Liza."

"Son, there's a lot you don't understand about family responsibility."

Lee shrugged. "You're right. I don't understand."

John Wilson propped his chin on his fingertips and eyed Lee. "Are you worried about her or yourself?"

"Both of us. We make a good team. She's been a lot of help to me."

"Then give her the support she needs now. You're an only child, and the day may come when you're forced to set aside your life to care for aging parents."

"Dad's shared his plans to provide care for their senior years."

"The haves and the have-nots," his uncle said. "The Stephenses don't have that kind of money. They're working-class people who depend on that farm for their livelihood. Paul Stephens doesn't know anything but the land.

"And if you knew anything about Liza, you'd know she's struggling with this decision. She's the most dedicated employee I've ever had, and frankly I'm willing to limp along without her for a while rather than risk losing her completely."

Lee felt like a thoroughly chastened little boy. He might as well reveal the rest of his role in this situation. "I don't suppose she asked you about me taking over the firm?"

His uncle's chair shot up straight. "I thought we agreed not to tell her until after we finalized things."

He nodded, sharing the grim news. "We did. And that was my intent until I let my emotions take control of my tongue and blabbed. I tried to explain, but I'm not sure she accepts my apologies."

"You'd do well to treat that girl right," John advised. "Losing her would be the worst thing that could happen to this office."

And me, Lee thought. "What do you suppose it is about us? She frustrates me faster than anyone I know. It starts out innocently enough. I ask a question, and she gives me the answer I don't want to hear. Next thing I know, the situation escalates into an argument."

"Are you attracted to her?"

Was he? Lee found it difficult to define exactly how he felt about Liza. "She's a beautiful woman inside and out."

John nodded agreement. "She is. Always has been—even before she lost all that weight. She's got the sweetest spirit. If Clara and I had a daughter, I'd want her to be just like Liza. Perhaps you're disappointed because you can't see her every day?"

"Perhaps." Lee pushed himself from the chair. "Guess I'd better start sorting through the mail."

"Liza's already taken care of that. She worked while she waited to talk to me."

Lee felt almost relieved.

"The temp will be in tomorrow. Rhonda has a different working style than our Liza," his uncle warned. "Don't expect miracles."

"I'm missing Liza already."

70

Chapter 8

Much to Liza's dismay, the confrontation with Lee stayed on her mind. The lengthy periods when she had time to think were definitely a negative of farm work. She knew Kit and Dave would string her up if she didn't attend their engagement party tonight. Without a doubt, Lee would be there. Hopefully they wouldn't argue again. What a mess.

Liza's friends had banded together to help her retain her sanity. Rick had been a daily blessing, and in the beginning she depended heavily on him. He explained things she couldn't to her dad and cheered her on as her confidence level increased. It hadn't taken long to gain the self-assurance she needed to get the job done. She attributed the change to all the prayers being offered up on her behalf.

Excited about the party, Kitty called several times to remind Liza and just to chat about what they would wear. Liza planned to use the outing as an excuse to dress up.

The strain and worry served one positive purpose—that of getting her over her plateau. Those first few days of not having her mom around to insist she eat did the trick. While running back and forth to the hospital, Liza frequently made do with little or nothing at night. Her last ten pounds and five more were gone, and she felt pleased that she had met her goal.

The accident brought about a number of changes in the Stephenses' home. When she started dieting, her mother became her biggest opponent, arguing she didn't need to lose weight. Then she claimed Liza lost too much weight and concentrated on fattening her up.

Now Sarah Stephens asked for her daughter's help. The heart attack frightened her mother into accepting that healthy eating was as necessary as breathing. Her father complained about the tasteless food and lack of things he loved, like homemade biscuits and gravy, but the changed eating habits helped everyone.

After combing her hair up into an elegant chignon, Liza removed the pale pink sheath from the hanger and pulled it on. The dress skimmed her body, stopping at her knees. The color complemented the tan she'd gained as a result of spending more time outside. Slipping on her sandals, Liza looked in the mirror and gave her hair one final pat.

Rick's eyes widened appreciatively when she answered the door, and his wolf whistle made her laugh. "Hello, gorgeous."

"I didn't think you'd notice."

"How could I not?"

"It's the first time I've been out since the accident, and I intend to celebrate." Rick grinned.

Liza walked over to kiss her mother good night. "You have a nice visit with Granny and Aunt Mary," she ordered. "And get to bed early. You've had a stressful day."

"Yes, ma'am." Her mother winked. "Have a good time, honey."

"Night, Granny, Aunt Mary. Make sure she minds you." Liza squeezed her mother's hand gently.

"If she does, it'll be a first," said Granny. "You look pretty."

"Thanks."

Her father smiled at her from the recliner. "I'm not sure I should let you out of the house in that get-up."

"Your little girl is all grown up." Liza kissed his cheek.

Family and friends of the couple filled the country club's restaurant. Liza waved at several people as she made her way over to where Kit and Dave were receiving their guests.

"Well, look at you," Kitty said. "Don't you know you're not supposed to outshine the bride-to-be?"

"What? This old thing is nothing compared to those stars in your eyes," Liza teased in return.

Kitty giggled, and Liza joined in.

They were complete opposites, both in looks and personalities. Kitty was fair-haired and vibrant, where Liza was dark and subdued. It always amazed Liza that they were best friends, the closest thing to sisters.

Over the years, Liza had become used to being dragged along to various events as one of the town's eligible young women. Kitty never hesitated to get Liza an invitation along with her own, and they made up the numbers more times than Liza cared to admit. Thanks to her friend, she'd had more than her fair share of party invitations and blind dates, few of which she'd been thrilled over.

Of course, tonight was a different story. What would she do once Kit was married? It would never be the same again.

Liza moved on down the line, hugging Dave and then Kit's parents. "You're looking mighty handsome," she told Jason.

"And you're stunning."

Dave's parents were next in the line. "I'm so happy for them," she told his mother.

Mrs. Evans smiled at her son. "It's about time. I want grandchildren before I'm too old to enjoy them."

Liza and Kit had never discussed children. She assumed they would have a family, but probably not right away. Hopefully Mrs. Evans wouldn't start pushing the newlyweds. No doubt Kit would stand her ground. Her outspoken friend wouldn't be pushed into anything before she was ready.

"How are your parents?" Mrs. Evans asked.

"Doing better. Granny and Aunt Mary are visiting tonight. Daddy's chafing at the restraints, but we're pleased with his progress."

"I can imagine," Mrs. Evans agreed. "Liza, can we borrow Rick for a while? He really should be in the receiving line. So many people are asking after him."

"Mom, don't be rude."

The woman looked shocked. "I didn't mean. . . I just thought. . ."

"She's right," Liza said quickly. "I'm sure everyone is eager to say hello. No sense in them having to chase you down to do it. I'll catch up with you later."

"Traitor," Rick whispered.

"Hey, I'm the queen of family responsibility," she mocked, grinning broadly before she walked away.

Liza paused underneath the ceiling fan to appreciate the cool breeze. It was warm inside tonight. Hopefully the predicted thunderstorm would wait until after Kitty and Dave's guests made it back home.

"Liza."

She turned, searching the crowd.

Jason motioned her over. "Here's a guy who needs some legal advice."

The group of people standing in front of the couple blocked her view. Liza smiled, gesturing that she'd be there in a moment. Despite her earlier anxiety, a thrill of anticipation touched her when she spotted Lee standing next to Jason.

"Hello, Lee."

"Hi. Liza knows paralegals don't give advice, Jason. She could get into serious trouble."

Jason laughed and winked at her. "But she gives good advice."

"What did you want to know?"

Lee's eyebrow rose a fraction. He started to speak, then stopped himself.

"Tell him how many years you get for not enjoying yourself at a Berenson party."

Liza shifted her gaze to meet Lee's penetrating, pale blue gaze. "Ten years to life as a social outcast."

Jason laughed, clapping Lee on the shoulder. "Hey, it's a joke. You didn't think we were serious?"

Lee appeared to relax, a slightly sheepish smile creeping over his face. "You had me going there for a minute. I wondered how long she'd been advising people."

"I've never started," Liza assured. "I play along because Jason gets such a kick out of the joke."

"And I only use it on lawyers," Jason said. "Got to go. Judy's either planning a career switch to a contortionist or motioning me over. Catch you later."

An uncomfortable silence hovered. "You look good," Lee said.

"Thanks. One of the pluses of worry is weight loss."

"You've caught the attention of more than one person tonight."

Liza shrugged. "The metamorphosis."

"Just how much did you change?"

"Around a hundred pounds."

His mouth dropped open. "You're kidding."

"Not at all. Ask anyone here. Most of them told me I'd be a pretty girl if I'd lose the weight."

"That's cruel."

"I was used to it. My real friends didn't mind."

Liza wondered how Lee would have reacted if he'd known her then. Thanks to her mother's efforts to grow the tiny daughter who had entered the world prematurely, she'd been overweight for as long as she could remember. She'd quickly turned into a chubby toddler. Her weight increased with each of her school years until it stabilized in her twenties. Last year, after the doctor started talking about high blood pressure and cholesterol problems, she'd taken a long look at herself and decided she didn't like what she saw.

"Looks like that line is dwindling. We should find our table," Lee commented.

They moved around the room, reading place cards. She was shocked to find herself seated with Lee. Kitty's doing, no doubt. Where had they put Rick? She glanced at the card on the opposite side. Not there.

Lee pulled out her chair. "I'm glad they seated us together. I don't know that many people in town."

"You and Jason seem rather friendly."

"We've run into each other a few times. We eat lunch at the same restaurant on occasion."

"He's a great guy."

"You're in my seat."

They looked up at Rick.

Lee indicated his name on the card. "No idea where they seated you, but it wasn't here."

"Come on, Liza," Rick said, reaching for her hand. "There's obviously some sort of mix-up."

"I'm here, too, Rick." She pointed to her card.

His mouth thinned with displeasure. "This is crazy. Why wouldn't they seat us together?"

Jason stood at the main table, calling for everyone's attention. "I don't know, but things are about to get underway. You need to find your seat."

"Looks like there's a chair up there," Lee pointed out. "I imagine they saved you a seat with the family."

"Keep out of it, Hayden. Liza's with me."

Lee stood his ground, not wavering when he said, "She's seated at this table. Unless you plan to toss someone out of his seat up there, I don't see anywhere for her to sit."

Liza looked from one to the other. Their antagonism surprised her. This was ridiculous. Surely they weren't fighting over her. "Stop it," she ordered. "I don't believe you two."

"But, Liza. . ."

"Excuse us." She laid a hand on Rick's arm and gestured to the side of the room.

"What's going on?" he demanded.

"I have no idea, but this is Kitty and Dave's night. Please, don't make a scene."

"Why would they seat us separately? They knew I was picking you up."

"I'm sure they wanted all the family together. I'll find you right after dinner," Liza promised.

Rick walked away without another word, and she watched him find his seat at the front table before moving back to her chair. Matchmaker was written all over the seating arrangements. Rick had been placed next to a single woman closer to his age—no doubt someone his mother hoped would entice him home. Liza settled in her chair, picked up her napkin, and draped it across her lap.

Lee leaned closer and whispered, "Why don't you clue me in as to what's going on here."

"I don't know," she insisted.

"Yeah, right," he said sarcastically. "Where does Evans come into the picture?"

"I came with him."

"I thought you were alone."

Lee's scrutiny made her feel uncomfortable. "He got caught in the receiving line. Whoever arranged the seating must not have known we were together."

"I doubt that. You two got something going?"

Liza shushed him when Jason began to speak, welcoming them all to the celebration.

"It took Dave a long time to get around to popping the question," Jason kidded. "You'd think he would have asked her to marry him when they were seven, but he's always been slow."

"Not so slow I couldn't keep up with you," Dave called.

Laughter filled the room.

"All joking aside, the Berenson family would like to take this opportunity to welcome Dave to our family. Kit, you couldn't have done better if we'd chosen him ourselves."

He sat, and Rick stood. "The Evans family is getting the prettier addition. I can't remember a time when Kitty wasn't around, so it's only fitting that she becomes Dave's life partner. She's been his partner in every other kind of mischief you can name."

"Hey, is this a roast or an engagement party?" Kit demanded. "I might have to rethink this. Dave never mentioned his brother was a comedian." Chuckles filled the room again.

"No way," Dave said, grabbing her hand in his. "It's a tradeoff. I get your comedian, and you get mine."

Rick reached for his water glass. "Let's all toast the happy couple. May God bless their union richly, and may they provide my mother with all the grandchildren her heart desires."

This time unreserved laughter filled the room.

Jason stood again. "Pastor Clemmons, will you bless the food?"

As they ate the salads and breads that were already on the table, the waitstaff moved in and served the entrées. Liza picked up her fork and knife and cut into the chicken. It might be disguised with all sorts of other things, but she'd eaten enough of the stuff in the past year to recognize chicken when she saw it.

"You never answered my question."

She didn't have to be reminded. "Rick is a good friend. He went off to college, then he worked overseas. Until the Evanses' party, I couldn't tell you when I saw him last. We've been renewing our friendship."

Accepting her answer, Lee immediately abandoned the conversation and launched into the subject near and dear to his heart. "Liza, we're lost without you."

"Please, Lee, not tonight. Daddy needs me," she said softly.

"He'd have a fair year without you."

"He needs a better-than-fair year, or he'll go under. There are lots of farmers being forced into bankruptcy, seeing their equipment and everything they've worked for sold at auction. No one's focusing on long-range goals. They're concentrating on survival, one year at a time."

"If he's a good farmer. . ."

"The best farmers are being forced out. I won't let that happen to Daddy. I won't," she repeated stubbornly.

"It could happen anyway, Liza."

"Not as long as there's a chance I can help prevent it. Do you have any idea how old my parents are?"

"Forty-six? Forty-seven?"

"Try fifty-six and fifty-eight."

"I thought people of their generation had children early."

"They did. My parents buried three of their children before I came along. I was born late in their lives, and I've been their life since I came along. That's the reason Daddy fights so hard to keep his farm, my birthright. I've never left home because they need me, and because I need them. I won't forsake them now, Lee."

"Nobody's asking you to do that."

"You can't farm in the dark, Lee."

"It's not fair to you."

"It's not fair to Daddy either. He's proud of the farm because he helped make it what it is. My great-great-grandfather sharecropped for years to earn the money to buy the acreage. He built the house himself. It's a legacy worth fighting for."

He clutched her hand with both of his. "I know I said I wasn't going to argue with you, but I need you."

I need you. Liza stared at Lee. How she'd longed to hear those words, only to hear them now and know he meant them in connection with the office. Not that. Never that.

He looked almost desperate. "Uncle John took off again yesterday. He's gone for a month this time. Rhonda's great with the phones, but she was out all last week with the flu. I was hoping you could get me organized again."

"A month?" she repeated. That was strange. Mr. Wilson had always been so dedicated to their clients.

"I guess he sees this as an opportunity to see if I can make the grade when the time comes for me to take over."

Liza tensed. Why did he keep bringing that up?

"Nothing will change, Liza."

"Just now when you said you needed me, did it occur to you that other people have needs, too?"

"Tell me what you need, Liza."

You, she almost shouted. No sense in being petty about it. She owed Mr. Wilson, particularly since he'd been so understanding about her extended leave of absence and continued her salary. Besides, it was her office. She'd have to contend with the mess when she returned. "Okay, Lee. You win. Sunday afternoon, after church, I'll meet you at the office."

"Thank you," he cried, grabbing her in a big bear hug. "I'm forever in your debt."

Liza managed a smile. Forever in her heart was what she preferred.

Chapter 9

Liza slept very little Saturday night, her mind churning with all of the things going on in her life. The need to escape was overwhelming, and after dressing, Liza left a note for her mother.

After saddling Majesty, she allowed him free rein to trot along the dirt paths. The early morning air blew the cobwebs and night's dreams away, giving Liza a fresh outlook on the day.

The breezes rustled through cornstalks, their whisper like that of a woman in silk walking. Dew glistened on the grass like newly cut diamonds. Liza spotted a large garden spider and stopped to marvel at the web he'd woven between two large old oaks. The dew made the unique pattern even more evident.

Though not many acres, the farm still required a lot of attention and expertise. Her father was born and bred to this life. Would she be as successful?

In the Bible, James compared patience in suffering to how a farmer waited for the land to yield its valuable crops and how the farmer waited for the autumn and spring rains. She certainly was beginning to understand the concept of patience.

Time slipped away, and Liza knew she needed to make an appearance at home before her parents began to worry. After taking care of Majesty and the other chores, she washed up on the back porch.

In the kitchen, the refrigerator door opened with a gentle tug. She poured juice for everyone, then contemplated the breakfast choices. Deciding on pancakes, she pulled out a carton of eggs and the other ingredients.

"Morning, Mom," she said, chuckling as the woman's gaze flashed protectively about her kitchen. Liza gave her a quick peck on the cheek and removed milk from the refrigerator. Stirring the pancake batter, she said, "I was going to surprise you with breakfast in bed."

"It would have been a surprise," her mother agreed, bending to pick up a tiny fragment of eggshell from the floor. "Drink your juice," she said, passing Liza the glass.

Liza took a couple of sips, then set the glass on the counter before she rummaged for a frying pan. "Where is that flat one I like so much?" She jumped back when the pile unbalanced and several pans slid onto the floor.

"Honey, as much as I appreciate your efforts. . ."

"Okay, I get the message. You hate people in your kitchen. I'll go shower for church."

Liza whistled cheerily as she went upstairs. Her father slept in the downstairs bedroom at the front of the house so she wasn't concerned about waking him, although she knew he was already wide awake.

The cool water felt wonderful as it washed away the stickiness from her early morning activity. After she toweled dry, Liza slipped into a sleeveless knit dress she liked to wear around home and went to see her father. He sat on the edge of his bed, putting on his robe.

"Hello, Pops," she said, smoothing back the hair on his forehead and kissing him there. "How are you feeling?"

"I'll get by, I guess. No real complaints, other than this thing," he said, slapping a hand against the despised cast.

"You'll have one on your hand if you keep that up," Liza warned. "It won't be much longer."

"Dr. Mayes said another three weeks. That's pretty long, if you ask me."

"It is," she consoled, patting his hand, "but you're blessed, Daddy. You're alive, and, God willing, in a few weeks, you'll be able to walk again. You still have your leg and your life."

"I know that," he allowed, "but, honey, I'm out of my element here. I need to be doing my work—not laying around, forcing you to do it."

Liza gazed sympathetically at his stricken face. He was like a child whose favorite toy had been taken away. "I wish you were out there, but I'd rather see you well again than see this farm make thousands of dollars. Your health is worth much more than that. If anything had happened to you. . ."

She dropped down on the bed and wrapped her arms about his neck. "You're right there with me every minute of the day."

"Liza, baby, you're worth a dozen sons and daughters. I love you."

"I love you, too, Daddy," she whispered.

"I know."

"Let me help you to the kitchen."

"I'm too slow. Better go eat your breakfast. It's getting on toward church time."

Back in the kitchen, Liza said, "Let me get some flowers for the table." She ran out the door, smack-dab into Lee.

"Ah, the farmer's daughter," he drawled after getting a glimpse of her bare feet.

"Why, of course," she drawled, emphasizing her Southern accent. "Just a li'l ol' farmer's daughter who loves the feel of God's good country dirt under her feet. Don't y'all?" She fluttered her long eyelashes at him.

Liza started at the admiring glint in the laughter-filled eyes. "I all wouldn't know," he said. "I all's from the city. We only have good city concrete."

"Why, you poor thing," Liza said, walking around to the backyard.

Lee trailed after her. "You really think so?"

She cut both a yellow and a peach-colored rose and breathed their heady aromas. "No. It was the best life for you, I suppose. What brings you to our neck of the woods?"

"I thought I'd see if I could do anything for you this morning since you're doing me a favor this afternoon."

"You really are a city boy. I've been up since dawn." She didn't add that part of the time had been spent on horseback.

"I thought there was always something to do on a farm."

"The Sabbath is a much-needed day of rest."

He shrugged. "You can't say I didn't offer."

There was something not right about his early morning appearance. "Come on, Lee, you know this visit is suspect, at best."

His whistle pierced the air. "I give in," he said, holding up his hands and crying, "Truce. Cease-fire. If I had a white flag, I'd wave it."

Liza's face turned red.

"I honestly did want to help. I feel guilty about heaping more on you with all your work here. How are your parents?"

That didn't sound like a selfish act. Was he beginning to understand? Liza sighed, shaking her head. "I've never known anyone like you."

"Because I asked about your parents?" Lee asked, mischief glinting in his eyes.

"You really get a kick out of keeping people guessing."

"This is a beautiful spot," Lee said, stepping closer. Their gaze met, and his lips slowly descended to meet hers. Like a moth to a flame, Liza felt herself being pulled in. She was powerless to resist his kiss.

"Liza, where are those flowers?" her mother called.

Lee's smile was as intimate as the kiss when he bent to retrieve them from the ground.

"Here, Mom," she managed, taking them from him and hurrying toward the house. "I'd have been in a few minutes ago if a certain early visitor hadn't waylaid me in the garden."

Her mother pushed the screen door open and greeted Lee with a warm smile. "Lee! Come in. How have you been?"

"Fine, Mrs. Stephens. And you?" He eyed Liza as she attempted to retrieve a vase just out of reach. "Let me get that."

He handed it to her. "I asked after you a few minutes ago, and your daughter tried to pick a fight."

"Liza!" her mother exclaimed.

"It was his fault, Mom."

"I'd declare you were enemies if I didn't know better."

Liza glanced at Lee, wondering what he thought about her mother's statement. "Sometimes we are," he said. "All good friends should be at times."

Mrs. Stephens set the filled plates on the table, resting her hand on her husband's shoulder as he shook pills from the containers. "Maybe so," she allowed. "Make yourself at home. Would you care for breakfast?"

"I wouldn't mind coffee."

Paul Stephens snorted.

"This is a no-coffee environment," Liza said. "There's juice or milk in the refrigerator. The glasses are over there," she added, pointing to a pristine white cabinet.

Lee laughed heartily, his deep laughter sounding throughout the kitchen. "Don't put yourself out on my account."

"I won't," she said, continuing to pour syrup over her pancakes.

"Sarah Elizabeth Stephens," her mother wailed, returning the tray to the countertop. "Have you forgotten your manners?"

Liza leaned her elbow on the table and rested her chin in her hand. "Most of them."

"What did I ever do to deserve this?" her mother entreated, lifting her gaze heavenward.

"Okay, Mom," she relented, passing Lee the plate of untouched pancakes. "Excuse me, please. I have to dress for church. Mom, Lee says thanks for breakfast."

"That child," her mother said, shaking her head as Liza left the room. "You'll have to excuse her. We spoiled her terribly."

"She really is delightful," Lee said.

Liza heard them talking as she walked toward the stairs. She didn't need her mother sharing all of her secrets with Lee. The sooner she returned, the better.

Liza dashed for the stairs. She came down minutes later dressed in a pale green, two-piece summer suit, her long hair flowing down her back, the bangs secured in a barrette.

Lee stood and watched her cross the room. "Would you like an escort to church?"

"You want to go to church with me?"

He shrugged. "Sure. If you think I'm dressed okay."

Far removed from the suits she generally saw him in, Liza found Lee quite handsome in his casual khaki slacks and short-sleeved, button-down shirt.

"Of course, I'm not Rick Evans."

"No, you aren't," Liza agreed.

"Your lifelong friend. Will we ever be friends like that?"

Liza picked up her purse and Bible.

There was a great deal of difference between liking a man as a friend and being in love with him. Awareness generated a chemistry of its own. "We are friends, Lee."

"If you say so. Sometimes I think you really do dislike me."

"We'll be late for church," she reminded, taking a step toward the door.

"Then let's go, but don't think this is the last of it." His expression grew more determined as he held the screen door open. "I'm going to be your friend yet."

Chapter 10

Liza settled comfortably into his car, watching the familiar scenery roll by. "I can't believe half of July is already gone. Doesn't seem possible that we'll get it all done, but Daddy declares we will, and he's the expert."

Lee glanced at her, then brought his gaze back to the road. "What I know about farming, you could put on the sharp end of a stickpin."

"That much, huh?" Liza grinned.

"City through and through," he agreed.

"Well, you're a country lawyer now, and you're going to have to learn better."

"Yes, ma'am," he agreed solemnly. "What does a greenhorn like me do to 'learn better'?"

Liza hesitated, blinking as the crazy thought coursed through her head. What if he spent a day with her on her own ground? No way. "Come for dinner one night. You can pick Daddy's brain."

"Sounds like a plan to me," he said, parking the car in the church lot and coming around to open her door. "Of course, with all the experience you're getting, I'll have my own resident expert in the office."

Attending church with Lee resulted in curious reactions from the people she'd known all her life. Several members came forward to ask after her parents and who her gentleman friend was. Every time, Lee stuck out his hand and introduced himself before Liza could explain. Most people said how glad they were to have him there and invited him to come back soon. She almost felt his sigh of relief when they sat down in the pew.

"Nice church."

Liza agreed. The congregation had bought the land and built the new sanctuary only two years before. The stained glass windows depicted a number of biblical scenes and sparkled beautifully in the sunlight. The padded pews were much more comfortable than the old wooden ones.

"How long have you attended?"

"Since before I was born. My ancestors were charter members. Mom and Dad married here."

"That's quite a history."

The minister of music stepped forward and directed them to secure a hymnal and turn to page one. Lee stopped Liza when she reached for a second book. "We can share."

The opening music of "Holy, Holy, Holy" filled the sanctuary, and the words of praise to her Lord poured from Liza. She noted the way Lee looked at her, almost as if shocked.

As was normal practice, the pastor welcomed the members of the congregation and asked them to turn and greet their neighbors. More people came forth to welcome Lee.

"Friendly bunch," he whispered when the music began again. "By the way, you have a beautiful voice."

Liza smiled. "Thank you."

Pastor Clemmons stepped into the pulpit minutes later. "Today I want to speak to you on your witness for Christ. For those who would like to read with me, turn in your Bible to Romans 12:1."

Liza quickly flipped through the tissue-thin pages to the chapter and verse he named and leaned to share with Lee.

" 'Therefore, I urge you, brothers, in view of God's mercy, to offer your bodies as living sacrifices, holy and pleasing to God—this is your spiritual act of worship,' " he read.

"What kind of witness are you? When people look at you, do they see Jesus in your actions?"

Thinking of the picture she'd presented to Lee with her combative behavior, Liza squirmed inwardly. How could she ever hope to show him God's love when she constantly battled him?

True, she prayed for him daily. Though she knew a wise Christian woman would never consider a relationship with a man who didn't share her beliefs, she allowed herself to ask "what if" more than she really should. If he couldn't understand why she had to help her parents, how could she ever think he would willingly accept her beliefs?

Perhaps she was being judgmental. The sermon continued as the thoughts coursed through her head. The pastor definitely caught her attention with his next words.

"Examine your actions daily. Ask yourself: Would Jesus have behaved this way? Remember that people have certain expectations of believers. Sadly, more often than not, they're looking for that one little slip, be it anger or a weakening of spirit, to say, 'I knew you weren't what you claim to be.'

"What they fail to realize is that we're all sinners—sinners saved by the grace of our heavenly Father. People with all the human failings who have been made whole by the love of the Lord. As we sing the closing hymn, the altar is open to all. If you haven't experienced God's grace for yourself, step out into the aisle and take those first difficult steps."

Two of the youth stepped out into the aisle, and Liza's heart filled with joy. Each time someone made the decision, she was moved to tears. She glanced at

Lee. He seemed lost in thought.

They continued to sing as the pastor prayed with the new converts. He introduced them to the congregation and asked everyone to extend the right hand of fellowship to their new brothers in Christ.

Liza felt torn—she knew these boys and wanted to speak to them, yet she hated to delay Lee for fear he would be uncomfortable.

"Go ahead. I'll wait here."

She smiled and stepped into the line forming down the aisle. Several times, she glanced back to see church members stopping to speak to Lee.

Within minutes she was back, gathering her Bible and purse. "Ready whenever you are."

"I told your mom I was treating you to lunch. Anything special?"

"Why don't we pick up something and take it back to the office?"

"The least I can do is take you to a decent restaurant."

In reality, she would love to have him take her to a nice restaurant, but it wasn't meant to be. There were differences in their lives that allowed friendship but certainly precluded a relationship—the first being Lee's lack of awareness of her feelings for him.

"I really don't have much time. If we eat while we work, we can get lots more done."

"Okay," he agreed, sounding reluctant. "But promise you'll let me make it up to you."

They discussed the fast-food possibilities and ran through the drive-in of a local chicken place Liza liked. After they bought their food and drinks, Lee drove to the office.

Well, Lord, a few seconds to organize my thoughts would have been nice, Liza thought, but an opportunity immediately presented itself to make things right between Lee and herself. "Today's sermon really danced on my toes. I apologize for being so prickly lately. I haven't given you much reason to believe I'm a follower of Christ."

"You're kidding, right?"

Confusion filled her. "No."

"Liza, I marvel at your goodness and kindness. Sure, you get angry. Everyone does when they're shoved against the wall. I'm the one who owes you an apology. I've pushed you ever since I came to the office, never stopping to think about all you do there. I came from a partnership with a huge list of names on the door. I knew there was no hope I'd ever see my name there. We had lawyers, paralegals, secretaries, and investigators so eager to advance, they stabbed each other in the back to accomplish their personal goals. I'm career oriented, but not like that.

"I realized today that this job isn't your life. It's only part of who you are. Your religion, your family, your friends, and lots of other things fit into that picture as well. I know I'm spoiled. All my life, my parents catered to my every whim. Since I was the only grandchild in the family, Uncle John and Uncle Dennis did their share to help. 'Me' has been the biggest word in my dictionary for a long time. In the past, everything centered on what I wanted, when and how. Thanks to you, I'm beginning to think it shouldn't be that way."

Lee parked the car and took the bag with their lunch. Flabbergasted, Liza grabbed the soda cups and followed him inside. Stepping into the office was like coming home, and she smiled to herself upon realizing nothing had changed.

She missed her work and felt a sudden longing to return. The situation presented an entirely different dilemma for her. Her parents weren't always going to be around, and one day she would be forced to choose between her job and the farm.

In her heart, Liza knew the office would win out, but she didn't want to disappoint her parents either. No sense borrowing trouble. She had plenty on her plate right now.

"Let's take this into the break room."

"But, Lee, we don't have much time."

"We can take time to eat our lunch," he said, overriding her protest with an easy smile. "Besides, I'd prefer not to have your greasy prints all over my papers."

They spread the meal on the table and sat down. Liza whispered grace and started to eat.

"I enjoyed your church this morning."

"I'm glad. You know Mr. Wilson attends First Church on Madison Street, don't you?"

"I've seen that church."

"Why don't you attend church regularly, Lee?"

"Believe it or not, my parents took me to church every week. I believe in God and His grace and majesty, but I've let other stuff become more important over the years. I also happen to believe there's a certain commitment to religion."

"You mean a focus like you have on law?"

"Well, yes. I know it's important to attend and participate in church, but I have so much going on in my life that I just don't have time."

"Jesus took time to die for your sins," Liza reminded. "Sorry. There's that witness thing again. Guess I came on too strong."

"Sometimes it takes strong to make people understand. And you're right. I shouldn't wait until it's convenient for me. I'll think about what you've said."

"That's all anyone can ask." Liza tore open a wet wipe and cleaned her hands. "We'd better get to work."

"You can't be finished already?"

She glanced at the remainder of her meal and felt guilty at her wastefulness. "My eyes were bigger than my stomach."

Lee started packing his food in the box.

"No. Finish eating. I know where to start."

He leaned back and asked, "Is that how you lost the weight?"

Liza could hardly tell him being in his presence curbed her appetite. "I ate enough." She left him in the kitchen, finishing his meal.

The place was a mess. The in-basket overflowed into the out-basket with files, transcription tapes, and mail.

"You're kidding, right?" she asked minutes later when he walked in. "This would take a lifetime to clear up."

"We're not exactly the most organized lawyers when it comes to the office. Tell me what to do."

Every time he made a statement like that, the craziest thoughts ran through her head. What would he think if she told him what she really wanted from him?

He glanced at her curiously. "Liza?"

She leaned against the desk. "Why don't you sort through that jumble?" She indicated the pile on the right side of the desk. "Put the files and tapes in stacks, then separate your mail from Mr. Wilson's. After you finish sorting, check the files and put away those you've finished with. I'll see if I can determine what Rhonda has typed."

He grabbed a chair and sat down in front of the desk. "Thanks, Liza."

She nodded, recalling the number of times he'd accused her of being disloyal to the office. *Stop it,* she chided. *Remember you're supposed to be a good witness.*

Liza found only a couple of tapes hadn't been completed and slipped the first cassette into the transcription machine. Only a small amount of actual typing needed to be completed—a few letters, a will, and a couple of briefs.

There was a point of inquiry on one of the briefs, and Liza went to the research library for the volume she needed. She spotted it on the top shelf and pulled the ladder over.

When the book didn't move, she pulled harder, the tug dislodging the book along with three others stacked carelessly on top. Liza overbalanced and fell back on the carpeted floor. The heavy volumes thudded about her.

"Liza? What happened?"

The room went dark as the last volume smacked her on top of the head.

She awoke to find Lee leaning over her prone form. "That hurt," she moaned, her hand automatically going to her forehead.

"I've told Rhonda at least half a dozen times to put them back where they belong. She has this thing for stacking and putting them away later. I should have warned you."

Liza struggled to sit up, feeling woozy from her encounter with the thick text. "She'll kill somebody."

"Are you okay?" Lee asked, his fingers gentle as he touched the bump on her forehead.

She nodded. "I'll have a whopper of a headache tomorrow, though."

Lee helped her up off the floor and to the waiting room sofa where he placed a pillow beneath her head and demanded she lie still. "I'll be right back."

He returned with an improvised ice bag, which he rested against her forehead. Liza winced at the coldness of the cloth, gradually accepting the numbing effect. She moved to sit up, holding it in place. "Thanks. This is helping."

"Lie still," Lee commanded, resting his arm across the chair as he sat on the edge. "I'll take you to the hospital."

She savored the satisfaction of his concern but felt an overpowering need to reassure him. "No, I'll be okay. Honestly. We Stephenses have tough heads."

"We should file a worker's comp form," he said, pushing her shoulder back to the sofa.

So much for caring. "Let me up, Lee," she insisted.

"No more work."

"What's the matter? Afraid I'll sue you?"

He managed a weak grin. "Very funny."

"For heaven's sake," she cried when he trailed after her into the library. "You're worse than a mother hen with one biddy. Give me that volume," she requested. "No, the other one."

Liza took the reference book back to her desk. She accepted the aspirin and water Lee brought, thanking him briefly before dropping her gaze back to the book.

She couldn't help but be aware of the way he watched her, almost hovering over her desk as he sorted and filed. He had gone through to Mr. Wilson's office to put some papers on his desk when she finished the brief and called out to him, "Lee, I've got. . ."

His look was anxious when he rushed out, relief obvious when he realized she was okay. "Does your head still hurt?"

"Not really. It's more like a dull throb. I need to get home to feed the animals."

"I called the hospital. They said I should bring you in."

She rolled her eyes. "They would. Believe me, it's not that bad. Take me home. I'll be fine tomorrow."

"I heard that you're not supposed to sleep after a head injury."

"It's at least five hours before bedtime."

She preceded Lee out the door, waiting for him to lock up. He took her arm, ignoring her protests that she could walk by herself. Lee unlocked the door, handing her into the vehicle with great care. He pushed away her fumbling hands and fastened her safety belt. Her heart pounded at his closeness, and Liza was glad when he backed away from her.

She leaned back in the seat, the smooth hum of the motor making her drowsy.

"Liza, wake up." Lee shook her arm, then depressed the window control to fill the car with cool evening air. "Are you all right?"

"I wasn't asleep. Just resting my eyes."

"You always breathe that deeply when you're resting your eyes? We can turn on the radio or talk," he said, offering two practical solutions. "Just don't go to sleep."

"All right," she muttered, shifting forward in the seat to fiddle with the knobs. She watched him out of the corner of her eye, seeing his curious expression.

"You can't find anything to say to me, can you, Liza?"

She frowned at his accurate evaluation of the situation. The entire day had been a big mistake. It only served to increase her agony over loving someone she could never have as more than a friend. She had to be strong. She couldn't let him know her true feelings.

"We can exchange all the pleasantries you like."

"What happened, Liza?"

"I don't know what you mean." She tuned the dial to a Christian station. She adjusted the volume, almost drowning out his voice.

Lee frowned and reached to lower the volume. "Yes, you do. We used to be friends. What happened?"

"Why do you keep asking that? We're friends. We don't see each other as often, nor do we have the same things in common. Like most people, it's awkward when we meet."

"You see to that," he agreed. The car surged forward as he depressed the accelerator. "I wouldn't want to keep you in my company a moment longer than necessary."

When he stopped at the house, Liza fumbled with the door handle in her haste to get out of the car. "By the way, tell Rhonda to put those books away before she really hurts someone. And tell her to check those. . .Lee!" she protested when his hand went to the back of her neck and pulled her forward, his lips touching hers. She wrenched away, hiding the vulnerability in her eyes. "Can't you behave?"

"Who'd want me to?" he inquired. "Certainly not you."

"It'd be a nice change. To finish what I was saying, tell Rhonda to check the tapes for some research Mr. Wilson wants done. Good-bye."

Liza got out of the car and moved toward the house, intent on changing clothes and feeding up, only to find Lee right behind her. "Where do you think you're going?" she demanded.

"To help with the chores."

"Not in those clothes."

"I'm not leaving."

"Oh, all right," Liza conceded ungraciously. "Come in."

Her mother was watching television in the family room when Liza showed Lee into the room. "He insists on helping me, even though I told him he's not dressed properly."

"It's the least I can do." Lee launched into the story of Liza's injury, raising her mother's concern.

She frowned at both of them. "I'm going to change."

"Are you sure you're okay?" her mother asked.

Liza nodded and hurried upstairs.

"Why don't you visit with Mom?" she suggested a few minutes later.

"Stop trying to discourage me. I said I'd help, and I intend to."

She scowled at him. "Stubborn."

"Right back at you."

In the barn, Liza found the feed bin was empty and went into the storeroom. Refusing to ask for help, she hefted the fifty-pound bag into the wheelbarrow. She caught her hand underneath. "Ouch!"

"Are you trying to kill yourself?" Lee lifted the bag. He reached for her hand, holding it between his own as he checked for damage.

"No," she denied. "Let go. I can take care of it."

"No, you can't. You think you're the most self-sufficient person in the world. Sometimes you even manage to act like it, but I know differently. You're as needy as the next person, and it's time you realized the truth."

She glared at him. "You don't know me very well at all, Lee. I have the support of people I love. I don't need another mother or father. You're the one who needs people when the mood strikes—when you're ready to take advantage to fulfill your own agenda."

Liza's voice rose until she was yelling at him. The pain in her head and hand didn't compare to the ache in her heart. She hated this bickering caused by her overwhelming awareness of him. It was driving her crazy. "Go home, Lee," she cried brokenly, her eyes glistening with unshed tears.

He took a step back. "I'm sorry. I can't."

"Please." The tears were flowing freely down her face. "Just go."

He stepped toward her. "Liza—"

"No, Lee." She pushed him away. "Just go. Please."

"I'm sorry, but I can't leave you like this. You have to calm down." He pulled her into his arms.

"I am calm," she whispered against his chest, her voice breaking as she allowed herself to remain in his arms. Realizing what was happening, she pulled away. "Please leave."

"I'll go, Liza, but remember—you're the one who keeps pushing me out of your life."

Lee walked from the barn without so much as a backward glance. All the strength drained from her legs, and she dropped onto a nearby bale of hay, her head resting in her hands as she gave way to the threatening sobs. She heard him return, and her gaze was drawn upward, meeting his.

"Liza?" he whispered, his face ghastly white in the late-afternoon light.

"Just stop, Lee," she moaned, turning away from him. "Stop saying things like that. You play on my vulnerability, begging me time and time again to be someone I'm not. Don't ask me to give any more. I can't handle it. Go away. I don't want you here."

This time he didn't return. Liza sat in the barn for some time, considering what she should do. Her prolonged absence brought her mother in search of her. "I heard Lee leave. I thought you finished."

"Sorry. I lost track of the time."

"What's going on with you two? I could hear you yelling out here, clear in the house."

Oh, Mom, if you only knew. Lee was gone, this time without so much as a good-bye. . .and she'd driven him away. "He doesn't understand."

"Neither do I. I know you're attracted to him."

"He's not a Christian, Mom."

"I see."

Liza wished she did. She didn't see anything but heartache for allowing herself to fall for a man she couldn't have.

"He went to church with you today."

"And look how it ended."

"Never doubt the power of God," her mother said. "Remember He's capable of changing all things we can't understand. Everything will be all right, if you trust Him."

"How, Mom?"

"Where's your faith, Liza? I know you believe in miracles. Don't you think God can work a miracle for you and Lee?"

"It would take one."

"It's getting late. You need to finish up and come inside."

Later, much later, after she finally went to bed, Liza gave way to the tears. They flowed until she could cry no longer. She lay wide awake for the next several hours, her mind refusing to forget what had happened that day.

Chapter 11

Lee's words continued to play around in Liza's head. Did she push him out? Yes, but only because he wanted more than she could offer right now.

With days that started at the crack of dawn and ended late at night, Liza felt bone tired. Tonight was the first night in weeks she promised herself a break, and she left the supper table without offering to help with the cleanup. In the family room, she stretched out on the sofa and settled in to watch a little television. Maybe later she'd call Kitty to see how the wedding plans were progressing.

Lately she'd worked twice as hard to accomplish the tasks she wanted finished. As if their farm didn't demand enough, she volunteered to help the neighbors in whatever capacity she could. Of course, she felt she owed favors to everyone; but at the rate she was paying them back, it might not take the rest of her life.

There hadn't been much time for a social life lately. Not that it mattered. She didn't feel like seeing other people. By the time she finished work each evening, the thought of going out lacked appeal, and she often ended up eating dinner with her parents and going to bed early.

The phone rang, and she pushed herself up to reach for it. "Liza," Kitty called cheerily. "Just the person I wanted to talk to."

"What's up?"

"Your friends are feeling like you don't have time for us anymore."

"I've been busy."

"I know, but Dave and I were talking. What if we come over and bring a movie, or just play games?"

So much for her quiet evening. "Sure. Come on over. Look for me in the family room. I'm the lump on the sofa."

Kit giggled. "Girl, you've got to get some exercise."

"Please don't mention that word in my presence."

Liza hung up the phone and went upstairs to exchange her old shorts and shirt for a sleeveless blouse and Capri pants. She was making popcorn when Kitty let herself in.

"We're here," Kitty announced, hugging Liza. Dave and Rick followed on her heels.

"Just in time to help with the snacks," Liza said, hugging each one. "What does everyone want to drink?"

They agreed on soda, and everyone pitched in. Carrying their food into the sitting room, they chatted through the movie credits.

"I figured you'd rather watch a movie than do anything to work your brain," Dave said.

"My brain thanks you." She glanced at Rick's glass. "You need a refill."

"I wouldn't if you two hadn't added a box of salt to the popcorn. My mouth is as dry as the Sahara."

"You were the one who bumped my shoulder," Liza said, throwing a kernel in his direction.

He retaliated, and Liza caught it in her mouth, grinning at his surprised look. "You coming over tomorrow?"

"For what?"

Liza slipped her hands beneath her hair, lifting it up and over the back of the sofa. "To be in the way."

"That's the truth of it," Rick admitted. "Your dad was bragging on you yesterday. Said you're doing beautifully."

She shook her head in denial. "I couldn't have done it alone."

Dave let go of Kitty's hand and leaned forward. "Don't be so modest. You're doing a wonderful job. We couldn't do better ourselves, could we, Rick?"

"You're making it look easy," Rick agreed. "Want to share your secret?"

Slightly embarrassed by their tag-team compliments, Liza made a joke out of the situation. "No way. I might need a job next year. Your dad can hire me on. Of course, he'd have to hire my team of experts—most of the town, in fact. Everyone's been so helpful."

"It's a community, Liza," Kitty said. "Friends help friends. You've done your bit as well. How many times a week do you go out of your way to help someone else?"

"As often as possible, but everyone's been so good to us. We'll never be able to pay them back."

"They don't expect you to," Rick told her.

Liza knew they didn't. The eggs she'd eaten for breakfast came from a nearby farm. For lunch, they'd eaten cake a neighbor brought over. One man visited with her dad while his wife took advantage of the opportunity to get her mom out of the house. Even the children brought handfuls of wildflowers they hoped would brighten Mr. Paul's day.

She knew farmers shared a belief in hard work, commitment to family, community, and rural life. It was certainly obvious as the neighborhood helped them through each and every day.

Liza sat on the sofa beside Rick, twisting until she got comfortable. Tomorrow she needed to pick butter beans. Her mother hadn't had time to do it, not with taking care of her father and the house and helping around the farm.

She thought she had it rough, but Liza had recognized her dad's cabin fever from the beginning. He was starting to help outside more and grew so irritable at times that he shouted at her. Her mother just shook her head and gave her one of those "don't argue" looks.

Not that he complained all of the time. She couldn't forget the look on his face when one visitor told him what a fine job she was doing. "More dedicated than my boy, that's for sure. I should have had a girl."

"That's right," her father agreed, catching her hand and giving it a gentle squeeze. "Wouldn't take anything for her."

"Maybe we can marry her off to my boy," their neighbor suggested, winking at Liza.

She felt her cheeks burn at their teasing. "I'm going inside before you start talking dowry."

The men laughed, their conversation turning to a recent fishing trip.

Kit asked her a question, and Liza pulled her attention to the movie. After seeing the trailers on television, she had planned to see the movie in the theater but never made it.

The movie ended, and they turned to the nightly news.

"I don't like the look of this one," Dave said when the weatherman talked about Hurricane Bobby.

"You think it'll make landfall?" Liza asked. Her dad had mentioned the storm's projected path that morning, but she hadn't thought about it much. Most days, she just hoped it wouldn't rain until after dark.

"This area hasn't been too blessed in the past few years. They're coming in near Wilmington."

"Losing electricity is the worst part," Kit said. "Mom almost lost the contents of her freezer with that storm last year. She made sure Daddy bought a generator after that. Said she put too many hours into freezing those vegetables to lose them."

"And you lost those long, hot baths and showers you're so fond of," Liza teased.

Kit grimaced at her. "We didn't have water for three days."

"You're supposed to make preparations," Liza reminded. "Things like filling the bathtub so you have water."

"I hate bird baths," Kitty said, looking at Dave. "You know, if we lived in town we'd always have water and sewer services."

"And I'd have a commute every time I needed to do something at the farm. Sorry, honey, you're marrying a farm boy. There's always the pond if you're desperate."

Kitty made a face and pretended to shiver. "No thanks."

"Like you've never swam there before," Dave mocked.

"Let's pray this one goes out to sea and does no harm," Liza said.

"Amen," Rick agreed.

"Fill me in on the wedding plans."

"We're about ready to elope," Dave said. "We've come to the conclusion it takes so long to plan a wedding because you're trying to decide who to invite."

"Our mothers keep adding to the list," Kit added. "Our intimate wedding has turned into a packed house. They've decided that everyone who can't attend the ceremony should be at the reception."

"Everyone you invite won't show up," Liza pointed out.

"We'd need the stadium if they did," Kit moaned. "Dave's not kidding. We've discussed eloping. I've got my dress, and with you and Rick to stand up for us, we could get it over with in a few hours."

Horrified they would even consider running away to get married, Liza exclaimed, "Don't do that. You'll regret not having the wedding you've always wanted."

Kitty glanced at Dave and nodded reluctantly. "I guess you're right."

Dave linked his fingers with Kit's. "I'll be glad when it's over. I can't wait to have you as my wife."

"Well, you certainly took your time asking."

"Give a man a break," he said. "I just wanted to be sure we were both ready."

Kit grinned and kissed his cheek. "Honey, I've been ready since I was ten years old."

"Back then, all you and Liza wanted to do was play bride."

Both women smiled as he triggered their memory of the times they had dressed in old castoffs and forced the guys to play their grooms.

"I won't be playing in a couple of months," Kit reminded.

Their eyes glowed with their love. They were perfect for each other. Of course, Liza knew their friendship would change once Kit and Dave married. . .just as it had when Jason got married and dropped their foursome in favor of Judy.

For a moment, she wished it were her, then pushed the thought out of her head. Such fantasies always led to thoughts of one person. She didn't want to go there tonight.

"Guess we'd better get out of here and let you catch a couple of hours' shut-eye. Talk to you tomorrow," Kit said. "We've got to get you fitted for your dress. No poufed sleeves or flounces," she promised.

"Or big bows either, I hope?"

She hugged Liza and promised, "Sophisticated and elegant are the key-words. Well, except for the color. How do you feel about lime green or Day-Glo orange?"

Liza scowled in mock horror. "You know, I really do need to recheck my calendar. Now that I think about it, I believe I have a prior commitment."

Laughing, they headed for the door.

Liza straightened the living room and took their glasses and bowls into the kitchen. She yawned widely as she checked to make sure they were gone before turning off the outside lights and locking up for the night.

Thank You, God, for my wonderful friends. She felt blessed to have them in her life. No matter what the future held, she would always have the love of her family and friends.

Chapter 12

W hat else did you expect?" Liza mumbled a couple of days later when the weatherman announced coastal North Carolina was under a hurricane warning.

"Wind and rain are the farmer's worst enemies," her dad said as they sat at the breakfast table, discussing this latest problem. "Once they flatten and drown the crops, there's not much hope left."

"What do I need to do?"

"Main thing is securing everything. The yard furniture needs to go into the barn. You can turn the rockers over and tie them to porch railings. The hanging baskets and planters need to come down, too."

As the list of chores grew, Liza wondered if she'd ever get it all done. "Barney hates storms," Liza pointed out.

"Majesty, too. Hopefully we'll be on the fringes of Bobby."

Her mother slid a cooked egg onto Liza's plate.

Liza quickly placed it between two slices of toast and wrapped a paper napkin about the sandwich. "Time to get busy," she said, heading for the door. "Are we taping the windows?"

"It's not worth the trouble. The sheet of plywood for the picture window is in the barn. I don't know how you'll get it in place, though."

Liza patted her father's shoulder reassuringly. "Someone will check on us."

He reached for her hand. "Just a little more breeze and rain than normal."

As she stepped outside to begin work, Liza noticed little indication of menacing weather. The hot overcast July day felt no different from any other, but after surviving three hurricanes in two years, she knew what to expect.

The office crossed her mind. She'd heard Mr. and Mrs. Wilson were on a cruise. That left Lee on his own, with no one to tell him what to do. Later, when time allowed, she'd check with him.

A couple of hours passed, and Liza paused to mop her forehead when Lee's car pulled into the yard. "What are you doing here?" she asked when he stepped out of the car.

"Hello to you, too. I've been sent as a reinforcement. The rest of the troops couldn't make it. Kitty called and said Dave and Rick are working like crazy at their place, and she was afraid they wouldn't finish up in time to get over here."

Kitty. She should have known. That woman was a determined matchmaker.

97

Each time they discussed the situation, her friend insisted Liza could make a difference in Lee's life.

"What about the office? Mr. Wilson's house?"

"The office is secured. I sent Rhonda home to take care of her place and went by Uncle John's before I came over here. His handyman has handled everything. He's not taking any chances."

"Daddy doesn't think we'll see much more than wind and rain, but we're not taking any chances either. I've been lugging this junk around all morning."

"Junk?"

"Well, it definitely seems that way when it's an inconvenience. I got smart and hooked up the trailer to load the lawn furniture and other small pieces. It's backed into the barn. Now all I have to do is pull it back over here and unload."

"I knew you were a smart lady. What can I do to help?"

Liza's thoughts went to the sheet of plywood propped against the house. "I need to cover the front window."

"Let's do it."

Working together, they soon had everything finished.

"I appreciate this, Lee."

"Hey, I owe you one for helping out at the office the other day. Besides, I have been known to lend a neighborly hand now and then."

"Have you thought about where you'll go?"

"Not really. I suppose I could stay in my apartment or go to a shelter."

"Or you could stay here." When he looked surprised, she offered, "There's a spare room, if you can sleep. This storm looks like it's going to come in at night, so I doubt anyone else will."

"My adrenaline is pumping like crazy at the thought of Bobby making landfall. I suspect the excitement of my first hurricane will be enough to keep me awake as well."

"How did you know what to do?"

"Uncle John gave me a crash course before he left."

"What about Mr. and Mrs. Wilson? They aren't cruising in the middle of the storm, are they?"

"Last I heard, they're headed for Alaska."

The news pleased Liza. She didn't want to think they were in danger on open seas.

"Well, we'll just have to pray this one isn't bad." As if a portent of what was to come, the rain began to fall.

"This rain has me worried," her dad said when the downpour increased in intensity.

The forecasters kept talking about the far-reaching rain bands radiating from the distant storm and predicted an early morning landfall. Meanwhile, Liza felt a bit more apprehensive with every deluge. She dropped the curtain back into place. Darkness made it impossible to see anything.

"They're giving the new coordinates," Lee called.

Liza joined him on the sofa. The stations had been running continuous coverage ever since the warning went into effect, making announcements, and keeping everyone current on Hurricane Bobby's coordinates. The weatherman repeated the warning, indicating the storm's extent on the map.

"Looks like he's veering this way," Lee said. "How much rain is too much?" he asked her father after watching Liza plot the coordinates on a hurricane map she kept nearby.

"It's hard to say. If the rain keeps up like this until daylight, I'm sure we'll have some serious flooding."

"Now, Paul, what does the Bible tell you about worrying? You're not helping yourself at all."

"I know, Sarah, but—"

"No buts," she insisted, reaching for his hand. "Let's pray about this and leave it to the Lord."

When her mother began to pray, Liza glanced at Lee to find he had bowed his head. After her mother spoke her words to Jesus, her father took over and prayed for His mercy to surround them during this storm and keep them safe. Liza added a hearty *amen* and smiled when Lee did the same.

Around ten thirty, her mother insisted on getting a snack and something to drink. Liza went into the kitchen to help. Back in the family room, all four of them were watching the news updates when the phone rang.

It was Kitty, and she was in a mood to chat. "Yes, Lee helped out. He's here now, waiting out the storm with us." Liza could hardly answer her friend's questions with Lee sitting at her side. She hoped he hadn't heard Kit's excited gasp. "This rain is incredible," she said instead. "I hate waiting around to see what's going to happen."

She almost laughed when Kitty said, "Girl, you've got a handsome man sitting there with you, and you're worried about time. You better seize the moment."

"Any progress on the plans?" Liza asked, ignoring her friend's advice.

"We're getting there. This dream wedding I always thought I wanted isn't what it's cut out to be. In fact, it's a lot of hard work. Right now, I'd like nothing better than to go down after church, say our vows, and take off on our honeymoon."

"So has Dave filled you in on the dream honeymoon?"

"No," she pouted. "It'll be a miracle if I can get him away from the farm for that long. He'll probably want to go to some farming convention."

"I don't think so. Dave's going to make a wonderful husband."

"I know. I just hate competing with the farm."

"Don't think of it as a competition. It's his career choice. You'd better get used to it now, or you'll be miserable."

"I know. I really do love Dave, and I know he's the man God intends for me. He's been farming for most of the time we've dated, so I have a pretty good idea what our life will be like."

"I don't mean it in a bad way, Kit. But when people are happy in their chosen career fields, that's one less problem a couple has to contend with."

"Amen to that. Wow, listen to that wind. I'd better go. Mom's got the guest list out, and she's waiting for me to hang up. I told her it's late, but she says we won't sleep anyway. Would you please tell me why it's an insult not to invite cousins I haven't seen in ten years to my wedding?"

"It is a good time to get your family together."

"Yeah, but I hate it when people I haven't heard from in a long time suddenly remember I exist."

"Particularly when a gift is involved," Liza added.

"Exactly."

A sudden loud crash caught Liza's attention.

"What was that?" Kit demanded.

The same words echoed about the room. Lee and her mother jumped from their seats. Her dad followed at a slower pace. "Gotta run, Kit. Something just happened outside."

"Be careful."

The others were looking out the kitchen window. "See anything?" Liza asked, straining to see for herself.

"No. It's pitch-black dark out there. I think something fell on the house," her father said.

"I could probably see better from the upstairs windows," Liza suggested.

"It might not be safe," her mother said quickly.

"I'll go with her," Lee said.

Liza was glad to let Lee lead the way as they moved from room to room.

"Found it." Lee pulled back the curtain at her bedroom window to reveal the large pine tree resting against the house.

"Can you tell if the roof's leaking?" Liza asked, studying the ceiling. There were no signs of water damage.

"Doesn't appear to be. Let's get a flashlight, and I'll go outside and see how bad it is."

Following him down the stairs, Liza protested, "You can't go out in this."

"Just long enough to take a look. Put up a tarp if it's needed."

"Let me get the raincoats. I'll go with you."

"Stay inside. No sense in both of us getting wet."

In the hall closet, Liza pulled yellow slickers off hangers. "Then you should stay in. You're the guest."

Her parents stepped into the hallway. "What happened?"

"That pine on my side of the house snapped. It's resting on the roof. We're going to check it out."

"Give me my coat."

"No, Daddy."

"We'll take care of it, sir," Lee said.

Her mother jumped into the fray. "You're not going out there, Paul. I don't care if the tree comes into the house. You're not strong enough to fight that wind and rain."

"I am not a weakling, Sarah."

Liza slipped on her boots. "Listen to Mom, Daddy. I'll check and come right back in."

Lee snapped the hooks on the raincoat he wore. "And I'm going with her."

The force of the winds nearly took her breath away as Liza opened the kitchen door. The moment she moved from the steps, Liza realized just how much rain had fallen. The yard was flooded, water coming up around her ankles.

Ducking his head, Lee grabbed her hand and pulled her around the side of the house, flashing the powerful beam of the light toward the roofline. The tree appeared to have broken the face board around the top and knocked in the roof a bit, but as far as she could tell, it hadn't gone through.

"Do we need to cover it?" Liza shouted.

Lee shook his head.

They splashed back around the house, avoiding fallen limbs. Inside the kitchen, they removed their shoes and dumped them into the box her mom kept for that purpose. Sarah handed them towels while her father impatiently demanded a report.

"There's some damage. We'll be able to tell more in the morning. The yard's flooded." Liza pointed to the watermark on Lee's pants leg.

Her mother quickly crossed the room to her father's side. "It'll be fine, Paul. We'll get through this."

Paul Stephens wrapped his arms about his wife, holding her tight. After so many years, they were even more in love. They looked to each other for support during bad times. Liza constantly prayed to one day find love as strong as theirs.

"Is he okay?" Lee asked softly.

"I should have kept my mouth shut about the flooding. He's already worried about the crops."

"You can't keep it a secret. He's not blind."

"True. Thanks for going out there with me. It's nasty."

"Weather's not even fit for ducks. Let's go see if we can cheer them up."

While they were out, her mother had set the lanterns and candles about the room. A battery-operated radio sat on the coffee table.

"It's just a matter of time before we lose power," she explained, handing Lee a pair of socks. "I can't offer you pants, but I figured you would appreciate these."

Lee cuffed his khakis several times and pulled on the dry socks. "Thanks, Mrs. Stephens."

True to her prediction, they lost power within the hour. Liza flipped on the radio, and they listened to the deejays talk nonstop about the storm that had given everyone a common cause. No music punctuated their discussion as they allowed callers to describe their storm experiences. The announcers issued constant warnings to stay inside. They talked about the eye of the hurricane, warning the population not to assume the storm was over when the calm arrived.

Their small group sat in silence, hearing the fury of the wind and rain as it battered the house. Now and again, one of them commented about an act of stupidity the announcer reported on the radio.

"Back when I was a young man, Hazel ripped through the area," her dad said. "That lady did a lot of damage. Almost wiped out some areas."

"Back in the old days, they named all the hurricanes after women. At least they're equal-opportunity storms now," Liza joked.

Lee jostled her with his shoulder. "And old Bobby is proving himself as capable as any woman, right?"

She nudged his shoulder in return before she turned her attention to her mother.

"Your grandmother said she stood on the porch and watched Hazel take away a tobacco barn."

"On the porch?"

"Yes," her mother said, sounding amazed. "I'm surprised she didn't get blown into the next county—particularly if the winds were anything like this."

"That's exactly why so many people died back then. At least now the forecasters can warn people in plenty of time to take shelter."

The old house creaked and groaned with the incessant winds. Torrential downpours seemed never ending. The deejay spoke of the spotting of tornadoes, adding something else to worry about. Liza certainly didn't need to add that experience to the night.

"Thanks for letting me stay," Lee said. "I don't think I'd want to be in my apartment right now."

"I wouldn't want you to be there alone," Liza told him.

The candles reflected the satisfied light that came into Lee's eyes.

Lord, please help me remain strong, Liza prayed silently. She knew she couldn't change people. She was proof positive of that. Until she had decided to lose the weight, she told herself she was as God intended. She carried the extra pounds, at times hating the restrictions they placed on her physically and mentally. Once she made up her mind, nothing could stop her from achieving her goal. She wished she could say the words to convince Lee to change his life to one of service to the Lord. She could plant the seed, but only God could grow it to greatness.

As the night deepened, the resonant snores of her dad and the gentler ones of her mom could be heard. "Glad they can sleep," she whispered to Lee. "Maybe we should pull out the sofa for them."

"Those recliners look pretty comfortable."

"They are. I've snoozed in them a few times myself."

"Liza. . ."

"Lee. . ."

"You first."

"No, you."

"We're getting nowhere fast," he whispered.

Liza chuckled softly. "You're right. I appreciate your help today."

They had sunk down into the cushions of the sofa and propped their stocking feet on the coffee table. They sat shoulder to shoulder, whispering in their intimate little world.

"You've been on my mind a lot over the past few days. Ever since that incident last time we were together, in fact."

"I was okay."

"I know. Why do you think we have such volatile fights? Every time we get together, we end up arguing."

"Probably because we both expect more of the other person than they're willing to give."

"What do you expect?"

"Not so much expect as want you to understand," she said. "As a Christian, it's my responsibility to be here for my parents now when they need me most. I love my work, but life sometimes has a way of throwing us curve balls."

"It sure threw me one," he agreed.

"In what way?" Liza asked curiously.

"You."

"Me?"

"Let me finish," he insisted. "I had great expectations when I came here. Uncle John more or less guaranteed that once he retires, his business is mine. He felt it was important that his clients adapt to me so they'd stay when he does retire.

"I hope you realize your value to the firm. There's no way everything could get done, if not for your dedication and intuitiveness. You're more than a fixture in the office. You're the lifeblood. In truth, from the first week we worked together, I knew we were a great team."

"I don't always get the impression you're a team player," Liza admitted, voicing the question that had been on her mind. "For instance, why did you choose to live in a hotel instead of Mr. Wilson's home? They would have loved having you there."

"I knew they planned to travel and didn't want the added responsibility of their house. Plus, I didn't care to rattle about alone in that big old place."

He makes sense, Liza thought.

"Besides, I like my privacy," he admitted. "I haven't lived with my parents since I was eighteen. No offense, Liza. I didn't mean. . . ," he muttered. "Well, it's different for a young, single woman."

"You think so?" she asked. There were times when a place of her own sounded wonderful, but Liza accepted the fact that she needed to be with her parents.

"And I like living on my own."

I bet you do, she thought glumly. A good-looking single man like Lee would never want elderly chaperones.

"Our arguments have a deeper foundation than work. My need for your presence goes far beyond the office. I know you have to be here for your parents, and I'm impressed with the way you've pulled things together.

"Take Kit, for instance. She couldn't have done what you've done this summer. Had the situation arisen, I'm not even sure she would have tried; but you did, and while I've been critical and made some accusations I shouldn't have, the truth of the matter is, my main frustration has been missing having you around.

"We were doing pretty well there at the beginning, but then things started to change. I decided too many changes wouldn't make a good impression on the clients. If Uncle John stepped out of the picture, I at least needed you to make them comfortable. Then things started to change. I know exactly when it happened: the moment I began seeing you as Liza the woman instead of Liza the coworker. That time you accused me of thinking the office was more important than your happiness was really a time I was afraid Rick would steal you away."

She couldn't help feeling shocked. Lee was so off base. "Rick's a very good friend, but this is the first time I've seen him since I was fourteen."

"You were a young teen then. Now you're a beautiful woman. He looks at you differently."

"We don't feel that way about each other," she protested.

"He could, with very little prompting on your part."

Lee shrugged and admitted, "You're very important to me. And not because you can run the office with one hand tied behind your back. I've fallen in love with you, Liza Stephens."

A tree limb banged on the house, and Liza jumped, realizing the storm raging inside caused the surge of emotion.

"Lee. . ."

He squeezed her hand. "Go ahead, I've had my say."

Liza feared she wasn't strong enough to withstand after what he'd told her. "Lord, guide me," she whispered fervently. "I love you, too, but there's a problem—a reason we're not ready to advance this relationship." The candlelight played off his frown. Liza forced herself to say what must be said.

"I'm a Christian. I pray for God's guidance in my life, then do my best to accept the answers He gives me. One thing my Bible tells me is that I cannot choose a man who doesn't share my beliefs. In order for a home to prosper and love to grow, two people have to be of the same mind about everything, including their beliefs. I want my children to know my strength comes from above. I want them to share that strength, and I want the man I love to avail himself of it as well."

"I could change."

"I don't want you to change," she objected, struggling to keep her voice down. "I want you to accept Christ as your Savior, but not because it's what I want. I can't get you a place in heaven, and salvation without commitment is meaningless. You need to experience what it means to turn your life over to God."

"Does this mean that I'm going to lose you?"

"No," came her emphatic response. "Daddy is getting stronger every day and hopefully, by the fall, he'll be capable of handling some of the day-to-day work. Chances are, he'll have to pare down his activities considerably, but we should be able to continue as before."

"What about the farm? Won't it be too stressful for him?"

"The doctor said Daddy's surgery added years to his life."

"No, I meant what do you plan to do. . . ?" Lee began, stopping when her dad spoke.

"Still bad?" Paul Stephens asked, stretching his arms as he came more fully awake.

"Hasn't stopped raining yet," Liza said.

He grunted his frustration.

"How are you feeling?" she asked. "Is it time for your medicine?"

"I'm fine. Don't fuss over me." He glanced over at his wife, watching her doze peacefully. "Your mother does enough of that."

They shared a knowing smile.

"So, Lee, how are you liking our area?"

"I'm getting used to it. Finding that most people are as rooted to the area as their crops."

Paul chuckled. "They believe in hard work. Farming's no playtime operation."

Lee and her father discussed farming and investments in new machinery and technology.

"None of this newfangled laborsaving equipment can operate itself."

"That's true."

"A lot of it is expertise gained through trial and error spanning generations of farming," her father said. "Most farmers are born and bred to the life."

"Of course, not everyone's cut out to be a farmer." Lee flashed Liza a meaningful look.

Her father nodded agreement. "It's a career of choice. You two had better try to get some sleep. I suspect tomorrow is going to be a busy day."

Chapter 13

They left the house at the crack of dawn, feeling like prisoners released from extended exile. Curious and afraid, they went out to determine the extent of the damage. The day dawned clear. A lingering breeze reminded them of the night. Water like never before greeted them.

Both she and her mother argued that her father needed to stay inside and let Liza report to him, but Paul Stephens insisted he needed to see for himself. He promised not to go far.

Liza glanced at her father, afraid the situation might be more than he could bear. Lee noted her concern and stepped to his other side.

"It's gone," he whispered, drooping like the soon-to-be-drowned crops.

"Daddy?" Fear clutched Liza. So much had happened to him over the past couple of months. Could he withstand yet another shock? She slid her arm about his waist and prayed softly, "Please, Jesus, give us strength."

"Amen," he agreed. "I need to climb up to the second floor in the pack house."

"Daddy, no," Liza exclaimed. "You can't."

"I have to see."

"I'll do it. Just stay here."

Liza scurried to the upper floor and threw open the double doors. As a child, she'd sat and dreamed in this loft, but today the dreams of her father's farm plummeted as she surveyed the flooded acreage.

Crops stood in water as far as the eye could see. Tears stung her lids. She glanced at Lee when he came to join her.

"Oh, Lee," she whispered, turning her head against his chest when he wrapped his arms about her.

"Honey, I'm sorry."

"I had no idea it would be this bad."

"You'll have a better idea once the waters recede."

"The damage is already done."

"The government sets aside money for this. I'm sure FEMA will assess the damage quickly. The governor will probably declare this a disaster area within the next couple of days."

Her father's roar caught their attention.

"You have to tell him," Lee urged.

Liza slowly walked down the stairs, trying to formulate the words to soften the blow. How much more could her father take? His hopeful look broke her heart. "It's bad."

His bones seemed to give way to the overwhelming defeat. "Tell me."

She wrapped her arms about him. "It's like a gigantic lake—water as far as I can see. The corn blew over. The vegetables, cotton, and soybeans are standing in the water. I'm sorry."

He stayed silent for several minutes as he continued to hold on to her. "We've been blessed over the years never to have the flooding and total devastation others endured," he said finally.

Lee stood on the sidelines, looking surprised by his reaction. "How can you speak of blessings?"

"We're alive, son. Our house may have a tree lying on the roof, but it's still standing."

"So that's where Liza gets it from."

"Gets what?" her father asked curiously.

"Her ability to see blessings at the worst of times."

Paul Stephens shook his head. "I can't take credit for that. It comes from her faith in the Lord."

"You should go back inside, Daddy. Mom will be worried sick." Barney barked, and Majesty joined in with a neigh of his own, protesting their confines. "I'll check the animals."

"They hear us out here," Dad said. "Don't let Barney out in this mud."

Liza scrutinized her dad's progress. His step was a bit slower than before, but she knew he would survive because that was what farmers had done for hundreds of years. They faced adversity head-on, and with God's more-than-able assistance, farmers came out victorious more times than not.

"I can't believe it's this calm and normal now," Lee said.

She picked up a branch from one of the old pecan trees and dragged it to the side of the yard. "That's the way of a hurricane. Except for the damage, you'd never know the storm had come. Then the assessment and cleanup begins. Given the damage I see here, I'm afraid this is going to be one costly storm."

"What about the tree on the house?"

"Mom will call the agent. Probably would help if we can get it down to check the damage. I wonder if the phone's working. Last time we lost electricity and telephone."

"What about the roads? You think they're flooded?"

"Probably. I'm sure the ditches are overflowing into the roadway. Those dirt roads will be muddy. Looks like you're stuck with us for a while longer."

"Can't think of any place I'd rather be."

Liza longed to throw her arms about his neck. Instead, she reached for another branch.

Lee grabbed another and said, "I hope the phone's working. I need to call my parents. My mother worries."

"Don't they all? Where's your cell phone?"

"At the apartment. I let the battery go dead. In all the rush, I walked off and left it at home."

❧

Rick and Dave showed up later that morning in one of their big, expensive tractors. Mud caked the huge wheels. Dave opened the cab door and climbed down. Rick followed. "Glad to see you made it okay. Kit's ready to get out of the house. I told her to stay put."

"I wouldn't be surprised to see her show up on horseback," Liza told him.

"I don't think she's thought of that yet. Maybe I should borrow a white horse and go to her rescue," Dave teased. "Nah, he'd be brown with mud and probably break a leg, to boot. We're headed over that way next."

"You shouldn't have come out."

"It's our spirit of adventure, the need to explore."

Liza eyed Rick skeptically. "The need to get yourself pinned under a tractor? Possibly even drowned?"

"We're in contact with the house," Dave said, reminding Liza of their two-way radio. "Besides, we know Dad will skin us alive if we mess up his tractor. That's plenty of incentive to be careful."

"Is it as bad as I think?" Liza hoped to hear things were different elsewhere.

Rick nodded his head. "The entire state is reporting flooding like you wouldn't believe. The river won't crest for days yet, and we're already in trouble. Twenty-one inches of rain fell in less than twenty-four hours. Looked pretty bad from what I saw on Mom's battery-operated television. Your mom said there's a tree on the house. We bought the chain saw to get it down for you."

Liza appreciated the fact that they were willing to help their neighbors. Given the size of their farm, no doubt they had plenty to do at their place. "Thanks, guys."

Rick hefted the saw from the tractor and glanced at Lee. "You want to help?"

The men seemed intent on measuring each other up from a distance. Lee stepped forward. "Tell me what to do."

"Grab a ladder from the barn."

"I'll show you where it is," Liza offered. She forgot about Barney, and when she opened the door, the dog charged outside, knocking her into a nearby mud puddle.

The three men laughed heartily at her plight as they dodged the dog. Barney ran from person to person, slinging mud as he allowed them to pet him. "Exactly why was it you wanted that dog?" Dave asked, reaching down to offer a hand.

Liza refused to comment. "The ladder's in the corner. I'm going to change."

Barney trailed after Liza to the house, keeping his distance.

By the time she returned, Rick was on the roof, and a rope dangled with the chain saw attached.

"Everyone stand clear," he yelled. The powerful roar of the saw echoed throughout the area, the volume changing as he worked his way through branch after branch and dropped them to the ground. Once Rick removed the top of the tree, he killed the saw and leaned over the edge.

"Doesn't appear to have damaged more than the overhang. We can tack down a tarp until the insurance adjuster comes. Watch out. I'm going to see if I can move this trunk."

Luckily, it wasn't one of their biggest trees and with a mighty heave, he shoved the remaining trunk of the tree from the house. It hit the ground with a thump, falling just short of the shrubbery.

"Here comes the saw," he called.

Dave grabbed the saw and started it again, carving the trunk into smaller pieces.

Rick climbed down the ladder and walked over to where Liza stood. "What's he doing here?" he asked in an undertone, nodding his head in Lee's direction.

"I invited him."

Rick's brows raised.

"He lives in an apartment. Besides, he was a lot of help yesterday."

"You're going to get hurt."

"No, she's not."

Liza jumped when Lee spoke from right behind her. "We have an understanding," he told Rick, glancing at Liza when he said, "I love Liza, and I would never intentionally do anything to hurt her."

Rick glanced from one to the other. "Good. I don't care to see anyone break my friend's heart. Let's clean up this mess."

Chapter 14

On Sunday morning, Liza looked out from the choir loft into the sea of faces and was surprised when Lee waved at her. She smiled back and nodded her head slightly.

Why is he here? Surely he isn't attending church to change my mind? The thought upset her so much that she couldn't even remember the words of the song. She wasn't being fair. Lee wasn't that kind of person. Liza forced her attention back to the service.

Afterward she shed her robe and hurried out to find him chatting with her parents.

He kissed her cheek. "How are you doing?"

His welcoming smile filled an empty place in her heart. "Fine. It's been a busy time, though."

"Getting everything sorted out okay?"

"Sure. What about you? Rhonda told me about the mess at the office."

"Maybe a foot of water entered the building. We had to strip out the carpet. One of the file cabinets burst from the force of the wet paper. I've never seen anything like it."

"Anything important?"

"Copies of old invoices. Thankfully no client files. No great loss."

Her parents said good-bye to Lee and walked over to speak to their friends. "I'm glad you came today," Liza said, pushing aside her earlier doubts.

Lee reached for her hand. "I enjoy being here. I saw an angel in the choir this morning."

His regard was almost embarrassing. "Are you flattering me to get an invitation to lunch?"

"Would it work?"

"Probably."

"Actually Uncle John and Aunt Clara are expecting me. I wanted to say hello. Could we go out to dinner one night soon?"

"I'll see. Kit's had me so busy with plans for this wedding of hers. Four more weeks and it'll be over. I can tell you this much: I think I'll be as happy to see them off on their honeymoon as they will be to go!"

"You won't say the same when it's your turn." Lee flashed her a knowing smile. "Do you have an escort for Kitty's wedding?"

"Not really, but I suppose I'll be too busy anyway."

"We'll discuss it later." He kissed her cheek and waved good-bye to her parents.

❧

Despite her efforts to restrain herself, Liza's hope grew with each passing week as Lee continued to meet her at church. He attended faithfully on Wednesday nights and Sundays. He enrolled in the Thursday night Bible study class, which surprised her, given how busy he was at work. She knew from experience that the course was no lightweight study.

"Want to go for ice cream?" he asked after the group disbanded.

The subject that had been troubling her came to mind. Seemed like as good a time as any to discuss the matter. "Sure."

The little shop's popularity made it a difficult place to talk. Several people tried to beat the heat with a cone of their favorite flavor. Liza and Lee stood in line, Liza opting for a tropical-flavored yogurt while Lee chose chocolate ice cream.

"This is good. Want to taste?" She held out her cone.

"No, thanks. Chocolate is my flavor. Let's sit outside."

They found a bench and enjoyed the late August night.

Lee caught the melting ice cream running down his cone with a swipe of his tongue. "I'm really enjoying this Bible class."

Liza licked her frozen yogurt and asked, "When do you find time to study?"

"Early in the morning. At night after I get home. Don't tell Uncle John, but the Bible has replaced my briefs."

The revelation surprised her, but then God was in the miracle business. "You've slowed down a bit."

Brilliant blue eyes focused on her. "Now that a particular lady has stolen my heart, I've found other interests."

His openness about his feelings stole her breath away. Liza could hardly believe he loved her. "Lee? I need to ask you something. Please don't take this the wrong way," she pleaded, "but I wonder about your church attendance. You aren't. . ."

"Attending because of you?"

He didn't answer, just stood and walked over to the trash can to dispose of his napkin and the remainder of his cone.

Feeling she'd made a serious mistake, Liza wiped her sticky fingers and balled the napkin tightly in her hand. She walked over to his side and dropped her trash into the can. "I've offended you, haven't I?"

He looked at her and shook his head. "No. It's not what you think."

"I don't understand."

"I like what I feel in your presence, what I hear coming from your lips. You're spiritually grounded, and you don't center on yourself."

112

In the past, her focus on her emotions had caused her to treat him badly. "I wouldn't go that far."

"I would. Ready?" Lee took her hand as they walked toward the car. After helping her inside, he came around and sat in the driver's seat. "My relationship with God has been too long in coming. I believe He put you in my life for this reason—to open my eyes. I was afraid you might think my newfound need for religion had to do with your ultimatum."

"No, Lee. I never meant it as an ultimatum."

"Well, you should have. A woman needs a committed man. My devotion to the almighty dollar didn't give me much comfort. Possessions just don't fill the void. And I'm finally accepting the void. I searched for years but was never able to give a name to the emptiness.

"When I left Charlotte, someone told me a big-city lawyer couldn't be happy in a small town. Boy, were they wrong. I've never been happier. Never felt more fulfilled. I'm not fooling myself, though. For the first time in my life, I know I'm on the right track spiritually. I've reprioritized my life."

"Thank God," Liza said, her eyes drifting closed as she drew a deep breath. "I want you to know Christ as your Savior for all the right reasons."

He leaned to kiss her cheek. "I know. Believe me, I'd never try to fool you into believing I was something I'm not."

"I'd better get home. Mom and Dad will worry about me."

"How about that dinner?"

"I'll call you soon and set a date."

&

Time had a way of getting away from her as Liza worked around the farm, trying to salvage what she could of their crops. A week before the wedding, Kit showed up at the house on Saturday afternoon and found Liza working in the garden.

"What are you doing out here alone?"

"Hoeing." Liza grinned at her friend. Her mother had planted a late garden, and it was doing well. The weeds, in particular, flourished. She didn't add that she needed the private time for reflection. In time she'd confide the truth, but not now.

"I can see that, silly. Why isn't your mom helping?"

"She did until lunchtime. Daddy's not feeling well. I suggested she stay inside with him. Even with those tests, the surgery, and medication, we're still nervous about his heart condition."

"Want some help?"

"Sure. How's life treating you?"

Kitty pulled a handful of weeds and tossed them to the side. "Can't complain. It's hot. I'll be glad to see fall."

Liza's face creased in a grin. "Thought you couldn't complain?"

"I've been working hard. I do believe everybody in town has been to the office this week. I didn't think farmers had time to be sick."

"They don't exactly have a choice in the matter."

Kitty took her time, careful not to damage her manicured nails. Liza dared not offer her a hoe, or she'd be sporting blisters at her wedding.

Her own hands were rough, her nails chipped. *I could do with a manicure.* Liza promised herself one as soon as work slacked off to the point where it would be worthwhile—definitely before the wedding next week. Meanwhile, she would find time to file her nails and put lotion on her hands.

"You didn't mention the late-afternoon thunderstorms."

"Dave's having a time because of them. They've been running behind all week. He all but stood me up last night."

Liza glanced up, curiosity lighting her eyes. "What happened?"

"We were supposed to go to a movie, but he didn't get to the house until almost nine. He was so tired I hated to insist, so we just sat on the porch and talked."

"And?"

"Don't be so nosy," Kitty said, wrinkling her nose at Liza. "Dave's a wonderful man. We have so much in common."

Liza feigned surprise. "Really?"

"Rub it in," Kitty said good-naturedly. "I know you've been saying we'd get together for years. He's perfect for me. Of course, he is a farmer. That part's not great, but I suppose things could be worse."

Liza froze at her friend's comments. "You wouldn't try to talk him into doing something else?"

"Don't be silly. Liza, I recognize the hints you've been dropping. I've lived around farmers long enough to know you can't change them. If the land makes Dave happy, I'm okay with it. I love Dave Evans enough that I'd rather have a few minutes a day of his time than nothing."

"I doubt it'll be a few minutes," Liza said, the tension easing from her body. "Wedding plans under control?"

"Finally. We've got the group down to a manageable number, and come next Sunday afternoon, I'll say 'I do' to the man of my dreams."

The man of her dreams. How Liza longed to say those words herself. In her heart and mind, Lee fit the position perfectly, but their relationship was far from Kit and Dave's happy beginning.

"Sorry I can't stick around and help you finish, but Dave promised to come by tonight and help with the birdseed packets."

"I'm glad you stopped by." Liza hugged her, tears stinging her eyes as she watched Kitty run for her car, carried along in the euphoria only true love could bring. She turned back to the row that seemed to stretch forever.

Even though she was happy for Kitty, envy kept interfering with the excitement she should be feeling. She didn't want to feel this way.

❧

Rick stopped by on Wednesday. Refusing her offer to come inside, he remained in the truck. He handed her a small brown paper sack of boiled peanuts he'd picked up at the tobacco warehouse. "Dave said you love these things. Don't know why. I can't stand them."

"They're an acquired taste," Liza explained, unrolling the top of the small bag. "How are things over at your house? Getting crazy?"

"Mom and Kit's mom keep trying to make changes to their plans. Last night Dave warned Mom to stop or they'll elope."

"Doesn't sound like Dave."

"Mom didn't think so either. She was still fussing this morning. Blamed Kitty, but what she doesn't realize is, her baby has become his own man. She'll have another fit when she learns they're fixing up a house near Kitty's father's place."

"Where did she think they were going to stay?"

"At the house, I guess. She'll be lost when we leave."

Liza stopped shelling the peanut and looked at Rick. "You're leaving? When?"

"Sunday night. I've got to get back to England. Kit and Dave are going, too. Tell me I'm not a glutton for punishment."

Liza leaned against the truck, crossing her arms in the open window. "Why didn't you tell me earlier?"

"I planned to. There's been so much going on."

She pasted on a smile. Everything was changing so fast. "Well, I guess I'll see you Sunday." Liza pushed herself away from the truck.

"Liza, wait." His fingers closed about her arm. "I don't suppose I should expect you to cry every time I leave?"

She touched his hand. "You can if you insist on waltzing in and out of my life every fourteen years. Seriously, though, I want you to do the things that make you happy. I'm not the same child I was all those years ago. I know you're cut out for greatness, and I'm glad you have the guts to go after it."

His smile widened in approval. "You're some woman, Liza Stephens. When do you go after what you really want?"

She knew exactly what he meant. "When God says it's time."

"It's going to happen, Liza. I know you love Lee, and he loves you. God brought you two together for a reason."

"I believe that, Rick. I'm seeing a real difference in Lee. He's attending church, and I know he's going to turn his life over to God one day soon. He may not realize it yet, but he's already changed from the man he was when we first met."

"Love has a way of doing that to a guy," Rick said. "I see it in Dave's eyes when he looks at Kitty, and I see it in Lee's eyes when he looks at you. One day soon I hope to have others see it in my eyes when I look at the woman I love."

"You will."

❧

Sunday dawned beautifully clear—not a dark cloud in the sky, not on Kitty's wedding day. Thinking of all the things she needed to be doing before the wedding, Liza considered missing church, but the feeling she needed to attend was strong.

She missed Sunday school but managed to pull into the parking lot shortly before the eleven o'clock service. Looking around for Lee's car, she spotted it on the far side of the lot. It was too late to get into her choir robe, so she decided to sit this one out. The opening hymn began as she headed for the pew. Lee glanced up and waved for her to join him.

He shared the hymnal with her. Liza felt so happy standing by his side, experiencing the little things couples did for each other. The hour passed quickly. The pastor preached a stirring sermon on love, reminding them how powerful God's love was for each and every one of them.

During the altar call, Liza sang the hymn from memory, her mind wandering to her list of things to do before she went to Kitty's. It took her a second to realize Lee had left the pew. Surprised, she looked up to find him talking with the pastor up front.

Joy greater than anything she'd ever known burst forth in her heart, and tears of delight filled her eyes. He and the pastor bowed their heads as the choir and congregation continued to sing. Liza's voice rose in volume at the wonder of the moment.

"Ladies and gentlemen," the pastor said, standing before them with Lee by his side. "Lee Hayden has come forth today to make a profession of faith. He plans to follow up his commitment with believer's baptism and a request to join our church. Please step forward and extend the right hand of fellowship to him today."

Liza knew she hardly had any time before she was expected at Kit's. She needed to go home and pick up her dress. Still, there was no way she would walk out of church today without sharing her joy with Lee.

Never had a line moved so slowly. By the time she reached Lee, she had few minutes to spare. Her handshake turned into a hug, and she smiled, her eyes watery with tears of elation. "I love you," she whispered, smiling when he lowered one lid in a conspiratorial wink. "I can't stay. Kit's going to kill me if I don't get over there now."

"Can't have her doing that. Go. I'll see you at the wedding."

❧

"Where have you been?" Kitty demanded when Liza stepped into the bedroom. "Where are my hose? I won't ever be ready in time."

After knowing Kit for so long, Liza thought she knew every facet of her personality, but she'd never seen Kitty panic before. Good thing Kitty didn't get married every day; Liza doubted her nerves could take it. "So they'll wait. You're the star of the show," she comforted. "Settle down. You're doing fine."

Liza was glad she'd decided to dress at home. Kitty had chosen a very classy dress for her, insisting there was no reason for them not to be dolled up. Two pieces, the lace top had a scalloped neckline and a tiered georgette skirt stopped about mid-calf. The lilac color complemented Liza's dark hair and tan.

Kitty refused to let her pay for the dress, insisting she cover the cost herself because she had only one attendant. Liza felt it had more to do with her being out of work and explained she was still being paid, but her obstinate friend refused to budge, so Liza finally gave in.

"I've got flowers for your hair," Kitty said, going over to sort through the bouquets to find them.

They tucked the tiny white rosebuds and baby's breath in place in her dark curls. Liza looked in the mirror and nodded. "Everything's perfect. I can't believe you did all this in a couple of months."

"Me neither. Did I tell you Daddy finished my gazebo?" Kitty continued to touch up her makeup.

After a great deal of argument, Kitty's parents had accepted her plans to turn her wedding into an outside event. Any sort of ceremony with relatives and friends was preferable to missing their only daughter's wedding. "He's going to take it to our house after the wedding. He painted it white, and I got ferns and ribbons. It's pretty, even if I do say so."

"Did you call the photographer?"

"He promised to be here on time. Oh, Liza, I'm so scared and excited. Dave called earlier to tell me he loves me. Sometimes I just can't believe it's happening."

After Lee's decision, Liza couldn't help but hope there was a future for them. She didn't want to take anything away from her friend's day, but the need to share the news overwhelmed her.

"Liza, that's wonderful," Kitty exclaimed, hugging her.

"I left him standing at the altar to get over here."

"I'm sorry. I know what a struggle that must have been."

Liza picked up the wedding gown from the bed. "I didn't want to leave. Let's get you into this so I can see him again."

"Hey, slow down, girl," Kitty said. "If he's worth having, he's worth waiting for. Besides, I'm trying to stretch these minutes into memories to last a lifetime."

Kitty had gone the whole nine yards with her dress. "A girl only gets married once," she said when they visited the bridal shop. She'd stood on the pedestal, looking every inch the perfect bride and asked, "It'll be fine, won't it?"

The question surprised Liza. Kitty was a confident person, always so certain of what she wanted. "You like it, don't you?" she'd asked.

"Love it."

"Then that's all that matters."

As Kitty slipped the bishop sleeves over her arms and smoothed the lace-draped neckline into place, Liza almost cried. Even the plainest girl made a beautiful bride, but Kitty looked like a fairy princess. Dave would never forget the vision she made when she walked down the aisle to meet him.

"Button me. Mom had a fit about this," she said, indicating the full-tiered lace chapel train. "I took care of that, though. Jason agreed to pull a runner over the grass just before the ceremony."

After posturing to get a better reflection in the mirror, Kit picked up the Victorian lace collar and passed it to her. "Help me with this. I'm all thumbs."

Liza stood behind her friend, looking at her in the mirror. "You're beautiful."

"We make quite a picture," Kitty agreed. "Promise you'll always be my best friend."

"Always."

The last thing was her veil. Liza fitted the lace cap over Kit's shining blond curls and pinned it carefully. "You want this in place now?" She held out the netting.

"What time is it?"

"The photographer is waiting to take pictures. By the time he finishes, it'll be time for the wedding march."

"You'd better get Mom and Dad."

The photographer took his shots, and Liza picked up their flowers, leaving Kitty for a few private moments with her parents.

From the window, she watched the guests assemble in the garden. Clearly Kitty and Dave failed in their attempt to curb the number. Nobody wanted to miss this wedding.

Kitty appeared at her side. "Looks like we're playing to a packed house."

"You should have charged admission," Liza teased, moving Kit's blusher veil into place. "Where's your father?"

"He's coming. Poor Daddy," Kit sympathized. "I still think he wants to lock me in my room instead of walk me down the aisle."

"Probably. Remember, I was there when he said you couldn't date until you were thirty." Liza kissed her cheek and squeezed her hand before putting the bouquet into Kitty's hand. "I love you. Be happy."

There were tears in both women's eyes as they walked out of the house. Liza moved down the aisle, smiling at Dave and Rick when she took her place on the opposite side.

Dave's expression spoke volumes when Kitty came forward. Another picture came to Liza's mind. She pushed it away. All in God's time. He'd already worked a miracle. She couldn't hope for more now.

The vows rang in her ears and in a fight to regain her composure, Liza allowed her gaze to touch on the crowd. A tiny smile touched her lips when she spotted Lee in the group. His grin was huge as he mouthed, "I love you."

"Liza," Kitty whispered, "the ring." Bringing her attention back to her duties, Liza found the item in question and placed it in her friend's hand.

Within minutes, Kitty became Mrs. David Evans. After a photo session, the wedding party entered the tent where the guests awaited them. This time Liza greeted guests in the receiving line.

"We seem to be waiting in line to see each other today," Lee said when he finally got to her. "You look beautiful."

"Thank you. Wasn't it a pretty wedding?"

"Very. We need to talk."

"Liza, the photographer wants to take more photos," Kitty called. "Sorry. I didn't realize you were talking to Lee."

"Save me a cup of punch," Liza told him, waving good-bye as she continued her attendant duties.

The next couple of hours were filled with picture taking, cake cutting, helping Kitty change, and entertaining guests. Several times, Liza found herself headed in Lee's direction, only to have her plans upset. They waved the newly-weds off to Dave's decorated car in a flurry of birdseed.

"Think the cans are a bit much?" Rick asked, grinning as they clattered down the highway.

"The shaving cream and toilet tissue would have been enough," Liza said.

She had vetoed his suggestion of packing the couple's luggage with confetti, reminding him of the mandatory payback they would set themselves up for as the remaining singles.

"Miss her already?"

She turned to face Lee, her dress whispering with the movement. Rick disappeared.

"She'll be back."

He brushed birdseed from her hair. "How did you manage that?" he asked, pointing to Kitty's bouquet.

"It helps to have your best friend as the bride. She all but put it into my hands."

He grinned and reached into his pocket. The blue-beribboned garter dangled from his index finger. "She must have instructed Dave to make sure I got this."

"Probably." Liza giggled at the thought.

"Would you like to attend church services with me tonight?"

She turned his arm to check his watch. There was just enough time to get home and change clothes. "I'll meet you at church."

"Why don't I go with you and visit with your parents while you change?"

"Let me get my things."

After talking with Kitty's mom and finding things were under control, Liza headed across the yard to her car.

She stopped when Rick came out of the house, calling her name. "I'm leaving early in the morning to meet Dave and Kit at the airport to fly to London. I wanted to say good-bye and tell you it's been wonderful seeing you again this summer."

"I'll miss you. Don't be a stranger."

Rick wrapped his arms about her and said, "I'm praying for you and your family."

"Liza?"

They glanced at Lee.

"Coming. Stay in touch, Rick."

"You, too. I'll be praying for you and Lee. God bless."

She kissed his cheek. "I'm praying for you, too."

Chapter 15

Three weeks later, Liza bleakly surveyed the mess before her, knowing there was enough work to keep her busy for more than the day she allotted. Served her right. She should have had better sense than to start such a job. The barn hadn't been cleaned properly in years. Stubborn determination made her push on with the latest of her keep-busy tasks.

It wasn't really necessary, but neither were the other jobs she'd done in the past few days. Thanks to Hurricane Bobby, the majority of their harvest had been a bounty of paperwork. They had managed to get a few fall crops in the ground, but it would be awhile before they began to produce.

Her father was doing much better—so much so, Dr. Mayes released him the day before, saying that if her dad exercised his leg, he wouldn't have a limp. The heart condition was something he would have to accept, but he could live a normal life.

He worked, but Liza insisted that he rest often. She knew he didn't really need her any longer, but she put off making her final decision.

Her life hadn't been the same since Lee Hayden came to her rescue all those months ago, and Liza knew it never would be. She saw him often but was so confused by his behavior. They attended church together, went out to dinner, and Lee often told her he loved her, but he hadn't brought up the subject of marriage.

Liza thought maybe Lee felt he needed to give them time to get used to the idea of being a couple, but now that they seemed to be comfortable in each other's company, his hurry had slowed down to a crawl.

"A woman's work is never done."

"Kit!" She whirled about, dropping the bucket and hurrying over to hug her friend. "How's married life, Mrs. Evans?"

"I won't say perfect, but let's say the ups make the downs worthwhile," she teased, appearing lit from inside. "Actually I highly recommend marriage. What about you? Did our subtle hints inspire Lee to propose?"

Crestfallen, Liza's smile quickly faded. "I think he's changed his mind."

Kitty's mouth fell open. "No way."

"I don't know what else to think. He's attending the new-Christian class at church now. We see each other at church fairly often and go out when we can, but that's all."

"I think you're wrong about Lee. If I guessed at a reason, I'd say he's like Dave and me. Adapting to change can be all-consuming. I thought I knew everything about Dave before we married, but I haven't even scratched the surface yet. It'll take another fifty years, I'm sure."

Liza sat on a nearby bale of hay and pulled one leg underneath her. "At least you're committed to figuring him out."

"Don't give up on Lee. I'm sure he never expected to find a relationship with Christ and the woman of his dreams when he came here."

"Maybe not. I just hate this state of limbo. I want more. Tell me about your honeymoon."

Kitty talked for several minutes about London and all they had seen. "Rick was a pretty decent guide. He gave us a quick tour, then we'd get together every couple of days for him to make suggestions on what we should do. Otherwise, he left us alone."

"Doesn't hurt to have someone who knows the area," Liza agreed. "So what are your plans now that you're home?"

"Dave's already deserted me for the land," Kit said. "I'm getting the house organized this week and going back to work next. We've decided to start a family soon."

"Don't you think you should give yourself time to get used to being married first?"

"Neither of us are getting any younger. We both love children. We've decided on at least three. One at a time, of course."

"Wow. Kids."

"Flighty Kitty, huh? I surprise myself in so many ways. It's like I woke up from a deep sleep and found I didn't want to exist without Dave. Funny, don't you think?"

"No. Perfect," Liza whispered. That was the way she felt about Lee.

"I wanted to let you know I was back and give you this," Kitty said, handing Liza a souvenir from London. "I'd better head home to fix Dave's lunch. Me cooking—can you believe it?"

She considered her friend's lack of experience in that area and asked, "What's on the menu?"

"Sandwiches. I'll throw in a can of soup if he's really hungry."

"He must really be in love."

Kit continued to laugh as she walked out the barn door. A new husband and home now kept Kitty busy. Liza missed the times they shared.

Right now she didn't feel she could talk to anyone about her feelings. She couldn't bring herself to voice her fears to her parents, not with them having so many problems of their own. Things were finally looking up for them. They didn't need her dragging them into her despair.

And in truth, she was afraid not even the open, honest relationship she shared with them, trusting them as friends and confidants, could handle this one. Deep down, she prayed her doubts would go away.

Hunger gnawed at her empty stomach. According to Kit, it was lunchtime. Liza strolled toward the house. *The yard needs to be mowed,* she thought, noting yet another task to be completed.

She stopped to wash up. The water from the faucet on the back porch was cold against her skin. Lathering her hands heavily with soap, Liza scrubbed vigorously to wash away the morning's grime, wishing desperately that she could do the same with her thoughts.

Liza cupped her hands, filling them with water before tossing it onto her face. The coolness unsettled her lethargic state, and in quick, jerky movements, she tugged a towel from the rack and dried her face and hands. The screen door slammed shut with a bang behind her.

Her father was seated at the table, studying one of his favorite farm journals while her mother moved about the stove, spooning the vegetables into serving bowls.

"What's for lunch?"

"Fried chicken."

Liza looked at the plate holding a couple of pieces of golden bird her mother placed in front of her. The other plate held baked chicken. "You didn't have to go to all that trouble. I could have eaten baked."

"I wanted to do something special for you. Oh, here's a letter," her mother said, pulling the envelope from her apron pocket. "Very fancy. Engraved and everything."

Liza noted the Wilsons' address and laid it aside.

"Aren't you going to open it?" her mother asked.

"Later."

She bowed her head while her dad said grace and reached for the salad bowl in the center of the table.

"Open it, Liza," her mother encouraged.

Taking a deep, steadying breath, Liza picked up the envelope and snapped the seal with her finger. Quickly scanning the contents, she dropped it to the table. "Mr. Wilson's retirement party."

The news came as no surprise to her. Lee had everything he'd worked for, thanks to his uncle. Liza found the reality unsettling. Even though she'd known this was coming, now she found herself worrying about the future. Could she work for the man she loved? Picking up her fork, Liza made a desultory attempt to eat her meal.

"How nice," her mother enthused, shaking out her napkin as she settled into her chair. "When is it?"

"Didn't you open your invitation, Mom?"

Sarah Stephens set the bowl on the table with a thump. "I hoped you'd talk to us again. You've shut us out of your life."

Liza pushed her chair back from the table. She glanced at her father, sensing his concern and knowing he wouldn't interfere. He would be there when she was ready to talk. That was all he could do. "I'm sorry. I don't mean to. It's just that I'm trying to sort out my life right now. Excuse me, please."

"Liza, honey, wait," her mother called, her voice strained.

Liza stood frozen in the doorway. She loathed herself for hurting the two dearest people in the world.

The chair scraped as it slid backward, followed by the whisper of her mother's slippers across the linoleum floor. Her hand rested on Liza's shoulder. "Never deal with anything alone. Talk with God. He can provide the answer. And promise me you'll attend this party."

Liza shrugged, pushing hurriedly out the door. "We'll see, Mom. We'll see."

She went into the barn and started the mower in hopes of taking her mind off the incident. But as the mower cut a swath through the grass, her thoughts continued to bother Liza. God waited for her to ask what He wanted for her instead of what she wanted for herself. As usual, she selfishly orchestrated her life to her own specifications, not praying for answers. She'd decided that Lee would be perfect for her if he was saved, but had God?

She was a hypocrite. All those times she'd accused Lee of being selfish, of looking out only for himself, and she did the same thing. The realization jarred her. Liza mowed the path around the curve where her parents couldn't see her and turned off the mower. She sat in the silence and, for the first time in weeks, opened her heart to the Author and Finisher of her faith.

❧

"How's my girl?" Lee asked later that evening when he called.

"Good. And you?"

"Busy." He launched into a description of his life for the past few days. "What time should I pick you up for Uncle John's party?"

The way he took it for granted bothered Liza, but her prayer sessions helped her curb her tongue. If God planned something for Lee and her, Liza would await His answer. "I thought you called to ask when I planned to come back to work."

"We can discuss it at the party."

"You promised no business on our dates."

"If you insist on holding me to a promise made under duress. . ."

"I do," Liza said. "Pick me up at six thirty."

❧

Liza spent the hours while she worked thinking about what she would wear. She wanted to look good, if only to give her the confidence she needed, and spent intervening days in preparation—some with feverish activity, but always in prayer.

As she applied her makeup, Liza tossed the eyeliner back onto the dresser, her hands too shaky to even try.

At times, she considered their differences—a lawyer and a farmer's daughter—and her doubts resurfaced. Lee didn't understand what this farm meant to her family. "You should just give up before you get hurt," she told the face in the mirror.

Don't, a small, insistent voice deep inside prompted. Where would she be if Jesus Christ had given up?

She twisted her hair up on top of her head and secured it with enameled combs. Slipping on the dress she'd chosen, Liza hoped Lee would be proud of her.

The deep red complemented her dark hair and made her feel feminine. Downstairs, the first person she saw was her mother.

"Liza, you're breathtaking."

"Think so?" she asked, the uncertainty of her thoughts running over into her words.

Silently mother and daughter stood, carefully handling the fragile relationship between them. Liza's feelings were still too raw to discuss, but their love was a tangible thing, strong enough to carry them through any storm.

"Honey, you've always been beautiful to me," her mother assured, her lips curving in an unconscious smile. "From the moment you came into the world," she reminisced. "My precious baby girl."

With a sob, Liza moved into her arms. "I'm so sorry. I love you and Daddy so much."

Protective arms sheltered her child. "We know. Now stop crying before you ruin your makeup."

With a teary smile, Liza stepped back, sniffling occasionally. Her hand clutched her mother's. Nervously she moistened her lips, trying to swallow the knot of tension that remained. The silence was so absolute even her breathing sounded loud.

"Mom," she whispered, "what do you do when you don't have the slightest idea what the man you love intends?"

A sympathetic smile flitted across her mother's face. "It's hard, isn't it?"

Liza was puzzled by her response.

"Don't look so shocked," her mother said. "I was a reasonably attractive woman in my day."

"Beautiful," Liza corrected.

"I made a decision, too. But when it comes to love, there's no choice to make. I loved your father, and as the only son, he accepted the responsibility. Not that he ever wanted a different life, but he always said no child of his would be pressured into doing something he didn't want to do. That's why I regret not having more children."

"What are you saying, Mom?"

"Wait for Lee. You won't regret it."

"I don't even know what he's thinking."

"Take a chance, Liza. Don't be one of those women who spends her life wishing she had done something."

"Promise me you'll be around to pick up the pieces."

Her mother squeezed her hand, the loving warmth of her smile touching Liza's heart. "Come show your daddy."

They entered the living room together. Her father sat in his recliner, watching his favorite television program.

"Paul," her mother called softly, stepping away from Liza's side. "What do you think of our daughter tonight?"

He glanced sideways, his head snapping back. "Whooee. That boy isn't going to know what hit him," he teased. Slowly he stood, his arms outstretched in loving welcome.

Liza took the steps eagerly, running to him. "I love you," she whispered. No matter what the future held, they would never suffer again because of her, Liza vowed. The doorbell rang, and she smiled at them before going to open the door for Lee.

"Wow."

"Is that all you can say?" she asked, striking a model's pose. "Not too shabby for a farmer's daughter?"

He shook his head. "Not shabby at all."

"You look very handsome tonight." Liza smoothed his expensive silk tie.

He kissed her. Liza led the way into the family room.

"Hello, Lee."

"Hello, Mrs. Stephens, Mr. Stephens. I can see I've got my work cut out for me tonight with this beauty."

"Have fun. We'll see you both later."

"It's going to be a wonderful evening," Lee said, promise lighting the eyes that rested on her when he spoke the words.

❧

The party was in full swing when they arrived at the Wilsons' home. Liza greeted Mr. and Mrs. Wilson, then Lee pulled her farther into the room.

"Mom, Dad, there's someone I want you to meet. Liza Stephens, James and Sheila Hayden, my parents."

Disturbed by his lack of warning, Liza managed a smile and cordial greeting. "Nice to meet you."

"You, too, dear. Lee has told us such wonderful things about you. How are your parents?"

"Fine. They should be here shortly."

His mother beamed at her. "We can hardly wait to meet them. They've raised a wonderful daughter."

Her praise sounded sincere, but it confused Liza. Lee's mother knew nothing of Liza or her parents. What had Lee told his parents about her? "Thank you. You have a great son."

Lee leaned over to whisper in her ear. "Visit with Mom and Dad a bit. I need to talk with Uncle John in the library. I'll be right back."

"But, Lee," she objected. Already he'd forgotten his no-business promise.

He patted her arm. "You'll be fine. This will only take a few minutes."

Her pride took a beating when it came to holding Lee's attention for any length of time. She considered it unfair of him not to warn her, but on the other hand, common sense told her they'd be there.

"So, Mr. and Mrs. Hayden, how are you enjoying our little community?" she asked, afraid her efforts to make conversation were stilted at best.

Lee's mother smiled. "Call us Sheila and Jim. I lived here until I went off to college. We prefer larger cities."

Real smart, Liza thought. *I knew that.* "I've never lived anywhere but here."

"After you and Lee. . ." Lee's father touched his wife's arm and shook his head slightly. "So how long have you worked for John?" she asked instead.

"Since I graduated from high school."

Sheila Hayden's animated gestures reminded her very much of her son's. "I know John feels you're an asset to the firm."

The woman's flattery made Liza feel uncomfortable. "I was the fortunate one. Mr. Wilson has taught me a lot about law."

"Lee says you should get your degree. Have you ever considered going to law school?"

Lee's mother should be a lawyer. Sophisticated and beautiful, she could cross-examine with the best of them.

Still, Lee's opinion of her ability pleased Liza. "I like what I do. I'm not really courtroom material."

"Liza."

"Kit," she cried, hugging her friend and then Dave. She introduced them to Lee's parents. "This is Dave and Kitty Evans."

"The newlyweds. Lee told us he attended your wedding. I dated your father years ago, Dave. How is he?"

"Great. Busy with the farm."

"Lee mentioned you honeymooned in London."

Obviously Lee enjoyed a better relationship with his parents than she realized. He seemed to have kept them current on everything.

Dave placed his arm about Kitty's waist. "Yes, ma'am, we did."

"We've been to England a couple of times. It's wonderful," Sheila enthused.

"We plan to go back again," Kitty said. "By the way, Liza, Rick called earlier. He sends his love."

"Rick?" Lee's mother asked curiously.

"Dave's brother," Kitty explained. "Our built-in tour guide in London."

"That sounds wonderful. Clara is looking a bit overwhelmed," Sheila told her husband. "You should tell John and Lee to come back to the party."

"I'll go," Liza volunteered.

"Thank you, dear."

She tapped on the study door and opened it. "Mr. Wilson, you really should. . ."

Lee glanced up from the papers he was studying. "Give us a few more minutes, Liza."

His words hit her like a shock of ice water. "Your mom asked me to let Mr. Wilson know Mrs. Wilson needs him out here." Just before she shut the door, she heard Mr. Wilson's chuckle.

"Come on, Lee. We can finish this later. This party is in my honor. If I want to enjoy my retirement, I'd better show my face."

❧

Piqued by Lee's dismissive attitude, Liza stepped out into the Wilsons' garden and strolled along the beautifully landscaped walkway, trying to work through the growing apprehension she felt.

Why couldn't Lee wait until a better time to talk with his uncle? She settled in the swing and pushed herself back and forth for several minutes.

Realizing pride controlled her, Liza frowned. She needed to go back inside and celebrate with her employer. After all he'd done for her over the years, he deserved her appreciation. Besides, she wanted to see his face when she gave him the hat she had found. She knew, without a doubt, the hat with a big fish through the center would make him laugh.

"There you are."

Looking at Lee, she asked, "Finish your business?"

"We were tying up loose ends."

"Organizing your life into nice tidy bundles?"

Lee dropped down beside her in the swing. "You could say that."

"So which bundle did you put me in?"

"Liza—"

"You shouldn't have taken Mr. Wilson from his guests."

Lee slipped an arm about her shoulders. "You're right. I'm sorry. I shouldn't have deserted you either. Forgive me?"

She wasn't finished. "And thanks for the advance warning about your parents."

He nodded. "Are you going to make me apologize all night?"

"I should. You keep pricking my stupid pride."

"Not stupid, my darling," he said, flashing her a loving smile. "That Carolina pride was my undoing. It's one of the things I love most about you. I was tying up loose ends so I could get on with the next phase of my life."

"What could possibly be so important?"

"This." Confused, Liza stared down at the family Bible he handed her.

Lee reached to open the leather cover. A gasp left her throat as Liza stared down at the names written on the matrimony page and the beautiful diamond solitaire looped on the ribbon bookmark. "Name the date and place. I'll be there. And God willing, one day we'll fill in our children's names."

Tears of joy ran unchecked down her cheeks.

"I know you're upset with me now, but I wanted everything to be taken care of before I asked you to be my wife. Uncle John and I have come to an agreement about the practice, so I can promise you we'll be close to your parents and the farm. And I know you were concerned about my commitment to God."

"I never should have judged you."

"Liza, I don't want anything to cloud your feelings for me, including doubt. That's why I waited to ask until after I completed my new-believer class. I now fully understand the step I've taken and embrace my faith openly."

"What about our differences, Lee? You've got law, and I've got the farm. How do we get past that?"

"Easier than if we throw our love away. We can have a family, Liza. Perhaps our son, or maybe daughter, will have the same passion for the land you and your father share. Just give us a chance."

"I want to—more than anything in the world."

"With God in our corner, we'll make it," Lee promised. His arms became her haven. "So how do I ask? Do you want a grand proposal like Kitty's? Me on bended knee in front of everyone?"

"No," she insisted, hugging him tighter. "Just us. Tell me you love me and ask me again. This time I'll be proud to say yes."

"And I'll be proud to have you as my wife. You're the second-best thing that ever happened to me, Sarah Elizabeth Stephens."

She knew his relationship with God held the number one slot, and Liza willingly accepted Lee's choice. "So are you going to ask?"

Lee untied the ring and knelt before her, taking her hand in his, "Will you do me the honor of becoming my wife?"

Thank You, Lord, she whispered softly. "Yes, my love. Yes."

Look to
the Heart

*To my aunt Inez, the woman with a heart
big enough to share with all her nieces and nephews.
Thanks for always being there for us.*

Chapter 1

What had he gotten himself into now?

Eli McKay paused in the doorway, tightening his hold on his daughter. Lynnie had started to bounce excitedly in his arms on seeing the other children squealing and running around the day care center.

"Oh, excuse me!" the young woman behind him cried. His sudden stop had caused her to plow into his back.

He turned toward her and grinned. "I'm sorry. I'm not used to seeing so many kids at once."

Adults dotted the playground, their attention focused on the children. He watched as an older woman spoke to an active little boy then bent down and hugged him. Eight months of fatherhood had shown him one child could be a handful. He admired these people.

Minutes earlier he'd been waiting in the office of the day care center to fill out an application. The same young woman, a staff member named Gina, had come in to telephone a child's mother. Eli couldn't help but overhear when she asked for Janice Gore, only to find her away from her office. After he explained that he knew Janice and her son, Davey, Gina told him why she was calling Janice—Davey was holed up in a big pipe and wouldn't come out. Eli had offered to help.

Perhaps he'd been too quick to respond. But he owed Janice. After all, she had suggested the day care center to him.

"Come on, baby girl," he said to his daughter. "Let's see what our friend Davey's up to now."

The baby cooed as she took in the new sights and sounds. She patted her hand in his hair, and Eli prepared for the inevitable tug. She had a mighty grasp when it came to her daddy's hair. He'd be lucky if he had any left by the time she started walking.

Eli followed Gina over to what had to be the strangest playground equipment he'd ever seen. The large, round plastic pipe stood on stilts, a bend dividing the ten or twelve feet before dropping off into a five-foot slide.

Somewhere in the bowels of the contraption, he could hear a woman chatting with a child—it had to be Davey—as though they were in a bright, cheery classroom.

"The bogeyman is in here, Ms. Dee," the small voice said. "Billy says he lives in the dark."

"Davey, there is no bogeyman. Billy's just trying to scare you."

"Mommy and Daddy stay with me when I'm afraid."

"Grab my hand," she said at his wavering response. "We won't be afraid of the dark any longer."

Soft and distinctly feminine, Eli found her words reassuring and intriguing. "Who's in there with him?" he asked Gina.

The young woman giggled. "Our fearless director. I hope she doesn't get stuck inside that pipe."

Eli chuckled and continued to eavesdrop, his imagination running wild as he visualized the female who told Davey she could eat a zillion chocolate chip cookies in one sitting. Not and fit in this tube, she couldn't.

He jerked himself back to the emergency. "Davey? It's Mr. McKay. Come on out."

Lynnie bounced against his chest, babbling her own request.

"It's dark." The tiny voice sounded as if it were in the bottom of a drum.

"Must not be the Davey Gore I know," Eli said. "That Davey sleeps in his own room without a night-light. His mom thinks he's the bravest little guy in the world."

The child cleared the opening in a flash. "It's me, Mr. McKay."

Eli feigned shock. "Why, it is my Davey. Come on out, buddy." He reached out to help, but the child plunked down on the slide and raced to the bottom, landing on his feet.

Davey ran off to play, and Eli turned back to the apparatus, catching the woman's voice again, this time mumbling dire warnings about the monster's future existence.

"Owie! Oh! Owie!"

As the groans and grunts blended with what sounded suspiciously like giggles, Eli called, "Are you okay in there?"

"I'm—" the voice began, a groan taking over. "My toe—cramp."

Her head cleared the opening. Blinded by the sunny light of day, she squinted, her even white teeth flashing with her wide smile. Light brown hair, almost blond, worn short and brushed back in a windblown style, framed the ivory skin of her face. She stood only a couple of inches over five feet and wore well-washed jeans with one of those comfortable floppy shirts.

Her mouth widened in surprise when her feet shot out from beneath her. She quickly came down the slide, landing solidly on the ground.

"How graceful," she murmured, her face reddening.

Eli offered his hand. "I'm sure it's easier when you're three feet tall."

Her laughter rippled through the air, her teal eyes closed slightly with merriment. *Probably in her early thirties,* he guessed, after spotting a few character lines.

Striking, Eli added to his earlier appraisal as he helped her to her feet. When her brows lifted and she pulled gently, he released her hand.

She dusted off the seat of her pants. "That was a masterful rescue. I didn't know how I was going to get Davey out of there."

"I'm thankful it worked," he said. "His mother is an exhausted woman vowing to wreak havoc on the older child who introduced her son to the bogeyman."

The young woman heaved a sigh. "After this escapade I'd almost be tempted to give her his name."

Lynnie took that moment to dive forward, her arms outstretched. Eli reacted quickly, securing her in his hold. One of these times she was going to take a nosedive right out of his arms.

"And who is this little beauty?" she asked, tickling the baby's chin.

Lynnie hid her face in his shoulder. Eli smiled. "My daughter. We're here to discuss enrolling her in your center."

"Do you have a couple of minutes?" She glanced around the play area. "I need to make sure Davey's okay, and then we can go to the office."

"Sure. We can wait."

He watched her work her way across the playground and found himself thinking of the Pied Piper when several children trailed behind.

His attention was diverted to two boys who were chasing each other. He stepped back to give them room, his gaze drawn back to the director as she sank to her knees in the sandbox beside Davey.

Did he really want this for his daughter? Very much so. This woman obviously had a remarkable rapport with kids.

She caught Davey's hand, leading him back to where Eli waited. "Thanks again for helping," she said.

"I've known Davey far too long not to help. Janice works for me."

She nodded. "Welcome to Kids Unlimited. I'm Diedra Pierce." She reached to shake his hand.

"Eli McKay."

Davey fidgeted at her side, obviously unimpressed by the adult conversation. "Ms. Dee," he said, tugging impatiently at her shirt, "can I play?"

Her hand dropped away and came to rest on Davey's shoulder. "Thank Mr. McKay first."

The little boy mumbled the words then ran off to the swings.

"So much for undying gratitude," she said with a shrug.

"That's some playground equipment."

Her expression came alive with her grin. "A former enrollee's father created the tunnel slide. I should have refused, but he insisted. It's too dark in the tunnel."

"You could always install low-voltage strip lighting."

She smacked her forehead and groaned. "Why didn't I think of that?"

"Do they all call you Ms. Dee?"

She nodded. "It's easier for the kids. Why don't we go to the office?"

Diedra turned to go inside when the two boys ran ahead of her and collided. They fell in a jumble of arms and legs and pained cries. Diedra helped them up and checked to make certain they were okay. "Stop chasing each other," she instructed firmly. She glanced at Eli and shook her head. "It must be a full moon or something. Today has been one of *those* days."

Eli pulled open the door and waited for her to enter. "I imagine all your days are action packed."

"Definitely," she agreed.

A huge contemporary desk and a credenza holding all sorts of computer equipment occupied one corner of the room. A cushy but worn navy leather couch sat against another wall, with a floor lamp next to it, and a small children's activity area filled the opposite corner. He sat in one of the two blue leather wingback chairs she indicated.

"Did Sarah give you an application?"

Eli reached for the clipboard that rested on the chair arm. "I think I answered everything. I got sidetracked when your staff member came in."

Diedra settled in her desk chair. "So why are you considering day care?"

Eli pulled a toy from his coat pocket and handed it to his daughter. "I've run the gamut from babysitters to housekeepers to a nanny. My nanny just quit without notice to get married. Guess she figured she wouldn't need a referral. I'm desperate."

"I see."

From her tone he knew she'd misunderstood him. "What I mean is that I need people I can depend on to be there on a daily basis. I wouldn't be here if I didn't think day care would work for my child."

She nodded, and the room grew quiet as she studied the pages. No doubt his atrocious handwriting caused her difficulty. Even he had trouble reading the bold black slashes at times.

"Gerilyn?" She glanced up for confirmation.

"Actually it's pronounced Gerry-Lynn. It's a combination of my parents' names," he explained.

"Father—Elijah," she read aloud. "Gerilyn's mother is. . . Oh, I'm sorry."

Her gaze focused on him once more. He'd dreaded this moment from the time he had written "deceased" in the space allotted to the mother's name.

Eli nodded at her sympathetic words. Even if questions filled her head, she didn't ask. He had to give her that. Diedra Pierce didn't allow curiosity to cross the boundary of professionalism.

"She's eight months old?"

Relieved she'd moved on, he nodded again.

"The problem is we don't have an opening for her age range," Diedra said.

"Surely you can make an exception. Janice raves about your center."

She shook her head. "I'm thankful our parents think highly of our day care, but state law prohibits overcrowded classrooms. We do maintain an application backlog. I'd be happy to put your daughter's name on the list."

Nothing seemed to be going right lately. "I suppose it's the only choice I have. What sort of time frame are we looking at?"

"We never know. Parents may withdraw their child today, or we might not have an opening for months. I can tell you we have one parent who is considering withdrawing her child. Gerilyn would be at the top of the list if that happened."

"I'd hoped to get this sorted out today."

"There are other centers," Diedra said.

"True, but yours comes with high recommendations."

"Recommendations are great, but we have to make sure Kids Unlimited is a good fit for your daughter."

He'd seen more love, warmth, and caring than he'd ever dreamed of finding for his child. "I already know your center will be a perfect fit. How many directors do you think would crawl into that tube to get to a child?"

Her cheeks colored.

"You did that because you cared about Davey," he continued. "You took care one extra step, and that's what I want. My daughter's happiness is my only goal."

"It's our goal, too."

Lynnie jumped in his lap, and Eli tightened his hold again and glanced down at her. Sometime in the past few minutes she'd managed to lose a shoe and sock. He straightened the tiny pink bow that circled a wisp of dark hair and smiled when she tried to stuff her toy into her mouth. He looked at Diedra. "Tell me about this backlog."

She leaned forward as she began to talk. "Basically I conduct an interview today. When a slot in her age group becomes available, I contact you. You get her physical form completed, and we enroll Gerilyn. Do you want to proceed?"

"Definitely."

Eli waited as she finished reading the application. The back of the chair cushioned his head, and he allowed his thoughts to drift to the work waiting for him. He'd spent a great portion of the past few days and nights sorting through designs for next year's furniture line. Those same hours included rescuing Lynnie from the things she'd managed to find during her crawling excursions.

Taking her to the office wasn't the solution. Now that she was more active, he couldn't keep up with her and work. He often placed her in the playpen and listened to her whine until she occupied herself with a toy or fell asleep. It made concentration nearly impossible.

Now she had her day and night hours confused and spent half the night wanting to play. Probably because he encouraged her to take longer naps during the day.

A nap didn't seem like such a bad idea right now. His eyelids were so heavy. He allowed them to close. Just for one second.

Chapter 2

The baby's cry caught Diedra's attention, and she glanced up to find Eli McKay asleep and his daughter reaching for the toy she'd dropped on the floor. Diedra hurried around the desk and retrieved the plastic ring. The baby flashed a grin before hiding her face against her dad's chest. Diedra found her shyness adorable.

Eli jumped with the baby's movement, his eyes opening. "What happened?"

"She dropped her toy."

He swiped a hand over his face. "Sorry. I dozed off."

"I noticed. You want to continue this later?"

"I'm tired, but I don't know when I'd find time to come back."

The baby dragged her father's tie toward her mouth. He quickly diverted her attention and tucked it back inside his coat. Diedra's gaze rested on the delicate baby girl. The "I Love My Daddy" on her ruffled pink stretch suit said it all. "She resembles you."

He grinned. "Poor baby. She'd have done better to take after her mother."

"Oh, but she's a beautiful child."

Heat crept over Diedra's face. She might as well have told the man he was handsome. She did find him attractive, but it wasn't something she needed to point out to him.

"Lynnie and I thank you," he said with a smile and a nod of his head. "Thanks for coming to her rescue."

"Let's finish this so you can catch a nap." Diedra sat on the edge of the desk and reached for the clipboard and pencil. "Primarily we need to know a little about Gerilyn. Let's see. No allergies. Unique behavior characteristics? Eating? Sleeping?"

Eli answered, and she jotted the information on the page. She covered the entire questionnaire, asking and receiving clear, concise responses. Several times Diedra found her attention drawn to the bass textures of his voice.

Diedra reached for a brochure and went over the information listed there before passing it to him along with a form for a doctor's physical. Lynnie grabbed at the colorful paper, but Eli quickly tucked it away in his coat pocket.

"We use age-appropriate activities to stimulate the child's development. Is she this active all the time?"

"Yes. She's smart, but then I'm her father. What else do you expect me to say?"

"Why don't you leave her with us for a couple of hours? Go home and get a nap," Diedra suggested when he yawned widely. "Think of this afternoon as an experiment. See how she adapts."

"I don't suppose you have an extra cot tucked away somewhere? I didn't realize how tired I was until I sat in this chair."

Concerned, she asked, "Should you be driving?"

A wry smile touched his face. "Probably not."

"Use the couch over there," Diedra offered. "I can vouch for its comfort, but I can't promise peace and quiet. Not with children on the premises. Expect some laughter, loud talking, a little screaming, crying maybe. Then again, after the day we've had. . ."

"I'll take my chances. Though I doubt anything will wake me once I close my eyes."

"I'll put Gerilyn in the nursery." Diedra held out her arms, and the baby moved willingly into her hold.

"Lynnie," he said. "I call her Lynnie."

She nodded and walked out into the hallway. "You're a pretty girl," Diedra cooed to the baby as they headed down the hall.

The nursery was quiet with most of the babies sleeping. "I have a visitor for you," she told Gina. "Her dad is dead on his feet."

"Not bad to look at either, from what I saw," Gina said, smiling.

Diedra knew the direction this conversation would take. All the women in the center wanted her to have someone special in her life. A few of them had tried to set her up with blind dates, but she had managed to resist their plans. "Don't even think about matchmaking." They smiled, and Diedra slipped into the hallway.

She returned to the office to find Eli McKay fast asleep, his tie loosened, shoes off, looking comfortable all stretched out. Diedra looked at him for a few seconds longer. Why had she offered her couch? Perhaps because of the dark circles under his eyes or her suspicions that fatherhood proved more difficult than he'd expected—and then again probably because she wanted to help him in some way. His obvious disappointment at hearing they didn't have a slot open for his daughter bothered Diedra.

She studied him for several moments. Good-looking in a rough sort of way, he wore his blond-streaked brown hair brushed straight back in a style that reminded Diedra of swashbucklers of old. His scraggly beard gave him the unkempt look an actor had made popular years before. He was long and lean, and the tailored suit fit him superbly, as did the white silk shirt.

Quit ogling him, she chastised herself, moving to her desk to focus on the food orders for the upcoming week. Diedra found herself struggling to justify the frequent glances in Eli's direction.

He slept restlessly, his frequent tossing and turning making the old couch creak and groan. Feeling the chill in the room, Diedra drew an afghan from the back of another chair and covered him. She fought the urge to sweep the hair from his eyes and decided it was time to find somewhere else to be.

"No!" His shout filled the room.

Diedra froze, her head telling her not to get involved, her heart saying it was too late. She knelt by the chair and found herself staring into his startling pale blue eyes.

"You didn't leave."

Confused by his statement, Diedra knew she should say something, but shock wedged the words in her throat. His eyes drifted closed, and she realized he'd been talking in his sleep.

Diedra studied his face. Warning flags shot up in her head. *Be sensible.* She couldn't be attracted to this man. She hurried from the room.

❧

The after-school children arrived, and Diedra busied herself with her tutoring duties. She fought the desire to check on Eli, to assure herself he rested comfortably. At the thought, apprehension gripped her. She returned to the task of explaining algebra to a young man.

At six o'clock Diedra said good night to the last of her staff. Gina hesitated at the front door, motioning toward Eli on the couch. "He's still asleep?"

Diedra nodded. "I should wake him."

"He must be exhausted. Want me to stick around for a while?"

Diedra considered Gina's offer. In all fairness she couldn't ask the woman to stay. "No. It's okay."

"Lynnie's in the baby swing. See you tomorrow."

"Thanks, Gina."

Diedra made her final daily walk-through of the ground floor rooms in the old two-story Victorian house. She'd had the entire area reworked into functional classrooms. The primary goal of every activity area was accessibility to the children. Crayon and finger-painted artwork, bearing the names of the creators, covered every available inch of bright, cheery walls.

As always, she thanked God for giving her this oasis of peace, for filling her life with so much love. Kids Unlimited was Diedra's commitment to the future. She and her staff were more than caretakers. They were more than teachers. They loved these children as if they were their own.

"Diedra? Are you there?"

At the sound of Janice Gore's voice, Diedra moved toward the side door. Surely it wasn't six thirty already. When Janice had mentioned her anniversary earlier in the week, Diedra had arranged for her to bring the children over for the night.

"Diedra?" Janice's voice grew louder.

She opened the French doors, and Davey shot past her, making car sounds as he sped his toy car through the air. Taking Janice's nine-month-old daughter, Kaylie, into her arms, Diedra kissed the baby's forehead and spoke to Janice. "I met your boss today. He rescued your son."

Janice groaned, looking around for Davey then finding him by the toy box. "Sarah told me when I picked them up earlier. Did Eli enroll Lynnie?"

"We discussed it. Nothing's been finalized."

"I was certain he'd enroll her. Eli's been frantic with trying to find a place for Lynnie and dealing with the business," Janice said. "He's been bringing her to work this week. From what he says, they're sitting up half the night. I hoped you'd be able to help."

"I'm sure we'll discuss it further. Once a slot becomes available."

Janice frowned. "I didn't think about that."

Lynnie's cries turned Diedra's gaze to the now idle swing. She walked across the room, with Janice behind her, and attempted to placate the baby with a pacifier.

"Why is Lynnie here?"

"Her dad's sleeping in my office."

Janice smiled. "So that's where Eli's been."

Davey raced by, shouting at the top of his lungs, and Diedra took advantage of the confusion to catch her breath. Janice's sigh made her laugh.

"Evidently he's over his earlier scare," his mother said. "I'm sorry that happened."

"Davey provides the excitement in my boring life," Diedra told her.

"Excitement?" Janice repeated. "Is that what you call it?"

Diedra grinned. "Well, some people might refer to Davey as a challenge."

"Definitely a challenge," Janice agreed. "I need to run. David's waiting in the car. He made reservations for eight o'clock. You have our cell number, just in case?"

Diedra nodded. Strong longing filled her as she listened to Janice's plans for the evening. If her life were normal, maybe she'd be planning a romantic evening with her husband. Instead she was babysitting another woman's children so her friend could have time alone with her husband.

Don't think about this now, she told herself as she waved good-bye to Janice. Not that she had time to think. Juggling two babies and an active four-year-old tonight would keep her on her toes. While Lynnie played in the swing, Diedra gave Kaylie a bottle. Suddenly the silence struck her.

"Davey?" she called. What was he up to now?

Eli staggered into the room, the toy car in one hand and Davey's hand in the other. "Do you have any glue?"

"Davey, you shouldn't have awakened Mr. McKay. I'll take care of that," she said, reaching for the car.

"No. I want him." Davey hugged Eli's legs.

Eli smiled. "I can't resist four-year-olds who ask me to fix their broken cars."

Diedra went to the storage cabinets and located the glue.

Eli knelt in front of the swing then glanced at Diedra. "How's my girl doing?"

"She did fine. Slept on and off all afternoon then enjoyed being the center of attention."

"All afternoon?" He looked at his watch, his eyes widening. "Why didn't you wake me?"

"I figured you needed the rest."

"I guess I did," he agreed, running his hands over his bristly cheeks. "I'm starving."

"I need to fix something for Davey and me. Would you like to join us?"

"Thank you, but no," he said quickly. "I've taken advantage of your kindness too much already today."

"Leftover spaghetti and cheese bread," she said with a shrug. "Nothing fancy."

"No, really. I couldn't."

"One more won't make a difference," she said, overriding his protests.

"You make it difficult to refuse," Eli said. "What can I do to help?"

"Watch Davey and the girls."

He grinned. "Hmm. Maybe I should run out for burgers."

Diedra laughed. "I'll have supper ready by the time you glue that wheel back on."

Minutes later she had the meal on the table. She put a booster seat in one chair for Davey and pushed two high chairs to the table for the girls.

She walked into the nursery to call them to the table and paused to study the group on the play mats. Eli seemed right at home with the kids. Davey hung on to Eli's arm, and the two babies lay on the floor, kicking their legs in response to Davey's giggles.

"Dinner's ready."

Diedra picked up Kaylie, and Eli lifted Lynnie. Davey followed.

They settled around the table, Lynnie at her father's elbow, Kaylie at Diedra's, and Davey in the middle.

Eli kissed his daughter's forehead, and Diedra's heart skipped at the obvious show of love between father and child. She wished more kids had fathers like him.

Here's the well-rested Eli, Diedra thought as he settled into his chair. From what Janice had said, Eli had his hands full with both the business and Lynnie. With rest he had become charming and eager to please.

"Davey, would you like to say grace?" she asked.

"Mr. McKay can."

Eli asked a blessing on the food and started twirling spaghetti around his fork. Diedra almost laughed when Davey tried to mimic Eli's action.

They talked and laughed, and when Diedra led the conversation into casual topics, Eli responded. Davey quickly tired of the adult conversation, demanding their attention with his restlessness. Eli pulled him onto his lap and rubbed his whiskers against the boy's face.

Davey giggled. "You tickle."

Eli rubbed his hand over his face. "Guess I could use a shave. I thought a beard might be less trouble, but I'm not going to survive the growing-out period."

Diedra's attention veered to Davey, who was moving toward Kaylie's chair. "Don't you dare!" she said sharply.

Eli started. "What?"

"Not you." She glanced at Eli then jumped up to intercept the little boy. "Kaylie can't eat toast."

"But she's hungry. See—she wants it," Davey said, dangling the crust in his baby sister's face.

"Kaylie has to eat special food," Diedra explained, guiding Davey back to his seat. "I'll take care of her. Eat your spaghetti."

Diedra settled into her seat again and tried not to stare at Eli as he watched Davey. She enjoyed Eli's infectious laughter when the boy sucked down a strand of spaghetti and managed to get more sauce on his face than in his mouth.

"I never thought I'd enjoy kids so much," Eli told her. "Seeing Lynnie change on an almost-daily basis has been wonderful."

"It's exciting," Diedra agreed. "It won't be long before she's walking and getting into everything."

"She's already getting into everything."

Kaylie's loud cry brought Diedra's attention back to her. She concentrated on soothing Kaylie, afraid the baby's agitation would set off a similar reaction in Lynnie.

"Janice told me Kaylie fights sleep," Eli said.

"She doesn't want to miss anything." Diedra rocked the baby in her arms.

"That must be Lynnie's problem, too."

They glanced over to where Davey played peekaboo with Lynnie. She hung over the side of the chair to look for him when he darted away, all smiles when he popped back up.

Eli stacked the dishes and carried them over to the sink.

"I'll take care of those," Diedra said.

"You cooked. I'll clean."

By the time he had finished, Kaylie had fallen asleep. "Looks as if she's down for the night," he said softly. He nodded toward Davey. "What time does he go to bed?"

"Eight thirty. After I put her down, I'll put him in the bathtub to wash off the spaghetti and read him a story before he goes to sleep."

"Come on, baby girl," he said, scooping up Lynnie from the high chair. "That's our cue to hit the road."

"I'm sorry I couldn't help you today. I'll call as soon as I know something for sure." She stood and followed him to the kitchen door.

"You helped more than you realize," Eli said. "I'll look forward to hearing from you."

She accepted his outstretched hand. "You're welcome to my couch anytime."

Eli squeezed her hand. "It was more than that," he said. Then he was gone.

⁂

After putting the children to bed, Diedra curled up on the sofa. The television kept her company as she updated her financial records. She would never become a millionaire, but she had decided her well-being was more important. She'd dedicated her career to the children in her day care center. Besides her time with God, her time with them seemed to be the only right thing in her cockeyed world.

She shut off the laptop when the vision of Eli McKay appeared in her head. *Why does he intrigue me so?* Diedra wondered, frowning when the answer refused to present itself.

Suddenly the loneliness seemed overwhelming. Diedra reached for the phone but realized it was too late to call her friend Granny Marie. The older woman had probably turned in for the night around the same time as Davey.

She'd met Marie Wright the first Christmas after her grandparents died. Diedra carried on their tradition of visiting the nursing homes, and Marie had been more than happy to have a visitor.

They had grown close, and she had asked Diedra to call her Granny Marie as her grandchildren did. Granny Marie's unhappiness at losing her independence in the nursing home led Diedra to help. Now she came to the day care center during the day and went home to her son's at night.

Recently Granny had admitted feeling she was intruding on her son and his family. Diedra had given the matter a great deal of thought and prayer before inviting her to share the upstairs apartment. She knew the offer tempted her, but Granny feared she would hurt her son's feelings.

Diedra reached for the Bible on the end table and opened it to one of her favorite verses, John 14:27. " 'Peace I leave with you; my peace I give you. I do not give to you as the world gives. Do not let your hearts be troubled and do not be afraid,' " she read aloud, feeling grateful that her Comforter was always near.

"Lord," she whispered, "I come to You, seeking Your guidance in my walk with You. At times I feel like a newborn, uncertain how to proceed with the tasks You've set before me. I want to be the Christian You would have me be. I pray for strength to show love to those with whom You would have me share Your message.

"Support me in this task I've dedicated myself to. You know my weaknesses, and

I pray You give me peace and understanding in the way You would have me go."

She whispered, "Amen," as Kaylie's cries began. She rocked the baby and wondered if Eli had gotten his daughter to sleep. She hoped so.

Eli tried to move, fighting his way out of the darkness.

He opened his eyes to find the hour predawn, his stiffness the result of yet another night in his recliner. *The dream,* he thought.

Eli missed his wife. He remembered their last morning together as if it were yesterday, rather than nearly ten months before. Kelly was excited about traveling to Ohio to visit the young woman who had become an integral part of their lives. He'd kissed his wife good-bye and talked to her a couple of hours later when she called to tell him she'd arrived safely.

Sometime later he'd been doing his practice laps at the racetrack when they waved his car in. Kelly was dead. Another car had run a red light and struck her in the intersection. The police said she didn't see it coming. No doubt she was still excited. If only he'd been there with her. Perhaps she would have lived to see her dream fulfilled.

His gaze focused on the child sleeping peacefully in his arms. Kelly would have loved their baby girl. One thing was for certain: Finding someone to care for her would not have been an issue if she were alive. His wife had wanted nothing more than to mother their child.

Eli glanced at the clock on the table. The brightly colored Kids Unlimited pamphlet caught his eye. Janice praised the center, raved, in fact, assuring him he'd find no better in the city.

And with a child like Davey, Janice would know. Why ever would he want Lynnie enrolled at the same center as Hurricane Davey? He did, though—ever since he'd heard Diedra Pierce inside that tunnel.

Eli sighed. Why did things have to be this way? He prayed she would find a spot for Lynnie. She struck him as a loving woman. Efficient, attractive—someone he could like if he gave himself the opportunity.

But no matter how fascinating he found her, Eli knew he had a lot of healing to do before he could consider a relationship with any woman. Of course, that didn't preclude friendship.

"No one ever told us this was going to be easy, did they?" he whispered against his daughter's curls.

And if he were truthful, Eli would admit he didn't mind Diedra's attention. It seemed like a lifetime since he'd had a woman's interest, particularly one as loving and caring as Diedra Pierce appeared to be.

Chapter 3

The feeling that she'd let Eli McKay down in his time of need weighed heavily on Diedra's mind. She tried to think of some way to assist him with child care, but beyond giving a few hours now and then, no solution seemed to work. Eli and Lynnie crept onto her prayer list, and she asked that God's will would be done in the situation.

And on Friday morning she received an answer to her prayers. One of the mothers decided to care for her six-month-old son at home. Diedra pulled the McKay application from the file and dialed his home number. "This is Diedra Pierce from Kids Unlimited."

She explained her reason for calling. "I wanted to let you know there's an opening. We can take Lynnie as soon as you get the form for her physical completed. I can give you a couple of days to make your decision."

"You have it now," Eli said without hesitation. "We'll see you on Monday at eight."

Diedra noted satisfaction in his tone. "I'll look forward to seeing you both."

The day passed quickly, and that night Diedra prepared dinner for Granny. She stirred a bubbling pot of green beans and prepared a tossed salad before checking the roast in the oven. "The nursery slot's filled. An eight-month-old girl named Gerilyn. She's so sweet. Absolutely beautiful."

"That didn't take long," Granny said, not missing a stitch as she rocked and knitted at the same time.

"It's just her and her dad. They came in the other day." Diedra placed the salad bowl on the table before taking plates from the cabinet and rummaging in the silverware drawer. "Knowing Lynnie doesn't have a mom breaks my heart."

"You can't take all the children's losses to heart, Dee."

"I know what it's like not to have someone when you need them," she said, a faraway look glazing her eyes. The nightmare she'd lived with her husband before he died and her parents' failure to help haunted Diedra.

"Despite how you feel about them, you have a family, Diedra."

"They believed Benjamin's lies. They cared more about their precious name than they cared about me. I can't forgive them for that."

"They're only human."

Hearing Granny defend her parents hurt; Diedra was overwhelmed by the pain. Realizing Granny didn't know what had happened, she turned to her friend.

147

"Benjamin killed my child and nearly killed me. They wanted me to drop the charges."

"Oh, honey, I'm so sorry," Granny said, dropping her knitting onto the seat and gathering Diedra in her arms. "Life dealt you a hard blow, but you know you'll have to forgive your parents—and Benjamin."

Diedra wiped her hand across her face. As always, the memories brought a flood of tears. Would she ever stop hurting? "How, Granny? How can I trust someone else when I can't trust myself?"

"You can trust God," Granny said. "You accepted Jesus Christ as your Savior and Lord, and that means you have faith that He will love and care for you. Faith equals trust. What if He sends the right man your way, and you shut him out because you don't believe He'll take care of your needs?"

"You can't understand what it was like for me," Diedra whispered.

Granny leaned back and looked at her. "No, I can't. For all of my seventy-seven years, I lived a sheltered life. I went from the home of loving parents to a man who treasured me, and now my son is dedicated to doing the same. I'm abundantly blessed.

"I'll never understand why your husband hurt you." Granny handed Diedra a tissue. "It's not your fault. To believe anything less is to give another undeserved victory to the same evil that allowed Benjamin to harm you. Why not give your fears to God?"

Diedra wiped her eyes. "I'm trying, Granny. God must be so disappointed in me."

"He isn't disappointed in you, dear. God loves and accepts you just the way you are. Don't forget that becoming a Christian is a growth process. We don't change overnight. It will get better."

Granny sat back in the rocker. Diedra washed her hands and returned to setting the table.

"What's Gerilyn's father like?"

She focused on telling Granny about the McKays rather than dealing with her own problems. "You should see him with his daughter," Diedra said, smiling. "He obviously loves her a great deal."

"So you like him?"

Everyone she knew seemed determined to see Diedra in a happy relationship. Even Granny looked at every man as marriage material. She wouldn't hesitate to play matchmaker if she thought she'd found the right man for Diedra.

"Not like that."

"Gina told me how handsome he is."

"I did my good deed for the day by letting him nap on my couch. And I'm committed to doing what I can to help them both," Diedra said, watching Granny's expression as she added, "the same commitment I give to all my parents."

Granny had told her more than once that she should stop giving so much of herself, but Diedra couldn't. Helping others made her feel her chosen path was worthwhile.

"Let's eat."

"I imagine Mr. McKay will be most appreciative of your help," Granny said as she took a seat at the table.

On Monday morning Eli stood in the doorway of her office, watching Diedra straighten the children's area. When he'd received her call, he'd been relieved to know Lynnie would be with people who cared. One person in particular—Diedra Pierce—stood out in his mind. He knew she would take good care of his daughter. And the idea didn't bother him at all.

But he feared his own fascination with Diedra. A fascination he couldn't afford. So many times since he and Kelly had decided to bring their child into the world, he'd questioned whether they'd done the right thing. But the moment he'd laid eyes on Lynnie, his daughter had grasped his heart in her tiny hand. He would do anything to protect her from harm.

Diedra tucked the stuffed animal in the basket and turned around. "Eli, come in." He held Lynnie in one arm and carried a huge bag stuffed with items in the other. Diedra doubted she'd ever seen one that large, even with the most protective of mothers. "Let me show you where she'll be."

Gina met them at the door. She greeted Lynnie and gave her time to warm up to her before taking her from her father's arms.

"I brought her favorite toys," Eli said. "Several bottles of formula, diapers, wipes—everything on the list you gave me. If she needs anything, call me."

Eli continued to talk, almost rambling, about the baby. Diedra understood his separation anxiety. It would take a few days for both Eli and Lynnie to settle into the new routine. She touched his arm, and he paused.

"Feel free to check in often," Diedra said. "I doubt you'll find Kids Unlimited lacking. Did I tell you about our video monitoring?" He nodded. "Come into my office, and I'll give you instructions on how to check on Lynnie from your computer."

Eli kissed his daughter good-bye and walked to the door. He glanced back once more before following Diedra into the hallway. "You operate quite a business."

"I consider it more of a life mission. These children are important to us. They're our future, and we owe them a good start."

"Do you have a life outside this place?"

The personal question surprised her. "Not much of one," Diedra answered truthfully.

Silence engulfed them as they continued walking. A door opened, and an aide led a child out of a classroom and down the hall.

"I'd better get that information about the monitoring and head for my office," Eli said abruptly. "It'll be time to pick her up before I know it."

After he left, Diedra settled in her office and managed to get Eli off her mind long enough to focus on the lesson plans for the coming week.

❧

"Thanks, Diedra. I'll see you at eight thirty." He hung up the phone as Janice entered the office with two cups of coffee.

"Did you make your arrangements?" she asked. "David could have picked up Lynnie."

"He already has his hands full," Eli pointed out. "Diedra's keeping Lynnie until eight thirty."

Strange how contented he'd become in only one week. At first he couldn't go through a day without checking on Lynnie. It hadn't taken long to realize how much the staff loved her. The staff and Diedra Pierce.

Diedra. Lately he'd taken to spending a few minutes in her office before collecting the baby. He loved hearing in her soft-spoken way how Lynnie had done that day. When she shared tidbits about her workday, he often did the same.

He smiled at Janice. "I've been meaning to thank you for referring me to the center."

"You'd better thank the Lord. She's the answer to my prayers, too."

"I have. Lynnie and I are particularly thankful."

"Diedra's a great person."

He picked up his cup and tilted back in his chair. "I didn't mean for her to take care of Lynnie tonight. I just asked her for a babysitter recommendation."

Janice sorted through the ring of fabric samples. "I think Diedra's a workaholic."

"She doesn't date?"

Janice shrugged. "It's a shame if she doesn't have someone in her life. Diedra suggested the kids stay overnight with her on our anniversary. She said we deserved adult time."

Workaholic. Eli understood that. McKay Design and Showrooms had become his life after Kelly's death. He'd surrounded himself with the business, embracing the tasks with open arms, hoping to keep his mind occupied until he could fall into bed each night so exhausted he couldn't think.

"We'd better get through these, Eli," Janice said, pushing the fabric bundle at him. "Are you still thinking this shade of blue for the McNeils?"

❧

Where has the time gone? Diedra wondered when the doorbell chimed. There never seemed to be enough for all the things she wanted to do. Grabbing a towel, she wiped her hands and hurried down the hallway. She could see Eli's image through the leaded glass panels of the front door, their beveled edges clouding his strong masculine profile. Maybe she should abandon her plan to invite him to dinner.

Diedra pulled the door open. "Hi. Come on in."

Eli stepped inside. "I'm sure you're busy. I'll just get Lynnie and go."

"Not really." She drew in a breath. "Have you eaten?"

He paused, his steady gaze boring into her. "I'll scramble some eggs later."

"Stay and have some chicken l'orange. I found the recipe in a magazine—main dishes in twenty minutes or less."

"No, really, I couldn't."

"You have to eat," Diedra reasoned. "There's plenty of food. I'm a fairly good cook. So if you don't stay, I'll think it's the company."

"Can't have you thinking that." Eli smiled. "Should I check on Lynnie?"

"If you want. She's asleep in the nursery. I have a monitor in the kitchen."

"It won't last. By midnight she'll be ready to rock the night out." Eli grimaced. "I can remember when rock had a completely different connotation. I'm praying these late-night play sessions end soon."

"Everything will be fine once she gets on a regular schedule," Diedra assured him, closing the front door.

Diedra could hardly believe she'd invited Eli to dinner. It hadn't been as difficult as she'd feared. For the first time in five years, she'd taken a step forward.

She enjoyed talking with Eli in the afternoons. A time or two she'd caught herself watching the clock, anticipating his arrival.

"You can wash up in the half bath under the stairs," she told Eli before he went to check on Lynnie.

"Anything I can do to help?" Eli asked when he came into the kitchen a few minutes later.

He'd removed his coat and tie and rolled up the sleeves of his pristine white shirt. Eli definitely rated a second look. And a third, Diedra allowed. "Everything's ready. How do you like your broccoli?"

"In the grocery store vegetable bin." He grinned.

"Now, Eli, we need our veggies," Diedra teased, stirring the cheese sauce before grabbing a pair of oven mitts. The silence caught her attention, and she turned toward him. Slight creases had formed in his cheeks, giving him a foreboding look. "Something wrong?"

He indicated the two plates and two glasses on the counter. "Did you plan this, Diedra?"

She couldn't deny she'd thought of him when she planned her evening meal. She disliked eating alone. Still, she hated feeling like a woman out to capture a man with her cooking. "If I say yes, will you accept it in the spirit intended?"

"Which is?"

Diedra opened the oven and lifted out the casserole dish. She placed it on a trivet and pulled off the oven mitts. "I admit to some selfish intent but with good motive. I wanted to cook. I knew you were coming and figured two friends could share a meal. Go ahead and sit down. I'll dish up the food."

"My social graces are obviously rusty," Eli muttered. The chair scraped across the wood floor as he pulled it away from the table.

Diedra filled two plates and placed one in front of him then sat down. "Nothing's wrong with your manners. Would you say grace?"

He bowed his head. "Heavenly Father, we thank You for the food You've provided for us and ask that You use it for the nourishment of our bodies. Thank You for the loving care You provide us each and every day. In Jesus' name we pray. Amen."

"Amen," Diedra repeated.

He forked a portion of the mixture into his mouth and nodded approval. "Good."

"Thank you," Diedra said, offering him a napkin. "Hope you don't mind eating out of pots."

"Is there another way?"

She laughed. "Well, I have been known to allow my guests to serve themselves on occasion. Of course, this way is easier with the kids."

"You sound like Kelly. Kids were important to her, too."

"Kelly was your wife?"

Eli nodded.

"She must have been special."

Eli smiled. "The first thing she asked when I proposed was if we could have a dozen kids."

"And did you agree?"

"I suggested we have half that many. I had no idea then that children could be so rewarding."

He had touched on her favorite subject. "Yes, they are, and they're so challenging and full of love and inspire the strongest emotions. And they respect you when they know who's in charge."

"And here they know." Eli smiled again. "Your day care seems to be one of the most innovative around. How did you come up with the programs?"

Diedra took a sip of tea from her glass. "They revolve around two groups of people with pretty basic needs. We can fill their stomachs and keep them comfortable, but everyone needs someone who cares. Kids Unlimited cares."

"And Diedra Pierce. Why do you care so much?"

"For me, Mark 9:37 says it perfectly: 'Whoever welcomes one of these little children in my name welcomes me; and whoever welcomes me does not welcome me but the one who sent me.' I want people around me who care. There are never enough."

"That is certainly true," Eli agreed, a smile spreading across his face.

The way he looked at her made Diedra pretend renewed interest in the food on her plate. "Tell me about your work."

"What's to say about furniture design and sales?"

"You have to be kidding. It's one of the hottest things going in High Point," Diedra said. "I've read about the Southern Furniture Market. I'd love to go, but I know it's open only to members of the trade. I read that buyers come from every state and several foreign nations."

"We have another market coming up soon, but I'm not ready for it yet. In fact, I'm not sure I'll ever catch up on my work."

"I never seem to either," Diedra said. "But then if I did, I suppose I wouldn't have a job. Would you like seconds?"

"No, thanks. You're a good cook, though."

Diedra thanked him. "I have some great cookies if you'd care for dessert." She stepped over to the counter then returned with a half-dozen white chocolate macadamia cookies on a plate.

Eli sampled one. "Hmm. My favorite. Did you make them?"

"Granny Marie is my cookie baker. I'm sure you've met her. She helps out in the nursery."

Eli nodded. "So the kids get homemade cookies all the time?"

"Not always. We serve healthy snacks, too."

Eli ate the remainder of the cookie. "So tell me more about Diedra Pierce."

"I like helping others."

She thought back to the time five years earlier when she had shown up on her grandparents' doorstep in North Carolina. They shared their faith in God with her and did everything in their power to help Diedra realize her own self-worth.

She knew she had to put the past behind her, but it took time for a heart to heal. Hers still had a few rough edges. Forgiving and forgetting took time. Pain had a way of renewing itself when she thought of the past and all she'd lost.

Eli leaned back in the chair. "What else?"

"There's not much to tell. I have a master's degree in early childhood education. I'm a widow," she added, barely managing to get the words past the lump in her throat.

"I'm sorry. Recent?"

She shook her head. "A couple of years."

"What about other family? Parents? Siblings?"

"Only child. My parents live in California. Your turn."

Eli sipped his tea and returned the glass to the table. "You know I'm a widower. My parents died when I was twenty. My mom had cancer, and I suspect my dad died of a broken heart. I was an only child, too. They were older when I was born. I wish they'd had a chance to know their granddaughter."

"Perhaps they're smiling down on her from heaven."

"Are you a believer?"

She nodded.

"I came to know the Lord just a few months ago."

"Where do you attend church?" Diedra asked.

"Cornerstone. My parents went there. I attended as a child, but other pursuits became more important than serving the Lord."

"That's a huge church. I attend First Church. It was my grandparents' church."

"It's good having a church home."

"And a church family," Diedra added.

"I've met lots of good people in the last few months. Including those here at the center. I've been meaning to tell you I like the center's name."

"My grandmother suggested it," Diedra said, reaching for his plate. Eli moved to help, and she pulled back when their hands touched.

Diedra noted the way Eli hesitated, his speculative look, and found it impossible not to return his disarming smile. "My granny said she hoped I'd have so many kids these old walls would groan with the pleasure of their presence." Diedra paused. "Would you like coffee?"

Eli reached for the bread basket. "I'll help with these and then clear out so you can have a few minutes to yourself."

"I have a lot of those, Eli. This place is like a tomb when everyone leaves."

She reached for the coffee can on the top shelf. Too late, Diedra felt her sleeve rise just enough for the ugly scar to show itself.

She glanced sideways and saw Eli staring at her arm.

"That must have been painful," he said.

She couldn't hide the scars forever, at least not that one.

Diedra jumped, and the coffee can slipped from her fingers, coming to rest on the edge of the countertop. Grounds flowed to the floor in a steady stream.

Eli reached past her to set the can upright.

She jerked her sleeve down. "It's nothing." Diedra refused to look at him. "I'll get the broom."

"Let me," he insisted.

The only sounds in the kitchen were those of dishes being washed, the swish of the broom, and, after Diedra summoned the energy to make coffee, the dripping of water into the pot.

Why hadn't she told him the truth about the scars? *Because you can't,* a little voice cautioned. *He'll lose respect for you.* Oh, why had she invited him to dinner in the first place?

Eli emptied the dustpan into the trash and replaced the items in the broom closet. "What's wrong, Diedra?"

"Nothing."

"I don't believe that, Diedra. You were fine until"—Eli broke off, resting his hand lightly on her arm when she tried to walk away—"I mentioned the scar."

Warning lights flashed in her head as Diedra stared down at his fingers. They seemed to tighten around her arm, and she became frantic, her skin paling and her breath coming in short gasps.

"Let go!" she demanded, jerking her arm away. "Take your hand off me. You have no right."

Eli dropped his hand at the terse request. As if on cue, Lynnie began to cry. Diedra could see him warring between his child's needs and wanting to understand what had just happened.

Tears squeezed from the corners of her eyes as she turned away from him. "You should take her home. It's past her bedtime."

"Diedra?"

"Just go, Eli. Please."

"Okay. We'll go. I'm sorry."

Chapter 4

Diedra glanced at the clock for the tenth time in a minute. Her stomach churned with apprehension. They were late. He wasn't bringing Lynnie back.

Why should he? Diedra knew she'd frightened him with her behavior. She'd frightened herself as well. She could only attribute her reaction to fear. Fear she'd be hurt again. Fear someone else would let her down.

But that naive young woman her husband had tried to destroy no longer existed. And given a few years in this environment in which God had placed her, surrounded by children and good friends, she would get past the nightmare that had been her life.

Maybe it would be better if Eli didn't come back. If she didn't see him, didn't experience the pull of his charm every time they were together, perhaps she could avoid letting him overwhelm her life.

The front door opened. Eli stuck his head in the office, and Diedra's breath whooshed out.

"We overslept."

She moved to take Lynnie from him. Gently pulling the pink knit hat off her head, Diedra smoothed the fine hair back in place. "Another bad night?"

Eli frowned. "I couldn't sleep. I kept thinking about last night. What happened?"

Diedra looked at him. "It's not you. Maybe one day I'll be able to explain what happened. Right now I'm not sure myself."

"Enough said."

He smiled, and Diedra's smile blossomed from within. "I'll take her to the nursery if you're in a hurry."

"That would help tremendously. Bye, baby girl," he said, touching Lynnie's cheek with his finger. "See you both later," he added.

❧

Eli waited for the light to change then pulled into the line of traffic. Things had gone better than he hoped. In the early hours of the morning, he'd worried that he'd done irreparable harm to their strange friendship–working relationship. He'd startled Diedra by touching her arm like that. And by being nosy. He had no business interfering in her life. When it came to emotional baggage, he had a full freight car of his own.

As for pursuing a relationship with Diedra, it was too soon. Kelly hadn't been dead a year. He had to deal with his grief before getting involved with anyone. For now, his priorities were God, Lynnie, and the business.

Diedra's role as child care provider to his daughter had to be of prime importance. Of course, that didn't mean they couldn't be friends. Eli believed the more he learned about the woman influencing his daughter's life, the more comfortable he would feel. Whatever the case, there could be no repeats of last night. The warm, almost datelike atmosphere of the evening had made thinking about the future seem almost too easy.

Diedra ran into Granny Marie coming out of the nursery on Friday morning. "Well, hello, stranger."

"I could say the same."

"Come and visit me in the office when you get a chance," Diedra suggested.

A couple of hours later she sat in a chair next to the older woman. "So how are things with your family?" Diedra asked. "Any better?"

"Everything's rolling along just as Jimmy wants it."

Diedra noted Granny's irritation. She understood the woman's frustrations about growing old. Granny spoke freely of the curses, fragile bones, and declining health while her mental capacity remained undiminished.

Things had changed dramatically for Granny since her accident. She'd moved in with her son and his family and tolerated living in another woman's home—a difficult task for a woman who had run her own home for so many years.

"They're trying to make an invalid of me," Granny complained. "Jimmy hovers over me as if he's afraid I'll shatter. I'm surprised he hasn't wrapped me in cotton batting."

"He loves you."

Granny dropped her hands into her lap. "I know he does, but he's talking about selling my house and moving me in with him permanently. What kind of life is that? Francie and I are already driving each other crazy. Jimmy's focused on me like a germ under a microscope." Granny frowned. "He'd stay by my side day and night if I'd let him."

"He'll settle down eventually," Diedra said.

"Let's hope so. I can't stand much more of this. I wanted to bake a cake for Sunday dinner, and Francie started talking about how we didn't need the extra fat and calories. You'd think one little slice would kill her."

"She seems conscientious about her diet."

"Too much so. Jimmy and the kids shouldn't suffer because she gains weight by just looking at food. I miss my kitchen." Granny sighed.

"Feel free to use mine anytime," Diedra offered. "Go on a baking frenzy. These kids go through a lot of cookies."

"Not only the kids," Granny teased.

Diedra smiled. "Okay, so I can be bought with a handful of your double chocolate delights."

The older woman laughed. "I'll remember that. I miss having people enjoy my cooking. Francie assesses every dish I prepare as if she can feel the fat corroding her arteries."

"Now, Granny, eating healthy isn't a bad thing."

"I don't want to interfere with her home, but I refuse to be treated like a child."

"You're always welcome here."

Regret filled her friend's expression. "I know. I just wish I could convince Jimmy to let go."

Diedra laid a hand on Granny's shoulder. "He will. Just give him time to get comfortable."

"Jimmy's just like his dad. He thinks everything is fine and dandy as long as the peace is maintained."

"Well, you know how to regain control of your life."

"Blessed is the peacemaker," Granny said.

Diedra shrugged. "It's a two-way street. Sometimes you have to fight for your own peace of mind."

"Honey, I have to remind myself it's in God's hands. He'll show me the way to go."

❧

"You're lost in thought," Janice told Eli that afternoon when she stepped into his office.

"It's been a busy week."

"That it has. Any plans for the weekend?"

"Not really."

"Too bad. I imagine Diedra doesn't have any plans either."

He ignored her obvious hint. "I wouldn't know."

"But you could find out easily enough," Janice prompted.

"Why are you interested in my plans or hers?" he asked curiously.

"I think you two would make a nice couple."

Eli shook his head. "I'm not ready to be part of a couple. It's too soon."

Janice settled in his visitor chair. "But you like her, don't you?"

"It's too soon."

"Kelly wouldn't want you to grieve your life away. Not when you have a chance at happiness."

"You didn't even know Kelly," he countered, saddened by the fact that so many of his new friends never knew what a wonderful, supportive woman his wife had been. In fact, he'd noticed Diedra shared some of her traits. Kelly would appreciate the fact that Diedra was taking such wonderful care of Lynnie.

"I know Kelly loved you, and you loved her," Janice said. "I know that when a woman loves a man, she wants him to be happy. You were blessed with a good wife."

"I was. And God took her away when Lynnie and I needed her the most."

"God works in mysterious ways, Eli. Don't close your mind if He sends someone to replace her. Grieve for her and move on. You deserve to find love again."

"I don't have time to invest in developing a new relationship."

Janice laughed. "Falling in love isn't something you schedule on your calendar. Once that feeling comes into your heart, nothing else seems as important. You find ways to be together even when you both have too much to do. You make time for everything else, don't you?"

"We'll see," Eli said brusquely, hoping to put an end to the conversation.

"Yes, we will," Janice said. "Just remember your heart has a mind of its own."

Janice's words confirmed the thoughts that had seemed to consume him. He missed Kelly. He missed being half of a couple. Kelly had been his sounding board and his confidant.

"Go home to David. I get the message."

"Sounds like a plan to me."

She started for the door, humming something that sounded like "Love Is in the Air."

"Very funny," he called to her.

If only falling in love this time could be as easy as the first. He'd felt this drawn to only one other woman. He'd found Kelly irresistible from the moment they met as seniors in high school. She listened to him dream about one day racing formula cars, and it became her dream, too.

They'd just celebrated their tenth anniversary the year she died. They'd been there for each other when their respective parents died and during the loss of their babies. They'd even come to know the Lord together. But they'd never had time to settle into a home life. And Kelly hadn't lived to mother the child she wanted so badly. How could he expect any woman to understand the decision he and Kelly had made?

Eli sighed. He didn't have time for this now. Besides, he didn't have a clue if Diedra felt the same. As always when his mind was troubled, Eli bowed his head and sought God's help in prayer.

⌘

That afternoon Diedra worked in the kitchen, preparing for the fall festival at church later in the evening. She had signed up to bring candied and caramel apples. She stirred the caramel and reached for one of the apples.

Diedra could hardly believe October was nearly gone. The year had rushed by with alarming speed. Before she knew it, Thanksgiving and Christmas would arrive. She wouldn't think of that now. She had a lot to finish before she left for church.

~∞~

Pushing the kitchen door open, Eli watched Diedra pursue her task with the single-mindedness he'd come to expect. "Hello, Dee."

A soft scream accompanied her jump of surprise. She grabbed the apple out of the caramel coating. "Eli? What time is it?"

"A little after four."

"You're early."

He walked across the kitchen and settled on a stool. "I gave myself an early day. I was thinking I owe you a meal. Want to join Lynnie and me for dinner?"

"I can't." She gave the apple one last twirl and set it on the waxed paper. "We have our fall festival at church tonight. Didn't you get a flyer?"

"I didn't read it."

"Several parents have said they'll bring their kids. I'm working at one of the games. Why don't you come, Eli? It'll be fun."

Granny pushed open the swinging door. "Eli, when did you get here?"

"A few minutes ago. Dee just invited me to the fall festival at her church."

"You're coming, I hope."

"I think we will."

"Good," Granny said, smiling broadly. "I'm heading for home. I need to pick up the cookies. See you later, Eli."

"Nice woman," Eli commented when Granny disappeared as quickly as she'd come. "Does she attend your church?"

"Sometimes." Diedra wrapped the candied apples in some cellophane.

"Want to ride with me and Lynnie tonight?"

"If you think there's room for everything I have to take."

"We'll manage," he said with a wink. "Need some help with those?"

"Two pairs of hands always get the job done faster."

Chapter 5

L ooks like a good turnout," Eli said as he drove through the crowded lot a second time, hunting for a parking space.

When she was appointed coordinator, Diedra and her committee had planned for the fall festival to be part of the church's homecoming celebration. They made a long list of activities that included games, prizes, food, a cakewalk, clowns, bobbing for apples, and a hayride in a horse-drawn wagon.

The committee posted notices around the city. Diedra sent public service announcements to the radio and television stations, and she'd seen to it that every Kids Unlimited parent received a flyer. A number had said they would see her at the church, but she knew to expect only a few.

Inside they'd decorated the large fellowship hall with the bounty of fall—pumpkins, bales of hay, colorful fall leaves, and scarecrows.

Eli looked around and nodded. "It looks good."

"Everyone pitched in to help," Diedra said. "I need to bring in the apples and drop off these prizes. I have the balloon board tonight. I can watch Lynnie if you'd like to explore."

"What's a balloon board?"

"The players attempt to burst balloons with darts as the board spins. They get tickets they can trade in on prizes at the end of the night."

"Sounds like fun. You're sure watching Lynnie will be no problem?"

She sat down on a nearby bale of hay and removed Lynnie's jacket. "Go have some of that fun I promised. We'll catch up with you later."

"I'll bring the apples in. Where should I put them?"

Diedra pointed to the table then took Lynnie with her to the area where they had set up her game. Occasionally Diedra caught glimpses of Eli in the crowd, talking with people or playing games. She propped Lynnie on her hip, and together they spun the wheel, staying well out of range of the flying darts. When someone made a hit, Diedra gave tickets to the winner then replaced the balloons.

"You should have a few of those," a fellow church member commented when Diedra tickled Lynnie and made her laugh out loud. "You're a natural."

Diedra thanked her, choking back the fiery pain that welled in her throat. Had it been only five years ago the doctor told her she could never have children? The memory of it hurt as much now as his words did then.

When they were dating, Diedra never would have believed Benjamin capable of hurting her. In the end he'd deprived her not only of love but also of her dream of children. The old familiar lump closed her throat, and tears stung her eyes. Would the time ever come when she wouldn't hurt? When she wouldn't feel so empty?

Granny had walked up in time to hear the woman's comment. Diedra smiled faintly when her friend slipped an arm around her waist and hugged her. At times Diedra hated herself for the self-pity. If only she'd known about her husband's emotional problems. Perhaps her life would be different.

"Why don't you take a break? Find that handsome man who brought you," Granny said. "I'm pretty sure I can handle this thing."

Diedra smiled. "Thanks, Granny. Lynnie and I could do with a bit of liquid refreshment."

"Take your time." She turned to the line of people and smiled. "Okay—who's next?"

Diedra grinned when Granny expertly touted the merits of the spinning balloon board. Then she spotted Eli serving the kids and talking and laughing as he passed out cookies and candy. When one of the toddlers snatched another one's cookie, Diedra laughed at Eli's startled reaction. He immediately offered a replacement to the brokenhearted child.

She made her way to his side. "Having fun?"

He tousled the child's hair and stood. "Yes. I'm glad you nagged me into coming."

"Nagged?" She laughed. "You jumped at the opportunity. Did you bring a bottle? I think Lynnie's hungry."

"I had the ladies stash them in the fridge. I'll get one."

"Stay where you are. I need to get something to eat anyway."

In the kitchen, members of the refreshment committee surrounded Diedra. They warmed the bottle and cooed to the baby, all the while asking about Lynnie and her handsome father.

"You should snap him up," one lady suggested.

"We're friends," Diedra said.

The women looked at each other. "I wouldn't let him get away. No reason you should be alone when he's available and so needy."

Diedra had never considered Eli as anything but self-sufficient. Definitely not needy. What did it matter anyway? Even if he were, she couldn't be what Eli needed. *Don't think about him*, she told herself, knowing she would only become more depressed.

"I'd better feed her." Diedra tried to juggle the baby, a hot dog, and a cold drink. She smiled gratefully at the woman who carried the items out for her.

Eli came over to her then. "Let me take her so you can eat."

Father and daughter seemed lost in their own world as the baby lay in his arms, drinking her formula and playing with his face.

Diedra pushed her plate away. "Guess I'm not as hungry as I thought." She took a couple of sips of soft drink. Lost in her melancholy, she fell silent.

"Are you okay?" Eli asked, concern filling his voice.

She nodded, refusing to admit the turmoil inside her.

The baby drained her bottle and fell asleep across her father's lap. Eli made Lynnie comfortable and took Diedra's hand in his. "Want to talk?"

His caring gesture made her feel like crying. She shook her head and changed the subject. "I'm tired but happy the event is so well attended. Our homecoming is Sunday. You should come. We have dinner in the fellowship hall after church services. We have some great cooks."

"I've never eaten church food I didn't like."

"Me neither," Diedra agreed. She picked up her trash and rose to her feet. "I'd better relieve Granny."

Diedra was glad when the evening began to wind down. Kids agonized over how to spend the coupons they'd won while parents prompted them to hurry. Several children from the center stopped to tell her good-bye.

"So what did you think?" Diedra asked Eli as he drove her home.

"I enjoyed myself. Several members invited me to come again."

"They're a friendly bunch," Diedra said. "They've been a blessing to me. I missed my grandparents so much, and everyone helped me through that period of my life."

"Losing loved ones is difficult," Eli agreed. "I don't understand why it has to happen. Kelly was so young. She had so much to live for."

As he spoke the words, Diedra considered her losses and the times she'd questioned God. A few tears of self-pity trailed down her cheeks; she welcomed the darkness. She hated these uncontrollable bouts of emotion.

In the backseat, Lynnie whimpered.

Diedra looked back at the baby. "She's tired."

"Not Lynnie," Eli said, looking at his daughter in the mirror. "She's a real night owl."

"I thought she'd be sleeping the night away by now."

"I wish. Are you okay?" Eli asked. "You don't sound like yourself."

"I'm fine."

"Are you crying?" he asked, glancing at her.

"I'm okay," she murmured, turning her head to the window as she swiped at the remaining traces of tears.

"What happened?"

Diedra closed up at his question. Why couldn't she ever admit she'd been a battered wife? Because she felt shame about allowing it to happen? Because she hadn't been smart enough to stop Benjamin?

No matter how she tried to justify her behavior, she couldn't. She'd allowed Benjamin to use her for battering practice, to degrade and hurt her. As a result, she'd lost more than she cared to think about.

"Everyone gets the blues," she told him.

If only she could tell him why. But spousal abuse wasn't something one shared casually. Most of the time she presented a bright facade to the world and managed admirably, except for times like now when depression overwhelmed her.

"I'm sure even you have your moments," she said as he parked in the driveway. "Would you like to come inside?"

"I'll listen, you know."

Eli removed Lynnie from her car seat and attempted to calm the baby as they walked toward the house. The porch lamp cast a glow over his face, and Diedra saw Eli's sincerity.

It wasn't that she didn't want his help. Just not right now. His caring words had a powerful effect on her, and those silver blue eyes touched her with the delicate probe of searching fingers. "It's nothing. Really."

Lynnie's continued crying took their attention from Diedra's problem. Diedra laid her hand on Lynnie's forehead and found it warm. She groaned. No matter how hard they tried, communicable diseases were a pitfall of day care. "Oh, Eli, I hate—"

"What?" He looked at her. "Diedra, tell me what's wrong with Lynnie. She's been crying for almost an hour. I don't know what to do."

"Calm down," Diedra said quietly, touching his arm. "We'll work on bringing her fever down, and if she doesn't get better, you should call her pediatrician."

"What?" The shouted word startled the baby into complete wakefulness, and her cries began in earnest. "Shush, honey. Daddy's sorry. Don't cry," he begged, rocking her gently.

Diedra's heart melted at Eli's frantic look. "Give her to me."

"How could this happen?" he asked, his voice rising again.

"You might as well prepare yourself," Diedra said. "As long as she's in day care, Lynnie will be exposed to everything."

He looked incredulous. "Don't you quarantine the sick kids? Send them home or something?"

"We try."

As Lynnie continued to cry, Eli moved closer to Diedra, her back blanketed by his chest as he reached over her shoulder to soothe his daughter. "Sweetie, please don't cry. Daddy's sorry you don't feel well."

Diedra found herself transfixed by the hand that consoled Lynnie. The gentle touch applied with just the right amount of control. His words were soft against her ear. "What can I do for her?"

"Come upstairs, and we'll see what we can do," Diedra said.

Eli followed so closely he bumped into Diedra when she stopped. Instinctively his arms cradled both her and his child. She stepped away quickly.

Upstairs in her sitting room, Diedra placed the baby on the sofa.

Eli paced the length of the small room.

"Eli, take it easy." Diedra reached up and pulled him down beside her.

She watched his hand go over his face in the gesture she'd begun to associate with him. "All it takes is exposure. The rest comes naturally. We are particular about sick children, but we can't spot everything."

He stood and paced again. "I know. I'm sorry. It's just that—"

"You hate to see her sick," Diedra finished for him.

He shoved his hands into the pockets of his slacks. "What should I do?"

"Let's sponge her off," Diedra said, trying to ignore the emotions swirling inside her. "Did you bring her bag in? We need to see if we can get her to eat."

He tapped his forehead. "I forgot her bottles at church. I'd hoped the car ride would lull her to sleep."

Diedra smiled. "Car trips worked in the past?"

He nodded. "Pitiful, isn't it?"

"Lots of parents, both mothers and fathers, use the same method," Diedra told him. "Look in the upper right-hand cabinet in the kitchen. We keep extra formula there. You should find a sterilized bottle as well. I'm going to put her in a cool bath."

Eli returned with a bottle of liquid medication. "I found this in her diaper bag." He disappeared again.

Diedra considered his reaction to Lynnie's illness. She'd never met a man with Eli's qualities.

"Hey, I can't find—" Eli entered the room and stopped, gazing at the scene before him. "How did you manage that?"

The crying had ceased. Lynnie lay there quietly, grasping Diedra's finger in her tiny hand.

"Lynnie loves the movement of the cradle swing. We have one in the nursery, too."

Fifteen minutes later they sat on the sofa, sipping the soft drinks Eli had poured in yet another kitchen run. Lynnie's eyes drifted open and closed with the sway of the cradle.

❧

Eli's gaze settled first on Diedra then on his baby in the cradle. "I have to ask you, Diedra. What have you done to my daughter? You know she cries when we leave the center."

Diedra looked up and smiled. "She's a discriminating baby."

His half smile changed to an expression of concern. "I worry that she's becoming too attached to you and the others."

"Lynnie will bond with the people who care for her, but I doubt she's crying because you take her away. More likely she knows she's in sympathetic arms."

"Are you saying she's spoiled?" The warmth of his smile permeated his voice as he looked at his child. "I love her so much."

A smile touched Diedra's lips. She stifled a yawn and murmured an apology.

"You're tired. I shouldn't have—"

"Nonsense," she interrupted. "I'm glad to help."

"Looks as if I'm going to get another break. I've just found the top of my desk in a couple of places. Oh well, no one ever said parenting was easy."

"No, but then everyone doesn't have access to Kids Unlimited's multifaceted plan. You work, and I arrange to go to your home until she's well enough to return to the center."

"You don't offer a program like that," he said. "Do you?"

"Well, no," she admitted, "but I think it would be a good idea if I could figure out the technical stuff."

Eli frowned and shook his head. "Probably not. Parents need to accept some responsibility for their children, you know."

"I can still help with Lynnie."

The idea tempted Eli. Letting Diedra take over Lynnie's care at the house would be too easy. While putting ice in the glasses earlier, Eli found himself thinking of the woman with his child. He shouldn't have stuck her with his problems. Her job demanded so much of her, days filled with kids, parents, and senior citizens. She didn't need to babysit a panicked father in the evenings.

But she wouldn't tell him that. She'd willingly do everything she could for him and Lynnie. He'd noticed that about Diedra Pierce. Along with her sharp mind, caring heart, beauty, and the other things that added up to make her a unique individual. She gave so much love to those around her.

"No," he said firmly.

"But—"

"You give too much," Eli said. "I could take advantage and let you come every day, but who's going to do your work here? I won't make more work for you."

Diedra flushed, and Eli knew he had hit on the truth of the matter.

"I care about her, Eli."

"And we care about you. I'll find a way. Now tell me why you were upset earlier."

Again he watched her close herself off from him. What was she hiding?

"Just one of those things. I let myself slip into the past and realized I'd made a mistake."

"I'll listen if you want."

"I think Lynnie's dropped off to sleep."

His gaze rested on the baby for a moment before coming back to her. "Thanks for putting up with us," he whispered, his arm dropping around her shoulders and squeezing her closer. "You're a lifesaver. I honestly don't know how we would manage without you."

"You'd do fine."

"I'm not so sure."

Eli wrapped her in a comforting hug, marveling at his attraction to Diedra. Her head rested against his chest. They both sighed at Lynnie's cry of protest when the cradle swing came to a gentle halt.

"I'd better get her home," he said. "Tomorrow's another long day."

"Not so long. Saturday sessions," she reminded him. "If you need to work, I can see if Granny's available."

"I have the weekend off," he said.

"You should monitor her temperature. If it rises again, contact her pediatrician. And feel free to call if you need me."

"I will."

As they wrapped up Lynnie, his shoulder brushed against hers. Diedra stepped aside to let him finish tucking his daughter into her carrier. She followed him downstairs and to the front door. Eli glanced over his shoulder to where she stood silhouetted in the lighted doorway.

"Good night," he called with a wave of his hand.

"Good night." She was still standing there when he turned the corner.

Lynnie slept through the drive. At home he placed her in the crib and turned off the light.

He paused outside the nursery and listened for a moment to see if she stirred. Eli couldn't believe Diedra had offered to come to his house and care for Lynnie. That went far beyond the call of duty.

Her capacity for giving amazed him. Already she lavished it on the kids and senior citizens but still had enough left over to share with him and Lynnie.

If only he could put his grief behind him, she would be the type of woman he could love forever. She would love a man despite his faults. But he wasn't ready. And what would Diedra think if she knew the truth?

Chapter 6

After he left, Diedra straightened the kitchen and did a few tasks downstairs before locking up and turning out the lights.

Upstairs she ran hot water in the tub and sprinkled in some of her favorite bath salts. She put her favorite Christian music in the player and slid into the fragrant water.

Emotion choked her as the words of one of the songs brought tears. "I'm so sorry, Jesus," she whispered, knowing nothing she had endured could ever be a fraction of what her Lord had suffered on the cross because of His love for her.

After her bath Diedra prepared for bed. She knelt by her bedside and turned to God in prayer, seeking His help for all the burdens on her heart that night. She thought for a moment about Eli's concern for her. What would it have been like to tell him the truth? To share her burden? She might tell herself Eli was only a friend, but she knew things were going beyond that. She was feeling emotions she'd suppressed for so long, but she knew she couldn't lose sight of the way things had to be. She'd spent the past five years trying to forget, trying to trust again.

Eli employed her to provide his daughter with the best of care. And that was all they could ever share. She wouldn't consider love again until she came to grips with the past. Others might think she gave too much, but only she knew how little she could give.

After her "shopping-care" kids left at noon on Saturday, Diedra called Eli. "How's Lynnie?"

"We spent the early morning hours in the emergency room."

"Oh, Eli. What did the doctor say?"

"She has an ear infection."

"Poor baby. How can I help?"

"There's nothing you can do."

Diedra knew Eli was exhausted but accepted his refusal. "Let me know if I can help."

"Enjoy your night off. You deserve it."

❧

On Sunday Diedra didn't ask if he needed help. She arrived at Eli's after church, using the bottles she'd retrieved and the plate of food from the homecoming meal as excuses to stop by.

Eli met her at the door, cradling the crying baby against his shoulder. He seemed almost desperate when he handed Lynnie over, taking the items she carried and disappearing into the kitchen. Diedra rocked the baby against her shoulder. She cooed soothing words as she reached for her tote bag and pulled out a water bottle.

"What do you plan to do with that?" Eli asked somewhat skeptically as he returned to the room.

"Heat helps. Granny mentioned a warm bag of salt or tea tree oil, but I figured this would be easier. I don't have a clue about the oil."

"I gave her pain medication a few minutes ago."

"Let's try the water bottle. It can't hurt."

Eli heated water and retrieved towels from the linen closet. Diedra wrapped the bottle and maneuvered the baby against the warmth. Lynnie continued to cry. Diedra rubbed her back and whispered words of comfort, praying the medication would take effect soon. She whispered a prayer of thanks when Lynnie calmed down and her eyes drifted closed.

"You think that thing really did the job?" Eli asked.

Diedra shrugged. "Sometimes the old-fashioned remedies work best."

"You mind if I hold on to that until I can buy one?"

"It's yours. I didn't know if you had one, so I picked it up at the drugstore on the way over."

After Lynnie's crisis passed, Diedra felt like a kid in a candy store. The nursery of pink ruffles and lace had everything from a canopied gleaming brass crib to a large wooden carousel horse. "This room is fantastic!" Diedra exclaimed, trying to take in everything at once.

"Lynnie's mom picked out the furnishings. I can't tell you how long we looked for that crib."

"It was worth the effort. This room is so feminine."

Eli reached to turn back the pink-striped comforter. "My baby girl is pretty feminine."

After Diedra laid the baby down, Eli took his time smoothing the covers over her. She stirred when her father kissed her head, then settled herself.

He pulled the shades and turned off all the lights except for a tiny night-light, then he pushed a few buttons on a panel by the door. "This activates a monitor wired into the house's sound system. I can hear her wherever I go."

"You've thought of everything," Diedra said. "This room, the monitoring system, even the way you handle her. She's your little princess."

"She sleeps like there's a pea under that mattress," Eli said, his grin turning into a wide yawn.

She laughed. "You need a nap, too. Did you want to eat first?"

He led the way into the kitchen. Diedra caught her breath at the sheer elegance of the room. Lynnie's discomfort had taken priority, so she hadn't paid much attention to her surroundings. She'd seen rooms like this only in decorator magazines. Her gaze lingered on the stained-glass cabinet doors before moving to the large bay window and the assortment of plants. "You did this?"

He smiled at her. "I own a design and furniture showroom."

"I'm impressed."

Eli retrieved the plate he'd placed in the fridge earlier and removed the foil wrap. "Did you eat?" He put the plate in the microwave.

Diedra nodded. "There was a ton of food at the church."

The microwave timer beeped, and he took the plate to the granite-topped island. Diedra leaned against the counter. "So what can you do with an upstairs apartment in an old Victorian?"

He held up a finger as he chewed and swallowed. "Ah, the potential is boundless. I see a blue-flowered, overstuffed sofa with a matching armchair. Cream walls, hardwood floors."

Diedra laughed as he described her own furnishings. "Exhaustion must have drained your creative genius. Maybe you'll do better after a few hours of sleep."

"Or a few weeks," Eli countered with a grin. He ate a few bites of food and rewrapped the plate. "That's enough for now. Let's go into the sunroom. I'll stretch out in my chair, and we can talk."

Despite his plan to talk, Eli soon dozed off, and as he napped, Diedra struggled to contain her curiosity. She wanted to explore, to learn more about Eli.

Instead, she flipped through a magazine. Being here was important. She knew that. Not even Lynnie's cries woke him. Diedra took care of the baby's needs and comforted her until she drifted off again. The hours stretched into late afternoon, and Diedra would have stayed longer if she hadn't invited Granny to attend the concert at church with her that night.

Even in his semiawake state, it took Diedra several minutes to convince Eli to let her and Granny help with Lynnie's care. He relented, but only for one day.

"She's going to be sick for more than a day," Granny argued when Diedra shared the plan with her that evening.

"He knows that, but we have to convince Eli this is not a problem for us. He feels he's taking advantage," Diedra explained at Granny's puzzled expression. "I told him the center is covered, but he only agreed to let you take care of her tomorrow while he sorts out things at work. I wouldn't be surprised if he's home early. He could be feeling guilty about leaving Lynnie when she's sick."

"I'll talk to him and try to make him understand he shouldn't stand in the way of people intent on doing good deeds."

"Do that. And convince him to let me stay with Lynnie on Tuesday," Diedra added.

Granny smiled. "So when are you going to tell me about you and Eli?"

"There's nothing to tell."

"Now you know better than that," Granny told her. "You care a great deal more for Eli McKay than you're letting on."

Diedra shook her head. "I can't. I'll hurt him."

"That's a possibility with any relationship, but if you follow God's leading, I doubt it would happen."

"I'm trying, Granny."

❧

On Monday morning Diedra eyed the pale blue page of the checkbook. Spending money had never seemed less interesting. She needed more coffee before she started on the payroll and bills.

Diedra stood and reached for her mug then sank back into the chair. At that moment Granny walked into the room carrying a thermal carafe. "Ready for a refill?"

She held out her cup. "You're a lifesaver. Caffeine is the only thing keeping me going."

"Heard from Eli and Lynnie yet?"

"No," Diedra said. "I hate it that she's sick."

"Me, too." Granny closed the cap before setting the carafe on the desktop.

"He should be here any minute. Remember to talk him into letting me stay with Lynnie tomorrow."

"You're needed here. They were telling me just now what Davey's been up to lately. A play for your attention, I suppose."

"How can that be?" Diedra asked, smiling. "Davey spends nearly as much time in my office as I do."

Davey's antics were legendary around the center. Every staff member had a Davey story that topped the one before. Diedra didn't even want to know what he'd done today but knew she'd hear soon enough. "By the way, we have Janice Gore to thank for referring Eli."

"So Eli knows Davey," Granny said.

"They're old pals."

"No doubt Eli figured you could handle anything if you could handle that boy."

She shuffled the papers into a pile then picked up her pen, tapping out a rhythm against the desktop. "Maybe I should ask Janice about Eli."

Granny looked confused. "What exactly are you hoping to find out?"

"I have to know he's trustworthy," Diedra admitted.

"That's something you need to determine for yourself, Dee."

"I don't even know why I feel this way. I'm not sure I believe in love anymore."

"There's too much love in you to allow apathy to rule your feelings toward anyone, including Eli. One day you'll get over what Benjamin did. You'll live and love again."

Diedra wished that could be true. "What man would want me, Granny? I can't give him children. Until I let go of the past, I can't even offer him the love he deserves. It's not fair to ask anyone to wait until I'm ready."

"Fairness rarely has anything to do with falling in love. You know that. You can't fill the loneliness in your heart with the children and old people in this place. A man who loves you would help ease the loneliness. And scars fade in time, just like memories."

"Oh, Granny, I want to believe that."

"You'll see. That's what love's about. Trust God to provide."

How many times would Granny have to remind her to trust God? Diedra believed in God's provisions, but she had so much to work out before she could ever hope to have a normal life. The ringing phone jarred the silence in the room. "Kids Unlimited."

"Dee, it's Eli."

"Hi. How's Lynnie?"

"We're leaving the doctor's office now. He gave us antibiotics and eardrops. Guess that means we won't have to find that oil you told me about."

Diedra laughed. "I could ask Granny if she has any. Did she wake again last night?"

"Around two. Is Mrs. Wright there now?"

Diedra winked at the older woman. "She's right here. What time will you pick her up?"

"Ten minutes," Eli said. "I won't bring Lynnie in."

"I'll have Granny meet you outside."

"Are you sure she'll be okay?"

"Without a doubt. What about you? Don't you need to rest before you go to work?"

Eli's sigh sounded slightly regretful. "I wish. If I weren't up to my neck right now, I'd stay home with Lynnie."

"It'll be okay," Diedra assured him softly. "Ten minutes then."

Diedra watched Granny hurry away to collect her belongings. Her cheerful bustle, much like when she helped around the center, assured Diedra one of them had something to look forward to that day.

It took all of her willpower to stay in her chair and wave good-bye to Granny a few minutes later. She wouldn't even look out the window. No matter how much she wanted to see Eli and Lynnie.

"Got a minute?"

Diedra's heart flip-flopped at the sound of Eli's voice. "Sure. I thought you weren't coming in," she said, happiness warming her from the inside out.

"I just wanted to say thanks for everything."

Diedra's heart thumped wildly. *Fairness rarely has anything to do with falling in love.* The words seemed to rebound through the room. *Don't be silly,* she chided herself. But there was no denying the truth. She cared a great deal for Eli McKay.

"Do you feel better about Lynnie? Did you ask the doctor about the late-night sessions?"

Eli nodded. "He agrees with you. Thinks getting her back on schedule will take care of those episodes." He glanced at his watch. "I have a ten o'clock appointment. I need to drop them off at the house."

"I'll stop by later and check on them if you want."

"You don't have time," he pointed out.

"It's no problem. Honestly."

"We went over this yesterday," Eli said.

"What if I charge you? Would that make it better?"

He chuckled. "I suppose it would seem less like taking advantage."

"My price is ten minutes of your daughter's time." Diedra smiled. "Payable upon arrival, of course."

Eli laughed. "It's a deal. I have to run. Mrs. Wright will think I got lost."

Bemused, Diedra lifted her hand then let it drop. She was teetering on a crazy emotional seesaw, but Sarah pulled her back to earth when she entered the office with one of the children from her classroom.

"What's up?"

"Eddie and Davey are fighting over a quarter."

"It's mine," Eddie said, breaking into tears. "I got it for my tooth. See?" He indicated the gap in the front of his mouth.

"How did Davey get your money?"

"I lost it. Davey says finders keepers, but it's mine."

The tears fell even faster, and Diedra knelt to hug the child. "It's okay, sweetie. We'll find your quarter." She slipped her hand into her pocket and fingered the coins before coming across the right change. "Here—let me look behind your ear. Maybe you lost it there."

Eddie shook his head. "It was in my pocket."

"Well, perhaps it slipped out. Why, look here," she cried as she fingered his hair. "Here's a quarter."

"Where?" Eddie demanded, squirming to see when she pulled the coin from behind his ear. Diedra showed him, and his sad eyes brightened.

He reached for the money. "I'm going to put it in my bank."

"Why don't you let me keep it for now?" Diedra held out her hand. "We wouldn't want it to get lost behind your ear again." Taking his hand, she led him over to the desk and placed the money in the wooden box that sat there. "See—I'll keep it right here for you."

Eddie nodded and wrapped his arms around her legs.

Diedra hugged him again. She glanced at Sarah. "I'll walk down with you and talk to Davey."

Sarah reached for Eddie's hand.

Davey denied having Eddie's quarter, and Diedra decided to let the matter drop for now and talk to his mother that afternoon.

After leaving the classroom, Diedra made her way to the nursery. "Hi, Gina," she said, plucking Timmy from the crib.

"Busy morning?"

Diedra sat in a rocker and accepted the bottle Gina handed her. She settled Timmy in her arms, enjoying the baby smell of him as she fed him. "You know, it just occurred to me that Davey starts school next fall. What will we do for excitement around here?"

"He's probably been training Kaylie."

Diedra laughed and nodded, her gaze touching on the baby who moved around on the play mats. "Please tell me he started crawling at home."

Gina settled in the rocker next to hers with a baby and bottle. "His mom's delighted. She thinks the other babies inspired him."

Diedra felt relieved. Too many times parents experienced guilt when they missed a milestone in their children's lives.

"How's Lynnie?" Gina asked.

"Ear infection."

"So we won't be seeing the gorgeous Mr. McKay this week?"

"Lynnie may be back later in the week."

"So Mr. McKay did make his daily stop by the director's office this morning?"

Diedra looked at Gina. "He's checking on his daughter."

"Funny. He always asks me how she's doing," Gina pointed out, her eyes twinkling.

"That's because I pay you to tell him," Diedra said. She lifted Timmy to her shoulder, and he rewarded her with a resounding burp. "You need something to occupy your time with this cushy job."

Both women laughed at the absurdity of Diedra's statement and settled the babies in their cribs.

"I'll be back later," Diedra said.

She took advantage of a lull in activity to run by Eli's house. She rang the doorbell and studied the outside of his home. Not a mansion but definitely not a cottage either. The painted woodwork gleamed in the sunlight. The lawns and shrubbery were meticulous, not a fallen leaf in sight.

"Hello, Granny," Diedra said, kissing the woman's cheek in greeting before she lifted Lynnie from her arms. "How's she doing?"

"She seems comfortable for now."

Granny poured two glasses of soda, and they sat and talked while Diedra played with Lynnie. The time passed quickly. "I'd better get back to work," she announced reluctantly as she transferred Lynnie into Granny's arms. Diedra smoothed a hand over the baby's head and squeezed Granny's arm gently. "Call if you need me."

"I will. Thanks for checking on us."

"You're too smart for your own good," Diedra told her.

Granny laughed. "Have a good afternoon."

Back at the center Diedra recalled Gina's teasing about Eli's daily visits. The woman had been right. Eli did make an effort to see her every day. She would miss not seeing him while Lynnie was out sick.

Don't do this to yourself, Diedra cautioned. She knew exactly where self-examination would lead. She picked up the day's mail and found that the licensing packet had arrived. She needed to help Gina with the babies again, and then she would find time to read the information. She still had to check next week's menus, order supplies, and contact a couple of parents.

As Diedra worked, her thoughts drifted back to what she'd asked Granny that morning. What harm would it do to ask Janice about Eli? Just a conversation between two friends. Eli would never know. Janice had to collect Davey's quarter anyway.

The phone rang, and Diedra felt guilty when Eli's voice filled her ear.

"Glad I caught you. It looks as if I'm going to be an hour late getting home. You aren't going to charge me sixty dollars, are you?" Eli asked, speaking of the dollar-a-minute late charge.

"I can't charge you, but you need to see if Granny can stay."

"I'd better call and ask."

"Talk to you later," Diedra said, glancing up at the tap on the door. She waved Janice in.

"Diedra!" Eli called just as she started to hang up. She pulled the receiver back to her ear. "Come over for dinner tonight. I can fix something, or we can order in."

"Okay. See you around seven."

Diedra focused on replacing the receiver before meeting Janice's smile. "Eli."

"So I gathered. Sarah said you wanted to see me. You aren't giving Davey his walking papers, I hope?"

"No, nothing like that," Diedra said. "There is something about Davey, but I had another matter I wanted to discuss with you."

Janice let out a sigh as she sank into a chair, resting her hand against her heart. "You take five years off my life every time you summon me to your office. I feel as if I'm going to the principal's office. As long as Davey's secure, go ahead."

"What can you tell me about Eli?"

"Probably no more than you already know," Janice said, shaking her head. "He's handsome, charming, well-respected in his business, and adores his child. I wish I could tell you more."

The feelings of guilt returned. What on earth had made her think Janice could enlighten her? "I'm sorry, Janice. I shouldn't have put you on the spot like that."

"Never be sorry for caring for someone, particularly Eli. I think you're good for him. I know you care about him."

"Janice. . ."

"Don't deny your feelings, Diedra. Caring is one of your best traits, but you have to allow people to care for you in return."

If only she could share how difficult it was for her to let people get close. Children were different. Every one of them stole away a little of her heart, but they gave so much more in return.

The thought of giving her heart to another person incapable of returning her love scared Diedra. "What I really need to discuss with you is Davey's quarter."

Janice frowned. "Davey doesn't have a quarter. We never allow him to bring money to day care."

Diedra explained the situation then summoned Davey to the office.

"Do you have Eddie's quarter?" Janice asked her son.

Davey produced the coin from the tiny watch pocket of his jeans. "I found it."

Janice took the money from his hand and gave it to Diedra. "You knew it belonged to Eddie. What you did was wrong, Davey. We don't ever make other people cry." Janice stood and captured his hand. "We'll see what your dad has to say about the matter."

After they left, Diedra found herself thinking about the life lesson that had transpired in her office. She wished Janice's claim to her son that "we don't ever make other people cry" could be true. The world would certainly be a better place.

Janice had forced her to face another truth—one she fought to deny. She cared a great deal for Eli. Myriad emotions filled Diedra with the truth—fear, excitement, and a tremendous anxiety. What would happen if she allowed herself to love Eli? Would doing so bring pain or untold joy? Was she willing to take the chance?

Chapter 7

Eli paced the living room, looking out the full-length glass windows every time a car drove down the street. He waited for Diedra, and despite his apprehension, Eli knew he wanted her there with him.

He'd gone inside the center that morning for one reason. He didn't want to go through a day without seeing her. And he'd invited her to dinner for the same reason. He wanted—no, he needed—to spend time with her.

Headlights flooded the room as a car pulled into the driveway. "Act your age, man. You're not some sixteen-year-old who's never dated," he muttered, rubbing his sweaty palms on his jeans.

Eli jerked the door open and watched Diedra approach. She'd changed into jeans and a fuzzy pastel pink sweater. She smiled, and the doubts evaporated.

"Get all your charges home safely?" he asked, returning her smile. She nodded, and he invited her inside. "I'm glad you came. I wish we could have gone out to dinner."

Diedra set her bag on the small bench in the foyer, her keys jangling as she dropped them inside. "This is better. You don't have to worry with a sitter. Did I tell you I love your home?"

Eli enjoyed the way she assessed the room. He'd seen the look often when his customers fell in love with a piece of furniture or room arrangement. "After the initial shock, you mean?"

She laughed. "I had no idea you were so talented. Are these original pieces?"

"They're one-of-a-kind pieces. I designed everything here exclusively for myself."

"It's a great showroom." Diedra glanced at him. "Don't your buyers want similar designs?"

"They don't see these," Eli explained. "I'm fortunate my business associates understand it's easier for me to have dinner parties at restaurants."

Diedra pointed to the oval stained-glass window. "Where did you find that?"

"I made it."

Her mouth dropped open. "It's fabulous."

"Thanks." He lifted his shoulders and stared moodily at the piece. The window had been the largest item he'd ever done. A flower garden in glass, his instructor had called it.

He'd been so depressed after Kelly's death that his doctor suggested Eli take up a hobby to help work through his emotions. And it had helped. The creative pieces had passed the time, vented his frustrations, and left him this memento to show that sometimes beauty comes from pain. "I need to take Mrs. Wright home, and I—"

"Granny's still here?" Diedra asked.

He nodded. "In the nursery."

"I'll go say hello."

Not ready to share her yet, Eli wrapped his fingers lightly about Diedra's wrist. He noted the way she stiffened then relaxed in his hold. "I thought if you stayed with Lynnie, I could pick up dinner on my way back."

Diedra looped her arm through his and urged him toward the nursery. "Sounds good."

Eli watched as she kissed Granny Marie's cheek and fingered Lynnie's curls. The older woman said something, and Diedra's soft laughter filled the room.

You've got it bad, old man, Eli thought. Diedra touched his life in ways he hadn't thought he'd experience again—her concern for Lynnie, Granny, the children in the center, even him.

"Eli's picking up supper. Want to stay?" Diedra issued the invitation then glanced at Eli and smiled.

He returned her smile. Inviting Granny wasn't his choice, but if Diedra wanted the woman to stay, he wouldn't refuse her.

"No, thank you," Granny said, careful not to disturb the sleeping baby as she put her in the crib. "Francie's already upset because I didn't rush home tonight."

Eli noted Diedra's dismayed expression. "Who is Francie?" he asked.

Diedra turned to him. "Her daughter-in-law." Then she looked at Granny Marie. "Why didn't you say something earlier?"

"Jimmy knows where I am, and Francie needs to learn things don't always go as planned."

No, they don't, Eli agreed, thinking her words sounded almost prophetic. He and Diedra had been trying to arrange their relationship on their own terms, but he had the feeling God planned to move it along a completely different path.

"You'd better get me home, Eli." Granny tucked the covers about Lynnie then folded a blanket, placing it over the back of the rocker.

"Wait," Diedra said. "Let me tell you what Davey did today. But let's go downstairs so we don't disturb Lynnie."

❧

Both Granny and Eli chuckled over Davey's latest stunt as they left the house. Diedra waved and closed the door.

She paused in the living room, the stained glass catching her attention, then walked over to examine it more closely. A work of art, filled with talent and emotion. Yet somehow Eli seemed unimpressed by his accomplishment.

Diedra checked on Lynnie again and decided to wait in the sunroom. The darkening shadows of the late fall evening showed through the glass walls. She flipped a wall switch and flooded the backyard with light. A large expanse of deck stretched across the back of the house next to a covered pool.

Another switch lit the lamps. This room fascinated her the most. Unlike the rest of the house, the eclectic mixture of modern furniture and antiques made the room a place where people lived. Again an abundance of healthy plants dotted the room along with exquisite pewter figurines and china plates. Walls of bookcases overflowed with a mixture of leather-bound collector's editions, popular hardcover fiction, action-adventure paperbacks, and volumes on furniture and antique history. Diedra trailed her finger along the spines, stopping on the ones of formula car racing.

A photo of a man in some sort of zippered suit sat on the bookcase. She lifted the carved wood frame to examine the photo in detail. A helmet made it impossible to tell who leaned against the formula car, his fingers forming a victory sign. Maybe someone Eli knew. Perhaps this explained his interest in racing.

Puzzled, Diedra replaced the photo and moved to the collection on the sofa table. There were several with Eli as a member of a group. Probably his parents, she decided upon seeing a resemblance between him and the older man in the photo. One of him in a porch swing with a beautiful woman caught her eye. Diedra reached for the silver frame.

Could this be Kelly? They looked so in love. Her fingers trembled as she replaced the picture and managed to knock over another. As she set it upright, she found the photo that told her all she needed to know about Eli McKay.

Apparently it was a recent shot, for the photographer had captured Eli's contentment as he presented Lynnie to the camera with happiness so real it stole Diedra's breath. She knew he loved his child, but she hadn't realized to what degree.

"There you are."

She screamed, stifling the sound with a hand over her mouth when she whirled to find Eli standing behind her. "That was quick."

"I know the shortcuts."

"I remembered this room from Sunday night. I thought it might be where you spend your evenings."

"This mishmash of design is my favorite room in the house. Both Kelly and I loved to read. The pewter pieces belonged to my dad, and the china plates belonged to Kelly's family."

"And someone definitely has a green thumb."

"I love plants. I never feel a room is complete without them. Are you ready to eat?"

"Let me wash up, and I'll meet you in the kitchen."

She stopped by the nursery to check on Lynnie. Diedra smoothed the blanket over her tiny form and watched for a second longer before going downstairs.

Eli had spread the meal over the kitchen island and settled on a stool. Diedra sat across from him. "Lynnie's resting comfortably. I'm so glad she's doing better."

"Probably resting up to give her daddy one tough time tonight," Eli said. "I hope you like Chinese."

"Love it. I never know exactly what I'm eating, though."

"I'm a Chinese takeout expert. I ordered wontons, chicken and broccoli, beef with green peppers, sweet and sour pork, egg rolls, and fried rice," he said, indicating cartons as he ticked through the list. "I wasn't sure what you liked."

"I know I've ordered one or two of those items. But how many people did you plan to feed?"

"One very hungry man and one little lady who looks as if she can't eat very much."

"You'd be surprised," Diedra said.

Eli asked a blessing on the food, thanking the Lord for His continued care for him, Lynnie, and Diedra.

"Thank you," she told him, accepting the carton Eli passed her way. "I appreciate your adding me to your prayer list."

"I hope I'm on yours, too," Eli said.

Diedra nodded. "Oh, look—it's a full moon," she whispered as the brightness filtered into the room.

"I ordered that today," Eli teased, bringing a ready smile to her face. "Right after you agreed to have dinner with me."

"I'm glad you did."

"Order the full moon?" Eli asked, his gaze lingering on her until Diedra dropped her head, feeling about as shy as Lynnie.

"No—invite me to dinner."

"I'm glad, too. Now try these wontons. They're the best I've ever eaten."

Eli kept the conversation flowing as they ate. His comment of how much he appreciated Granny Marie's help reminded Diedra of the older woman's home situation. "I hope Granny and Francie got everything sorted out."

Eli nodded. "I didn't want to say anything in front of Granny Marie, but I thought you said it wouldn't be a problem."

Diedra didn't know what to say. "It wasn't supposed to be. I think Granny and her daughter-in-law experience conflicts when Francie tries to control Granny's life."

"She offered to come back tomorrow, but I don't want to get in the middle of a family conflict."

"I'm sorry, Eli. I'm sure they've worked things out. So tell me—who's the race fan? I noticed the books."

His jaw tensed. "I raced formula cars until last year. I started right after I finished college."

The driver in the photo is Eli. An ever-changing mystery, he'd just revealed something she'd never have guessed. Diedra tried to cover her shock. "You miss it, don't you?"

"At times."

"Why did you quit?"

"Driving was all I ever wanted to do. After Kelly died and Lynnie was born, I knew I had to give it up. I'd rather not talk about this."

"You should," she insisted.

"Quitting was my choice. There's too much risk. My daughter needs her father."

His stance tugged at Diedra's heartstrings. All her life she had wished for a man who put his family before everything else. Now she'd found one and knew she should run the other way, but she couldn't.

"I have to establish security for my child. I want to be around to see her grow up. I refuse to make Lynnie worry the way Kelly and my parents did."

Diedra laid her fork on the plate and looked at him. "I think you're a very special man, Eli McKay."

"Do you mean that, Dee?"

She found his intense regard unsettling.

"Dee?"

She nodded, managing a shaky smile. "Yes. Telling myself to keep this strictly business is not working. I'm not sure I can deal with this right now."

"You're going to have to, aren't you?"

Diedra tried to tell him the truth but found she couldn't. Lynnie's cries echoed over the speaker system. His daughter had a knack for crying right on cue.

"I'll take care of her," Eli said. "Eat. We'll discuss this when I get back."

Anxiety replaced hunger. She couldn't allow this situation to go any further. Diedra hurried to the living room, her movements almost furtive as she picked up her purse and started toward the door.

"Where are you going?" Eli asked as she laid her hand on the doorknob.

"I thought I'd go home. . . ." Her voice faded to a hushed stillness.

"You're not going anywhere until we talk," he said.

"Lynnie needs you."

"She's fussing in her sleep. We need to talk."

"I can't." Diedra fidgeted with her purse strap.

"Why did you accept my dinner invitation?" Eli asked.

"Because. . ." She should never have come here tonight, particularly after realizing how she felt about him. He deserved more than she could give.

"The first time we met, I looked you in the eye and knew right then that you would play an important role in my life." He paused as if considering his next words carefully. "I've grieved for Kelly and known I couldn't afford to get too close. But I couldn't deny I wanted to be near you. I used Lynnie as an excuse to see you, and you didn't discourage me."

Diedra started to protest but accepted that he told the truth. She didn't confer with other parents on a daily basis. Only Eli. They shared a spark that had flamed despite their combined efforts to extinguish it. She nodded.

"What are we going to do?" he asked softly.

"I don't know," she said. "I've never become involved with an enrollee's father before. I'm not even sure it's good business sense."

"This isn't business, Dee. This is you and me and this new experience we're sharing." He moved around the sofa. "We have time to get to know each other better, see where it leads. That is, if you're interested."

Her eyes closed. She wanted to believe love was a possibility for them.

"What do you want, Dee?"

What did she want? *Please, God, help me,* she prayed silently.

"Diedra?"

A battle raged within Diedra. She longed to say yes, but she knew that wouldn't be fair to Eli. She wrung her hands in frustration.

"I never should have let things go this far. You should go, Diedra. It's late, and tomorrow's another early day."

She gasped, her eyes widening. Eli had made the decision for her. He'd taken her silence to mean no.

Chapter 8

The enormity of Eli's words hit Diedra hard when he stormed from the room. He'd suggested they see what the future held for them, and she'd upset him with her silence.

Dazed, Diedra felt the sudden need to do something. Back in the kitchen she closed the cartons and placed the leftovers in the refrigerator.

A wry smile touched her lips. Maybe she should just disappear into the dark without a word. In the end that would be best for them both.

Several minutes passed before Eli returned. "I thought you'd be gone."

She scraped her plate into the garbage disposal.

"Look, Diedra. It would be better if you left. You're right to avoid further involvement with me. I'm not over Kelly's death. I might never stop grieving for what I've lost."

His face, tight with suffering, mobilized her into action. "You have a right to grieve for the woman you loved. She was a part of you. She's a part of your child. No woman who loves you will ever expect you to forget Kelly."

"Then why did you hesitate?"

"It's a trust issue for me, Eli," she said. "I'm afraid to let go. Afraid of what will happen if I do."

"You can trust me, Dee. I wouldn't hurt you."

"I hope not. That's why I stayed. I want you to know—"

Lynnie's cries interrupted her, filling the room.

"What's that old adage about children being seen and not heard?" Eli seemed disgruntled by his daughter's poor timing.

"I'll get her," Diedra volunteered.

"I'll warm a bottle."

The night-light provided sufficient illumination for Diedra to see that Lynnie was awake. "Hey, sweetie," she whispered.

Lynnie rewarded her by kicking her legs in recognition and reaching out to her. She lifted the baby and carried her to the changing table. Afterward Diedra smoothed the long gown over her legs. "You're a blessed little girl," she cooed, cuddling the infant against her chest. "Your daddy sure does love you. And I think I love him, too."

The truth stunned Diedra. She did love Eli. She loved everything about him—his kindness, his loving nature, his dedication to his child and business, all the things that made up the man he was.

"Diedra?"

"Coming," she called.

Eli met her in the hallway, and they walked into the sunroom. She placed Lynnie in his arms. "I checked her temperature. It's normal."

As he became more focused on his daughter, Diedra felt in the way. "I should go," she said.

"Stay." He tugged her down on the sofa beside them. Time slipped away as they spent the remainder of the evening on the sofa talking. Eli told her about his wife and parents. Content to listen, Diedra didn't share her personal story. As the hour grew late, she noted Eli's exhaustion and Lynnie's wide-eyed alertness. She glanced at her watch. "It's almost one o'clock."

"I feel guilty for keeping you here so long. You have a day with the kids ahead of you. I was selfish."

"I could have left," she said. "I enjoyed this evening."

He squeezed her hand. "Me, too."

Eli followed Diedra to the foyer. She picked up her purse and turned the deadbolt on the front door, swinging it open.

"Good night," Eli said, kissing her gently. "I'll call you."

He stood in the doorway with Lynnie as Diedra walked along the lighted path to her car. Feeling the late night chill, she hurried. Diedra turned the ignition and waited for the engine to warm up.

Eli had said he'd call her. Those three words could be the kiss of death to a relationship. How would she feel if Eli didn't call? Was she strong enough to face the disappointment?

Diedra had loved only one man, her husband. She'd accepted that Benjamin hadn't known how to love. She'd tried to show him how, and he'd beat the desire out of her. Now she felt nothing but shame for being so weak-willed, for not standing up to him before he killed their child.

Her baby. What would Eli think when she told him she couldn't have babies? Would he understand? Diedra battled the emotions that tore at her. Fear of his reaction when he learned the truths she hid overshadowed the happiness of knowing he cared for her.

It didn't matter anyway. She loved Eli. She always would. But she could never marry him. She'd never deny him the family he wanted. The family he deserved.

Putting the car in reverse, Diedra glanced at the house once more before backing down the driveway. "Lord, help them both get some rest," she prayed as she drove down the empty street.

⌘

"It's going to be a long day," Diedra muttered at nine thirty, rubbing her gritty eyes. "Very long." If only she could slip upstairs for a nap. Or just lay her head on the desk. Maybe they wouldn't need her for thirty seconds or so. Her eyes drifted shut then jerked open when the telephone rang. Diedra groped for the receiver. "Yes? Kids Unlimited."

"Diedra?" Granny asked. "Are you okay?"

"Fine, Granny. How's Lynnie?"

"Better," the older woman said. "She must have slept badly last night, though. Eli seemed a little bleary-eyed." She paused. "So how was your date?"

Diedra felt guilty. Why had she done this to herself? To Eli? He didn't know of her self-doubts, of the hatred she felt for one man and at times for herself.

"Diedra?" Granny said when she didn't respond. "I didn't mean to pry."

"You weren't, Granny. How's Lynnie?"

"I told you she's better. Are you sure you're okay?"

"I'm fine. Eli and I talked last night. There are some things to be sorted through."

"What does that mean?" Granny asked.

"We care for each other," Diedra admitted. "Eli wants to see where it leads. But how can I do that to him?"

"Give it to God, then take it one day at a time, Dee. Get to know Eli. When the time is right, share your confidences and let Eli make the decision about what's right for him."

"I don't know, Granny. It doesn't seem fair to go any further without telling him the truth."

"Are you ready to tell him about Benjamin?"

"I can't. Not yet."

She heard Granny sigh. "I'm praying for you, Dee."

The unspoken disappointment in the older woman's tone weighed on Diedra almost as much as her own disappointment at not being able to tell Eli the truth. "What about you and Francie? Did you work things out?" Diedra asked.

There was silence on the other end of the phone. Finally Granny asked, "Does your offer for a roommate still stand?"

"You know it does," she said without hesitation.

"I want you to take some time to think about this first, Dee." Granny paused. "I don't want to burden you. I want your life to go on as if I weren't there."

"You could never be a burden. Now tell me what happened."

"Francie became very upset when I got home last night. She'd planned on my bathing the kids and putting them to bed while she prepared dinner for her guests. I didn't say anything until she started accusing me of caring more for others than for my son and grandchildren. I don't need that in my life. I'm a grown woman. I was married for forty-nine years, ran my own home, did volunteer work at my church, and managed to raise a son. I love them all, but I don't want to live with that kind of treatment or be in their way."

Diedra hurt for Granny. She knew things had to be bad for Granny to take action. "How did Jimmy take the news?"

Silence stretched over the distance. "He didn't have a lot to say last night. We had a private discussion this morning. I explained what I plan to do."

"Did he understand?"

"I think so," Granny said. "I told him that's why I went into the rehab center in the first place. I can take care of myself, Diedra. I know I can."

"We'll take care of each other, Granny."

"That we will. I need to go now. The oven timer just went off."

"What are you doing?" Diedra asked.

"Baking Eli an apple pie."

Diedra laughed. "How do you know he likes apple pie?"

"Everybody likes apple pie. Take care, sweetheart."

Granny probably had Eli's dinner planned, house cleaned, and clothes washed and ironed. Without thinking, she picked up the phone and dialed his direct office number, surprised to hear Janice's voice.

"Hi, Diedra. Eli's out front with a customer. Is it an emergency?"

"I can wait," Diedra said, leaning forward in her chair and tapping her fingers against the desktop. "You'll be happy to know Davey's been on his best behavior this morning."

Janice laughed. "Look out, afternoon. Then again, I think his father made an impression on him Friday night, and he'll behave for a day or two. Here's Eli now. See you later."

Eli's voice came over the phone. "Hi. What's up?"

"Granny just called—"

"Is Lynnie okay?"

"Lynnie's fine," Diedra assured him. "Granny called to tell me she's moving in with me."

"Are you sure that's a smart move? I don't think it's wise to get involved in family situations. What will you accomplish by offering her an opportunity to separate from her family? This could even cause a bigger rift in their relationship."

How could he question her when he had no idea of the true situation? "Granny's unhappy. Not being a burden to her family and managing her time will make her happy again."

"Are you sure? She's regaining that happiness at what cost? Alienating her son? Her daughter-in-law?"

"No. She's explained her decision to her son. She won't go back to her own home out of respect for him. He doesn't want her living alone."

"With reason, I'm sure."

"She's doing much better," Diedra insisted. Eli's disapproval disappointed her. "There's no basis for him to monitor her every breath."

"And what about her son's need to care for his aging mother? How can he do that if he's eliminated from the picture?"

"Granny and I have given the matter lots of thought and prayer, Eli. She needs her independence."

"I'm not sure why you feel you have to do this, but I get the impression there's more to the situation than meets the eye."

"Don't analyze me," Diedra snapped.

"I'm just suggesting you don't take a step you'll regret later," he said.

"I won't have regrets. Granny is my friend. I look forward to sharing my home with her."

"I'm not trying to pick a fight, Dee."

"You're criticizing me."

"And you're being defensive," he countered. "Friends give each other advice. I'm advising you to rethink your plans before you get hurt."

"I have to go," she said abruptly.

"I'll see you this afternoon."

She didn't respond.

"We are going to see each other again, aren't we, Diedra?"

The old fears and uncertainties loomed in her mind.

"Dee?"

"I don't know." The confusion-filled words came out in a rush. Last night had been a different place and time. She needed time to reorient herself, time he wouldn't give her.

"You're not upset because I don't agree with what you're doing, are you? Your life is going to change in a big way because of this decision. I just want you to understand how big."

"I expected support, not criticism. I shared good news with you, and you've turned it into the biggest mistake I've ever made in my life."

"I'm not going to tell you it's a great idea. If you thought I'd made a bad decision, you'd tell me, wouldn't you?"

"You already made that mistake getting involved with me."

"Why would you say something like that?" he asked, his voice agitated.

Granny's position hadn't changed. She needed help, and Diedra had to help her. "I have to go. Good-bye, Eli."

⌘

"Diedra?" he said into the receiver, only to find she'd hung up.

No matter how much he tried to understand her, he always ended up more confused. What did she mean that he'd made a mistake by getting involved with her? What was she hiding from him? Why was she pushing him away?

The worn leather chair tilted backward, the squeaking springs unnoticed as he lapsed into thought. He needed time to get to know Diedra, to learn all about her—her past, her dreams for the future. He needed to know what made her smile, what excited her, what caused her to be happy or sad. He wanted to eliminate the sadness from her life. He didn't want her to cry because of him.

Love made a person vulnerable, opened them to hurt. In one way he could understand she was upset because he hadn't shared her excitement. But he saw the other side of the situation. He understood the potential for pain for Granny Marie and her family.

Eli reached for the phone. He'd call her back. See if they could work things out. Before he could dial, he heard a sharp rap on his office door. "Come in!"

His secretary opened the door and stepped inside. "Janice needs you right away."

Eli paused by the desk. He wanted to call Diedra first.

"Eli." Janice entered the room. "We have 'enraged' times two out here."

Frustrated, he followed Janice into the hallway. Diedra would understand. Business came first for her, too.

Diedra stared at the phone as if willing it to ring would make things different. It wouldn't, and if anyone should know it, she should.

Benjamin Pierce had been self-centered to the core. Charismatic, handsome, everything she'd ever dreamed of in a man. Or so she thought. She married him, unaware of the problems he'd buried beneath the polish. He thought only of himself. Especially the times when he used her as a punching bag.

Desperate, she'd gone to her father, only to have him insist she stop her foolishness and return home. When Benjamin nearly killed her, her parents didn't want their precious name connected with scandal.

Diedra could think only of herself. She could accept his love and keep her secret. But she knew they both would lose in the end.

She could never do that to Eli. The first loving, giving man she'd ever known had been hurt too much for her to add to his pain. Let him remain angry with her. It would be best for them both in the long run.

Diedra wiped away the tear that trickled down her cheek. Before, she'd gone to counseling and managed to pick up the pieces and put herself back together. Then she'd had her grandparents. This time she had God. She would do it again. She still had her children, her center, and her best friend.

Chapter 9

Eli's gaze went immediately to the wall clock when he returned to his office. He couldn't believe it had taken two hours to placate the Albrittons. From experience, though, he knew they would probably decide they wanted a completely different design.

He needed to see Diedra. He refused to allow her to push him out of her life without his understanding why. Eli reached for the phone, propping it against the desk as he punched the numbers. He put the receiver back in the cradle. He couldn't make her understand on the phone. This required a face-to-face, look-her-in-the-eye discussion.

During the drive, Eli went back over Diedra's words, looking for something at odds with the woman he thought he knew. Last night she had been receptive to furthering their relationship. Today she wanted to put it on hold until she tied everything up in tidy little bundles. He had to know what had changed.

Eli opened the door to Diedra's office and stepped inside. He should have called first, but an advance warning would have given her time to raise her guard. Diedra sat at her desk, her eyes closed and her shoulders slumped as though the weight of the world rested there. "Dee?" he said anxiously.

"Eli?" She sat up straighter. "Shouldn't you be home?"

"I called Granny."

"What did you say?" she asked sharply.

Eli hesitated. "That I had work to handle. I wouldn't tell her I don't agree with what you're doing. It's not my business."

"Oh," she muttered uneasily.

Eli eyed the top of her head. "We need to talk."

She refused to look at him and flicked imaginary specks of dust from her desk. "You really think it's that simple?"

Just apologize, Eli told himself as her words rang in his ears. "You're pushing me away, Diedra. Don't run away from us."

"We're moving too fast, Eli."

He ached to lift her head and look into her eyes. "Then we'll slow down. Just give us a chance. I won't lie to you. Nothing about our relationship will be simple, but we've come a long way since we met. We can handle this."

He watched her, both in anticipation and dread. The sudden tenderness and fierce love he felt startled him.

189

"I don't know. You're the father of one of my kids," she argued weakly. "And Granny Marie is important to me. I can't risk making her feel unwanted."

"She's not your responsibility."

Diedra frowned. "I invited her to move in with me months ago. Can you imagine how she'd feel if I refused her now? Particularly since she's had a blowup with her daughter-in-law that involves me."

Asking her not to care was like asking a leopard to change his spots. Eli reached out to her in an instinctive gesture of comfort. "It's not my choice to make. I'm sorry I hurt you. Will you forgive me?"

※

Eli waited for her answer. *Tell him why you can't,* her heart urged. She wasn't ready. Not yet.

Diedra knew her attempts at breaking away would never work as long as they saw each other daily, as long as Eli intended that they wouldn't.

He moved around the desk and pulled her to her feet, encircling her with his arms and pressing a kiss on her forehead. "I had to see you. Will you come to the house after you finish here?"

Diedra knew she should say no. Everything in her said this wasn't right. But she couldn't. "All right."

She followed him onto the porch, watching long after he'd pulled away from the curb. She wrapped her jacket tighter as a sudden chill struck her; she stared into the darkness.

Could love sustain them through her doubts and fears? Without intending to, she'd made a commitment to their future. Her vow not to become involved shattered the moment she saw him. She turned to go back inside.

She loved Eli. But that didn't make her any less afraid. She couldn't postpone her day of reckoning forever. Each passing moment drew her closer to the time she would have to tell him the truth.

Diedra pushed the idea aside and went upstairs to change. She wanted to look beautiful for him and pulled out one of her favorite dresses. She showered, dried her hair, and slipped into the garment. After one last look in the mirror, she dabbed on her best perfume. Downstairs she picked up her coat and purse and headed for Eli's.

The heavy traffic demanded her attention. She was relieved to see the sign for Eli's subdivision.

Lights blazed throughout his house. Ringing the doorbell, Diedra listened for the sound of footsteps on the marble entry hall. The door swung open, and Granny greeted her with a smile. "You're looking extra pretty tonight."

Diedra shrugged. "Oh, I just felt like it."

Granny frowned. "Don't try to fool an old woman, Dee." Then she smiled. "I've never seen you so radiant."

She felt as transparent as glass. "Oh, Granny, I care for him so much it scares me."

"Will you tell him about Benjamin?"

Diedra drew in a deep breath. "I can't. I'll lose him."

"Don't keep secrets. They destroy a relationship faster than anything else."

"I'll tell him soon," Diedra promised.

"I suppose you know best." She turned toward the hallway. "Eli had better get me home. I don't want a repeat of last night's scene."

"You could move in with me tonight," Diedra offered.

"Francie may whine a bit, but I can always start packing."

"I'm sorry it's come to this, Granny."

"Me, too, Diedra. I don't want to come between Jimmy and Francie. I'm depending on you to see that I don't come between you and Eli either."

"Let's cross that bridge when we get to it," Diedra said. "What do I smell? Fried chicken?"

"I cooked supper. Lynnie's doing much better. I think she'll be ready to come back to the center next week."

"I'm sure Eli appreciates everything."

Eli walked up, smiling. "He's forever in her debt." He kissed Diedra. "I'll be back in fifteen minutes."

With her back to Eli, Granny raised her eyebrows and winked then hugged Diedra before stepping through the door. Eli reached over and squeezed her hand as he walked out the door.

Diedra went to check on Lynnie. The baby slept on her stomach, her bottom pushed up in the air. She envied Eli his daughter. He could watch her grow and benefit from her love. He'd rejoice with her in her successes and provide his shoulder to cry on in crises.

Tears welled in Diedra's eyes. She had no idea if her baby had been a Lynnie or a Davey. Grief as strong as that which she had felt years ago overwhelmed her.

Some minutes later Eli joined her in the nursery. "What is it, Diedra? Why are you crying?"

Diedra wiped her hands over her cheeks. "She's so beautiful."

"That's no reason to cry," he said, guiding her from the room. His gentleness spoke of his caring.

"You look beautiful. I wish I could take you somewhere special."

"Another time," Diedra said.

"It's a date. I'm starving. I skipped lunch today."

Eli fixed his plate, and Diedra couldn't help but smile at his combination. "Chicken and apple pie?" she asked. "I know Granny has vegetables in those pans."

He waited for her to serve her own plate and pour iced tea. She pulled out a stool at the counter and sat down. He asked a blessing on the food, and she lifted her fork, only to find her hunger had faded.

Eli studied her. "Are you still upset about this afternoon?"

"No."

"I don't have a right to question your decisions. The way I feel about your involvement in Granny's situation isn't going to stop you from doing what you have to do. You've made no secret of that."

Secret. The word left Diedra breathless. She had too many of them. Her gaze dropped to the plate as she idly rearranged the food. *Don't do this to him. . .to yourself,* her mind warned.

Eli reached for her hand. "I sort of understand about Granny, but I can't help thinking you're setting yourself up for hurt."

"You wouldn't do the same?" Diedra asked, looking him in the eye.

He shrugged. "I can't say that I would. What about when you're not there for her anymore? Will you have helped Granny by not encouraging her to work it out with her family?"

"Where am I going?" Diedra asked. "Kids Unlimited is my life, and for as long as I have a home, Granny has one."

"And if we become involved?"

Tell him about Benjamin.

An overwhelming desire to push the truth even deeper seized her. "I'll make that decision when the time is right. I'm not sure about us. There were issues with my marriage." *Don't stop there,* the voice prompted. *Tell him the truth.* She couldn't. Not now.

He looked at her expectantly.

"Trust issues. I know you won't intentionally hurt me, but I'm afraid."

"You were hurt this afternoon when I didn't agree with you," he said in an effort to prove his point. "But you're here now. You trusted me enough to come over tonight. Doesn't that say something to you about us?"

"I'm so confused," she whispered.

He wrapped her in his arms then hugged her tight. "We'll work through this, Diedra. Just trust God. He'll make it right."

After cleaning the kitchen, Eli asked, "Would you like to look at photo albums? I think one of them has my baby pictures." He chuckled.

"I'd love to," Diedra said, glad for an opportunity to change the subject.

"I want to see your albums, too," Eli said.

A momentary look of discomfort crossed her face. How would Eli react to the fact that her memories only focused on the last five years?

Chapter 10

They sat on the sofa, half watching a television program as they talked about their plans for the weekend. Eli studied the face he'd come to love. They'd seen each other every night this week. Though at times Diedra seemed content, he knew she struggled with something of gigantic proportions. Was he the issue? Instinct warned him not to push too hard.

"I'm glad tomorrow's Saturday," Eli said. "You have morning and afternoon sessions of shopping care, don't you?"

"Sounds as if you've memorized my brochure," Diedra teased.

"I have to if I want to see you."

She liked it that he'd taken the time to examine her business. Her shopping-care program did well. The center parents and a few others often arranged to bring their children by for a few hours while they ran errands. Diedra yawned widely. She moved from her comfortable position. "Guess that's my cue to hit the road."

"May I take you to dinner tomorrow night?" Eli asked, taking her hand in his.

Guilt was a strange thing. At times it nagged like a persistent child—always in the background no matter how hard she tried to push it away. Every day she loved Eli a little more, but she had no right. She didn't deserve his trust because she hadn't been truthful with him. And someday the old hurts could destroy everything they'd managed to build.

Diedra fought to swallow the bitterness that rose in her throat. Though she knew she had to tell Eli about her past, she found it easy to forget while in his presence. The moment became very important, and only when they were apart did she promise to do the right thing the next time she saw him.

Diedra let go of his hand then knelt on the floor and peered under the sofa, searching for her missing shoe. "Gina's picking up tomorrow's sessions so I can help Granny move. I don't know how long it will take. I hoped it wouldn't take more than two or three trips with the van."

"You two plan to move her things alone?"

"We'll manage." She tilted her head to listen as the monitors came alive with the sound of Lynnie's cries. "Your daughter's awake."

"What time did you tell Granny you'd be there?"

"Ten thirty."

"I'll help. Granny Marie can't move her things."

Diedra stopped searching for her shoe and looked up at him. A smile trembled on her lips, and Eli rewarded her with one of his own. "Do you think you should?" she asked. "Lynnie's been so sick."

"Lynnie can stay with her at your place while we pick up her belongings."

"I'll call Granny in the morning and fill her in on the plan." She looked at him. "You're sure you want to help?"

"I'm not totally against her moving in," Eli said. "Truthfully, I can't say what bothers me."

"I can't bear to see her miserable. Besides, she's afraid she's going to become a cause of disagreement in her son's marriage. I have room and can use the company. That's why I offered."

He folded her close. "I know I don't understand, but I'm trying."

Diedra lifted her hand and wiped away the tears then giggled. "You're good for me."

"I think we're good for each other."

She could only nod her agreement as he kissed her fingers before she left.

❧

"Eli is so kind," Granny said when Diedra outlined the plan to her on the phone the following morning. "Between him and Jimmy, my move should be no problem."

"Jimmy's helping?"

"My son admits he's smothered me since the accident. He promised he'd try to stop but not stop loving me. I told him I reckoned I could live with that," Granny added with a soft chuckle. "He wants me to make Thursday my weekly night for dinner and to spend every Sunday afternoon with him and the grand-children. I'm pleased he's handling it so well."

"How's Francie taking the news?"

"Who knows? She keeps to herself. I doubt that she minds I'm leaving."

"I'm sure she does. I have to go, Granny," Diedra said, quickly ending the conversation when she heard Eli calling her name. "Eli will pick you up around ten thirty. We'll go back for your things. Make sure you show him where every-thing is. Bye."

Diedra dashed out of her office to find Eli on his way upstairs with his daughter. When they got to the second floor, she reached for Lynnie, smiling at him when he relinquished his hold.

"Granny said Jimmy's going to help. She also said he's making plans for Thursday night and Sunday afternoon visits. Get moving. I'll have breakfast ready when you get back."

"But I'm starving," he protested.

"Hurry back."

She watched him go down the steps, her face breaking into a wide smile when he stopped to blow her a kiss. She had to tell him the truth soon. Otherwise she had no right to tell him she loved him.

194

Downstairs Diedra found Gina setting up for the day. "Hi, sweetie," Gina cooed to the baby. "She takes my breath away."

"She is gorgeous," Diedra agreed. Eli and Kelly had certainly created a perfect child.

What would their children have looked like? The vision of a blue-eyed, blond-haired baby filled her head and teased Diedra with its elusiveness. She pushed the image away.

"You were miles away," Gina said. "I asked why Lynnie's here."

"Eli's helping Granny move."

"He must be wild about you." At Diedra's curious look, Gina added, "Not too many people volunteered to help her move."

Diedra felt her cheeks grow warm under Gina's scrutiny. "Okay. Eli and I have been seeing each other."

Gina smiled. "I'm glad. There's something about the two of you. It's as if you both know exactly what the other one—" She stopped. "Oh, you're good for each other."

"He's a wonderful man."

"I detected an interest when he started making those daily trips by your office."

"So you told me."

Gina shrugged, lifting her hands in mock helplessness. "What can I say? I'm a romantic."

&

In the kitchen Diedra placed Lynnie in a high chair and gave her some banana slices to occupy her while she searched the refrigerator. Maybe she could convince Eli to stay for dinner. It would give him and Granny an opportunity to get better acquainted.

She cooked bacon in the microwave and placed it on a paper towel to drain while she cut up fresh fruit. Soon she had everything ready. Where were they? Maybe she should call. She picked up the phone as Granny pushed the kitchen door open.

"Good morning, Dee," she called, lingering to speak to Lynnie before coming over to hug her friend. "Eli's parking. It didn't make sense to waste a trip, so Jimmy helped him load some of the smaller boxes. I'll show him where they go."

"I promised Eli breakfast when he got back." Diedra ripped off a paper towel and dried her hands as she edged toward the back door. "I'll get him."

She stepped outside. He'd parked in the driveway and had the van door open. "Eli?"

"Look at these boxes!" he exclaimed. "And at least fifteen or twenty more are still at the house. Then there's the furniture."

She understood his surprise when she saw what they'd piled in the van on one trip. "Leave them for now. Breakfast is ready."

Eli drew her into his arms. She heard a knock on the center's window and turned to find a child standing there watching her. Diedra waved at the little girl then saw her giggle when Gina led her away from the window.

"Peeping Tom?" he asked.

She smiled. "Thomasina."

Eli laughed. "You live in a fishbowl. How am I supposed to tell you good morning?"

"Are you giving up so easily?" Diedra asked, her eyes twinkling.

"Never." He kissed her gently.

"Breakfast is ready. If I'd known Granny would change the plan, I'd have fed you before you left."

"I have a feeling Granny's going to change more than one of our plans." Eli smiled as he looped his arm around her waist.

By six o'clock Granny had settled into her new room. In between caring for Lynnie and preparing their evening meal, she had also unpacked a number of boxes.

"She's amazing," Eli whispered to Diedra when Granny insisted they stay put while she brought in the dessert. "When did she have time to cook?"

"She works rings around most people I know," Diedra told him. "I'm gasping for air when I try to keep up."

Granny set a chocolate chip pie topped with whipped cream before them. Eli inhaled his portion. "I can see why Diedra wants you for a roommate. That's the best food I've eaten in some time."

"What?" Diedra demanded playfully.

"Best food I've eaten since this morning," he amended.

"Oh, go on, Eli," Granny said. "Dee knows I'm a better cook. I taught her everything she knows."

Diedra laughed.

"Didn't you want to show Eli that new lighting system in the tunnel slide? After I do these dishes, Lynnie and I are going upstairs to watch our favorite program." She winked at Diedra and began stacking plates.

"Granny, don't. You're tired," Eli said, surprising Diedra with his concern.

"You did all the heavy work."

"We'll do the dishes later." He looked at Diedra, and she nodded.

Granny patted his shoulder. "Thanks for your help today. This old woman won't forget your kindness."

After she had gone, Eli and Diedra pulled on their jackets and stepped into the backyard.

"I see you're calling her Granny now."

"She asked me to today," Eli said.

He grew quiet as he scanned the well-kept fenced area. "You were lucky to find this much space."

"My grandparents lived here. I wish you could have met them."

"Tell me," he invited, taking her hand in his as they walked around the playground.

Diedra settled in a swing, smiling up at Eli when he gave her a push. "They were there for me when I needed them most," she whispered, the words almost lost in the wind that stirred the leaves on the trees. "They never looked for me to be different, and I loved them for that."

"What about your parents?"

She tensed. "Let's not talk about them."

Eli's hand covered Diedra's on the chain for a moment before he took the swing next to hers. Idly he pushed himself about with his foot.

"Moving takes a lot out of you." He sighed. "Jimmy's an okay guy. He seemed to be taking it pretty well. He told me the whole mess was his fault. He feels he didn't check on his mother often enough. He mentioned the accident and indicated he felt guilty about it."

She was thankful he'd changed the subject. "Granny fell and broke her hip. They didn't find her until the next day. After they operated, she stayed in the hospital for a while then went to a rehab facility for therapy. She doesn't blame him. She's just trying to get her life back."

"Maybe it's working."

"I hope so. That's her biggest concern. She doesn't want to alienate her family, but she wants to go home."

Eli twisted the swing to one side and looked at her. "That Francie's a different one. I thought she'd breathe fire for a minute when Granny pointed out the furniture pieces she planned to take."

Diedra found his comment puzzling.

"I suspect Francie's coveted them for a while, and when Granny moved in they became feature attractions in her decorating scheme."

Diedra shook her head. "I'd love to give her a piece of my mind."

"Not too much, I hope."

"Very funny," Diedra said.

"What did you have to show me?"

"You're not too bright if you can't see past that old matchmaker's way of encouraging us to spend time alone."

He laughed. "So I have support in the camp?"

"As if you need it," Diedra murmured.

Chapter 11

"I don't like the idea of your spending Thanksgiving alone," Granny repeated for the third time.

Diedra almost screamed when the subject came up again. Why was her lack of plans for the holiday causing so much concern? She retrieved the bread basket from the counter and offered Eli one of Granny's freshly baked yeast rolls. His eyes sparkled as he folded back the cloth and took out a roll.

"You're going to Jimmy's," she told Granny. "You convinced me to indulge myself in a mini-vacation. I have these fantastic plans in which I do absolutely nothing all day."

"But you'll be alone," Granny objected. "At least come for dinner."

"No," Diedra said firmly. "Jimmy and Francie's guest list is full. You go and have a good time with your family. I'm going to the nursing home in the afternoon anyway."

"I'll go with you," Granny said stubbornly.

"Please don't make a big deal of this, Granny," Diedra said.

"It doesn't make sense to me," the older woman grumbled. "Why would anyone want to spend Thanksgiving alone?"

Diedra turned her attention to her supper.

❧

While Granny was talking, Eli studied Diedra. He knew without asking that she wasn't going home for the holiday. He charged in, unsure how Diedra would react. "She won't be alone on Thanksgiving, Granny."

Both women stared at him. "I'm taking her to my house to taste the wonderful things I do with dressing. I'd tell you, but it's a secret family recipe."

A smile wreathed Granny's face. "I'm so glad. I can enjoy myself knowing neither of you will be alone."

His gaze lingered on Diedra's face. "Having her there will make a world of difference. It's Lynnie's first Thanksgiving," he said when Diedra started to object.

"Lynnie couldn't care less about the holiday," Diedra pointed out.

"You know how important family traditions are," Eli said with a grin. "Maybe we'll test the new food processor I bought. The salesperson told me I could make my own baby food. I wonder how Lynnie would like homemade turkey and dressing with a hint of cranberry sauce."

"You don't want to upset her stomach," Granny warned.

"Just joking. Her turkey and peas will come in a jar."

After dinner Granny took Lynnie upstairs while Diedra and Eli started on the dishes. She played with the suds that frothed in the sink. "Why did you tell Granny I'm spending Thursday with you?"

Thursday, Eli thought. *Not Thanksgiving. Even earlier she referred to it as a holiday, but not Thanksgiving.* "Because you are."

Frowning, she slid the plates into the sink, splashing water onto the counter. "When did I ask you to make plans for me?" she asked huffily.

"Give me one good reason why you won't come," Eli said, ignoring her angry question. He tossed the drying towel on the countertop and grabbed her soapy hands from the water, holding them tightly. "Please do me the honor of spending Thanksgiving with us. It's a difficult time for me. Mom, Dad, and Kelly always made a big deal of holidays. I've never spent a family holiday without being with family."

"You have Lynnie."

"As you said, she doesn't understand what Thanksgiving means. I want you there. Please say you'll come."

"Oh, okay. But I have to go to the nursing home in the afternoon. I always take flowers to those without families."

His eyes brimmed with tenderness. "It's a deal."

He dropped her hands, and she resumed washing the plates. "Tell me about the McKay family traditions."

Eli dabbed at his wet shirt with the drying cloth and proceeded to tell her how his family gave thanks.

෴

Thursday dawned overcast and dreary, and Diedra lay in bed considering the plans they had made. Eli would bring the brightness into her day. He would make her laugh and remind her of the things for which she should thank God. She threw back the covers.

He arrived early so they could go over to his church to package and deliver plates of food to shut-ins. They returned home shortly after eleven, just as Jimmy and Granny were leaving. After waving good-bye, they placed Lynnie in the playpen and began to transfer the cut flowers from the house.

"It looks like a flower garden out there," Eli said when he returned for another load. He lifted one of the remaining two boxes and tried to still the clatter of glass vases.

"This is it," Diedra said, taking the box of bows.

"There's another one over there."

"Granny's contribution to our dinner," Diedra said. "Sweet potato casserole and your favorite pie."

"Okay!"

Diedra laughed when he set the box of vases down and took the food first.

At his house Eli parked in the garage and began unloading boxes while Diedra removed Lynnie from her seat.

Eli lifted the two buckets of fresh-cut flowers she had purchased. "Why not have the florist deliver them?"

"I enjoy making them for each person."

"To brighten otherwise lonely lives. You're one special lady."

"Glad you think so," she murmured.

After she settled Lynnie in the nursery, Diedra found Eli watching the parade on a small television mounted under the kitchen cabinets.

"That isn't getting our dinner cooked."

Eli snared her hand, pulling her closer and resting his chin on her shoulder. His arms about her waist secured her into place. Diedra started giggling when he burst into song about loving parades. By the time he'd finished his emphatic rendition of the tune, her sides ached with laughter.

"I'd never have guessed," Diedra said as she watched the floats roll by the television cameras. Several minutes later she broke away and examined the items on the center island. She removed a peeler from the drawer and started working on the potatoes.

"I bought a turkey breast," Eli said as he stood and walked over to the oven door. "They don't make small birds."

"Maybe the growers think holidays are for big families," Diedra suggested.

"Only because they haven't realized there's something to be said for twosomes," he said, lifting his brows.

Diedra grinned. She finished peeling the potatoes and filled the bowl with cold water. "I'll go set the table."

"Do that. And make it cozy. I want my hostess beside me."

In the dining room Diedra reached for the fall centerpiece on the table and stopped when she read her name on a card tucked among the flowers. Her trembling fingers snapped open the sealed envelope. "With love on our first Thanksgiving."

Love. His thoughtful gifts always surprised her. Would they share another day like today? A Christmas? She had to tell him.

Diedra opened the antique buffet drawer and removed beautiful gold linen and hand-crocheted white tablecloths. After smoothing them over the table, she laid out the china and heirloom silver, all the while thinking of the McKay family traditions Eli had told her about.

Every family had them. At exactly seven o'clock on Thanksgiving Day, her parents sat down to their goose, never turkey. The twelve places at the Wynne table seated people who wouldn't dare refuse a Wynne family invitation.

As a child she had made an appearance before going to the kitchen to eat her meal with the staff. The years passed, and she joined the group at the dinner table; when she married, her parents welcomed Benjamin without reservation. Diedra shook her head as thoughts of Benjamin intruded. Enough of that.

One final adjustment to the table linen and she made another decision. Diedra hurried to the nursery and looked through Lynnie's closet. She pulled out the baby's prettiest dress—pale pink with a lacy froth of ruffles flowing from its waist. She located matching lace-trimmed socks and tiny black patent leather shoes. Perfect.

"Diedra?" Eli called from the hallway. "Where are you?"

"In here."

He found her in Lynnie's room laying out clothes for the baby. "She'll look beautiful." He glanced down at his jeans and flannel shirt. "Something wrong with these?"

"We're dining formally," Diedra said as she tucked the baby's socks into her shoes.

"And you?" Eli asked, his gaze lingering on her jeans and sweater.

"I'm going home to change into another outfit. You said you always dressed for dinner. Do you have a camera? I can bring mine so we can get a picture of you and Lynnie for the family album."

Her words brought back bittersweet memories of the arguments with his mother when she insisted they dress for dinner. Not that he or his dad ever won. But their time together always ended up being warm and inviting, a time of love. Eli wished they were here to meet Diedra.

"But we'll have to change before we go out again," Eli argued good-naturedly.

"A well-dressed group will never be turned away from anywhere."

"You won't be gone long, will you?"

She smiled. "No, I already know what I want. I can be back in thirty minutes."

"Okay," he agreed reluctantly. "Should I do anything else while you're gone?"

"We'll be eating at three. So you can work on dinner and have a sandwich to tide you over. If that doesn't keep you busy, start thinking about flower arrangements."

"Yes, ma'am, General Pierce!" Eli said, snapping his sneakers together and saluting her.

As Diedra started down the hallway, Eli dangled the car keys from his finger. "You'll need these."

Later that afternoon, they drove to the nursing home. Diedra considered Eli very handsome in his black suit. She wore a tobacco brown suit with a leaf-print blouse. All three of them brought smiles to a number of faces as they distributed flowers and visited with each person.

"How much longer?" Eli whispered. Lynnie had fallen asleep, and the flower supply on the cart had dwindled to three.

"We're finished. Those are for the nursing stations. Tired?"

"Sort of. It's been a busy Thanksgiving."

"Ready to get home to your game?"

"And a snack."

Diedra winked. "I think there's a sliver of pie left."

At the house Diedra changed Lynnie into a sleeper then went to the kitchen to make a snack.

In the sunroom Eli relaxed on the sofa. Diedra slid the tray of food onto the coffee table and smiled at him. "You look comfortable."

He pulled her down to sit on the sofa next to him then reached for a sandwich with his free hand. "Like football?"

"I never watch the game," Diedra admitted.

Eli spent several minutes explaining the plays. The conversation trailed off, and Diedra observed him while he watched the game. She smiled when he alternately cheered for and criticized the players, coaches, and referees.

At halftime Eli turned to Diedra. "When did you start visiting nursing homes?"

"My grandparents took me the first Thanksgiving I spent with them. Initially I didn't want to go. I couldn't imagine what I had in common with strangers until an elderly man shook my hand and told me how privileged he was to have met me. I understood then how important it was to them, and now I go whenever I can find the time."

"How can you be so selfless?"

"I get a lot of joy out of making them happy."

"I knew that. You always get joy from doing for others."

❧

Eli held her hand as he thought of how little he'd given in his lifetime. Once he'd visited the children's ward at the hospital. He'd injured himself in a crash; his doctor suggested he might be able to brighten the spirits of a few of the long-term patients who were also race fans. He'd given his share of charitable contributions, but that hadn't been as rewarding as giving of himself today. Besides, if it made Diedra happy, he'd invite the entire retirement home to Christmas dinner. "Dee?"

"Yes?" She looked at him through blinking eyelids.

"Sorry. You're tired."

"Just lazy," Diedra said. "I always get that way when I'm full and content."

"You have tomorrow off. What do you say to driving to the mountains for the day to pick out Christmas trees?"

"That's a long ride for a tree."

"Not just trees. I promise you some of the best panoramic views you've ever seen. Plus some old family friends live up there, and we could visit them. What do you think?" Eli breathed in the faint floral scent of her perfume.

"Oh, why not?" she said finally. "What will we do with the turkey?"

"Make sandwiches?"

Eli drove up the next morning in a borrowed SUV. "We need it for the trees," he said, indicating the luggage rack on top.

They were on their way by seven thirty, stopped at a drive-through for breakfast, then headed for the mountains.

The radio played softly, and conversation came and went as they traveled the miles. Eli took the scenic route, and Diedra enjoyed the views that seemed to go on forever. At times she could have stuck out her hand and touched the mountainside. "It's incredible."

"I want to bring you back next year in late September, early October," Eli said. "There's something spectacular about majestic mountains with a backdrop of colorful trees—palettes of orange, rust, red, gold, and green. We can even do the tourist things if you want."

Diedra recalled memories from her childhood. She'd been ten or so when her grandparents brought her to the mountains. She had memories of Tweetsie Railroad and the train robbers, the elevator up through the mountains, and the chairlift at Maggie Valley. "What did you plan for today?"

"Nothing strenuous. I talked to the Kings after you left last night, and they insisted we come for lunch. After that we'll visit the tree farm."

"Sounds wonderful," Diedra said.

"I thought you would appreciate it. We have Lynnie, but I don't think she'll be as demanding as a center full of kids."

"Compared to my usual number, she's a day in the park. I hope everything's okay at the center."

"No work talk allowed," Eli said, reaching for the radio as the hourly news came on. The reporter covered the world and daily news before mentioning a local murder trial. He highlighted the testimony of the victim's sister, who said the police had documented the husband's abuse numerous times.

Diedra's heart pounded. She could have been that victim, but she would have had no one to testify in her defense.

"I don't understand why women tolerate that," Eli said as he lowered the volume.

"Mostly because they don't feel they have a choice."

"But there's so much help," he said. "Family. The police. Domestic violence shelters."

"It's not always enough."

He grimaced. "I don't ever want to see Lynnie in that sort of situation. I'd probably kill the man with my bare hands."

"Then make sure she develops tons of self-confidence and tell her she should never take abuse from any man."

Aware of his gaze on her, Diedra grabbed her purse and pretended to look for something, finally settling on a roll of breath mints. She offered him one then carefully peeled away the paper to take the next mint for herself.

"I'm sure she'll be very confident, since I'm not letting her date until she's thirty," Eli said, chuckling.

Diedra's smile waned as she considered her own confidence level when she met Benjamin. A recent college graduate, she'd been ready to conquer the world. She couldn't remember when fear had taken over—maybe when she discovered no one believed her husband was capable of cruelty.

Overwhelming sadness filled her. Another right time and she hadn't told him. Knowing she hadn't trusted him enough to share the truth would probably infuriate Eli.

"Are you still with me?" he asked, turning onto the driveway that led to the Kings' home.

Diedra brought her thoughts back to the present. The past was not going to ruin their day. "Tell me about your friends."

"They're good people. They were my parents' friends." Eli pulled into a graveled area and parked the car. "I used to come up here often, but I haven't been for a long time. I couldn't make myself come."

"Why not?"

"My mom loved the mountains. We came here for three weeks every summer. That's how my parents met the Kings. They honeymooned in a cabin just down the road from their place."

Diedra slipped a hand over Eli's. "I'm sorry. I can understand why your mom loved this area. It's beautiful."

She opened the car door and stepped out. Diedra heard the rush of water nearby. "It sounds as if there's a stream."

Eli stood and stretched. "There isn't much to it right now, but come spring, when the snow melts, it overflows its banks."

Diedra admired the rustic log cabin. "What a beautiful home."

"Wait until you see inside."

Diedra unfastened Lynnie from her car seat and joined Eli as they walked toward the house. The door swung open, and an elderly couple stepped onto the wraparound porch.

"Eli," the woman said, smiling. "We're so glad you're here."

He hugged them both. "Mr. and Mrs. King, this is my friend, Diedra Pierce." He reached for the baby. "And my daughter, Lynnie."

"We're so glad you could come," Mrs. King told Diedra before her gaze focused on the baby. "Oh, Tom, look at her. Your parents would be so proud, Eli."

Lynnie started to whimper.

"Time for a bottle," Eli said.

"Then come on in," Mr. King said. "Let's not keep the little lady waiting."

Within minutes Diedra sat holding the baby and watching as Lynnie's tiny bud of a mouth worked greedily to assuage her hunger.

She couldn't imagine a homier environment. The stone fireplace occupied one full wall, the crackling logs warding off the chill of the day. Comfortable leather furniture suited the area, as did the large Christmas tree that stood in the corner.

"Your home is beautiful," she told Mrs. King after accepting the cup of coffee. "I love your tree."

"Thank you. We decorated it last night." She smiled at her husband as she joined him on the sofa. "How did you and Eli meet?"

"Lynnie comes to my day care center."

"I could tell she's very comfortable with you," Mrs. King said. "So, Eli, tell us what's been going on with you."

"Lynnie keeps me busy."

"How's your work?" Mr. King asked.

"Doing well." Eli sipped his coffee and set the mug back on the wooden coffee table. "It's been hectic this year. It's good to get away for a day."

"You have a standing invitation to visit anytime you like," the older man said.

"I miss coming up here. Seeing the area today brought back so many good memories."

The conversation drifted into the past years, and Diedra enjoyed hearing about Eli's escapades as a young boy. "He was a handful," Mrs. King told Diedra. "His parents never knew what he'd do next." She glanced at Eli. "Do you remember the time you jumped off the side of the barn?"

"Don't remind me. I wore that cast for eight weeks."

A timer buzzed in the kitchen. "Lunch is ready," Mrs. King said. "Hope you don't mind turkey potpie."

"Not at all." Diedra glanced at Eli and smiled. "We had the same dilemma with leftover turkey yesterday. We have sandwiches in a cooler in the car."

"I prefer turkey potpie any day," Eli said.

The meal consisted of a combination of Thanksgiving leftovers along with the hot dish and a salad.

"You're a wonderful cook," Diedra said after finishing the last bite of her slice of red velvet cake. "I need exercise."

"I promised Dee a walk along your trails," Eli said.

"Good idea. Why don't you leave Lynnie here with us? Let her finish her nap."

Eli glanced at Diedra.

"We'll help you clean up first," Diedra said.

"Nonsense. I'm going to load all this into the dishwasher."

"I'll get my coat from the car."

They headed into the woods, following the trail that led up to a roaring waterfall. Diedra stopped at every turn to gaze at the beautiful scenery. She enjoyed the peace and quiet most of all. The wind rustled in the trees and leaves. The same leaves crunched underneath their feet, until they spotted some wildlife and tried to be still. It didn't take long for the deer to catch their scent and dart away.

Eli wrapped an arm around her shoulders, and they continued to walk in comfortable silence. After a while he glanced at his watch. "We'd better head back. Time to buy the Christmas trees."

The Kings directed them to their favorite tree farm, and after a flurry of hugs and good-byes, they were soon on their way.

They found the tree farm easily and spent the next couple of hours searching for the perfect tree. Every time they thought they'd found one, another more just-right tree caught their attention.

"This is it," Diedra said, pointing to the tree she wanted.

"Isn't this the first one you liked so much?" Eli asked.

Diedra giggled. "Probably. I think we've been wandering in circles for too long."

They selected the four trees they wanted and watched as the man felled each one, running them through a machine that secured them in netting.

She stood to the side with Lynnie as the men struggled to hoist them atop the SUV. Just when she decided it was an impossible task, Eli flashed her a happy grin and fastened the rope the man tossed over the top of the vehicle. "Didn't think we could do it, did you?"

"I never doubted you for a minute," she teased.

They stopped at a picnic area on the way home and found a table a short distance from the vehicle. Lynnie drained her bottle in record time and drifted off to sleep.

The view was breathtaking. "The fog looks like smoke over the mountains," Diedra said.

"Probably why they call them the Great Smoky Mountains."

Diedra tapped his arm playfully and spread out the sandwiches, chips, and veggies he'd packed in the cooler.

"Good sandwich," Eli said afterward, balling up the wrappers and tossing them into a nearby trash can.

Diedra nodded. "I didn't think I could eat another bite after that lunch Mrs. King served," Diedra told him.

"But all that walking and tree shopping gave you an appetite?"

"I suppose so. I've enjoyed myself today."

He took her hand in his. "Me, too. I hope we can do this again."

Diedra found herself almost too tired to sleep when Eli dropped her off at home later that night. She tossed and turned restlessly and finally dozed off. A nightmare woke her in the early hours of the morning. She pulled on her robe and went downstairs to make a cup of cocoa.

The dream lingered in her head, and she felt guilty. Yesterday had been wonderful. She couldn't remember a nicer holiday, and Eli deserved the credit. Most women spent their entire lives looking for Mr. Right, the perfect man. In her case she had fallen at his feet that first meeting.

Pity she couldn't return the favor for Eli. In her dream Diedra had revealed the truth to him and he told her it was over. Not because of what she'd shared but because he hated deceit. Because she hadn't believed in him. Even thinking of the dream sent cold shivers down her spine.

She sat at the table and bowed her head. *Dear God, help me. I'm wrong to keep secrets from the man I love because I'm afraid. Give me the words to tell him what I should have from the beginning.*

Chapter 12

As Diedra listened to the drone of the television, she realized loneliness had not been a factor in her life lately. Since she'd started dating Eli and Granny had moved in, at times she longed for a few minutes to herself.

Granny's presence left little time for her and Eli to be alone, but the older woman also made certain Diedra didn't stay locked in the confines of her decision not to become involved again. She often babysat so they could go on dates.

Ever since their argument about Granny's move, Eli had kept his opinions on the subject to himself. When Diedra made excuses to stay home with Granny, his face revealed his disappointment, but he didn't say a word.

At first he'd picked up Lynnie from the day care center and gone home. Then after a few nights they drifted into a pattern of eating together. Eli usually refused at first but gave in to Granny's argument that he had to eat anyway. Afterward he would help with the dishes, and then they would join Granny in the upstairs sitting room.

Eli had even taken to attending church with them on Sundays. He placed Lynnie in the nursery then sat with them in the sanctuary.

His spiritual knowledge surprised Diedra more than once when Granny mentioned something from the sermon and Eli offered the view of a man who had read his Bible more than a few times.

Wanting things to be perfect for everyone placed Diedra in an impossible situation. She justified her actions, telling herself she deserved happiness for just a little longer. But the guilt increased daily, and she knew she had to tell Eli the truth.

She snuggled under the chenille afghan and watched the Christmas tree lights twinkle. She was thankful her staff had decorated the big tree downstairs, and Eli's staff had taken care of the one at his business. They had decorated the one at his house Tuesday night, and Granny had helped with this one last night. Eli insisted on themes, and they combed through their combined decorations to come up with sufficient ideas to make the trees original.

Not only had they finished the trees, but they also had hung garland and wreaths and placed other Christmas mementos around the living room. Eli's favorite was an old mechanical figure that had belonged to Diedra's grandfather. He was like a child crying, "Do it again," when she showed him how it worked.

She'd enjoyed herself immensely until the conversation shifted to families.

"Have you finished your shopping?" Granny asked as she picked up the tangled lights Eli had tossed down in despair.

Eli shook his head. "Who has time?" The lights flashed on as he tested the last bulb in another strand.

"Not me," Diedra agreed.

"Funny how certain things become less important as you get older," Eli said. "A few years ago I'd never have dreamed I'd be comfortable with having no plans for every evening of the week. You learn family's more important than good times."

Diedra couldn't hold back the grief that overwhelmed her every time she thought about the natural progression of the conversation. A suffocating sensation tightened her throat, and she pushed up the barriers that shut everyone out when it came her time to share.

Transported back in time, Diedra sat before her father's desk, trying to make him understand she needed his help.

"Things like this don't happen to women in your social status," James Wynne argued. "Do you have any idea how these lies will hurt Benjamin's reputation? No respectable firm would tolerate the bad publicity."

"I'm not lying, Daddy!" she had cried out.

"Go home, Diedra. You're a lucky woman to have such a successful husband."

Shame had kept her from confiding in others. She had no friends. Benjamin had long since made sure of that. The people they associated with as a couple would have listened only to gossip about the sordid details.

Given Benjamin's legal background, Diedra convinced herself the police would never believe her over him. Alone in her struggle, she feared the monster she'd married.

Two men had hurt her: the husband who abused, ridiculed, and made her feel worthless and the father who scolded and treated her like a little girl. At least she understood her father's reasoning.

Publicity had always been her parents' greatest horror. Nothing could defile the Wynne family name, the family honor, but in the end Diedra won.

"Mother expects to inherit the house," Diedra had protested when her grandparents told her their plans.

"Elizabeth sees this house only as prime real estate. She doesn't need it the way you do," her grandfather said. "It's our choice, Dee. Make two old people happy."

After weeks of agonizing she realized she had no choice but to agree. Diedra watched as both signed over their home to her in their lawyer's office. Before their deaths her grandparents spent a great deal of time helping her make and carry out plans for the center.

Elizabeth Wynne attended her mother's funeral then waited for the lawyer to read the will. She accused Diedra of turning her parents against her then refused to listen to any reply and returned to California. They had not spoken since.

Sometimes fear of becoming like her parents gnawed at Diedra, and she wished she were the child of more loving and forgiving parents. Diedra knew her mother had never been content with her lot in life and that she couldn't wait to get away from her parents' strict upbringing and do things her way.

James Wynne's money allowed her mother to live the life she coveted, and soon a wide chasm spread between her mother and her grandparents. Diedra suspected her mother sometimes felt guilty over the way she treated them but eased her conscience by sending them expensive gifts. Diedra had witnessed their sadness when their daughter didn't visit.

The door chimes echoed throughout the house. Diedra threw the afghan aside and fumbled for her bedroom shoes.

"I'm coming," she called when the chimes started up again the moment her foot touched the varnished floorboards of the hallway.

One glance through the side window and she opened the door quickly.

"Eli? Janice said you were working."

Diedra had offered to keep Lynnie earlier when he called to tell her Janice would pick up the baby. At first she'd been offended, but after giving the matter more consideration, she realized Eli was giving her a break.

"I have been. Sort of," he admitted with a sheepish grin.

"If you came for supper, Granny's out."

He looked relieved. "Good. Honestly, Dee—I've got to skip some of those meals of hers or buy new clothes."

"I've gained five pounds since she moved in."

"I bought you something," he said, placing a small box in her hand.

She untied the ribbon and opened the box to reveal four of her favorite chocolates. Surprised, Diedra looked at him. "How did you know?"

"I asked Granny."

"You make me feel so special."

"You sound as if no one ever did anything special for you."

Diedra chewed her lower lip and stole a look at him.

"Why can't you tell me about your past, Dee?"

She knew her inability to share this with him bothered Eli. A mute appeal touched Diedra's face. "Please don't spoil my evening."

"I want to get to know you."

Trapped in her own lie, Diedra knew Eli could never know the person she had been. He would never respect that woman.

Eli hugged her close, and some of the tension drained from her. He couldn't understand her feelings. Sometimes even she couldn't. She wanted to love her parents again. She did love them. She simply didn't trust them.

Eli released her. "I meant it when I said I want to know you, Dee. Show me what you looked like as a little girl. Tell me your favorite things. What was your best friend's name? What kind of grades did you make? What are your hopes and dreams?"

Diedra's misgivings increased with each word. She didn't want to remember Diedra Wynne. And she'd spent years trying to forget when she was Mrs. Benjamin Pierce. In her haste to change the subject, Diedra fumbled with the little box. "Time for dessert."

The amaretto filling of the chocolate candy oozed over her fingers as Diedra took a bite then gave him the remainder.

She sighed. "Hmm. Addictive."

"I couldn't concentrate tonight," he said. "I need to talk to you."

She looked at him curiously. "About what?"

He seemed very uncomfortable.

"I care a great deal about you, and I think you care for me as well."

"You know I do. What's wrong, Eli?" Was he experiencing doubts?

He looked at her. "Today is the first anniversary of Kelly's death. It's been difficult. I keep thinking about her."

"We don't forget those we love. We just pick up and go on with our lives because that's expected of us."

Eli studied her. "You understand. You lost your husband."

Her relationship with Benjamin had never resembled Eli's marriage. She pushed the thought away and considered what she could say to comfort him. The usual things—how it gets easier with time, with each passing year. She paused as the thought struck her. "You said Kelly's been dead a year. How can that be? Lynnie's only ten months old."

"Can we go into your office? There's something I feel you should know."

Diedra's eyes closed. *Not another man with a secret. Please, God, not Eli, too.* She had already loved one man who had hidden something terrible. Her apprehension grew at his solemn expression.

She led the way and sat in one of the blue leather chairs. Eli sat in the other one.

"Lynnie is our biological child," he began, obviously ill at ease. "But a surrogate brought our baby into the world."

Her eyes widened in astonishment. "A surrogate?"

"Yes," he said. "My wife wasn't able to carry a child, so the doctor took our biological child—our fertilized egg—and implanted it into another woman who carried it on our behalf."

His revelation threw her thought processes into a tailspin. "You paid someone to give birth to your child? Why, Eli?" she asked when he nodded.

"Did you ever watch someone grieving to death?"

Diedra thought of the times she'd done exactly that. She'd focused on what she'd lost instead of thanking God for what she'd gained.

"After she lost our second baby, Kelly slipped into a deep depression. She cried all the time. She barely ate. I watched her waste away. It killed me to have her want a child so badly. I suggested adoption, but she wouldn't consider that. She insisted I needed a son to carry on the family name.

"I argued that a child of the heart would serve the same purpose, but she wouldn't listen. This went on for months. She consulted doctors. She read everything she could find on the subject. Our marriage stopped being about us and became about having children. She was miserable. I was miserable.

"Then she told me she wanted a divorce. She'd decided that if she couldn't give me children she would free me to find someone who could. I told her she was being ridiculous. That having a child wasn't that important."

Diedra gasped.

"Not very understanding, I know," he admitted. "But I was at the end of my rope. I refused to consider divorce. I told her I would never marry again if she left me and she would be hurting us both unnecessarily. Things settled down for a while after that. Then she came up with the surrogate idea. She said we could have a biological child with another woman's help.

"Surrogacy was one of those things other people tried. But the more Kelly talked, the more I realized I couldn't come up with one reason to say no. Our decision wouldn't hurt anyone. The young woman liked being a surrogate. I weighed losing my wife against surrogacy and decided losing Kelly would be far worse. In the end it all came down to making Kelly happy."

"And was she happy?" Diedra asked.

"Ecstatic. Once our surrogate let us know we were expecting, Kelly was thrilled. She started planning the nursery right away. While I raced cars, she planned. We never passed a baby store that she didn't have to go in. I knew my life was about to change in a big way when she brought up buying a house and settling down.

"She'd stuck with me through the good and bad, so I knew it was my turn to show her support."

Diedra struggled with his revelation. She wanted to understand. "It never bothered you?"

"I think we blocked the reality and lived in the fantasy," Eli told her. "A couple of months after Lynnie was on the way, God began to work in our lives. We attended the funeral of a dear friend, and the message moved us both to repent that same day. Reality hit us hard, and we questioned whether we'd done the right thing."

"Lots of people make bad decisions before becoming Christians."

"I won't believe Lynnie is a mistake," Eli said.

"That's not what I meant," Diedra said. "I believe God knows the paths our lives will take. I believe that path often leads us to Him. I know I made more than one unguided choice of my own."

Eli took Diedra's hands in his. "Maybe so. But right or wrong, every time I see my wife in our child, I experience only joy. We joined a church and went to our pastor for counseling. He agreed we'd tampered in God's work, but he told us Jesus had paid the price for our sins and His grace would get us through.

"We couldn't undo what we'd already done. At that point we decided to raise our child in a godly home. A home filled with love. And then Kelly was killed by a speeding car."

Diedra understood his agony.

"God's strength was all that kept me going. That and the fact that I would be a father in a very short time. Kelly never got the opportunity to mother our child. The true irony is that despite her insistence I needed a male heir, we had a daughter. I've grieved for Kelly. I still do, but I have a responsibility to love and care for my child. I don't believe God makes mistakes. He brought Lynnie into this world as a healthy baby. And even when I have doubts, I can't take my eyes off God's promises. Lynnie is a precious gift. I don't know what the future holds, but I know God will be by my side. I want to prove myself worthy of the task He's set before me. I want to be the best father possible."

"You are one of the best I've ever known," Diedra said.

He squeezed her hand. "Do you want children, Diedra?"

She swallowed the lump in her throat. "I love children, and if possible I'd like a couple of my own."

Tell him the truth. Give him the chance to decide whether he wants to continue the relationship. Tell him.

"Eli—" Diedra began, desperation overcoming her at the thought of losing him. She couldn't. She watched the play of emotions on his face.

"You know what I think about? How Lynnie will feel when she learns the truth. Will she hate me for what we did?"

"Lynnie will ask questions. Your daughter loves you. There's no way she's going to stop."

"You stopped loving your parents," he pointed out.

Diedra's smile faded. "I love them. I need to forgive them for not supporting me at a time in my life when I needed them most."

"Oh, Dee," Eli said, drawing her to him.

She held on to Eli. How easily he and Lynnie had become part of her world. Her life would be miserable without them.

"Does knowing this make a difference to you?" he asked, tilting her face back to see her expression. "I understand you could find it morally offensive."

"Are you asking me to pass judgment on what you did?"

"People sometimes hold the circumstances of our birth against us," Eli said. "I couldn't bear it if the woman I cared for did that to my child."

Diedra stared at him. "I'd never do that to any child. Lynnie's a wonderful little girl. You're blessed to have her."

His relief was obvious. "Thank you. I didn't tell you this to pressure you into anything. You deserve to know before things go any further. Of course, I'm telling you this in the strictest confidence."

"I'd never share this with anyone," Diedra promised. She certainly knew how gossip could affect lives.

"I'd better go. It's getting late."

She followed Eli to the front porch. The enormity of what had just transpired hit Diedra like a ton of bricks. Eli trusted her with a secret. He trusted her with the truth, and she would never betray that trust.

God didn't make mistakes. Lynnie existed today because He intended her to be there. Diedra couldn't doubt that.

An even stronger realization hit her. Eli was serious about their relationship. He never would have told her this if he didn't have hopes for the future. Eli showed his love to her over and over again, while she couldn't even say the words.

She loved him. But did she have the right?

Long after Eli had gone, Diedra agonized over what he'd told her. Knowing he and Kelly had wanted a child badly enough to go the surrogate route reinforced how impossible it was for her to commit to a future with Eli. He'd asked if she wanted kids. As much as she loved them, she knew he wanted more children. Why hadn't she told him the truth?

Diedra fully identified with Kelly—the agony she must have experienced at not being able to give birth to her own child. The agony Diedra suffered at the thought of never being able to do the same. Diedra clutched her arms around her waist, and the tears began to fall. It hurt. So much.

She wasn't being fair to Eli. "Oh, God, help me!" she cried, seeking comfort from the One who loved her even when she couldn't love herself.

Chapter 13

A night spent agonizing over Eli's truth didn't make things any better the next day. The weekend had been wonderful, but a knot formed in her stomach when Gina came back to work on Monday morning wearing a diamond. She'd turned in her resignation, explaining she wanted to move to Virginia Beach to be closer to her fiancé.

While happy for Gina, her friend as well as her favorite staff member, Diedra knew it would take her a long time to find someone who worked with the babies so well. Gina planned to stay long enough to train the new employee for the first two weeks. Of course, that depended on Diedra's choosing from among the many applicants.

"Thank you, Mrs. Adams." She checked the name on the application. "I'll be making my decision within the next week."

After the woman left, Diedra sighed and placed the most recent response to her employment ad in her in-basket.

As if Gina's leaving wasn't enough, two staff members succumbed to a stomach virus, and Diedra had to work in their classrooms. Long days with the children and evenings of decorating for Christmas exhausted Diedra. She'd hoped to get to bed early the previous evening, but Eli's news had left her tossing and turning through the night.

Granny had plans to stay with her grandchildren, and Janice had invited Diedra and Eli over for family night. Diedra had agreed earlier in the week, but with so much happening, she wished she could stay home. It was too late to change the plans now. Eli would pick her up at six thirty.

Diedra had just managed to shower and dress when the doorbell rang. She hurried downstairs and greeted Eli and Lynnie. Eli relinquished the baby to her, and Lynnie smiled and cooed at Diedra.

Eli's bright smile told her he was happy.

"She loves you," he said. "And I do, too."

Diedra's heart began to pound so hard she could scarcely breathe. "You what?"

"I said I love you."

Her gaze fixed on the collar of his sport shirt. "Eli?"

"Is that all you can say?" he teased. "It's not every day a man says he loves you, is it?"

Diedra swallowed hard and smiled faintly. "No, it isn't."

215

She didn't know what to do. One part of her wanted to return his love and forget the past. Another part argued that the past would always rear its ugly head to spoil the present and future.

How would Eli feel about the truth? She'd learned long ago that hers wasn't a pleasant story, and she had witnessed the changed attitudes of people who knew. Would he lose all respect for her? Could she handle it if he did?

"We'd better go, or we'll be late," she said, seeing his expression grow sad when she didn't return his sentiment.

Diedra handed Lynnie back to Eli and reached for her coat on the hall tree. He held it with his free hand as she slipped her arm inside.

At the car Eli strapped Lynnie into her car seat then slipped behind the wheel. He started the engine, hitting the heat control. "It's chilly out tonight."

Cold air shot out of the vents, and Diedra shivered.

"Sorry," he said, turning it off. "I thought it would still be warm from the drive over."

Diedra buttoned her coat and reached into the pockets for her gloves. "Cold weather is definitely not my favorite. I asked Janice if I could bring something, but she said no."

"I picked up a gift basket. She's excited that we're coming over," Eli said as he maneuvered into traffic.

"I really like Janice. I've met her husband a time or two when he picked up the children. He seems very nice."

"They make a great couple," Eli agreed.

A few minutes later he parked behind Janice's green van. The Gores welcomed them inside, and Davey whisked Diedra away to show her their Christmas decorations.

A magnificent live tree stood in the living room and another in the family room. Davey fell to his knees and turned on the train that was spread out under the tree. They spent a couple of minutes playing engineer before he dragged her to his room. A small tree decorated in cartoon characters sat in his window seat. Diedra admired the nativity scene on Davey's nightstand.

"The baby Jesus was born at Christmas," Davey told her, picking up each piece of the set to tell her about it. "Kaylie has a tree, too." He caught her hand and led her to his sister's bedroom where Diedra viewed yet another small tree.

"Everything is beautiful," she said to Janice, who had come to tell them the pizza had arrived. "When did you find time to put up four trees?"

"Don't tell anyone," Janice said, "but we store the little trees already decorated. Remove the bag and fluff them out—instant tree."

Diedra laughed. "Wish I could figure out how to do that with the bigger varieties. I threaten to buy one of those prelighted artificial trees every year, but I never do."

"Me, too. David insists the kids would be upset, but I know who doesn't want an artificial tree. He goes on and on about the scent. Never mind the mess they make. Just so long as they smell good." They laughed together as they walked into the dining room.

"There you are," Eli called to Diedra. "I thought you'd gotten lost."

"Davey had lots to show me."

Janice smiled at that. "He loves Ms. Dee."

"I love him, too."

She sat beside Eli, and he leaned over and whispered, "I wouldn't mind hearing you say those words to me."

Davey dragged a chair over and placed it between them, and Eli said no more about it.

The conversation flowed as they ate pizza and drank soda. Eli told them about their day trip to the mountains, and Janice and David talked about their visits to both sets of grandparents.

Diedra helped Janice clean up while Eli and David took Lynnie and Kaylie into the family room. Janice put the leftover pizza into the other box and closed it. "I'm glad you came with Eli."

"I'm enjoying myself."

"I hope we can do this more often. I've never seen Eli so happy."

Diedra was suddenly struck by the feeling that Janice could soon see him miserable again. She didn't want her to be upset with her. "What if it doesn't work out?" Diedra asked finally.

"Do you think it won't?" Janice pulled out a chair and sat down. "Let's talk about it."

"I don't really see how we can make this work," Diedra said.

"You seem happy together."

Diedra wrung her hands in her lap, glad the wooden tabletop hid her action. "I've been keeping things from Eli. Things I should have told him. I've fought my conscience for weeks. Then tonight he said he loved me. I've been so unfair to him."

"Don't you love him?"

"If only it were that simple. I care a great deal for Eli, but I find it very difficult to trust. I'm afraid."

"God didn't give us a sense of fear, Diedra."

"I know. Granny tells me the same thing. In my heart I know if my secrets hurt Eli, I've wronged him. How can I expect him to forgive me when I've let this go on far too long?"

"Why haven't you told him before?" Janice asked curiously.

"I've meant to. But every time an opportunity comes, fear strangles me, and I clam up. I've hinted at some things, but I haven't told him the truth."

"You need to open up to Eli. Tell him what you're holding back and take it from there. You can't say how he'll react until he knows. Because he loves you, I'd be willing to say he'll be able to deal with the truth."

"I'm such a coward."

Janice patted her hand. "Falling in love gives us a different perspective. We stop thinking of ourselves and consider how our behavior affects others. You're definitely doing that. David and I learned early on that communication is key."

David stuck his head in the kitchen door and smiled. "Hey, what's keeping you two?"

"We'll be right there," Janice said then turned back to Diedra after he had left. "I'll pray for you. Trust God to give you strength to do what's right."

The men had already set up the game table. Lynnie crawled around the family room while Kaylie watched and clapped her hands. When Diedra sat down, Lynnie crawled over and pulled herself up against her legs.

"Well, aren't you a smart girl?" Diedra said, smiling when she lifted the baby into her lap.

"She's been doing that for a few days now," Eli said. "She's testing her sea legs, holding on to the sofa and coffee table."

Diedra glanced at Janice. "I've been watching Kaylie in the nursery. I pray she takes her first steps at home."

Janice patted her hand. "Don't worry about it. Tell Gina to record the specifics. And give me a call, of course. I'll check on the video monitoring."

"Gina turned in her resignation this week. She's moving to Virginia Beach to marry her soldier."

"I'm happy for her," Janice said, "but sad for us. She's excellent with the kids. Are you giving her a bridal shower?"

"We should."

"Let me know how I can help."

"Are we going to play or talk weddings?" David asked and winked at his wife.

"Diedra and I will play you and Eli," Janice told her husband. "Prepare to lose."

And win they did. Diedra had never been good at games, but Janice made up the deficit.

"We give up!" Eli exclaimed when the women won the fifth game in a row.

"You don't want to defend your manhood?" Janice countered with a wide grin.

Eli glanced at his daughter, who was sleeping in Diedra's arms. "It's past Lynnie's bedtime."

Kaylie had fallen asleep on a cushion on the floor, and Davey scooted his toy cars around the room while a children's video played on the television.

"They'll have to defend it another time," Diedra said. "Tomorrow's a workday."

"You'll have to be my partner again," Janice told her, smiling. "I never win against these guys."

❧

Eli arrived on time the following morning. His lighthearted mood caused Diedra to wonder if admitting her feelings for him would help her feel the same kind of joy. Or was it the relief he felt after revealing the truth about Lynnie? "I guess I'd better go," he said after a few minutes of reminiscing about the previous night. "Take care of my baby girl."

"I always do. Have a good day."

Diedra helped in the classrooms and monitored the playground, and after lunch with the children, she settled at her desk with the applications for the teacher position. A week of Gina's notice time had already passed. She'd barely started reading when the phone rang.

"Hello, sweetheart."

"You should wait until you know who's on the phone," Diedra said.

"Why? The chance I'll get a sweetheart every time is a hundred percent."

"Maybe not this sweetheart."

"Then I have a problem, because you're the only one I want."

His words thrilled her. If things could be different, Diedra couldn't imagine anything better than Eli's love.

"I called to see what your plans for the afternoon are."

"Plans?" she asked. "The same as usual—work."

"Let's take the afternoon off. I have to do some Christmas shopping."

She glanced at the piles of paper on her desk. "I have interviews to arrange."

"Just say yes or no."

"And if I refuse?"

Eli sighed. "I suppose I could go alone. Oh, say yes. I'd like to see you."

Diedra wanted to see him, too. "When and where?"

"In one hour at the mall. I'll buy you a hot dog in the food court."

"You go ahead. I ate lunch with the kids today."

As she stepped into the busy mall an hour later, Diedra searched for Eli. She waved when she spotted him at a table across the room.

"Just in time," he said, kissing her cheek before grabbing his trash from the table.

He took her hand and outlined the gifts he planned to buy as they walked through the mall. The toy store was first on his list, and they spent the next hour picking out items suitable for Lynnie.

"I love toy stores. I want to buy out the place."

"Just remember how many times you'll have to pick up every toy you buy," Diedra said.

"That's a good argument for controlling my buying impulse."

"Good. Now I can buy more for her," Diedra said with a burst of laughter.

He arranged for the toy store to hold his bags while they continued shopping. They strolled through the mall, and when they arrived at a jewelry store, he led her inside. "I want to get something special for Granny."

Diedra followed as Eli moved from case to case.

"What about that?" he asked, pointing out an exquisite enameled brooch.

"I'm sure she'd love it."

He asked to see the brooch then examined it closely. "I'll take it."

"May I show you something for the lady?" the salesclerk asked with a smile.

Eli glanced at Diedra. "Yes, I think you can. We'd like to see your engagement rings."

Her breath caught in her chest, and she feared she would suffocate for lack of air. Eli started to follow the woman.

"Diedra?" he called when she didn't move. Eli reached to touch the blond curl that nestled against her cheek.

"Eli, no," she managed finally.

"It's time, Diedra. Marry me?"

Her shocked teal eyes gazed into his silver-blue eyes. Frozen in limbo, a place where all decisions and actions were impossible, Diedra knew the time had come. The time when secrets were going to take from her everything she needed for survival.

Eli grasped her hand. "Marry me, Diedra. Help me give Lynnie the family she needs."

Her eyelids fluttered downward in an attempt to mask the fear. "I can't, Eli. I'll love you always, but I can't marry you."

"Why not?" His brows furrowed.

Diedra glanced at the clerk, and Eli told her he'd come back for the brooch. He led Diedra out into the mall toward the seating area.

The silence lengthened, making her uncomfortable. All along Diedra had been careful not to say things to destroy his illusions about her, truths that would make him think her weak. She could keep her precious control and never lose his respect. But she couldn't respect herself if she did that to Eli.

"I do love you, Eli." Diedra's voice cracked as tears trailed down her face. "I just can't let you tie yourself to a barren woman."

She turned and ran, weaving in and out of shoppers, looking for a place to hide.

"Diedra, wait!" Eli called. "Sweetheart, please."

She slipped out a side exit and prayed he wouldn't follow.

❧

Stunned, Eli moved faster than he would have believed possible. He searched the crowds. Where had she gone? A sense of inadequacy swept over him. This was his fault. He hadn't encouraged her enough to talk about her past.

❧

Diedra didn't feel relief when she reached her car and climbed inside. An angry woman stared back at her in the rearview mirror. "Why?" Her tortured cry rose with the pain that ripped through her. She'd had so many opportunities to tell Eli the truth. "Whatever made you believe you could get beyond your problems? Your self-doubts?"

She fumbled the key into the ignition and started the engine then backed out of the parking space. The blare of a horn forced her to slam on the brakes, rocking the car with the sudden stop. She pulled back into the space and rested her head on the steering wheel, her chest tightening so much she could hardly breathe.

The thought of losing Eli shattered her, but she couldn't gain her own happiness at his expense. It wouldn't work. In time he'd blame her, and she'd lose him, too.

Be fair to him, she told herself, biting her lip until it throbbed. *He deserves the best, and that's not you.* Diedra covered her face with trembling hands. *It'll never be you.* What had she done to deserve this? A stab of guilt penetrated her thoughts. What had Eli done?

He'd loved her. But she'd kept secrets. And secrets destroyed. Her teeth chattered when a chill as freezing as an arctic blast pervaded her soul. Where could she go? Not home. Eli would find her there.

❧

"You don't know where she is?" Eli asked again. He hadn't been able to think clearly since Diedra had disappeared in the mall.

Upstairs in the apartment, Granny sat in an armchair, her hands clasped tightly in her lap. "I don't know. I haven't heard from her since she left around two this afternoon. Eli, what happened?"

His hand swept over his face. "We were Christmas shopping." He hesitated. "I—I asked her to marry me. She said no." His neck throbbed from the tension knotted there; his stomach churned. "Where does she go to be alone?"

"This place is her refuge."

"And she won't come home because of me," he said, sinking into a nearby chair. "Oh, Granny, what have I done?"

"Nothing that wouldn't have happened sooner or later. You've forced her to confront the truth." Granny reached over and patted his hand.

"What truth? I thought we were heading in the right direction. Everything just blew up. I don't understand."

Granny looked concerned. "She didn't tell you why?"

"She threw out something about not wanting to tie me to a barren woman. What did she mean? Does it have to do with her rift with her family? Her marriage?"

Granny looked hopeful. "She told you?"

"She's tried to share some things. Vague comments about her parents and trust issues she has. I knew she was holding something back, but I figured I could wait until she was ready to tell me. I should have realized she was crying out for help. Instead, I selfishly took everything she had to give for myself."

"Eli, don't blame yourself. She's a giver. Diedra looks out for everyone but herself, but she'll have to do that now. She won't allow anyone else to help."

"You know something you're not telling," Eli said, shifting forward in the seat.

Granny nodded slowly. "She's been hurt, but not by you. I suspect she feels she's protecting herself. She's wary, afraid to trust another human being with her love. And rightfully so. She's been subjected to so much pain and misery, but I know she will overcome it."

"How do you know?"

"Dee loves you, but she loves God more. He won't let her destroy herself."

Yes. God was in control. Eli closed his eyes and opened his heart in prayer, thanking His Savior for the grace He gave him every day. He pleaded for God to provide Diedra a safe harbor and comfort during this time of tempest.

Chapter 14

Diedra closed the motel door and shoved the lock in place. The room had seen better days. The mattresses on both double beds had noticeable sags in the middle, and the scarred furnishings belonged to the fifties. She didn't care. Here she could find the privacy she needed to pull herself back into a semblance of a human being.

She slipped off her coat and kicked her wet shoes under the chair. She looked like a drowned rat. A heavy rain had started as she left the motel office, soaking her hair and skin. She was thankful her coat had kept her clothes dry.

The desk clerk hadn't asked questions. He had registered her and handed her the key that made running too simple. She could still see Eli's face when she told him the truth and rushed away.

She closed her eyes as the memories poured in. New memories, happy ones of Eli, Lynnie, her day care center, Granny. No doubt her friend would be worried sick.

Diedra paced the room, turning on the television to drive out the loneliness. It had been awhile since pain had engulfed her to this degree. Ever since Eli had come into her life, Diedra realized, clenching her hands until her nails made crescent-shaped cuts in her palms.

How could she have done this to him? She felt like such a bad person. She covered her ears as the accusations taunted her.

"No!" Her scream echoed in the room. She didn't want to hurt Eli. *But you hurt him,* the voice whispered. *You hurt him. You hurt him. . . .*

Unable to bear the agony, Diedra crumpled on the floor. The pressure gripped her head like a vise. She cried for her baby, for Eli, Lynnie, her family, herself, and all she'd lost, sobbing until she could barely lift her head.

Minutes turned into hours until slowly the trancelike state receded. A glance at her watch confirmed the late hour. She had to call Granny. She went to the bathroom and splashed cold water on her face. She stared at her mussed hair. Uncaring, she turned from the mirror. Moving like a sleepwalker, she returned to the bedroom.

When Granny picked up the phone, Diedra said, "It's me."

"Dee. Where are you?"

"I'm okay."

"Eli's looking for you."

Pain hit like an unexpected stomach punch. "I know. He asked me to marry him, to provide a family for Lynnie. I've never hated Benjamin more than I do at this moment."

"You don't mean that, Dee," Granny said softly. "Where are you? You shouldn't be alone."

"Don't ask. Please."

"God will bring you through this, Dee. Trust in Him."

She allowed the tears to fall freely. "How can God love me when I have so much hate in my heart?"

"He loves us, faults and all. And He'll help you find forgiveness if you ask. Eli's here now," Granny said. "At least speak to him."

She swallowed hard. "Put him on."

As she listened to the phone exchange hands, she accepted that Eli had broken through her fragile barrier. No matter how hard she tried, she would never forget him.

"Diedra, sweetheart, where are you?"

Painful emotion lodged in her throat. "I have to think."

He sighed heavily, his voice so filled with anguish she could barely understand his words. "I love you."

"I love you, too, but I should have told you."

"We can work this out," he insisted.

Oh, how she wished that were true. "Eli, please know this has nothing to do with you," Diedra said. "You're one of the few truly loving people I've known in my life. You deserve the best."

With that she cut him off, removing the last trace of happiness from her world.

❧

Eli held Lynnie close as he removed the bottle from her mouth. "Where is she?" he asked. Just hearing her pain had pierced like a knife through his heart.

"I'd say in town," Granny said. "She's probably found a place where she can grieve."

"This situation is not insurmountable," Eli insisted.

"To her it is."

He held Lynnie against his chest as he stood. "I need to find her. I know what she's feeling. She's hurting just as Kelly did."

"Maybe," Granny said. "But we need to give her time."

"That's the one thing I have plenty of," Eli said. "There will never be anyone else for me."

"God will work this out for you."

"I believe that, Granny. As you told Dee, He loves us—faults and all. He put her in my life for a reason. I know that much. I love her."

"And she loves you. Let's pray for her."

Eli reached out and clasped Granny's hand in his. Together they bowed in prayer. Granny squeezed his hand. "Diedra will come home soon."

Diedra awoke disoriented and frightened, staring at the strange room, aware of someone knocking at the door.

"Please, no," she breathed as everything rushed in on her. Eli couldn't have found her already. She needed more time.

Diedra crawled from the bed, frowning at her disheveled state. She staggered to the door and looked through the peephole, relieved to find the motel cleaning staff. She told the woman she didn't need her services. Closing the door, Diedra wondered what she was going to do. After Benjamin, determination had kept her going. What would give her that needed push now?

Anger toward Benjamin and her parents had pushed her into the new life she'd found with her grandparents. Her parents had never uttered one word of argument, never attempted to heal the rift between them.

She'd loved them, and they hurt her. She couldn't do the same to Eli. Already she'd done so much damage. Selfishly she'd allowed the love to grow, all the while knowing she should walk away. Diedra couldn't deny Eli a family. She couldn't see him again. Making him hate her was her only option. She was afraid. Afraid she wouldn't be strong enough to say no. Too afraid he could convince her it didn't matter. Maybe it didn't now, but one day it could.

Eli and Kelly had gone to extremes for Lynnie, and Diedra couldn't believe that having more children wouldn't matter to him. She sat in the room's only chair.

Diedra leaned her head back and dropped her arm across her eyes as the pain knotted in her stomach. She had to do this. No matter how much she hurt. No matter how long it took her to get over her loss. No matter if she never got over him. She had no other choice.

Eli rubbed his eyes, feeling the results of his sleepless night. Agonizing hours, filled with thoughts of Diedra and the total devastation on her face when she'd told him she was barren. In a way he wanted to be angry because Diedra hadn't trusted him enough to tell him earlier, and yet Eli understood because of Kelly. If only he had pushed a little harder for her to talk.

He recalled her response to his question about babies. She had alluded to the possibility. How it must have hurt to know that even if she wanted them, she could never have children of her own.

He loved Diedra far too much to lose her, and he'd fight as much as he needed to in order to get her back. He could convince her. As soon as he found her.

He dropped Lynnie off at the center and went to his office early. After a few minutes Eli knew he couldn't wait out the hours there either. He had to do something. He ripped a listing of hotels and motels from the phone book and took off. Two hours and he didn't know how many hotels and motels later, he dialed the office again.

"Janice, have you heard anything yet?"

"No, and I'm not likely to if you keep calling every few minutes," she told him.

"I have to find her." He grew more desperate by the minute. "Pray she doesn't hurt herself."

"Keep searching, Eli. I'll call the minute I know anything."

He tossed his phone onto the seat next to him and glanced at the dashboard to find the gas needle dancing over the empty mark. Pulling into a gas station, he propped against the car and squeezed the nozzle handle hard, as if doing so would make the gas flow faster. The next motel on the list was in this neighborhood.

He straightened and looked around. The area could do with renovation. He saw old restaurants with rusting signs, businesses that had changed hands so often the new owners had tacked signs over the larger painted names rather than bothering to paint. People wandered the streets as if they had nowhere to be. He hoped Diedra hadn't come here. It didn't look safe.

The aged motel sign caught Eli's eye. He glanced toward the parking lot, skipping over the cars that weren't the exact shade of blue as hers.

A transfer truck drove past, blocking Eli's view. He looked at the numbers on the pump. How long would this take? He sighed.

The vehicle passed, and Eli resumed his search, starting on the opposite side of the lot. His gaze drifted along then darted back, stopping on the far corner. It had to be hers. The color was right, and the rear door panel was dented in the same spot where a parent had backed into her car a couple of weeks before.

Eli shoved the gas nozzle into the holder. He ran inside and tossed a twenty onto the counter. "Keep the change."

Cutting across the street in the traffic, Eli was oblivious to the blaring horns and loud insults. He parked in front of the office and ran inside.

Despite all his pleading and badgering, the desk clerk stood firm in his refusal to give Eli the room number and threatened to call the police if he didn't leave.

Frustrated, Eli stepped outside. One of these doors hid Diedra from him. He fought the temptation to knock on every one of them until he found her. "Please, God," he prayed, "help me find her. Show me the way."

Eli could hardly believe his eyes when Diedra exited a room, carrying an ice bucket. He whispered his thanks before running toward her. "Dee," he called gently.

She stopped and looked at him. "Hello, Eli."

He felt overwhelming relief as his gaze swept over her, ignoring the stringy, uncombed hair, slept-in clothing, and red puffiness around her eyes. He wanted to touch her, to assure himself she was real. But Eli knew she wouldn't let him. "I love you. Please come home."

Diedra dropped her head. "I can't."

"Why not?" he asked sharply. He'd vowed to be patient, and yet he was already snapping at her. "I'm sorry. Forgive me."

Diedra tucked loose strands of hair behind her ears. "Don't, Eli. If anyone should apologize, it's me."

"Tell me why, Dee. I have to know."

She indicated two chairs by the pool. She sat down, placing the ice bucket on the nearby table.

"Have you eaten? Would you like to go somewhere for coffee?"

She shook her head. Eli sat opposite her.

"Why, Dee?"

"I can't be the mother of your children, Eli. I won't deprive you of the opportunity to be the wonderful father I know you are."

"I don't care if we can't have children. It doesn't matter."

"It does!" Diedra cried out, total despair hiding the loveliness of her face. "It matters a great deal to me."

"Dee, I understand," Eli whispered. "Kelly felt the same way. She wanted to divorce me so I could find a woman to give me children. I didn't want another woman. And I don't want another one now. I want you. Another woman can't fill your place in my heart."

Diedra looked up at him. "I lost a piece of myself when my unborn child was murdered. I'll never know what it is to hold my child in my arms."

Eli wanted to cry for her. All the time she'd loved his child, she'd been grieving for her own unborn child. "What happened, Dee?"

A pained look crossed her face. "My husband took offense at the news of my pregnancy. He slapped me so hard I fell backward down a flight of stairs. The banister broke, and the bottom rail impaled me."

The scars he had seen. And more he hadn't. Her husband had put them there. "Oh, honey, I'm so sorry," Eli murmured, reaching out to her.

She looked down, ignoring his hands. "Don't pity me, Eli. It wasn't the first time Benjamin abused me. It started on our wedding night. I was a textbook case. I kept making excuses for him. He was tired. I'd done something to upset him. He didn't mean to hurt me. Then I accepted the truth and went to my father. He sent me back to Benjamin. He said the lies would destroy my husband's career. My father called me a liar.

"The night it happened, I lay on the floor thinking I would die while Benjamin ranted and raved that the accident was my fault. It took him a long time to dial 911. The hospital staff called the police. I filed charges the day they told me my baby was dead.

"When my parents found out, they pressed me to drop the case. They said everything would be easier if it didn't appear in the press." She looked at him. "Easier for whom? Certainly not me."

"Dee, I've experienced the side of your nature that doesn't give up on people. Loving like that makes you vulnerable."

"I've dealt with the self-pity, Eli. Now my strength comes from God and the work He gives me to do. I can't let anything destroy that, or I'll be destroyed, too."

"I understand."

"I think you do," she agreed.

"Just remember you don't have to give birth to a child to love it."

For an instant, wistfulness stole into her expression.

"If having a child of your own doesn't really matter, why did you give in to Kelly?"

Eli hesitated. "I—I don't—"

"Why, Eli?" she persisted.

He owed her the truth. "Because Kelly insisted I be the father," he admitted. "She wouldn't accept anything less. I didn't want to lose her."

The sadness in Diedra's eyes tore at his heart. "I want children, too, but I can have only those who belong to other people. I'm angry, Eli, and until I deal with that anger, I can't love anyone as they need to be loved."

"You can. You already have," he said softly. "You've made a difference for me." He reached out to her. "Let me help you."

Diedra shook her head. "My emotions have controlled the situation for too long. I took something I had no right to take."

"You took what I freely gave," Eli said. "And you gave so much more than you took."

"It's not that simple, Eli."

Eli didn't want to frighten her with his desperation. "You think I didn't know something wasn't right? I should have pushed, but I never figured we couldn't handle whatever it was when the situation arose. You're an intelligent woman. You know it won't be simple, but we can work together."

Diedra pulled her overcoat tighter about her.

"Are you sure you don't want to get something to eat?"

She shook her head. "You'd think I was intelligent. High school valedictorian, summa cum laude college graduate, and a master's degree in education. But I refused to admit failure, and it cost me dearly.

"I tried to be a good wife. Benjamin was demanding, ruthless, overbearing. Nothing I did pleased him. I took it over and over until the night I nearly died. I kept trying to prove I could make it better, while Benjamin beat every ounce of love from me."

Anger shone in Eli's eyes. "Diedra, you don't have to—"

"I do, Eli. You have to know the demon I'm fighting. I accepted my failure as a wife and got on with the successful parts; but no matter how hard I try, my other successes can't compensate. I'm an angry failure, and I won't let myself hurt you, Eli."

She stood and started to walk away.

He jumped up and stepped in front of her. "You can't blame yourself, Diedra," he said, reaching out and grasping her hand. Tears filled his eyes. He drew a deep breath then pulled her to him. "You married a batterer. He wasn't capable of making his own life work, much less yours. With God's help and our love for one another, we can work this out. Are you sure there's no chance you can conceive?"

"Benjamin did the job well," she whispered. "The doctors used lots of technical terms, but the end result's the same."

"Have you ever seen Benjamin again or told him how angry you are?"

"I can't, Eli."

"You have to. You can't bottle these emotions inside. You're still afraid of the power he held over you."

Diedra rested her head against his shoulder. "Benjamin died following a long, difficult battle with cancer. He sent for me, but I refused to go."

"Oh." Eli was silent a moment. "What about counseling?" he finally asked.

She shook her head. "I went. I thought I'd worked everything out in my head. Then I met you, and things fell apart again."

"Oh, Dee, what will it take to convince you? You love me—us—and we love you. Let that be a beginning."

"Until I deal with this, there's a part of me I can't give. I have so much hate in my heart. I have to forgive, but I can't."

"God knows your heart, Dee. He knows you want to forgive and move on. Sweetheart, you showed me love. Let me do the same for you."

"I can't deny you more children, Eli. I just can't."

"We have Lynnie. She's enough."

Diedra shook her head and pulled away. She buried her face in her hands. "I can't. Not now."

"At least come home," Eli said. Diedra needed the routine of her life to fight this battle. And if it meant giving her up until she was ready, he would. "I promise not to push you to make a decision."

A police car pulled into the parking lot, and an officer got out and walked into the office. A minute later he came toward them.

"Is everything okay, miss?" he asked Diedra, glancing at Eli. She nodded.

"It's all right, Officer. I'm leaving," Eli told him. "Please come home, Dee."

"I'll think about it."

"Do that, please, and think about us. Life does go on, and you deserve to be happy."

Chapter 15

Dee?" Granny's voice floated up the stairs. "Eli's here. May he come up?" Diedra closed her eyes and sighed. Granny had asked the same question every day this week, and Diedra had responded in the same way. "Lynnie's in the crib. I'll be in my room."

"I'm not coming up," Eli called. "Are you okay?"

The question stabbed at her heart. She might never be okay again. She loved Eli and wanted to run down those stairs and let him make her world perfect. *But who would make his world perfect for him?* Diedra asked herself as Gina lifted Lynnie from the crib and started down the stairs. Certainly not her.

Diedra knew Eli struggled to understand, to be patient. But she doubted he'd wait forever. Fearful images built in her mind. If the past few days were an example of what life without Eli would be like, she knew she couldn't survive the future.

You deserve to be happy.

The words were as clear as the night Eli had spoken them. No amount of thinking, of trying to justify the part she'd played in putting herself in this situation, could change the truth, and Diedra accepted that. Life had no certainties and no promises, and no matter how much she loved Eli, she couldn't risk having him hate her because she'd denied him the love he deserved.

Diedra clutched her stomach in a useless attempt to stifle the emptiness. Her world had come to a standstill. Not even Kids Unlimited could fill the void, and that scared her. Not one day went by that she didn't miss Eli McKay even more than the day before.

❧

"How is she, Granny?" Eli asked as he turned from the stairs. It hurt that she wouldn't talk to him, but he refused to give up hope.

"I don't know," she said, shaking her graying head. "Diedra's withdrawing more daily. This place used to be her life, but she rarely comes downstairs. She's not taking care of herself. I'm worried."

Eli grimaced and massaged his forehead. He hated feeling useless. "I want to help, but short of storming upstairs and shaking some sense into her, I don't know what to do." He swallowed the lump that rose in his throat.

"You're helping. More than you know. This thing has simmered in the background for years. Like dynamite waiting to explode."

"And I provided the fire," Eli said with a grim look.

"Fire tempered with love," Granny said. "Diedra loves you, but she's more afraid of what she can't give you than what she can."

He looked at her. "She can love me. That's all I want."

"I'm glad to hear you say that. Diedra needs the love of a special man. One who is capable of returning her love. One who can accept that her past is a part of their future."

Eli lifted Lynnie from Gina's arms, smiling absently at the woman before he greeted his daughter. Lynnie smiled at him.

I envy you, sweetie, he thought. *You get to be in Diedra's arms, and I want so badly to be there, too.*

After Gina left, Eli said, "I'm trying to understand, Granny. I really am."

"Diedra thought she'd managed to put it all behind her."

The baby's smiles and arm-waving brought a smile to his own face. "When I brought Lynnie here, I wondered if this was best for her. I had no idea it would be best for us both. I pray for Dee several times a day."

A smile curved Granny's lips. "Diedra will come out of it. You'll see. We've let this go too long. Let me tell you what I have in mind."

❧

Diedra dried the tears of the latest grief session and went into the bathroom to splash cold water on her face.

"Diedra? Where are you?"

"In the bathroom."

"I'll wait for you in the sitting room. We need to discuss something," Granny said.

Diedra sucked in a deep breath and stared at the pitiful reflection in the mirror. "Granny, you know—"

"I'm not talking through a closed door," the older woman said. "There's been enough hiding around here."

Diedra threw the door open. "I'm not hiding!"

Granny sighed. "You've been hiding from the world for a week now. Or perhaps I should say from Eli McKay."

Diedra nodded her head and followed Granny into the sitting room. She settled on the couch, pulled up her legs, and wrapped her arms around them. "It hurts, Granny. It hurts so much."

"Ignoring the circumstances won't change anything. You can't even put the situation in the proper perspective until you admit that. Your inability to have children is a fact. Eli loves you, Diedra. He loves you a lot, and you're breaking his heart."

"He asked me to marry him, Granny. To help him give Lynnie the family she needs."

"Did you ask what he meant by that?"

"He wants a wife and children."

"Family has more than one definition. A man, a wife, and a child can be a family. What makes you think you couldn't be enough for him? He told me his wife had suffered as you are now."

Diedra's head filled with the things Eli had said to her after learning she couldn't have children. Could he really want her as a wife, a mother to his daughter?

"I know you haven't asked for my advice, but I have some for you anyway," Granny said. "First off, start praying and quit moping. If you're determined to deprive yourself of Eli's love and that's what God directs you to do, tell Eli and be done with him. Then get yourself straightened out. You can't solve the abuse matter alone. Go see a counselor.

"But if you want any kind of future, you'll welcome Eli McKay and his daughter into your heart. Put the past where it belongs. We have few second chances in life. There's no changing the past, but you can change your future with God's help."

Diedra hesitated. "I feel as though I'm cheating him. From the first I knew I shouldn't get involved, but my feelings for him prodded me on. For every step back I took, the emotions knocked me forward two. I didn't ask for God's guidance. I knew it wouldn't work; yet I couldn't refuse myself just one more minute with Eli. I took from Eli until it was too late, and now I'm hurting him."

"You're cheating him of your love."

The truth hurt. Unable to sit still any longer, Diedra jumped up to pace the room. "I hate myself for letting it happen, Granny. I never wanted to hurt Eli. I want to love him."

"Then show him."

"You really think it doesn't matter?" Doubt pervaded her voice.

"I think you could heal each other."

Diedra stopped in front of Granny. "I owe everyone an apology."

"We love you, Dee. The others don't know the full story, but they've stood by you every step of the way. Gina's even planning to postpone her move for a few months."

The idea of interfering with the happiness of yet another person horrified Diedra. "No. She shouldn't waste one minute of the time she can spend with the man she loves. Is she still here?"

Granny nodded. "Downstairs."

"I'm going to talk to her."

"That's my girl," Granny said. "Get on with life. Your world has been missing you. Can we pray first?"

Diedra nodded, bowing her head as they sought solace from their heavenly Father.

"Dear Lord," Granny began, her voice calling out to the One who could make things right. "We come to You tonight praising and thanking You for the love You freely give. We ask that You touch Diedra's life and heal her. Empower her to be able to forgive and grow in Your love each day. Help her to build a life with Eli that is both happy and pleasing to You. Amen."

Diedra spent the next hour convincing Gina she wouldn't allow her to change her plans. Afterward she went into the office and picked up the job applications. Granny made a lot of sense. Her grief served no purpose. She had a life to live, kids to care for, decisions to make.

Diedra made herself comfortable on the couch and began reviewing the applicants. Thoughts of Eli resting in this very spot the first time they met filled her head. Dropping the papers in her lap, she pleaded, "Lord, please tell me what to do."

She felt an overwhelming urge to share her fears and doubts with Eli. As she drove to his house, Diedra wondered how Eli would react to what she had to tell him. She wanted to give him all the love she had to give but knew overcoming the past would take no less than the miracle of God's love.

At the house, the length of the sidewalk seemed to double and then triple as she covered the few steps to the porch. Diedra hesitated. "You're a coward," she chided herself then pressed the doorbell.

She heard footsteps treading across the marble floor then saw light flooding the window. The dead bolt clicked, and the door opened slowly.

Diedra's heart lurched as she stared at Eli. His blue eyes had lost some of their sparkle, and shadows lay beneath them. "May I come in?"

Eli held the door wide. "Is everything okay?"

"It's going to be," Diedra said.

Eli smiled and opened his arms to her. "Thank You, Lord!"

She loved this man. Even after the hurt she'd inflicted, he still cared. "I'm sorry."

The house came to life with the sounds of Lynnie's stirring on the sound system. "You want me to get her?" Diedra asked.

He gathered her close, shaking his head. "Do you have any idea how much I've missed you?" he asked, his arms tightening as if he were afraid she'd disappear.

"Probably as much as I've missed you," Diedra admitted, wiggling to loosen his hold. "A bit of me has died every day since I sent you away, but I wanted to be fair."

"When will you be fair to yourself, Dee? You're not responsible for all the wrongs in your world."

She touched his cheek. Eli pulled her hand to his mouth and kissed it.

"I realized I'm still grieving, too. I thought I was past the hurt. Everything was fine as long as I focused on work, you, and Lynnie, anything but myself. My child would have been five years old," she said. "I'll never be able to give you a child, and that hurts more than anything else. I don't think I could bear it if you ever came to hate me."

"Hate you? Dee, darling, do you know what just thinking about not having you in my life did to me?" Eli said. "You shut me out."

"I need you to love me, Eli," Diedra replied in a tiny, frightened voice. "But I need to know the truth about how you feel about never having more children. I'll leave right now if there's the slightest possibility you could be unhappy because we can't."

His mood seemed suddenly buoyant. "But, darling, we have a child. And she needs two parents."

"Is that what you meant by making a family for Lynnie?"

"I meant whatever we could have," Eli said. "I didn't know the truth, but it doesn't change the way I feel about you. I'd want you even if I didn't have Lynnie. Even if it meant never becoming a father. I love you, Dee."

Tears of joy slipped down Diedra's face. "Then if you don't mind, I'd like to give my love to you and your daughter for the remaining time we have."

Diedra entwined her fingers with his. "I plan to see a counselor. There will be times when I'm unrealistic, unreasonable, and withdrawn. Times when the past will bear down on me in ways I can't handle."

"And I'll be right by your side, loving and supporting you in every way I can. Understand I'm here to help lessen the burden. Talk to me. Trust me to share the bad things in your life. Know I'll stand by you no matter what."

"I do trust you," she whispered, her fingers tightening around his. "I should have told you the truth."

"You couldn't. I know you wanted to. Your child's death was not your fault. Don't you see, Dee? Life does go on. I'm offering you a package deal. What's wrong with being my wife and providing Lynnie with a mother's love?"

"I can't think of a thing," Diedra whispered. "I already love Lynnie as my own. She's the most special child at Kids Unlimited."

"Spoken like a true new mother." He hugged her close.

"You're giving me motherhood, Eli," she said with a soft smile, "though maybe not in the conventional manner."

"I need you in my life. With God's help it's going to work for us."

"It will," Diedra agreed. "Everything that makes you happy is all I want. Can you understand that's what this has been about?"

"You make me happy, Diedra."

"Then I love you, and I'll marry you."

"I've wanted to hear that," Eli said, kissing her gently.

Diedra became aware of the baby's noises over the sound system. She tilted her head slightly, listening to Lynnie. "Eli, she's laughing."

His face was transformed, and his voice sent shivers over her. "See—I told you. Our happiness extends all over this house."

Her arms went around his neck. "I love you, Eli."

"Welcome home, Dee," he whispered.

Chapter 16

The next morning Eli arrived at the center to find Diedra in the nursery, already hard at work supervising the volunteer grandparents who were feeding and cuddling the babies. He ignored the interested stares of the others in the room when he kissed her. "Good morning, sweetheart."

Diedra nodded and smiled.

"So when are we going to make our engagement official?" Eli asked.

"The day I mark the last item off my list."

"What list?" Eli asked, puzzled by her comment. She hadn't mentioned a list the previous evening when they talked.

"Overachievers make lists. It helps keep us focused on the tasks at hand."

He could handle that. "So what can I do to help you get this list completed as quickly as possible?"

Diedra glanced over her shoulder at Granny, who had just entered the room. "Granny, could you take care of things here for a few minutes?"

Granny smiled. "Good morning, Eli. I'm glad to see you both looking so happy."

Eli's hand wrapped around Diedra's waist. "Not as happy as we are to feel that way."

Diedra led him to the office. "I've made a list of the things I feel I need to do before I can make it official. I crossed off the first item this morning when I called the domestic violence shelter. I spoke with the director and requested a counselor referral. We talked for some time, and she suggested I attend their group sessions. She says I've taken the first step. I believe her."

"I'm glad," Eli said, hugging her. "I know how difficult that must have been for you."

Diedra nodded. "I have also bought a plane ticket. I'm going to visit my parents."

Eli spoke without hesitation. "I'm going with you."

"What about Lynnie and your business?"

Eli knew she was trying to give him an out. "I'll ask Granny and Janice to help out. It's important that I be with you."

Later that afternoon on the plane, Diedra felt her love for Eli deepening. Once they arrived at the airport, she called her mother, and Eli rented a car and drove them to her parents' home.

"Are you okay?" Eli asked, his hand covering hers after they parked in the circular drive.

Diedra felt no great emotion at returning home for the first time in five years.

"Impressive," Eli said, looking around at the property.

Everything appeared perfect, from the roof of the three-story mansion to the beautifully landscaped lawn. Her parents had never planned one detail or planted one flower. The staff did everything. Her parents couldn't be bothered.

"I always thought it was ugly. This place never seemed like a home in the truest sense of the word." She smiled faintly. "Ready to meet your future in-laws?"

"You bet." He jumped out of the car and went around to open her door. Eli held on to her as they walked up the front steps and stopped before the heavy wooden door. "Ready?"

She nodded, and he reached to ring the doorbell. The butler greeted them, and Eli held on to Diedra's hand. It hurt her that there was no joyous reception upon her arrival. The man showed them into the drawing room where Diedra's mother waited.

"Diedra, do come in," her mother said when they paused in the doorway. Her gaze touched on their connected hands. "Are you going to introduce your friend?"

"This is my fiancé, Eli McKay."

Her mother's expression showed nothing. "Please have a seat. Your father's taking an important call. He'll be with us shortly."

His daughter has come home for the first time in years. Would it have been too much to ask someone to take a message? Diedra thought critically. Silence loomed as they all sat uncomfortably, waiting and wondering who would voice the next words.

"How long have you and—?" her mother began.

"Eli," Diedra supplied, angry that her mother pretended not to remember his name. "Elijah McKay."

"How long have you been engaged?" she asked, glancing at Diedra's left hand.

"Not long."

"Have you set a date for the wedding?"

"No. We have issues to work through first."

"There's no need to rush into anything."

The censure in her words didn't go unnoticed. As they continued their roles of polite strangers, Diedra couldn't help but wonder if her mother had ever cared about anything but propriety. Still, she refused to offer the words that would make Eli socially acceptable.

No doubt her mother would put aside her disdain if she knew Eli was a successful executive.

Tired of the verbal fencing, Diedra said bluntly, "We hope to marry soon."

The door opened, and her father stepped into the room. Diedra noted her mother's relief when she stood quickly and approached him. "James, this is Diedra's fiancé, Eli McKay."

"Diedra, Mr. McKay," her father said in curt acknowledgment of their presence as he joined his wife on the sofa opposite them.

"Mr. Wynne," Eli said with a nod.

"Hello, Daddy," Diedra said, her voice tight with emotion. "I suppose you and Mother wonder why I arranged this visit."

Her father frowned. "This is your home, Diedra."

"I haven't considered it my home for a long time."

"If you're trying to make a point, perhaps we should go into the study." His words were cold, overly polite. "And discuss the matter privately."

"No." Diedra shook her head and reached for Eli's hand. "I want Eli to hear this. My past affects him as much as it does me. I have to get rid of the anger I feel so we can get on with our lives."

"Diedra, it's past. Forget it," her mother said.

Terrible bitterness assailed Diedra. "How, Mother? How do I forget your accusations that I turned Granny and Gramps against you because of what Benjamin did to me? Did you really think I'd do something like that to spite you?"

"I won't have you speaking to your mother that way, Diedra."

Aghast, she turned to her father. "And you, Daddy, how will I forgive you for calling me a liar and sending me back to Benjamin?"

Her father's discomfort was obvious. He glanced at his wife and back at Diedra. "I had no idea of Benjamin's instabilities."

"Why didn't you believe me? Did you really think I would fabricate such a story? That I was some pampered little brat who came crying to Daddy because my husband spoke harshly to me?"

"You were happy at first," he said. "I couldn't help but feel some of the glitter had worn off."

Diedra stood up. "Oh, it wore off. Benjamin revealed his true colors on our wedding night. It's a good thing we were gone for two weeks. It took that long for the bruises to fade. But that's not why I'm here. Benjamin Pierce is dead. My marriage cost me a great deal, but you know that as well as I. Perhaps you even grieved a little for your grandchild."

"Diedra, I didn't know why his mother wanted money," her father replied in a low, tormented voice. "We were on a business trip when she called the office and said Benjamin needed money. I had my accountant write the check. We didn't know. You hadn't contacted us."

"I was fighting for my life in the hospital," Diedra said.

Strain marks appeared around her parents' tight lips. "Do you think we ever forget that?" her father asked.

"But you wanted me to drop the charges."

Her father's face was bleak with sorrow. "The press was having a field day. You were struggling physically and mentally. I felt it would be easier for you to handle the matter privately. A quiet divorce, and Benjamin would disappear from your life."

"And reappear in the life of another unsuspecting woman? I couldn't let that happen. I did what I had to do. The court forced Benjamin to seek help. Women need to speak up."

"I know that now, Diedra," her father said. "We wanted to protect you. Saying we're sorry probably doesn't mean much at this point, but we are."

"I don't want you to be sorry," Diedra said. "I want you to love me for who I am. With Granny and Gramps I didn't have to excel. I could be me, and for a long time I was no prize. Loving Eli has taught me I don't have to work so hard at pleasing everyone." Tears filled her eyes as she glanced at him then looked at her parents again. "I love you both, but I've spent years believing you didn't care. And you let me."

"We thought it best to stay out of your life."

"Because it was better not to have your errant daughter where people could pity her?"

"We don't deserve your anger, Diedra," her father said. "Maybe your mother and I aren't parents of the year, but you've never wanted for anything."

"Just one thing," she whispered. "I wanted your love. I felt guilty for not being the daughter you wanted. The trial and then Mother's reaction to the will magnified the feeling. I have to get past this to move on with my life. I wanted you to meet Eli. We're here to invite you to be part of our family—parents and in-laws."

"And grandparents," Eli added.

Her parents' eyes widened.

"If you'd like to visit, we'd love to introduce you to our daughter," Eli said.

Our daughter. Those were beautiful words to Diedra's ears. Eli had brought up the subject of adoption during the flight. As soon as they married, he planned to start the proceedings to see that Diedra McKay officially became Gerilyn Marie McKay's mother.

"Do you have a picture?" Diedra's mother asked softly.

Eli pulled out his wallet and handed her a photo of Diedra and Lynnie. "She's ten months old," he volunteered. "Her name is Lynnie."

Diedra's father studied the picture closely and handed it back to Eli. "Diedra will make an excellent mother."

"Yes, sir," Eli agreed, grasping Diedra's hand. "She's very good with children. Her day care center has an excellent reputation."

"You turned the house into a day care center?" her mother asked, looking shocked.

"That's what Granny and Gramps wanted. They helped me get started."

"Kids Unlimited," Eli said proudly. "You've never seen a place more filled with love."

"Diedra, I'm so sorry," her mother whispered as she stood and opened her arms. "Can you forgive us?"

Tears poured down Diedra's face as she allowed her mother to hug her close. "Yes."

"May we come to the wedding?" She glanced at her husband. "We'd like to be there."

Diedra sniffed and laughed as she accepted the handkerchief her father passed her. "We're not sending out invitations. The guests will be our loved ones and friends. I'll let you know when we set the date."

Her mother insisted they stay for dinner. They refused the offer of overnight accommodations to catch their eleven o'clock flight. Diedra knew it would take a long time for them to get beyond the pain, but at least they were on speaking terms again.

Later they sat in the car, Diedra wrapped in Eli's arms as she shed a few tears of joy. His embrace provided the comfort and security she'd needed so desperately. She didn't know how she had survived so long without him.

"I was a little nervous during those first few minutes," Eli said. "Your parents on one sofa and us on the other. I thought we were choosing up sides."

Diedra laughed at his apt description. "What do you think of your future in-laws?"

"With a daughter like you, they can't be all bad." Eli cupped Diedra's chin in his hand. "It's going to be okay."

She hugged him tighter. "I believe that, too."

They returned the rental car and went to the airport coffee shop to wait for their flight. On board they found their assigned seats. Diedra waited while Eli secured his seat belt and made himself comfortable.

She leaned her head against his shoulder. "I have a favor to ask. I want you to take me to a race."

He looked at her. "I didn't know you liked racing."

Diedra rested her hand on his arm. "I don't know if I do either. But you do, and I want to see what you like."

Eli shrugged. "Sure, if that's what you want."

"It is," she said with a degree of satisfaction. "By the way, I'm going to make an appointment with my doctor."

He sat up straighter. "Dee? You don't need to do this."

She touched his cheek. "I do."

A month later Diedra prepared dinner in Eli's kitchen while Lynnie banged on pots with a wooden spatula nearby.

Eli entered the room and stepped over to her. "What did the doctor say?"

Diedra stopped chopping tomatoes and smiled at him. She shook her head, feeling the familiar knot lodge in her throat. "She said what we already knew."

Eli's eyes clouded with tears. Diedra knew he wanted the news to be different for her sake. His arms wrapped around her waist, and he pulled her to rest against him. "Are you okay?"

Diedra relished the security she felt. "God has been very good to me. You and Lynnie are all I need."

"You're all I need."

"And how did you do?" Diedra asked, speaking of his errand for the day.

"Sweetheart, giving money away is never a problem. McKay Design and Showrooms is now a proud sponsor."

Diedra hugged him, enjoying the glow of excitement on his face. Eli had finally admitted he loved racing. They had attended a couple of races as fans then gone to see his friend race.

She was glad when his buddy convinced Eli to give his new car a spin around the track. On the way home he had acknowledged he'd enjoyed himself. "But my competitive edge is gone. I didn't think about winning. I thought about how much life I missed while I focused on racing. I don't want to go back to that."

"I don't care what you do as long as you realize you have an obligation to yourself, to your own happiness. Everything else, Lynnie, me, the business, should add to that feeling, not weigh you down."

"I know. I recognized your ploy from the beginning."

"And I thought I was being sneaky."

He laughed. "You were about as obvious as a speeding bus. I did push racing into the background, all the time pretending it didn't make any difference. Lately it seems I enjoy the business more, though. Probably because I'm happy in my personal life."

Excitement filled her with the words. Diedra knew exactly what he meant. Eli encouraged her participation in the spousal-abuse group meetings, urging her to share her experiences with the other women who thought they could make things better. Counseling convinced Diedra that the abuse wasn't her fault and that her self-blame served no purpose.

They'd even gone to couples' counseling. Knowing Eli loved her enough to be there for her when she needed him had helped Diedra see she was worth loving.

"We need to finish here," Diedra said. "Janice is bringing Kaylie and Davey over."

"I'm going to fire that woman," Eli said with a frown.

She laughed at his frown. "Janice promised to keep Lynnie while we're on our honeymoon."

"In that case I'll have to give her a bonus."

Diedra laughed. "Oh, you're crazy about Davey. And you don't mind having him over."

"The kid's a character. He's getting worse by the day."

"And you're doing your share to help. What were you and David thinking last week when you sent him into the kitchen to get those chips? Janice said she's still finding them everywhere."

"David sent him," Eli said. "How were we supposed to know he'd try to open the bag the way his dad does?"

"He had to climb up on the counter."

"Janice yelled at him," Eli added with a grin.

"And then she yelled at you and David," Diedra said, bursting into laughter. "Are you sure it's wise to let him be Lynnie's friend?"

"Our daughter knows a champ when she sees one," Eli said. "You see the way she follows him around?"

"Soaking it up like a sponge," Diedra supplied. "Have you forgiven me for her first word being *Mama*?"

Eli threw back his head and roared with laughter. "Why do you persist in believing that gibberish is *Mama*?"

"We're working on *Daddy* now," she said, draping her arms around his neck.

"I love you," he said.

Diedra's eyes brightened with pleasure. He could never say those words too many times for her. "I love you, Eli. More than I can ever express."

"I can't wait to put my ring on your finger and call you my wife."

"Our wedding day will be here before you know it."

Epilogue

The groom wore a black tuxedo and waited at the base of the staircase. His best girl was dressed in pink organza and sat in Janice's lap. The ring bearer played with the pillow, holding it upside down and swinging the ribbon-tied rings back and forth.

Their audience was alive with the assorted fidgeting of Diedra's honorary attendants in their child-sized chairs. It was standing room only as parents, staff, and other guests filled every available space on the ground floor of the day care center's hallway. Diedra's mother sat in the front row, looking spectacular in an ice blue designer gown.

The music began, and Eli lifted his eyes to where the love of his life would soon make her entrance. Granny Marie moved slowly down the stairs that were garlanded with greenery, pink roses, white ribbon, and twinkling fairy lights.

The music changed, and Diedra appeared at the top of the stairs holding her father's arm. Eli admired the elegant gown and noted she carried the bouquet of miniature white roses he'd sent up to her earlier. Diedra wore her mother's veil, made of exquisite lace that couldn't mask what he considered an even more exquisite face.

His gaze never wavered, and when she came to a stop by his side, Diedra smiled up at him. "Dearly beloved" was all Eli heard as he grasped her hand in his and returned the smile. They had come full circle. With God's help they had looked to the heart and found what they both once believed could never be.

A Sense of
Belonging

In loving memory of my mother, Martha,
who shared my love of the written word and taught me to persevere.
Special thanks to my sister, Tammy;
my friends, Dianne Abbott, Darlene Roberts, Trisha Sunholm;
my critique partners, Gail Martin, Lynn Coleman, Becky Dryden, Mary Gaskins;
and all the members of the Sea Scribes for their faith and encouragement.

Chapter 1

Sharley Montgomery closed her eyes and opened them slowly. Yep—there was a helicopter in her parking lot. Just sitting there, precisely parked within the white lines of a parking space, as though the pilot were confused about whether its identity belonged to earth or air.

Sharley felt no confusion. They were miles from the airport, so it had to be a joke. After all, her longtime employees had been struggling for weeks to come up with something to pay her back for the last prank she'd pulled on them. Devlin and Jack must have called in a lot of favors on this one.

Well, too bad. She'd learned the definition of a poker face at her father's knee. Jack and Devlin would crack before she did. She would act as though there was nothing out of the ordinary. That would surely drive them crazy.

Sharley slipped through the back door of Montgomery-Sloan. The austere surroundings contrasted sharply with the more formal front entrance. Sharley had grown up in these back rooms, watching her father and Uncle Ben, his brother-in-law, perform the tasks others considered morbid.

Jack sat with his feet propped on the ancient government surplus desk, his face hidden behind the few pages that constituted the daily release of the town's newspaper.

Sharley fixed a pleasant smile on her face. "Good morning, Jack."

The paper dropped. "Morning, boss. There's a guy waiting in your office. Flew in on that chopper."

She had to give it to him. He was putting on a good act, better than usual. "Did he say what he wanted?"

Jack shrugged. "Something about finalizing some arrangements."

"I take it he considered your break more important than his business?"

Jack grinned at her dry humor. "I'm not supposed to be here until ten. Besides, he wants to deal directly with the boss."

The boss. No way would she admit that those words always made her want to look for her father. "Thanks, Jack." She headed toward the front and stopped, turning back to add, "When you get here at ten, how about running out to pick up the chairs at the Adams place? Sheila told me her mom's going back to Raleigh with her this afternoon."

"Can do."

Sharley glanced in the mirrored hall tree just outside her office, taking a moment to smooth her hair and put on her serious facade. People had certain expectations of funeral home directors. They needed to be staid, grave, worthy of respect, and blend into their surroundings like one of the knots in fine wood paneling.

Sometimes, because of her appearance, she was hard put to convince them she was a knowledgeable professional. One who had already apprenticed at the hands of the best before obtaining her own training. Her father had done his job well. Sharley knew what needed to be done and prepared to do exactly that as she reached for the door's hand-carved knob.

⌘

What was taking so long? Kenan Montgomery's gaze swept toward the door for the hundredth time. Telling Sam about his vacation plans was his first mistake. This year he planned to fly a chopper along the coastline, but when he briefly mentioned the idea to the old man while seeking approval for the time off, the old man made him an offer he couldn't refuse. The company helicopter, all expenses paid, for two weeks with only one stipulation—one little favor. And truth be told, the trip had been a pleasure, Kenan admitted, dragging in a deep breath as he glanced around the tastefully decorated office—up until now.

Kenan tried to trick himself, to pretend he was waiting for one of the up-and-coming young executives he dealt with daily. When that didn't work, he thought about the pleasures of his journey—the beautiful scenery, wild ponies and dolphins at play, and touching down wherever the urge struck. The solitude had given him time for personal reflection, and he decided his life was pretty good. Or at least it was until about thirty minutes ago when he entered the ornate doors of Montgomery-Sloan Funeral Home.

Of all the tasks Sam had ever sent him to perform, this was the strangest. *The most ghoulish. Morbid. Unnatural.* The phrases jumped into his mind with frightening regularity.

Sam had been determined. Kenan's protests did little good, since his eccentric but wealthy employer thought nothing of sending his right-hand man to make advance funeral arrangements for him. The elderly man had bluntly announced he was old and dying and needed to make final arrangements for his burial while he was still alive, to be sure they were exactly as he wanted them.

Kenan argued that it was something best done in person. Sam countered that he wasn't up to the trip. The man ran a multimillion-dollar organization like it was child's play, so that one was a little difficult to swallow. But what could Kenan say? His masculine ego wouldn't let him admit that funeral homes gave him the creeps.

At six, he had attended his first visitation and managed to get himself locked in the funeral home for several hours. After that nightmare-filled evening of his young life, Kenan vowed never to subject himself to such incidents again. He hadn't set foot in a funeral home since, always finding a reason to be elsewhere, sending large, expensive flower arrangements in his stead.

"Then we'll wait until you feel up to it," he told the old man. "Or better yet, you can have Jamie drive you to a local business to make your choices."

"No!" the old man roared, something he did occasionally when he felt the need to exert his authority. "The Montgomery family buried my ancestors, and they'll bury me."

"Fine. We'll fax them information on what you want, and they can submit the plans for your approval," Kenan offered just as decisively.

Sam changed tactics then, fixing pleading eyes on him as his voice turned soft and shaky. "Kenan, do this one last thing for an old man. You're like a son. I trust your choices. There's no one else."

And because he owed Sam so much, Kenan had spent the last few hours dreading his arrival in the little remote North Carolina town. *Remote is the key word*, he thought; he'd had to touch the chopper down in the parking lot because the nearest airport was two hours away.

He couldn't help but wonder about Sam's ties to the area. Kenan knew it was more than a passing acquaintance. After all, the name of the town was Samuels. And though he knew there was no delaying the inevitable and that it was best to just jump on this task and get it over with, Kenan couldn't escape his desire to run and never look back. Why Sam thought it was necessary now was beyond him. The way he had it figured, the peppery old man would be around when Kenan himself was a grandfather.

～⊗～

The man sitting in her visitor's chair was obviously uneasy, Sharley decided. In fact, a corpse in the throes of rigor mortis would probably be more comfortable. Still, that white-blond hair was something else, the shade as light as a small child's before the passing of time darkened its color.

"Hello. Sorry to have kept you waiting."

The man jumped and shot to his feet. "Kenan Montgomery."

Sharley smiled and gestured toward the chair. "Any relation to the local Montgomerys?"

"None that I know of. I was raised in Texas."

"Strange how people can have the same last name and not be related," she mused.

"We're all descendants of Adam and Eve."

"That's true." Sharley swallowed hard as his obsidian eyes touched on her face.

"Then there's always the possibility that we're kissing cousins." She almost laughed when he shifted uneasily, barely managing a feeble smile before he added, "I'm here to make arrangements for my employer's funeral."

Sharley decided Kenan Montgomery was quite a man. Now that she was closer to him, she realized he was older than she had first thought. Fine lines creased the corners of his eyes and silver glinted in his blond hair. He was six feet tall, with a muscular breadth of shoulders that convinced her he was a weight lifter. His towhead and black eyes were a magnificent contrast to the deeply tanned skin. She jerked her eyes away, then seated herself and reached into the drawer for a folder containing the necessary paperwork.

"Please have a seat. When did your employer pass away?"

"He didn't."

Her head lifted, and she fixed her questioning gaze on him.

"He feels he's getting old and wants the arrangements made in advance," Kenan offered. "He sent me to make them."

"I see." *Stranger and stranger,* Sharley thought and stifled a grin. Just what were the guys up to with this one? A helicopter and a decidedly uncomfortable actor making funeral arrangements for a man who was not dead. She couldn't wait to see how this turned out.

"A number of people prefer making arrangements in advance," she said. "They feel it spares their loved ones the added pain during their time of grief. What does he have in mind?"

Sharley believed in the services her business provided. Every potential customer who stepped through the doors received her undivided attention. She had a drawer full of contracts for people who had planned their services to the minutest detail, some much more flamboyantly than she would have chosen, but it was their funeral. A tiny smile teased her lips at the pun.

"No insult intended, but in this case, I think it would be best if I dealt directly with the owner."

"No offense taken," she murmured. Steepling her hands under her chin, Sharley relaxed and said, "I'm Charlotte Montgomery. Montgomery-Sloan is my business. How can we be of service to you?"

Sharley hid another smile. If his jaw slackened any more, his mouth would be hanging open. An old, familiar feeling hit her, and her smile faded. As a child, she had endured the other kids' taunting. Things had changed little over the years. She had yet to meet the man who could get past her profession.

People still reacted strangely when she told them her occupation. Those were always the most inconvenient times when her rebellious nature struggled with the quiet dignity her profession demanded.

She weighed the situation and decided on business as usual. "If you'll accompany me into the display room, I'll show you our selection of caskets and vaults. Once those decisions are made, it shouldn't take too long to finalize the arrangements."

☙☙

Gooseflesh chased themselves over Kenan's arms, his stomach feeling as if he'd taken a deep breath and forgotten to release it. *The oxygen deficiency must be messing with my brain,* he thought, as he somehow managed to get to his feet and follow her.

Though she certainly did something for the pencil-thin black skirt she wore with a hand-painted blouse, not even Charlotte Montgomery's feminine sway could take his mind off the pending event. He couldn't believe this beautiful woman was a mortician. His first impression had been she was totally out of place, not belonging to the macabre profession.

"The markers are in the corners. Please feel free to look around. I'll be in the office if you have any questions."

Sales psychology is definitely at work in this room, Kenan thought. She had lavished great attention and care on the spacious room with its softly colored wall-to-wall carpeting, the lighting designed to enhance the inviting feel.

He felt panicky. "I'd prefer that you accompany me. In case I do have questions," Kenan added quickly. He didn't want her thinking he was a coward, but his voice shook like a house of cards in the wind. "It'll save time if I don't have to go looking for you each time I need information."

Sharley inclined her head slightly. "Certainly."

Her quiet dignity rattled Kenan even more. He wished she would strike up a conversation—about anything. Well, anything but her work. But she seemed to be waiting for him to say something.

Row after row of caskets lined the large showroom, dignified colors with lids open to show the adorned interiors and plush linings. "As you can see, the choice is unlimited." She had shifted into her sales mode. "Maybe you'd like a painted background? Some have verses. A particular color? Wood? This is our most expensive unit in stock."

Kenan wondered about the slight frown that crossed her face. "This particular model is lined with white velvet. The tiny tucks are impressive in themselves."

Kenan moved along the row, finding it difficult to focus. His gaze fixed on the woman's long slender hand as she lovingly stroked the wood, almost as though it was a living thing. For a few moments, he considered how that gentle touch would feel against his skin. Her hand moved to the brass rail that lifted the lid. "This one is solid oak. Impressive, don't you think?"

"Very nice," Kenan said and flinched as he considered what he had just complimented.

❧

Sharley watched Kenan's expression as she lifted the lid slowly. Things shifted into fast and then slow motion. Kenan Montgomery let out an Indian war cry and jumped backward. A serious whack sounded when he struck the casket on the row behind them. A fluorescent yellow smiley face helium balloon floated from the casket and danced along the ceiling.

"Devlin! Jack!" Everyone but the man who lay on the floor could easily hear the shout.

The tall, lanky man ambled into the room, a grin splitting his face. "Yes, ma'am?"

"Is this part of the act?" Sharley asked as she knelt by Kenan's side, noting the pallor of his skin. "He's good," she said. "If I didn't know better, I'd say he's out like a light."

"Act? What are you talking about?"

"This man. The helicopter. That balloon in the casket," Sharley enumerated as she patted the man's hand and cheek. "You guys wasted a lot of money trying to pull one over on me."

A frown creased her employee's face as he knelt by her side. "I don't know who this man is. Jack said we owed you. He knew you'd go in to check the display room, and we figured we could startle you at least."

"Devlin," Sharley said, the growing fear in the pit of her stomach making her nauseous, "please don't tell me this man is a paying customer."

"Sorry, Sharley." His hangdog expression spoke volumes.

"See if there's any ammonia in the first-aid kit." As she spoke, Sharley's hand went to Kenan's wrist. His skin was damp, as though he had been traumatized. Hopefully he hadn't struck his head when he fell. As it was, he would probably sue her into bankruptcy.

⁂

Kenan's eyelids fluttered open and shut as the pungent odor tore through his nostrils. He struggled for a few moments, grappling with the hand that seemed so intent on annihilating him. He opened his eyes and looked at the woman who sat back on her heels, obviously dismayed. He remembered where he was and fought his way up. They wouldn't be getting any personal business from him. Not for a long, long time.

"What happened?" A sharp pain shot through his head. Kenan reached to check his skull, wincing when his fingers came into contact with the goose egg.

Her shoulders pushed back, the flaming hair a nimbus around a face that was beautifully serene. Kenan had always thought of undertakers as creepy, but this one was gorgeous. Charlotte Montgomery was almost temptation enough to see if his opinion had been off base all along.

His gaze lingered on the fiery red hair and friendly hazel eyes. Long, the hair draped about her shoulders in curly spirals that made his fingers itch to touch them, to fulfill his overwhelming need to verify that something in this place was full of life. She was nothing like he would have expected to find in a mortician's office. He couldn't stop himself from wondering why she chose to work here when she was definitely suited for more desirable places.

"Do you feel okay? I could run you over to the emergency room if you think you need to be checked out."

He used his long arms to give himself an added boost and got to his feet.

"No, I'm fine." Kenan didn't mention the vision that fluttered about in his head. He glanced toward the oak casket and found it to be no more than a long, empty wooden box. His gaze swept along the interior. *Don't be foolish*, he chided his overly active imagination.

Sharley almost screamed when the heat kicked on and the balloon dipped into view. Kenan's face whitened again. So help her, she was going to fire the next employee who pulled a prank. The whole situation was getting out of hand. What had started out as good fun had turned into a nightmare.

"Everything okay, Sharley?"

"It's fine, Devlin. Why don't you get Mr. Montgomery a glass of water?" *And go away*, she cried silently as she noted Kenan's changing expression.

"Mr. Montgomery doesn't want any water, Devlin," Kenan drawled as he grabbed the balloon. "He wants to know why this was inside that casket."

Sharley swallowed and nodded for Devlin to leave her to confront the situation. "I'm sorry. They were playing a joke on me."

His incredulous expression turned the obsidian orbs even blacker. "Joke?" he demanded as he released the balloon and rubbed the bump on the back of his head. "Is that what you call scaring innocent people to death?"

Sharley watched the expressive face change with the mixture of embarrassment and anger. In a flash, she sensed his rage had a much deeper source. This man was no more comfortable now than he had been the moment they met. He was making a poor attempt to cover his fear.

"We're sorry. We never intended to involve anyone else in our little game."

Kenan shrugged this off. "For the life of me, I can't figure out why Samuel Stewart Samuels insists on being buried by you people in this one-horse town anyway."

Sharley's objections were lost at the mention of the man's name. *Samuel Samuels*. Her mother had once joked about parents loving their kids so much they named them twice. It wasn't possible. Was it?

Kenan Montgomery couldn't possibly be talking about the man her mother had jokingly referred to as Triple S. *He doesn't know*, Sharley told herself, fighting the haze that obscured her normal thinking. He couldn't know the man he spoke of was her maternal grandfather, the only living relative she had left in the world, and the man who had walked out on his wife, forgetting the existence of his only daughter.

"Let's just finalize this so I can get out of here," Kenan said, his step quickening as he neared the room's exit. "We'll take the most expensive casket you have."

That was fine with her. Getting him out before he decided to make them pay for his little blackout seemed the best idea she'd heard in a long time.

"Certainly. If you'll step this way, I'll show you the vaults."

A frown cut a groove in the broad forehead. "Don't you have a mausoleum?"

"We don't, but you can always invest in a marble companion mausoleum if you like. Does Mr. Samuels have other family he wants to be interred with?"

"Parents, a wife, and a daughter. They're buried in a family cemetery around here somewhere."

Had her grandfather discussed his family at some point in time with Kenan Montgomery? If so, why didn't he know about her? *Forget it*, Sharley told herself and turned back to the arrangements.

"Do you know if Mr. Samuels has considered cremation?"

"No," Kenan all but shouted. "Sam doesn't want to be burned."

She nodded briefly. "What about body donation?"

He seemed to grow paler with each question she asked. "For heaven's sake, he's seventy-nine years old. I doubt he'd think there was much of his body that's of use to anyone else."

Sharley stepped into the office. "Perhaps you'd like to use the phone to check on his preferences? I could speak to him," she said and then changed her mind. No, she wasn't prepared to speak to her grandfather. Not yet. "Or maybe it would be best if I worked up a proposal. If you'll give me an address, I'd be happy to mail it to you along with literature on the casket and vault for his perusal. I can price the mausoleums if you'd like. Do a couple of scenarios including grave-site burial and a mausoleum."

Her grandmother and mother were buried in the Samuels' family cemetery. Surely her grandfather didn't intend to place himself there as well. They would all turn over in their graves if he did.

❧

Kenan's breathing became shallower with her casual references. He knew that if he didn't get out of there soon, he was going to disgrace himself. How would Charlotte Montgomery react to his throwing up all over her nicely decorated office? He had a feeling she wouldn't appreciate his getting sick on top of her antique desk with its expensive accessories.

"Great idea." He quickly quoted an address. "Mail it to me there and I'll be in touch to finalize the arrangements."

"Is there a number? Just in case I run across something I should call you about."

Kenan watched the red lips speak the words and could think of nothing but removing himself from this nightmare situation. His gaze bolted toward the door. If only he could get his feet into motion.

"Running away won't change anything, Mr. Montgomery."

Her words halted his steps, and his stunned gaze fixed on her knowing expression. She had guessed his secret. Of course, it couldn't have been too difficult for her to pick up on the trail of clues he had left ever since his arrival.

"You're reacting out of fear."

Kenan found her words as chilling as a frigid blast of air-conditioning on a hot summer day. "Just as you're making these plans for someone you love who will one day die, others do the same. Funerals aren't for the deceased. They're for the living. They help people cope with their loss."

His broad chest heaved with the deep breath. He needed air. "Just send the proposal to the address I gave you. We'll be in touch."

Kenan Montgomery charged from her office as if the hounds of hell were nipping at his ankles.

Pity, Sharley thought with a reluctant smile. She could be interested in a man like Kenan Montgomery, and he couldn't get away from her fast enough.

Chapter 2

Kenan glanced about the hotel room, his gaze stopping on the laptop and cellular phone on the dresser. Not even vacation excused failure to contact the office. Sam provided state-of-the-art equipment and demanded that his execs use it at all times. Well, Kenan decided, he'd better check in before taking off for the next leg of his journey.

The phone rang a couple of times before his secretary picked up. "Hi, Marie. How's it going?"

"Kenan, we received an overnight package from Montgomery-Sloan Funeral Home today. It's a quote for funeral arrangements. For Sam."

The hushed fear in his secretary's voice had him rushing to explain. "Which he's not going to need for years. It was something he wanted done. Give me a minute to connect my laptop and fax me a copy."

"Oh." The word sounded more like a relieved sigh. "I'll send it right away."

Charlotte Montgomery must have worked overtime yesterday to assemble all the data she had described. "Give Sam the original packet. Tell him I'll be in touch after I review the information."

"Sure, Kenan. Sam's not. . . He's really okay, isn't he?"

"Sam's getting old. Old people start thinking about death. That's all." Kenan realized her concern was well-placed. Sam Samuels was well-loved by his employees. News of this magnitude in the wrong hands could do worlds of damage. "And Marie, let's keep this low profile. I'm not lying to you, but we don't want this getting out of the office."

The tiny printer produced a facsimile of the correspondence Marie had held in her hands only minutes before. Kenan fingered the letter that accompanied the packet. Charlotte Montgomery must have mailed it just after his departure. He still wasn't certain whether it was eagerness or efficiency.

The proposal workup was uncanny. Not one detail had been missed. That would impress Sam. In fact, it was an aspect Sam demanded in his business ventures. Kenan glanced at the thin gold watch on his wrist and reached for the phone. By now, Sam had reviewed the correspondence. He dialed Sam's private office number.

"Samuels here."

"Hello, Sam."

"Kenan. Glad you called. Enjoying your vacation?"

254

"Yes, sir. It's been pleasant."

"Good. Good. Just been looking over the information from Montgomery-Sloan."

"What do you think?"

"Very detailed."

"I noted that myself. Marie faxed me a copy." Kenan lifted the letter from the bedspread and glanced over it again. Charlotte Montgomery was obviously no lightweight when it came to business. The stationery lettering was an appropriate Gothic print. The letter had the appearance of being prepared on a computer and printed on a laser printer. The scripture verse caught his eye, Psalm 23:4: "Even though I walk through the valley of the shadow of death, I will fear no evil, for you are with me; your rod and your staff, they comfort me."

"That's weird. Charlotte Claire Samuels Montgomery," Kenan said as he studied the flowing, feminine script of her signature. "I knew about the Montgomery part but not the Samuels. Wonder if that's her maiden name or something?" But she hadn't been wearing a ring. He was sure of it. Kenan always noted details like that.

"What does this woman look like?"

Why would Sam care? Kenan shrugged and described Charlotte in great detail. In the brief time since he'd met Sharley, her beautiful face had imprinted itself on his brain. Once he'd been airborne after escaping her office, he found humor in the incident.

But making a fool of himself in Charlotte Montgomery's eyes annoyed him. It hadn't taken her long to recognize his eagerness to escape. And that one little episode had almost been more than his male ego could bear. Kenan turned beet red at the thought of fainting dead away at her feet. "Why do you ask?"

"I knew someone with that name once," Sam said. Kenan recognized the vagueness as Sam's thinking mode and waited. "Kenan, you've got to go back. I want her in Boston."

He wasn't given to questioning his boss's orders. Usually. But there was something about that place and that woman that got under his skin quicker than chill bumps on a freezing winter day. "Why? You have all the figures, and you have to admit she did an exemplary job." Charlotte Montgomery had covered every possible contingency.

"Very thorough. I want these arrangements finalized, and I want it done in person."

In person with Charlotte Montgomery—*the angel of death*, he thought to himself with a silent groan. In fact, she was quite desirable. Could he put aside his personal feelings of dread long enough to check her out more closely? To see if she was as warm and friendly as she looked?

"Let's just say I have my reasons. Because of that I want you to get to know this Charlotte Samuels Montgomery. I want to know everything you can find out about her."

"I'm not a PI."

"You're the only person I'd trust with this, Kenan."

That was enough for Kenan. Sam had taken him on when he had come home from Vietnam, a broken, confused man, unable to come to grips with what he had witnessed in the foreign jungles. Being placed on a medevac chopper from day one had exposed him to more suffering and loss than he'd ever dreamed possible. It had taken only a few months to come to grips with the fact that he was incapable of dealing with wholesale killing. Fortunately for him, his time had been cut short by the withdrawal of American troops.

Despite their efforts, his family hadn't been able to understand his private torment. His unwillingness to talk only made them more persistent in their efforts to draw him out, and at last he had escaped to Boston and the job with Sam.

When he first put in an application with the company, his experience in flying helicopters appealed to Sam Samuels. In the intervening years, he piloted Sam across the city to and from his country estate. Sam talked, and Kenan listened. Gradually he introduced him to various jobs and Kenan embraced them. He learned more under Sam's tutelage than he could ever have learned in school. Still, Kenan was surprised when the man offered him the position of CEO.

Nothing much had changed. He still flew Sam around the city, but now he handled company business on a daily basis. Sam treated him like a son, and Kenan loved him like a father. So now he did the only thing he could do under the circumstances. "What's the real reason, Sam? We've been together too long for you to start hiding things now."

"I have reason to believe Charlotte Montgomery may be my granddaughter."

Never once had he considered that Charlotte might be related to Sam.

"Her description sounds very much like my late wife," Sam said by way of explanation. "Also Charlotte was my mother's name. I wanted Glory to be named that."

"Glory?"

"My daughter, Gloria. Always hated that name." Sam sounded so distant, as though lost in the past. "I called her Glory."

"What happened? How did you get separated from your family?"

"I walked out on them."

"You did what?" Kenan doubted he had heard right. This was God-fearing, good-hearted Sam, not some sorry excuse of a man who would just walk away from his family and not look back.

"I'm not proud of the fact, but I'm not given to making excuses or apologizing either. Jean and I probably should never have married. We were too different. She wanted to live and die in that small town. I wanted to make something of myself."

Kenan was shaken by the truth. "How could you?" he blurted. "How do you justify hurting her like that? And just what do you hope to achieve by making contact with Charlotte Montgomery?"

"Don't judge me, Kenan. God forgave me for my sins. I'm just asking you to help me right a wrong."

"But your daughter. . ."

"Was just a little girl. She had a happier life without me and her mother bickering."

Kenan wondered about his justification. Maybe it made sense, but he felt sorry for the little girl who surely must have felt rejected by her own father. His disappointment at learning his hero had feet of clay weighed heavily on his heart. This certainly wasn't something he had ever thought Sam would do.

At forty-six, Kenan was ready to settle down. The longing for a wife and kids of his own grew stronger by the day. He believed marriage was forever and being a parent was something he could never walk away from. He couldn't understand how Sam could have done so without a backward glance.

"I didn't think it'd be this difficult to convince you," Sam offered.

"I don't want any part of this mess."

"It smacks of hypocrisy, doesn't it?" Sam asked. "I suppose I could order you to do this, but I don't want to. I'm asking you as a friend. There's a lot riding on this. It could be my chance to right a wrong. I didn't do right by my daughter. Perhaps I can do better with my granddaughter."

"I still don't understand how you could do this. It goes against everything I ever believed about you." Kenan's voice was sharp with outrage.

"I'm human, Kenan. Not perfect. I possess all the human frailties others possess, and for a while, I was not walking with our Father. I attribute the entire mess to complete stupidity. It started out with me thinking my wife should believe in me and trust me to do right. Then pride took over, and I decided if my wife didn't want to be with me, I didn't want to be with her. I missed Glory, but I didn't want her caught in the middle. I saw enough of that with my parents. At the time, I thought it my only choice. I can't change things now, I know."

"But you're trying," Kenan conceded. A new thought occurred to him, and he frowned. "What you're doing will affect not only your life but hers as well. Just because you want to relieve your guilt doesn't mean she'll want to cooperate."

Would Sam guess why he was so concerned about Charlotte Montgomery's feelings? Kenan wondered. This went beyond his fear of mortuaries. He found he didn't want Charlotte Montgomery hurt. And if she learned the truth, what an opinion she would have of him. Not only would she think him a coward, she would assume he had been dishonest with her. But if he didn't do what Sam asked, someone else would. Someone who didn't care about anything except the money Sam would pay.

"It's not going to be easy," he said finally, the words followed by a long sigh. "Charlotte Montgomery is an intelligent woman. She'll probably see right through me."

"You're an intelligent man. Healthy, handsome, certainly capable of getting information from this woman."

Kenan knew when he was whipped. "When do you want me to go back?"

"Whenever you're ready. I see no reason for you to interrupt your vacation. The return trip should be time enough."

❧

At almost five in the afternoon, Sharley was ready to hurry home. There was a visitation that night, and she needed to change, eat, and return before the family arrived. As she ran into her office to grab her purse, she was startled to find Kenan Montgomery waiting there.

She had submitted a complete, concise package she felt certain would answer any questions Samuel Stewart Samuels could ask. And though she'd been tempted, she resisted the urge to use the telephone number he'd given her. From Kenan's previous behavior, she was certain nothing short of his own funeral could have convinced him to return to her establishment.

"Mr. Montgomery," she said politely, lifting her hand toward him as she advanced. "I thought you were going to call with your final decision."

"Mr. Samuels preferred I handle the details in person. He was impressed by the proposal you submitted."

"Thank you." *So much for my dinner,* Sharley thought with a sense of disappointment. She had been looking forward to relaxing for a few minutes.

"I know this might sound strange," Kenan said, "but I didn't get lunch today. Do you think we might be able to discuss the arrangements over dinner?"

"I have about forty-five minutes before I need to run home and change for a visitation tonight. There's a barbecue place nearby that has decent food."

"Sounds good. Hope you don't mind driving. I don't think the restaurant would care for my flying us down."

He didn't know much about small towns. Just seeing the helicopter in the parking lot would give them something to talk about for years. "They'd love it, but I doubt it makes much sense to start it up for a few blocks."

❧

Dinner with Sharley, as she insisted he call her, was interesting. A constant flow of townspeople interrupted their conversation before seating themselves in the restaurant. People spoke to her with smiles and good humor, and she appeared to be well-known, well liked in fact.

Later that evening, Kenan recalled how he had picked up his fork and dug in when their food arrived. He felt like an unmannered oaf when she bowed her head in silent prayer.

He asked a few questions, hoping they didn't sound too contrived, managing to work a few personal points into the conversation, and found she was a woman who laughed often, and usually at herself.

"I owe you an apology. I guess it's more than a little obvious I'm uncomfortable with death."

"You're not alone. Many people are, Kenan. I often seek reassurance from a Higher Power."

"Higher Power?" Kenan frowned. What was she talking about? "What does that have to do with the way I acted?"

"I find that my belief in God helps me deal with a lot of the life and death issues."

In his own way, Kenan believed in God. As a child, he'd attended church every Sunday with his mother, but the years had separated him from his religion. In Nam, he prayed God would help him through, and He had. The prayers had come less frequently since his return home, though, and his life had moved on.

Kenan squirmed uncomfortably in the chair as Sharley's direct gaze bored into him. "So you're religious?"

"You make it sound like a dreadful disease."

"God doesn't have much use for an old sinner like me."

"We're all sinners, Kenan. Sinners saved by God's grace."

After dinner, they stopped by the chopper to pick up his flight bag, and Sharley dropped him off at the local bed-and-breakfast. Kenan didn't care much for using the phone in the hallway and opted to use his cell phone. It was almost seven. Sam was probably in the office of his palatial estate, going over the myriad details relating to his investments. The man was a workaholic. Perhaps that accounted for the money he'd accumulated in his lifetime. He dialed the private number. Barely half a ring preceded the answer. "Hello, Sam."

"Kenan. Did you see her?"

The eagerness in Sam's voice concerned him. "We had dinner. She's a popular lady. The kids love her. She teaches a Sunday school class of four-year-olds. I think most of them ate in the same restaurant we did tonight."

Sam chuckled. "What do you think?"

Kenan tried to come up with a suitable answer to Sam's question. Some of the thoughts he was having weren't exactly appropriate to share with a grandfather.

"What I think has nothing to do with the situation," Kenan said abruptly.

"Bring her to me."

Sam must think him a miracle worker. Sure, he'd had his share of luck with the opposite sex, but somehow he didn't believe she would agree to the suggestion without question. "Give me one good reason why Charlotte Montgomery would travel to Boston with me?"

"Because you asked her. Nicely, of course."

Kenan chuckled at that. "It might be better if you called and requested a meeting."

"Ask her."

"She might not come."

"Tell her I'm interested in a fifteen- to twenty-thousand-dollar funeral. That should generate enough interest to get her here."

Why not? If she said no, Sam would have to come up with another means of getting her there. "I'll go by the funeral home first thing in the morning."

"I'll see you both in a couple of days."

Kenan sighed as he replaced the phone and reached for his duffel bag. He had no guarantee he would get Sharley to Boston in his lifetime, much less two days. Sometimes Sam placed entirely too much faith in his abilities.

❧

"I'm sorry, sir. Ms. Montgomery won't be in until around eleven."

Kenan frowned. He had wanted to get this over and done with. "I'm really on a tight deadline. Do you have any idea where she might be?"

"Home, I suppose. Though she did mention some errands."

"Is there a cab in this town?"

"Don't need one. Sharley's house is about five blocks from here. Pink Victorian on Montgomery Boulevard. She hates it when we rib her about having her own street. Only right, though, considering the Montgomerys' contribution to this town. She's got the same blood as two of the town's founding fathers running through her veins."

A warning bell sounded in Kenan's head. The town's founding fathers. Was the Samuels family the other one of those families? "Where is Montgomery Boulevard?" he asked.

Kenan found himself strolling along the quiet streets, wondering how she would respond to his arrival and subsequent inquiry.

The house was just as her employee had described, and Kenan noted her car in the driveway as he rang the bell. When no one answered, he rang it once more. Figuring she was out with someone else, he turned away, stopping when the door opened.

"Kenan? Hello." Sharley pulled the door open wider, her hand going immediately to the barrette that pulled her hair back. She wore a long sweatshirt over a pair of jeans.

"Hope you don't mind. I needed to talk with you."

"Please come in. I was in the attic looking for my grandmother's journals." She indicated the stack of books she held in her other arm. "Samuels is celebrating its bicentennial in October. I'm on the planning committee. We almost have everything pulled together, but I remembered these the other day and thought they might add something to the history."

He nodded and reached to help her with the load. "I called Mr. Samuels last night, and he'd like for you to fly up to Boston with me to discuss your proposal."

"I'm sorry. That's impossible."

If he'd had to describe her changed expression, Kenan would have said Sharley disliked the idea immensely. "If you're worried about time away from the business, we could arrange to have you back within a couple of days." *Sam will kill me for this one,* Kenan thought as he added, "In the event that something should arise, I'm sure Mr. Samuels would be willing to reimburse you for any lost revenue."

They moved into an old-fashioned parlor, furnished with well-maintained antiques that suited the room perfectly. "Have a seat," she invited, indicating the sofa. "I'm afraid I'm a bit confused as to why he would feel it necessary for me to fly to Boston with you."

"Perhaps he was so impressed by your proposal he wants to tell you in person."

Sharley laughed at that. "I'm sure they have telephones in the big city."

Kenan chuckled. "More than you can count. Seriously, though. . . ," he said, waving one hand through the air. He gasped when he almost toppled the vase that sat on the nearby table. "Whew, that was close."

She moved the urn out of harm's way. *Oh, good,* he thought. Now she'd think he was clumsy, too.

"You'd enjoy the trip," he said, jumping immediately into his travel plans. "I could call for the company jet to meet us at the airport. I'd need to put the chopper in storage there. Have you ever flown in one?" At her negative head movement, he continued, "You'd like the chopper. There's nothing like it. Up there, just above land, close enough to see everything, your body vibrating with the machine."

"Sounds intriguing." She appeared thoughtful, her gaze moving to the vase and back to him.

"Will you go?"

She nodded. "On one condition."

"What's that?" he asked curiously.

"We scatter the contents of that urn."

Kenan glanced at the vase, and understanding knotted his stomach. "Who is it?"

"My father. He always wanted to go skydiving but decided it wasn't something a mortician would do," Sharley explained. "This would be the closest I'm ever likely to get. I'm not even the mental daredevil my father was. I don't fantasize about jumping out of a plane, and it's highly unlikely I could manage the vase and a parachute even if I did."

Kenan felt the color drain from his face.

"Of course I'd understand if you'd rather not," she tacked on hurriedly.

He wouldn't let Sam down. "When can you leave?"

"Not until tomorrow. We have a funeral this afternoon at three. And I'll need to make sure everything is covered here. Say eight in the morning."

"I'll be waiting. I have reservations at the bed-and-breakfast again tonight."

"I could pick you up if you'd like. I'll leave my car at the office."

"If it's not too much bother."

"Not at all," Sharley said with a broad smile. "After all, we'll be taking your vehicle to the airport."

⁂

Sharley spent the hours after the funeral making arrangements to have the office covered during her absence. Jack Jennings and Devlin Spear were her right hands. Though neither of them liked being in charge, they were more than capable.

Jack was as much a part of Montgomery-Sloan as the building. He was a distant cousin her dad hired when he took over the business. Sharley couldn't remember a time when he hadn't been around. Jack was in his fifties when she took over management. Sharley feared he would resent her or quit even, but he had turned out to be a valued employee and friend.

Devlin Spear was a more recent addition. In his early twenties, his friendly nature had impressed Sharley from their first meeting. Devlin was a good addition to their crazy crew. She felt comfortable knowing they were taking care of Montgomery-Sloan.

Her thoughts drifted back to Kenan Montgomery. Did he really think she had no idea who Samuel Samuels was? It might not have been a popular name in her house during her childhood, but it had been mentioned more than a time or two. Maybe she should just tell him she knew.

She grinned. On second thought, she wouldn't tell him anything. She wanted to carry out her father's last wish, and she doubted Kenan would be half as agreeable if he knew the truth.

She owed this to her father. Jackson Montgomery had let propriety keep him from enjoying life. Dealing with that same propriety was Sharley's greatest struggle. She expressed her opinion and dealt with the many qualities that kept her from being the proper mortician, but thanks to God's help, she managed to keep things under control enough to project a suitable image. Still, she rebelled from time to time. And then she prayed even harder for the Lord's help.

On his deathbed, her father had told her he should have done a few of those things he'd wanted to do. He encouraged her to try things before it was too late. That was when Sharley had promised herself to make sure his ashes were scattered from the sky. In the intervening months, she had been unable to work up the nerve to do it herself. She had considered hiring someone, but she knew the likelihood of finding a willing person would be less if they knew what she had in mind.

This would be perfect. Obviously Samuel Samuels wanted her in Boston badly enough that Kenan Montgomery was willing to go along with her request. Her father's last wish would be carried out, and she had found a means that didn't entail her jumping from a plane—and for that she would do anything, including meet her grandfather.

Sharley whispered a prayer for strength. Sometimes being a Christian was hard work. She didn't want to hold a grudge against Sam Samuels. She wanted to forgive and forget and maybe even get to know the man her mother had never known.

"Please, God. You know how hard this is for me."

Kenan had been right about one thing. Sharley loved the helicopter. She climbed into the front passenger seat and strapped herself in, accepting the headset he handed her. *It's like riding in a glass bubble,* she thought as she looked through the window at her feet. The steady whirring of the blades vibrated the chopper. Kenan set the chopper into motion, and they twirled in a circle, tilting to one side as they moved higher.

The view below held Sharley fascinated. The area was alive with the new growth of spring, lush greenery covering the formerly bare trees. Patches of color here and there indicated the spring flowers.

Every once in a while someone came along selling aerial photos of the houses in town, and most people purchased one of their home. Still the black-and-white shots did nothing to depict the true vision Mother Nature had bequeathed on Samuels.

"Look down." Kenan's voice filled her ears, and Sharley jumped. "See it?"

She grinned at him. "It's my house. And there's the funeral home." Sharley continued to point out various sites.

Soon, Samuels was behind them and she was initiated to more beauty. Furrowed rows in fields that had lain barren over winter months. Tractors moving slowly back and forth as farmers planted their crops.

"Is this what you had in mind?" Kenan asked as they flew past a group of trees.

Sharley looked down. Exactly the place she loved to roam through at her leisure. She nodded. They hovered as Kenan told her how to open the window. Wind gusted into the chopper, and the lid fell off the vase when she pulled back.

"Be careful with that thing," Kenan shouted over the noise of the blades. "I don't want your father's ashes in my face."

Sharley smiled. Kenan Montgomery didn't want anything near him that had to do with death. The psychologist in her made Sharley want to broach the topic, but she didn't think he would be very receptive to the discussion.

In seconds the deed was done. Her father's ashes blew over the field, the downdraft from the chopper blades helping to scatter them.

"Thank you," Sharley whispered as she refitted the headset into place.

Kenan's eyes held hers with a strange intensity. "You okay?"

She nodded, a glimmer of tears in her hazel eyes. When he reached out to her, Sharley offered her hand in return. In that brief touch, they shared something extremely important. Kenan cared. He didn't say the words. There was no need. Gladness and warmth filled her heart.

"It's going to be all right," he said, flashing her a reassuring smile as he set the chopper back on course.

Chapter 3

Sharley's first face-to-face look at the man who was her grandfather took her by surprise. He appeared younger than his almost eighty years. So much so that she found it difficult to imagine he was even thinking about his funeral. He looked to be in excellent health.

He stood and extended his hand. "Ms. Montgomery, thank you for coming."

"My pleasure, Mr. Samuels."

"Call me Sam."

Sharley tilted her head to one side, appearing puzzled as she asked, "Does one call their grandfather by his first name?"

"You knew?" Kenan's words sounded more like an accusation.

"Of course I did," she returned, her hazel eyes pinpointing him in a direct stare. "Even though we've never met before, my parents did acquaint me with my grandfather's name. I've even seen an old photograph or two."

"I'll be in my office if you need me."

Sharley looked at Sam as Kenan stormed from the room. "I think he's angry."

"He'll get over it."

"I should have told him," she said, shrugging at her run-in with good intentions. "I had always assumed you died years ago. My father only told me you were still alive shortly before his own death."

"I suppose you expect an apology for what I did to Jean and Glory?"

Sharley considered his statement, particularly his name for her mother. She liked it; Glory suited her more than Gloria ever had. Sharley herself rarely apologized for her own actions. Maybe it was a part of her genes she had inherited from the Samuels side. "No."

"Then maybe you realize I've got some money? Are you expecting your share?"

Sharley grinned. She had money, too. Her father's family hadn't been as wealthy as her grandfather, but he'd left her well provided for. Besides, her business fell into one of the earning categories. Along with taxes and birth, death was one of life's certainties, a recession-proof career. "Congratulations, but no again."

"Then what do you expect from me?"

"Absolutely nothing. You're hardly an old man with a deathbed plea for forgiveness. And I'm not a destitute young woman seeking reconciliation with her grandfather. I'm here for the same reason you wanted me here—curiosity. I'd like to know a little about the Samuels blood that runs through my veins. This is my chance to find out."

"So you don't doubt we're related?"

Sharley shook her head. "I knew the day Kenan told me your name. I've heard it often enough. Samuel Stewart Samuels. My mom called you Triple S."

The gray eyebrows were a sharp contrast to the snow-white hair as they jutted upwards. "Not always in the best of terms, I imagine."

"Actually neither Mommy Jean nor Mother ever said anything derogatory. Besides, I could hardly call myself a Christian if I sat in judgment of you. Grandmother and Mother made their peace with the situation."

The familiar smile showed itself on Sam's face. "You can't know how thrilled I am to hear you know the Lord."

Sharley smiled back at him. "I'm thrilled to have Him in my life."

Sam nodded, and Sharley knew he understood the feelings she tried to communicate in her witness to nonbelievers. "Praise the Lord, our God is a forgiving God," he said. "Have dinner with me at my house tonight? I could ask Kenan to join us if you like."

She considered it. She liked the idea a lot, but she didn't think Kenan would be interested. He'd been in a fine rage when he stormed out of the office. Probably more than a little ticked off at her for the condition she had set when all along she would have come anyway. "After what I put him through on the trip up, I'd think he'd rather not."

Sharley launched into a description of their two meetings that had Sam chuckling. "I don't think he's comfortable around death," she concluded.

"Few people are. Kenan has more reason not to be than others. He flew a medevac chopper in Nam for a while."

Maybe that was it, but Sharley sensed his fears ran deeper.

"What about dinner? Maybe I am an old man interested in making things right before I go. I'd really like it if you would stay at my house while you're in town."

She considered his offer. At this stage of the game it would be ridiculous for her to climb on her high horse to defend her mother's honor. Gloria Samuels Montgomery had been more than capable of fighting her own battles. If there had been something she wanted to say to her father, she would have done so in no uncertain terms. In death, as in life, she didn't need a protector. "It would be my pleasure."

He smiled, and Sharley found something else she had inherited from Sam Samuels. She flashed him a matching wide and friendly smile.

"Now about these proposals you sent me," Sam said, indicating the papers spread about his desktop. "Do I get a family discount?"

"Why should I?" Sharley countered. "A girl has to make a living, you know."

Kenan suggested she make herself comfortable for the drive out to Sam's country estate in Dover.

"We don't have to go through that tunnel again, do we?"

Sharley had been glad of the limo's dark windows when Kenan indicated they were traveling underwater.

"What? Does Sharley Montgomery have a phobia?"

"I don't swim."

Kenan laughed at that. "And I left all the life jackets at the office."

Sharley focused her attention on the passing scenery, and after a while, he asked, "Why didn't you tell me you knew?"

She looked at Kenan. "Why didn't you tell me?"

"It wasn't my place."

"I'm not going to argue the point with you, Kenan. I could have kept pretending not to know and let the truth come out later, but it wouldn't have served any true purpose. Sam's been out of my life forever. At least I'm trying to be civilized about the matter. He asked me to stay at his house, and I will. I'm not after his money or trying to hurt him. I just wanted to meet my sole surviving relative and maybe get to know him. And yes, I probably owe you an apology for that trick with Daddy's ashes, but I don't think you would have been as receptive to the idea if you hadn't wanted something, too."

A frown touched his handsome face. "To tell you the truth, I don't particularly care for the way either of you has used me."

"You think Sam knew I existed when he sent you to Samuels?"

At his hesitation, Sharley knew Kenan was giving the matter serious consideration. "Probably. When he saw the way you signed your proposal, he asked what you looked like and insisted on seeing you."

"It was his mother's name."

Charlotte found herself lost deep in thought, going back through the years to the time when a ten-year-old asked her mother why her grandmother always seemed so upset when her grandfather's name was mentioned.

Gloria Samuels Montgomery had hugged Sharley close. "The past wasn't kind to your grandmother, darling. She loved my father, and he went away. She sometimes blames herself for his leaving."

"Because she didn't name you Charlotte?"

Her mother had soothed a hand over her black hair. "Oh, Sharley, sometimes you're much too wise for your years. My father begged her to name me Charlotte after his mother, and she wouldn't. But no, it wouldn't have changed anything."

"Because she didn't like the name?"

"No, darling, it's a beautiful name. I'm glad your father wanted me to name you after your great-grandmother and my family. I only wish we had been able to give you a brother or sister to play with."

"Oh, Mama," she had cried when the tears trailed along her mother's cheeks, "I like being your only baby."

"And I couldn't have had a better one if I'd gone to heaven and personally picked you out," she always declared, brushing her lips against Sharley's cheek.

These special times with her mother had been the moments Sharley missed so deeply since her passing. It seemed more like forever than only a couple of brief years; time had a way of healing, though, and she was going on.

She liked to believe that her mother had been proud that she had followed in her father's footsteps. Gloria Samuels Montgomery had been proud of her husband. She had teased him out of his sometimes withdrawn stance and put a smile on his face that had changed him into a likable fellow.

Her mother had often claimed responsibility for changing his image with the public. Her eyes would twinkle as she teased him mercilessly about how he had frightened kids as a scowling old undertaker until she had turned him around.

Sharley had laughed with her father. As she had grown older and begun to understand the love her parents shared, she hoped that one day she would find a man she could tease and love as much as her mother had loved her father. She was still looking, though, sometimes wondering if there was a man who was capable of dealing with all the complexities that made up Charlotte Montgomery.

"Sharley?" Kenan's hand on her arm brought her back to reality. She reached up to dash away the tears that trembled on long lashes, covering her emotions with a trembly smile.

"I'm sorry, too," he said. "I shouldn't have taken part in the ruse to get you here. But he was determined. I didn't know who he would involve if I didn't help him. It's just that. . .Well, Sam. . .he's a wealthy man. . . ."

"And as peculiar as they come," Sharley offered, her face stretching in a wide grin. "I'm not exactly average either. Maybe that's another of those things I inherited from the Samuels side."

The conversation drifted to safer subjects as Kenan told Sharley about the area.

"I can't believe you've never been to Boston."

"I never traveled much. I even went to college in North Carolina. Mommy Jean took me to New York on a culture trip when I was about eight. I cried and told her I wanted to go home. I must have been really bad. She cut the trip short."

"I bet you were a character even then."

Sharley laughed and said, "I am what I am. No sense in pretending any different."

"We're here."

The mansion sat directly in front of where he had stopped his Mercedes in the driveway. Sharley let out an impressed whistle. "This is some house."

"Sam likes his space."

"I don't think we can find anything this big to put him away in."

"Please," Kenan said, shuddering with distaste. "Let's don't even discuss that. Sam asked me to bring you home and get you settled. He'll be home by seven. Dinner is served at seven fifteen."

"Are you coming?"

His eyes focused on her, and Sharley felt a growing warmth at the appreciation she saw in their depths. "He invited me."

She grabbed his arm. "Please. I think maybe you might serve as a buffer between us."

"Why would you need a buffer?"

"Because I suspect we're more alike than is good for either of us," she responded with a cheeky grin. "You already know we both like our way too much for our own good."

Kenan chuckled. "I do. The similarities between the two of you are incredible. What's strange is that I didn't even see them until you were both in the same room. I was floored earlier by how alike you are when you smile. I think maybe you've got him slightly off balance, too."

"So you'll come?"

"Sure. If you promise not to talk about your job."

"Why does it bother you, Kenan?"

His expression closed. "It just does. Let's get you settled in. I'm supposed to sit in on a meeting with Sam this afternoon."

He'd tell her one day, Sharley vowed. "Really? What exactly do you do for Sam?"

"My official title is chief executive officer but it should be gofer."

The car filled with the sound of her laughter. "Somehow I don't think that would impress the people with the big bucks no matter how appropriate it might be."

~⌘~

At dinner that night Sharley mentally prayed her thanks for living in a small country town. Sam's house was huge. Just leaving her bedroom was an adventure. She'd gotten lost twice trying to find the dining room. His table seemed a mile long, him seated at one end, her at the other. Kenan sat halfway down.

She responded to Sam's questions, repeating her answers when he couldn't hear what was said. This was ridiculous. Her table for six was far more desirable than this.

"Charlotte? Where are you going?" Sam demanded when she stood and grabbed up her plate and utensils.

"You staying down here in the echo chamber or moving up in the world?" she asked as she passed Kenan's chair.

He grinned and quickly gathered his place setting to follow.

Sharley sat down to her grandfather's right, leaving the opposite side for Kenan. "I refuse to raise my voice unless we're having a shouting match. This room is too big and too cold."

"Not when it's filled with guests," Kenan volunteered.

"Is that often?" Sharley countered.

"Fairly. Sam likes to entertain."

"Surely there's a smaller table in this house."

"The breakfast room seats twelve," Sam volunteered.

"Twelve?" Sharley repeated. "You don't do anything in half measures, do you?"

"There's a table for four in the kitchen," Kenan said.

Sharley could tell by Kenan's smile that the picture of his employer seated in the kitchen nudged his funny bone. "There's nothing wrong with that," Sharley said when his laughter broke free. "I often sat at the kitchen table while my mother was cooking and talked with her."

"Your mother cooked?" Kenan asked.

"My mother did a lot of things. Samuels isn't exactly a bustling metropolis, and while I may live in a nice home on a street named after my ancestors, my neighbors don't expect me to get above my raising."

"Jean was a marvelous cook," Sam reminisced. "What that woman could do with chocolate layer cake was beyond words."

"Mother improved on her recipe," Sharley said with a smile. "Daddy used to declare he was glory-bound when he took a bite."

Sam appeared thoughtful for a few minutes before he blurted out, "I hope Glory forgave me."

"She once told me you wanted a life without her. She learned to live that way. There were three times when I think she might have considered looking for you, but she never did."

"When?"

"When she married Daddy, when I was born, and when Mommy Jean was diagnosed with cancer."

Sam cleared his throat. "What did she do with her life?"

"Became the first lady of Samuels."

"First lady?"

Sharley grinned. "She got Daddy elected mayor. You should have seen him. He blustered and said he didn't want it. Told her to run herself. She told him she didn't want to be mayor, just first lady. And she was a lady. He was putty in her hands." Sharley's eyes teared with the thought. Her mother had been a regal and beautiful role model. "She also worked in the business and dedicated her life to showing people our human side."

"What did she tell you about me?"

Sharley laid down her fork and looked Sam directly in the eye. "That's the second time you've asked how Mother felt about you. What do you want me to tell you? That she hated you and would never have approved of my coming here? That she and Grandmother had to fight to get beyond the fact that the descendant of the town's founding father deserted the town?"

His expression told Sharley nothing, and suddenly she felt ashamed of the way she had allowed her temper to take control.

"She didn't, you know," she said softly. "Neither Mother nor Grandmother ever spoke a word against you. They believed in people being happy. Both of them hoped you were."

"I can't say whether you're your mother's daughter, but I can see Jean in you," Sam said. "Maybe I'm feeling remorse in my old age. Not that I'd change things. I wouldn't go back to Samuels, but maybe I would have tried harder to convince my family to come with me." Sam pushed his plate away. "I remember your grandfather Montgomery. Smoked a cigar with him when your father was born. Cecil Montgomery was a boring man."

"Yes, he was," Sharley agreed. "Mother once said it was a good thing most of the people he dealt with were already dead."

Sharley saw Kenan shake his head at her funeral home humor.

"I bet Cecil never walked away from the honor of being a founding father," Sam said.

"Daddy always said Grandfather considered it good for business. Mother said he was so delighted when she agreed to marry Daddy that he insisted Mommy Jean allow him to help with the wedding plans. It was quite some affair. I have the picture album and copies of the papers with the write-ups of the wedding at home. Mother made certain Daddy didn't follow in his footsteps. She kept him from getting stuffy. She loved Daddy. And she loved Samuels."

"And you? Is that small town enough for you?"

"My life is full. Work and church keep it that way."

"What about marriage?" Kenan asked. "You can't take a career and religion home with you at night."

"I'd disagree with you on that. My work is fulfilling, and my relationship with God gives meaning to my entire life. Mother and I were really close, and I'm very like her in the respect that I love Samuels. I love being a descendant of the town's founding fathers. And I have political aspirations of my own. I have no intention of merely being the supporting woman behind the candidate, though."

Out of deference to Kenan's request that she not talk about her job, Sharley didn't mention the elected position she planned to pursue. She also left it unsaid that her mother had always wanted a warm, loving relationship with her family. She knew now was not the time for recriminations, and her place wasn't to criticize her grandfather for what he had done to her mother.

Gloria Montgomery had once told Sharley she wasn't sure she ever wanted to see her father again. Her feelings for him had been more like those for a parent who had died during her childhood. She had said she couldn't even recall his face without the aid of her mother's pictures. Maybe that was where she had learned not to cry for what she couldn't have.

Her grandfather asked more questions about Sharley's mother, and she answered as best she could. "She was very popular in high school. A cheerleader and valedictorian of her class."

"I always knew Glory was smart, Charlotte."

"Very. I have a nickname, too, you know."

He nodded. "Just where did *Sharley* come from?"

She lifted her shoulders. "The Montgomery penchant for nicknames, I guess. Daddy called me his Charlie girl a time or two when I was three or four, and I told him I weren't no boy; so he started calling me his Sharley girl, and it stuck."

Sam nodded again. "Tell me more."

"I took after Mother. I was valedictorian, too, and graduated magna cum laude from college. I majored in psychology and minored in business management. I also have a mortuary science degree."

Sharley launched into the story of her parents' romance. "Mother and Daddy met right after she came home from college. When a great-aunt died, Mother attended her visitation, and that was when she met Daddy. He was training to take over for his father. She told me once that she was afraid to approach him at first. But attraction was stronger, and she made excuses to see Jackson Montgomery. Mommy Jean told her she was foolish to fall in love with an undertaker."

"Jean would feel that way," her grandfather agreed with a wry grin.

"Mom told her true love was never foolish. She and Dad had almost forty happy years together. She died in her sleep a couple of years ago."

"And your dad?"

"He died last year."

"So you've run the business alone for the past year?"

"Actually I've been in charge for longer than that. Daddy had emphysema. He was on oxygen for a couple of years before he died. He felt it was okay for him to work in the back, but mine was the public face. He listened to my presentations over the intercom and advised me on changes to make in the future. I learned a lot from him when it came to the business end of things."

"Have you considered leaving the business for something else? You could write your own ticket at Samuels Enterprises."

"Based on an acquaintance of a couple of hours?" Sharley said, disbelief coloring her words. "I'm truly honored, but no thanks. I don't want to make changes in my life."

"Are you trying to shock an old man by admitting that a beautiful woman like you prefers the funeral home business?"

"No. I don't mind admitting I love my line of work. I had a lot of options open to me, but I knew it was what I wanted to do. The psychology degree was so I could help the bereaved. A Montgomery has operated the funeral home in Samuels for almost two hundred years. I just hope my kids want to carry on the tradition."

"Speaking of kids, just when do you plan to have them? You're what? Twenty-five?" Sam guessed.

"Didn't anyone ever tell you about asking a woman's age?" she teased. Sharley didn't mind telling anyone how old she was. She wore every one of her years with as much grace as possible.

"Hey, I'll be eighty soon, and I'm proud of it. Besides, I'm not asking any woman. I'm asking my granddaughter."

"I'm thirty-five," Sharley told him. "We share more than a name, actually. I was born on your birthday."

She could tell he was pleased, but he merely said, "The biological clock's been ticking away for a few years, hasn't it?"

Sharley grinned at his less-than-tactful reference to her advanced years. She wanted a family more than anything else in the world, but she had yet to meet the man she wanted to father her children. "There's more to bringing a child into the world than just biology," she said softly. "I want my children to feel loved and wanted; I want them to grow up knowing God. In fact, I believe God wants me to wait for the man He created to help me raise my children in just that way. Hopefully he'll come along soon. Meanwhile, I have an entire group of children at church. A Sunday school class of preschoolers."

"But they aren't yours."

"Nope, but they're good experience for when I have my own. I love working with them."

Sam was silent for a moment. "What about you, Charlotte?" he asked at last. "How do you feel about what I did to your mother?"

Sharley fiddled with her napkin, pleating and then smoothing the creases from the fabric before she balled it up and placed it on the table by her plate. "I'm going to say this, and then I'm going to extract a promise from you, Papa Sam. I think that you cheated a lot of people with your actions. You deprived Mommy Jean of a husband, Mother of a father, me of a grandfather, and the people of Samuels of a leader and friend. You've accomplished a lot here in Boston, but I think maybe you could have done the same for Samuels.

"But it wasn't my choice to make, nor is it my role in life to judge. I can't promise you that I'm not going to remind you of Mother or some way she might have suffered because you weren't there—but I'm going to try not to. For you and me, life started today. So if you're willing to accept me as I am, I promise to do the same for you."

His hand covered hers, and she squeezed it, noting the misty sheen of his eyes. "It's a deal, Charlotte."

"I'd really like it if you called me Sharley."

They smiled at each other. "You know, I sort of like this new seating arrangement," Sam announced. "Kenan, remind me to tell Elise to group small parties like this from now on."

"Yes, sir," Kenan said.

"Why don't you take Sharley out and show her what I pay those gardeners a small fortune for?"

"Sharley?"

She stood, not too sure what they would see in the darkness. "I'd love to see the gardens. I caught a glimpse from my balcony earlier."

Side by side, they strolled along lighted pathways that were intricately worked between flowers and plants too numerous to count.

"It's beautiful," Sharley murmured as she stopped to smell a rose that had wrapped itself around the archway separating the rose garden from the other areas. "Makes my gardening efforts look shabby."

"It suits the house," Kenan said. "You suit this place."

Sharley waved her hands airily. "Do you mean I have a lady-of-the-manor look?"

Kenan pulled her into his arms, and their lips met in a soft, stirring kiss.

Sharley felt dazed by the impact as he released her, and they took a couple of steps apart. Her hand went to her mouth.

"Sorry," Kenan said, a strange catch in his voice. "I didn't mean to spring it on you like that."

"But you intended to kiss me? You were just going to warn me ahead of time?"

"I—I think so."

A giggle rose up into her throat, and Sharley forced it back as she considered his response. "So give me that warning next time. Okay?"

"Okay."

It was over and done with, and yet she knew the kiss had made a difference. Sharley felt slightly unsettled by the charge that shot through her when Kenan took her hand and pulled her arm through his. As they strolled, she realized he wasn't going to be just another man.

"Well, what do you think?" she asked in an effort to regain control. "Will Sam and I be able to keep the agreement?"

"I suppose you will if you both work at it."

"Probably so. When we're together, that is. Our lives are so far removed from each other."

"What do you mean?"

"Just that Triple S isn't moving to Samuels, and I'm not moving here. We should be capable of being cordial to each other on the rare occasions when we find ourselves in each other's company."

"But surely. . .I mean, now that you know you have a grandfather. . .and that's no way to refer to your grandfather."

"You think I'd give up my life in favor of developing a closer relationship with him?"

"Well. . .yes, I do. It's not every day you learn you have a grandfather."

"Kenan, I knew I had a grandfather when I was a small child. That didn't keep me from living my life up to this point. Nor did it keep Sam from doing the same. I don't think he expects anything to change, and neither do I."

"It's wrong. Both of you are throwing away something very precious here."

"No, Kenan. We've found something precious, and if it's precious enough, we'll both work to overcome the problems."

"Maybe you're right."

"I know I am." She hesitated and then added, "I've been thinking about what you said earlier, and I've decided you were right. I did use you today, and I'm sorry. Maybe if I had asked, you would have said no to my request for help with Daddy's ashes—but you would have been entitled."

Kenan was silent for several seconds before he trailed a finger along her cheek. "I wouldn't have said no. I could see it was important to you."

Sharley smiled. "Does that mean you never say no?"

"Sometimes I have to. When I was in Nam, I learned life was a big maybe. I guess maybe that still tempers a lot of my decisions."

"Sam was lucky to have found you," she whispered.

"I was the lucky one. We'd better go back. Sam's probably waiting for his coffee."

Kenan led the way to the room Sharley figured was probably Sam's home office and library. It was her favorite of the rooms she'd seen thus far. Book-lined walls, a massive fireplace with a fire in the grate, and sturdy, comfortable masculine furniture.

Sam asked Sharley to pour for them, and they settled in with their coffee and dessert.

"I need to be getting home," Kenan announced, placing his empty cup and saucer on the tray.

"You could stay over tonight and drive in with me tomorrow," Sam suggested.

"I have those files for our meeting to go over again."

"Don't understand why we can't reschedule."

"Why would you want to? It took two months to set it up."

"I'd like to spend time with my granddaughter."

"Then let's get things wrapped up as quickly as possible tomorrow."

Sharley's gaze shifted from Kenan to Sam. Was he considering canceling the meeting that had taken so long to set up? Surely not. "I'll be here when you get home," she told Sam. "Don't forget, you're dealing with a businesswoman here.

I know all about these important meetings."

"I'll see myself out then," Kenan said. "Good night, Sharley."

"Thank you again for everything," she said softly.

Kenan's gaze caught hers and held. "It's been my pleasure. Let me know if there's anything I can do."

"I will."

"Wait, Kenan. Let me get that other file for you."

Both men walked over to the desk and were soon involved in the papers Sam produced.

Sharley's thoughts kept going back to Kenan's surprise kiss. He was about as subtle as a teenage boy on his first date. *Should I?* she imagined him thinking. *Shouldn't I? Oh, go ahead and get it over with already.* This time her giggle erupted, and she covered her face, certain Kenan wouldn't care for her analogy of their romantic interlude. If that was what you called it.

She looked up and caught Kenan and Sam staring at her. Though she felt a little foolish, Sharley flashed them a brilliant smile. Kenan called good night and walked out of the room. After he left, Sam concentrated the conversation back on her. "Thank you for agreeing to stay with me," Sam said. "I hope your room is okay?"

"It's beautiful. Your home is magnificent."

"I've instructed the housekeeper to serve you breakfast in bed. There's an intercom near the nightstand. Just let her know when you're ready."

"That's not necessary. I can get up and eat with you."

Sam frowned even more heavily than he had when Kenan had reminded him of the meeting earlier. "Unfortunately, I have appointments scheduled for all day tomorrow. I hoped to get out of them, but Kenan assures me it's impossible."

"There's no reason why you should. It's business. I can certainly understand that."

"I don't like inviting you to stay with me and then leaving you to entertain yourself. I can't even ask Kenan to fill in for me because he's involved in these pesky meetings as well."

"It's no problem. Really."

"Perhaps you'd like to do some sightseeing. I can make the limo and driver available to you. You could go shopping."

"I think I'll stay put and enjoy my surroundings. For some reason, I just feel like being lazy."

"Do you swim? There's a heated pool—or a spa, if you prefer. If you'll tell me your size, I'll have Elise send for swimsuits."

Pools. Spas. Swimsuits just by mentioning my size. What luxury. Sharley smiled. "That's not necessary. Don't worry about me. I'll spend at least half the day finding my way around. In fact, I'll probably just be getting downstairs by the time you arrive home from work."

Sam laughed. "Perhaps I should ask Elise to provide a tour guide."

"That sounds like something I really could use. Now, tell me why you never contacted Mother," Sharley asked, making herself more comfortable by shifting her legs underneath her and leaning into the corner of the comfortable sofa.

"Glory visited me once."

Sharley sat up straight. "When? I thought you said you never heard from Mother."

Sam offered her a mint from the dish on the table and then took one for himself. He slipped it into his mouth. "She was eighteen, fresh out of high school and full of herself," he reminisced. "A beauty. She asked me to come back to Samuels. I told her I couldn't and never saw or heard from her again."

"Why couldn't you go back?"

"I had to be in a place where I could be me, Sharley. Not Stewart Samuels's hardheaded son. At least that's what I thought at the time."

"But what about Jean Samuels's husband and Gloria Samuels's father? Weren't those roles important to you?"

"We could go round and round on stupidity and pride, but we wouldn't accomplish any more than your mother and I did. The ties in Samuels strangled me."

"We're different in that respect."

"You got that from Jean. Sometimes I felt she loved my place in the community more than me. She changed even more when Glory was on the way. Started siding with my father. Saying things would be easier if I'd try harder. I tried. I really did, but I'm not a conformist. Never have been."

"Neither am I," Sharley argued.

"But you found a way to belong. I never did."

"Maybe it's different for me because I'm the only Samuels in town. There's no one for people to compare me to."

"I can't say why one person loves a place while another hates it passionately. I hated Samuels. I don't regret leaving. I do regret losing Jean and Glory and even you." He looked thoughtful. "My search for happiness ended the day I got back in the right relationship with God. Unfortunately it was too late by then to make things right with Jean and Glory."

"Did you know about me?"

"I knew Glory had married and had a child. But on the day she stormed out of here, she demanded that I stay out of her life. I honored her wishes. I didn't go to Jean's funeral because of Glory. I couldn't hurt her anymore."

"I understand."

He flashed her a grin. "Then maybe you'd care to explain it to me."

Sharley laughed and shook her head. "Papa Sam, you're one in a million."

"So are you, Sharley girl. So are you."

Kenan Montgomery unlocked the door of his Mercedes and climbed inside. The engine remained silent as he sat there in Sam's driveway, his thoughts filled with the woman he had discovered tonight.

To say Charlotte Samuels Montgomery intrigued him would be the biggest understatement in the world. He was intrigued, bedazzled, and amazed. There went again, his mind listing words quicker than he could blink his eyes. If nothing else, she was Sam's female equivalent. They were so alike it was shocking. He could have raised her.

Except for one thing: Kenan couldn't understand her love of small towns. Like Sam, he loved the bustle of the big city. He liked having things to do and places to go. What was there to do in a small town?

His thoughts took a different direction. With a woman like Sharley, a man could while away the hours without realizing they had passed. He had watched her hair ripple and flash in the candlelight as she talked. She had worn a simple dress that proved she liked the world knowing she was a woman, but she didn't feel the need to be overly informative in the fact.

And a psychologist. That news had floored him. What on earth would have made her pursue such a degree if she intended to run a funeral home? No wonder she had asked why death bothered him. His reaction probably intrigued her.

Maybe he should have told her. Kenan longed to shed the lifetime of fears that had bedeviled him, but he knew he didn't know Charlotte Montgomery well enough to unburden himself.

Not that he wouldn't like to know her better. But she was Sam's granddaughter. He owed the man too much to chase after his only living relative unless his intentions were honorable. In his heart Kenan knew they could never be. He was too locked up inside himself to ever be a good husband to a woman who was a mortician. And he sure didn't plan on fathering a bunch of little kids to push into the funeral business.

Chapter 4

I'll expect to hear from you by Monday." Sharley replaced the receiver and let out a long sigh. She had just spent over an hour trying to straighten out a burial policy and knew even less now than before.

One of those days—scratch that, one of those weeks with snafu after snafu. At least it was Friday afternoon, and her weekend appeared to be free. Sharley lifted the folder and came across the information on replacing the hearse and limos. It wasn't going to be cheap.

Ideally she would have ordered three vehicles in either pearl gray or white, whichever of the two colors she considered classier at the time. But as a business-woman on her own, working hard to keep her profits on an even keel, Sharley worried about the sizable investments.

Of course, at this rate it wouldn't make much difference anyway. There weren't any little Montgomerys to take her place. There wouldn't be any little Montgomerys anyway. Unless her husband took her name or she married someone named Montgomery. Someone like Kenan Montgomery.

Sure, like there was a chance of that happening. *Stop feeling sorry for yourself,* Sharley chided herself as a wave of dissatisfaction flooded through her. She had felt this way ever since Kenan had brought her home. Things had settled back to normal and though the Denton funeral went off beautifully, her former spirits were still not restored.

She couldn't erase Kenan from her thoughts. His strong reaction to death worried her, along with his closeness to Sam. Both were solid reasons for her not to become involved with him. But though she didn't want to be, she was attracted to him.

On one hand, a man who disliked anything to do with death as much as Kenan did surely couldn't accept a woman who made her living from it. And on the other hand, how could she be sure he was interested in her for herself and not for her wealthy grandfather?

She shook her head. Where had that come from? Kenan wasn't interested in her at all. The idea was so off base it was laughable. When he'd brought her home, he had all but thrown her out of the chopper before the rotors stopped turning. She had offered him a room, so he could get a night's sleep before he flew back to Boston, but he had claimed he needed to get back immediately. No, Kenan definitely wasn't comfortable around her. That much was obvious.

She glanced at the tiny clock on her desk and pushed her chair back. What was the use of rehashing the Boston trip? She hadn't had so much as a telephone call from Kenan or Sam in the week since she'd come home. She felt a certain degree of regret that her grandfather hadn't been in contact. Kenan, she could understand, but not Sam. She had cared enough about the fact that they were related to establish a relationship. Had he satisfied his conscience with one meeting?

Oh well, as Mommy Jean often said, "No sense worrying over it now."

Sharley walked to the hall closet and opened the door, jumping back as several items tumbled to the floor. Okay, here was an area of her life she could fix. She found the guys out back washing the cars.

"After you finish that, come on inside. That hall closet hasn't been cleaned in years."

"So what's another year?" Devlin asked playfully.

"Three hundred and sixty-five days," Sharley teased. Devlin groaned, and she flashed him a grin. "Ask a smart question; get a smart answer. I'll get started."

"We'll be right there," Jack said, picking up the bucket of sudsy water. "We're finished here anyway."

Back inside, Sharley hesitated over the daunting task.

"Are you sure you want to do this?" Jack asked, looking around the crowded space.

"This place has got to be the original lost-in-space room," Devlin added.

"I doubt anyone's cleaned in here since Sharley was a kid."

Sharley bent to pick up the things on the floor. "Come on, guys. It's long past time. We can probably toss half of it."

They were a group who rarely worked in silence, and today was no different.

"Tell us about your grandfather's place," Devlin called as he sorted through old papers.

Sharley took out a new trash bag and placed it in the can. "It's incredible. I toured the place the second day I was there while Papa Sam was at work. He's got a Dover country estate, and let me tell you, there's a bit of everything. He even has a gardener. Puts my yard to shame."

"Oh, come on, Sharley, you know you win the garden club award every year," Jack said. "Mrs. Gloria did a fine job fixing up that place, and you've kept it up real nice."

"Thanks. To tell the truth, his house was way too big. He's got a helipad for that chopper Kenan flies. There's stables with some of the most beautiful horses you've ever seen roaming about in white fences. His pool was fantastic."

Devlin stopped and looked up, "Since when do you swim?"

"Never, but if I had a place like that, I could probably learn. I lounged out by the pool and enjoyed being waited on."

Devlin hefted two of the filled garbage bags and nudged Jack's shoulder as he passed. "I'm surprised she lowered herself to this lowly work."

"Yeah, what should we call you now?" Jack asked.

"Sharley will do just fine."

"So did you like your grandpa?"

Sharley thought about the question, her thoughts going back to the three-day visit. Both she and her grandfather had made an effort to get to know each other better. She was at a loss as to how to catch up on a lifetime within a few days, but they covered a great deal of territory.

The library was her favorite room in the palatial house. The expensive leather furniture was comfortable, and there was a fire to ward off the chill to his old bones, as Sam put it. Briefly Sharley considered she could get used to the living accommodations, but just as quickly she realized she preferred the coziness of the home she'd grown up in.

"So how did the meetings go?" she had asked Sam the second night she was there, after he had apologized again for leaving her on her own.

"Successfully. Kenan probably could have handled them alone, but he's not comfortable with that extent of responsibility."

That surprised Sharley. Kenan struck her as very in command. "How long has he been with you?"

"Over twenty years. Started out as my pilot and then moved along until I made him CEO. He thought I was crazy. I think I got the best end of the deal."

"How so?"

"I've never had an employee with as much ability as Kenan. There's nothing I ask of him that he doesn't give one hundred and fifty percent. Well, maybe one area, but that's not work-related."

Sharley's brows lifted. "Personal, you mean?"

"His salvation. He's important to me so I stay on him. I'm sure one day he'll come to love the Lord. He's been so restless lately that I've been afraid I might lose him. Now he's perturbed about this latest revelation concerning your mother and Jean. I think he sees me as a hypocrite."

"You never told him the truth before?"

Sam shrugged. "I've never told anyone until now."

"Surely he understands that even Christians are not perfect?"

"I never claimed to be—but I was less than honest with him. Chances are I would have taken the secret with me to my grave if I hadn't sent him to Samuels."

Sharley flashed him a reassuring smile. "Kenan loves you and his job. Besides, if he were going to leave, it would have happened about the time you sent him to Samuels. I'm sure he called on the Lord a time or two while he was there."

"Wish I could have seen that," Sam said. "I've never seen him disconcerted. He's always so in charge."

"Not then, he wasn't. Speaking of Kenan, could you give me his home phone number?"

At the speculative look in Sam's eyes, she added, "I need to see what time we're leaving tomorrow. I have business waiting at home."

She had called Devlin and learned old Mrs. Denton had died that afternoon. The family was scheduled to come in and make arrangements the next day. The service would be delayed until some of the kids flew in. Devlin agreed to assist in the choices, but he didn't like to carry out the actual service, so Sharley had promised to be there for the visitation.

After saying good night to Sam, Sharley went upstairs and reached for the receiver. He might not even be home. Her thoughts were confirmed when the answering machine picked up. "Kenan, this is Sharley. . . ."

"I'm here," his voice interrupted.

"Kenan? I thought you weren't home."

"I screen my calls sometimes."

How could anybody just sit there and listen to someone recite a message into one of those stupid machines? "If you don't want to talk to people, why bother with a machine? Why make people think you'll call them back when you don't want to talk to them in the first place?"

"I talk to them. Eventually." He sounded defensive.

"I'm glad I caught you. I checked in and found that I need to be home by tomorrow afternoon."

"Did you tell Sam yet?"

"Yes."

"We'll need to leave early."

"I can make a reservation."

"I'll fly back with you. I have to pick up the chopper anyway." They said their good nights. As she dropped the receiver from her ear, he called her name so softly she almost missed it.

"Yes, Kenan."

"I think Sam's pretty impressed by you."

"I'm glad."

"I was pretty impressed myself. Yesterday, when you asked about my fears about death. . .did you ask as a friend, a mortician, or a psychologist?"

Two and two didn't always equal four, particularly when a person had time to put all sorts of new twists on the situation. Kenan had probably given the matter some thought and decided she was trying to analyze him.

"A friend," she said quickly. "It disturbs me that you're so on edge about death."

"I've seen a lot of it in my life."

"Sam told me about Vietnam." Sharley settled back on the bed, sticking pillows behind her back as she prepared to let Kenan talk as long as he wanted. Most times things just came out of their own accord if a person just took time to listen.

"It was pretty bad. I was lucky. I only had to survive a few months before I got out of there. Fortunately for me, I was all in one piece, even though my head was a little messed up. Sam helped me to come to grips with that. He's quite a man."

Sharley was glad Kenan had found Sam. God had used Sam's selfish decision, she realized with a sense of surprise. Gloria Samuels Montgomery had been more than capable of dealing with what life had given her. Jackson Montgomery and her child had helped. But Kenan might not have survived his return from Vietnam if Sam had not been in Boston to help him.

"I've got to go, Sharley. Someone's at the door."

She wondered if it were the truth—or if the conversation had become too intimate for him to handle and he needed an excuse to get away from the conversation.

"Good night, Kenan. I'll see you in the morning."

She had replaced the receiver and retrieved her nightgown and bedtime necessities. Her life had taken a decidedly odd turn, she mused. In the last few days, she had inherited a grandfather and become attracted to a man who had an almost pathological fear of death. Things couldn't get much weirder than that. Sharley shook her head. She never understood why people thought her career so macabre. It was indispensable, a loving service she performed for people. Something she and other morticians did because families couldn't take care of it themselves.

"Earth to Sharley," Jack said now, waving a hand in front of her face as he broke into her thoughts.

Sharley jumped. "Sorry. The visit was an experience, Jack. I'm still trying to understand why Papa Sam did what he did."

"I'm glad he contacted you. It's good to have family. You two work your problems out and enjoy the relationship."

Jack's words surprised Sharley. He was right on target with what she was feeling.

"Ooh, la la," Devlin said, holding up an intricately beaded, brilliant red dress. "What is this?"

Sharley touched the garment. "I haven't seen this in years."

"Isn't it a bit fancy for funeral wear?"

Sharley glanced at Jack. "You tell him. You were here when it happened."

"That dress has its own history," Jack said with a wide grin. "Made the headlines—FAMILY FEUD COMES TO SAMUELS."

"According to Daddy, it was legendary," Sharley said.

"Come on, guys," Devlin demanded impatiently. "Tell me."

Jack tugged a folding chair from against the wall, ignoring the tumble of items that fell to the floor. "Sadie Meares was well-known in this town. She had twelve kids, and they scattered like leaves in the wind when they grew up. One daughter, Marilyn, never married and lived at home. She was real protective of the old lady.

"When Sadie died, Marilyn decided it was her right to plan the funeral since she was closest to her mother. Marilyn was known for. . . Let's see, what's the best way to say this?"

"Her absolute lack of taste," Sharley suggested.

Jack laughed loudly. "That sums it up fairly accurately. She put together the most outrageous funeral plans I'd ever heard of in all my years with Montgomery-Sloan. She had us looking for white horses and a carriage. Planned to have a marching band and the family walking behind the carriage. Watched too many old movies if you ask me."

"What about the dress?"

"I'm getting to that. Red was her mother's favorite color. Marilyn was a seamstress, and she went out and bought the material, made the dress, and sewed on all them beads. It got crazy when the rest of the family showed up. They argued, vetoed each other's plans, took votes, changed their minds. Finally reached the point that Mr. Montgomery was ready to send them to the next county. Two of the girls got into a cat fight. I thought they were going to scratch each other's eyes out.

"Everything got changed but the red dress. Marilyn called every hour on the hour to ask what her mother was wearing. Anyway, it was decided that the casket would be closed for the ceremony. A couple of the girls asked for a few minutes alone with their mother after the final visitation. We found the dress in the casket room stuffed under a lining a week or so later."

"Did anyone tell Marilyn?"

"Are you kidding? She went to her grave talking about the fabulous dress her mother was buried in. Let's hope she wasn't too surprised when she ran into Mrs. Sadie up in heaven. Never saw so much hugging in all my life as there was at that funeral."

"Man, I missed out on all the good stuff."

"Thank heaven for that," Sharley said. "I don't think I could be as calm and collected as Daddy."

Later that afternoon, Kenan walked into the back room, half dreading what he would find. The sight that met his eyes astounded him.

Sharley knelt by the chair where Devlin was obviously deeply asleep, his snore reverberating about the room. A bottle of liquid shoe polish sat nearby, and she used a feather to tickle his nose. Only after Devlin swatted his face, rubbing his nose and leaving a black streak, did Kenan realize she was up to no good.

"What are you doing?" Kenan realized he was whispering.

Sharley whirled around, wondering if he were real or a conjured-up figment of her imagination. She decided he was real and grinned unabashedly. She dropped the feather and reached for Kenan's hand, pulling him from the room.

"Just having fun. Payback for the balloon."

"He'll know it was you. You left the evidence."

"I *want* him to know it was me. What are you doing here?"

Kenan seated himself in a wingback chair before her desk and crossed one jeaned leg over the other. "Sam sent me to finalize the papers."

"You could have done that by phone." Disappointment surged through her; she had hoped his visit was more personal. "Sam pretty much filled me in on everything he wanted at his office."

"He wants to see you again."

"And old Triple S couldn't pick up the phone and tell me that himself?"

Kenan frowned. "That's no way to refer to your grandfather."

Sharley rolled her eyes, shaking her head at his admonishment. "Well, excuse me if I'm a wee bit ticked at him right now. Besides, he's a stranger, Kenan. There's no instant bonding between people who never spent any time together."

"Isn't there?"

Sharley pinkened at the roguish tone of his voice. There was something almost tangible between the two of them. Sharley felt as though she should be able to reach out and touch the emotion. But it couldn't happen. Emotions were meant to be felt, not touched. Maybe the world would be a better place if a person could see them in a physical sense. Feelings were too transient, too difficult to understand.

"What gives with you two?" Kenan said. "Your attitude doesn't seem very Christian to me."

His words reminded Sharley of the Bible's charge to show her Christianity through actions. Kenan must be royally confused by their behavior. "Sam was never a part of my life. And though I hope he will one day be my very good friend, I don't yet see him as my grandfather. I don't think he sees himself in that role either."

"He doesn't have long left."

Sharley's greenish-brown gaze fixed on him consideringly. Were his words a gambit to gain her sympathy for his dear old friend, or was her grandfather near death? "Sam strikes me as being in pretty fair health. I don't think he's going anywhere anytime soon, and my personal opinion is that we're both getting what we expected out of our relationship. We were curious about each other, and now that the curiosity has been appeased, what's left? Obviously not much, since he can't take time from his busy schedule to call. What do you expect?"

Sharley wondered if she were being too blasé about the matter. Deep inside, she was happy that Sam cared enough to send Kenan. But another part was upset because he didn't care enough to make the contact himself.

"I expect a normal blood relationship. When he goes, Sam has no one else in the world to inherit his estate. You're his granddaughter. You should be the one to fill his shoes."

Sharley doubted she was up to the job. "You've been a son to him for years.

He can leave it to you."

"I don't want it."

"Neither do I. Between the money my dad left and my business, I don't do so badly." When Kenan shifted uncomfortably in his chair, Sharley asked, "How long do you suppose you can hide the fact that you don't care for my work?"

He ignored her question. "I don't understand either of you. You're both waiting for the other to make the first contact. If you want to talk to Sam, call him."

"If the old man's conscience hasn't bothered him before now, it's not my job to make it happen. I'm not going to take a chance that he's too busy for me."

"How can you just forget you have a family?"

"Blood doesn't always make it family, Kenan. And I haven't forgotten Sam exists. I'm glad to hear he was impressed by his granddaughter. I'm glad to know he wants to see me again. Unfortunately for us both, I have a business to run, and that business is a few hundred miles from Boston."

"Does it make that much difference?"

He doesn't understand, Sharley realized. Kenan couldn't begin to comprehend her need to belong to this community. Samuels was her home. Montgomery-Sloan was her heritage. "It matters to me."

"You're like your grandfather in more ways than you realize."

Sharley smiled at that and glanced up when Jack stopped in the doorway. "Hey, boss, ready to pop into the back for a cold one?"

Her gaze moved from Jack to Kenan and back. She indicated Kenan's presence with a subtle tilt of her head. Jack frowned and shrugged before making a hasty exit. "Sorry. Standing joke around here."

"Do you people ever tell regular jokes?"

"Sure. Want to hear a few?"

Kenan's hands came up to ward off her efforts. "I just wondered. I'm beginning to think my sense of humor has gone south for the summer."

"People have a tendency to accept death more willingly when you deal with it often."

"I'll take your word for it."

"You put your faith into a machine that carries you miles above the ground every day. Why is it so difficult for you to believe there's nothing to be afraid of here?"

"Give me a chance to mull that over."

"Maybe that's part of the problem," Sharley suggested, her eyebrows lifting in question with the statement. "Chances are you're spending entirely too much time mulling over the situation."

Kenan squirmed in his seat and changed the topic. "How have you been?"

"Pretty good. I spent most of the morning trying to decide on whether or not to replace my vehicles." She lifted two samples. "What do you think? Pearl gray or white?"

"The gray."

"It is elegant," she agreed, looking at it with new interest. "I was considering ordering a hearse and two limos, but on second thought, maybe I'll just order one limo. I can always rent if I need one. No sense in tying up more funds than necessary."

Kenan cleared his throat. "Sharley, there's another reason I'm here." She looked at him curiously, and he continued, "Sam's birthday is in a couple of weeks. He's planning a big bash. He wants you to be his hostess."

What did they expect of her? "What are you? His paid voice? Is it so very inconceivable that he could pick up the phone and tell me this himself? I haven't heard one word from him since we met."

"Don't get angry. He knew I was coming with the paperwork. He just mentioned the idea."

"So, tell him to call me. I'll see if I can fit him and his party into my schedule." Sharley shoved the papers into her desk drawer and slammed it shut. "I do hope he won't be too disappointed if I'm not readily at his beck and call. My job is demanding, too. I'm required to be available twenty-four hours a day. People won't put their dying on hold so I can attend my grandfather's birthday bash."

"I should have known." The words gushed from Kenan's mouth along with a defeated sigh. "Okay, the truth of the matter is, Sam didn't send me here to bring papers. He didn't ask me to ask you to act as his hostess. They were all excuses. Excuses so I could come here and see what it is about you that won't let me forget you exist."

Sharley felt more alert than she had in days. "Now we're getting somewhere. It scares you, doesn't it, Kenan? You don't want to be attracted to the mortician lady."

"Yes, it does, and no, I don't. But that hasn't stopped it from happening. I was scared when you came to Boston, and I'm scared now. I know you're just a flesh and blood woman. I know your work is something that has to be done. Still, I can't see us together, and yet I can't forget you either."

"Why do you want to forget me?"

"Because we're worlds apart."

Finally they were getting to the crux of the matter. Kenan had made more than one admission. "Why don't we go out to lunch? You'd probably be more comfortable talking in a restaurant."

"I'm not sure I want to talk."

"Make up your mind, Kenan. I am what I am. That is not going to change. If you're interested in me, you have to accept my life."

A war waged itself on his expressive face before the words seemed finally ripped from him. "Then I guess we'd better talk."

❧

They went to the barbecue restaurant where they had eaten before. Kenan held

Sharley's wooden slat chair for her and then moved around to seat himself at the wooden table. The restaurant lacked the big-city ambience he was used to, but Kenan found himself liking the homey atmosphere. The walls were painted a stark white, and the windows were open to the parking lot, a swatch of fabric across the top their only decoration. The walls contained painted pictures, tiny price tags tucked in the corner. The owners obviously collected pigs, and some of the pieces were fascinating.

Sharley removed the menus from behind the napkin dispenser and passed him one. A young waitress in shorts and a T-shirt took their orders.

"How do you deal with your job?" Kenan asked. "Those people. . .they're just so. . ." He shrugged. "Dead."

"Good thing. A living person might question my efforts to embalm them."

Kenan grimaced, and Sharley shrugged and grinned. "You accept it as a part of living. Everyone dies, Kenan. And when they do, I carry out their family's wishes. It helps them find peace."

"I've never found anything remotely peaceful about death. My personal history has to do with being six years old and locked in a funeral home for several hours."

"What happened?" Sharley demanded.

Kenan thanked the waitress when she set the plastic cup filled with crushed ice and tea before him. "My maternal grandfather died, and my mom took me to my first visitation. It was fun for the most part—a big place with plenty of places to play with my cousins while the adults sat around and talked.

"There were two things that bothered me. One was when my grandmother clutched my grandfather in her arms and sobbed out her grief. Then my mom touched his face and cried softly, saying how cold he was. I wanted to see for myself so I sneaked a hand over into the coffin. He *was* cold, and I was upset because he made my grandmother and mother cry. I decided then and there I didn't want anything to do with this death business.

"Later, I told my cousins how cold he was, and the older ones started telling ghost stories. I was scared and tired so I found a small room with a sofa and lay down.

"When I woke, it was very dark and the building was empty. For whatever reason, I had been left behind. As an adult I can see how easy it would be to lose one child in so many, but as a little boy I felt deserted. Mom assumed I was with my cousins, and my cousins assumed I was with my mother.

"I was afraid to move from the sofa. I kept calling for Mom until I started hearing strange noises. I got real quiet then because I was afraid my grandfather would come after me." Kenan shrugged. "My cousins' stories really did a number on me."

"No wonder you don't like funeral homes. How long were you there?"

"Four or five hours. It seemed like forever."

Sharley's hand covered his. "You must have been terrified."

"Terrified is a mild word for what I was. I didn't sleep with the lights off for months. My parents argued a lot about that. Dad told my mom she was babying me too much."

"But you were just a little boy."

"Not in my dad's eyes. When he was away, I was the man of the house. I was expected to take care of my mother and sisters. I haven't been to a funeral since."

The conversation halted when the waitress delivered two paper plates piled high with barbecue, coleslaw, french fries, and hush puppies. Kenan wasn't sure he could handle the man-sized plate he had ordered.

"And yet you flew the choppers that transported victims. How did you deal with that?"

"I told myself I was a man. That I could handle it. That my dad would be disappointed if I let him down. I pumped myself up, cajoled, belittled, anything I had to do to get myself through. It was pretty bad, but I guess I was lucky. I only had to survive a few months before I got out of there. Fortunately for me, I was all in one piece, even though my head wasn't the same as it had been before." He shook his head. "I can't explain the feeling that swamps me when I think about death."

"Mainly fear?"

"Yes."

Sharley offered a sympathetic smile. "That was a smart answer on your part."

"It was a coward's answer."

"No, it's not. Only by admitting to a fear can you learn to live with it. As long as you avoid dealing with it, the fear grows and consumes you more each day."

Their gazes locked. "This is not the conversation I planned to have with you."

Sharley chuckled and admitted, "It's not one I thought we'd have, Kenan. I find myself attracted to you, but I know we're going nowhere as long as you're overwhelmed by this fear of what I do for a living."

"How can you prepare a body?" he blurted. "What kind of emotions allow you to deal with someone who once lived and loved just like you?" Sharley saw him shudder.

"How does a surgeon operate on a human being?" she countered. "Is what I do really so different from that? Except for the fact that I don't have to worry about losing my patient on the table, that is." When her smile received no answer, she turned serious. "Truthfully it's no picnic. I've reconstructed accident and suicide victims so that family members could have a final viewing. And this may strike you as gruesome, but I'm as proud of what I've accomplished as an artist is of his paintings. I believe in the business. I'm also not your ordinary undertaker."

That caught his attention. "In what way?"

"I often rush into things. I'm aggressive. I have millions of ideas, and I love a challenge. I like to be the center of attention. I like to socialize. I try to be diplomatic, but I have a temper. I get furious when people think I can't do the same job my father did because I'm a woman."

"I didn't know," Kenan said, recalling how he'd asked for the manager that first day.

"I realize that, but it's a preconceived notion I've been fighting for years." Sharley speared a chunk of the succulent pork and put it in her mouth. She swallowed and said, "Humility and anger aren't a very good combination. People expect me to be staid and respectable. It's not in my genetic makeup to fade into the woodwork. I have to work hard at it. My dad passed up a lot of things he wanted to try in life because he felt they weren't proper activities for a mortician.

"Personally I feel that life is too short not to experience everything one can. I see people every day who will never have the opportunity to try the things they missed. I've performed funerals for stillborn babies, for children, and for teenagers. Those touch me the most deeply. When a seventy- or eighty-year-old comes through my doors, at least I can think, 'Here's someone who has had a full life.'"

She thoughtfully sipped her iced tea. "I suffer for the bereaved, too. That's another reason why I have to do my best. I want them to have what it takes to help them live in peace with their losses. It's not a money thing. But when all is said and done, it becomes something you do. A job." Sharley broke off as an idea occurred to her. "Maybe if you actually saw what goes on. . ."

Kenan shook his head, dread filling his eyes.

"Maybe not," Sharley agreed. He wasn't ready for that step. First, he had to get past his fear of death. Then maybe he could understand that preparation and burial were the logical conclusions. "I wish I knew the magic words that would make you more comfortable, but there aren't any. Besides, I told you once I was concerned as a friend. I don't think we'd get very far if you kept thinking I was trying to analyze you."

Kenan picked up the check the waitress laid on the table and escorted Sharley to the checkout. He paid, and they walked out to his rental car.

"Did you want to come back to my house for coffee?"

"I was hoping for a repeat on the room offer you made last week," he admitted with a grin. "I didn't think to make arrangements for somewhere to stay. The B and B is full."

Sharley hesitated. "After what we've just discussed, do you think it's wise?"

"I have no dishonorable intentions, Sharley," Kenan said quickly. "I need a place to sleep. I'll take you up on that cup of coffee, and we'll talk some more. I could tell you about the Sam I know."

"I'd like that."

The sun was dropping fast over the horizon as they neared the town's flashing caution light. Kenan's gaze caught on a flurry of political posters for seats on the board of education, sheriff, state and congressional representatives, and, of course, coroner.

"So that's your political aspiration. Nice poster."

Sharley glanced over at him. "Thanks. Samuels is located in one of the few North Carolina counties where coroner is an elected position." She noticed his expression. "Somebody has to do it, Kenan. I'm qualified."

Silence eased back into the car as they turned up Montgomery Street toward her house.

"You don't have to do this if you don't want to," Kenan said.

"It's okay. The house is full of guest rooms."

"Will my staying over compromise you in any way?"

Sharley smiled and shook her head. "My great-aunt Liza happens to be spending some time with me. She goes to bed early, so you won't meet her tonight, but she's the perfect chaperone."

Kenan climbed out and went around to remove his flight bag from the trunk. "Lead on, Ms. Montgomery."

Sharley showed him inside the house. "Let me show you where you'll be sleeping, and then I'll pour us a couple of glasses of iced tea. We'll take it out onto the patio. It's too nice a night to stay cooped up inside."

She left Kenan to change and came back downstairs.

"Sharley?" he called a few minutes later.

"In here."

He followed her voice into the neat kitchen. Sharley's eyes lingered on the muscular forearms exposed by the shirt. "How do you keep up your regime when you're traveling?"

"I generally try to stay in hotels with fitness centers."

"You certainly have an admirable physique."

"I could say the same of you," Kenan returned, grinning at her bold compliment.

She laughed. "There's a weight machine in the basement if you're interested. Dad and I used to do a few reps now and then."

Kenan poked her upper arm. "Oh ho, another bodybuilder."

"Not exactly. I haven't been near the thing in months. Daddy needed it for muscle tone, and I encouraged him. You're welcome to use it."

"I might just take you up on it later."

Sharley led the way through the utility room, stopping long enough to retrieve cushions for the chaise lounges. They made themselves comfortable, and she tilted her head to stare at the full moon. The unlit area glowed with its eerie but iridescent light.

"Hard to believe it'll be pitch-black dark out here in just a couple of nights," she mused.

"Full moons bring out strange behavior in some people."

"Even in small towns?"

"Particularly in small towns," Sharley pointed out. "So tell me about the plans for this gala affair for Sam."

"Just an intimate party with a few hundred of his closest friends." Sharley heard the tinkle of ice against glass as Kenan took a sip of tea.

"He'll be eighty?"

"Yes. How old was your mother when she died?"

"Sixty."

"So Sam was a father at eighteen?"

"That sounds about right. That would have made him a grandfather at forty-five." Sharley felt too lazy to attempt the mental math and shrugged her shoulders. "How did you end up in Vietnam?"

"Family tradition. Dad was retired Air Force. He wanted his only son to have a military career, but I refused to allow him to rule my life. I graduated at seventeen, got in a couple of years of college, and joined the army. They gave me more flight training and made me a warrant officer pilot. I ended up on a chopper in Nam. I learned very quickly that the only career I wanted had nothing to do with the military."

"Do you have a lot of bad memories?"

"Every Nam vet has at least one good nightmare. I was scared. It wasn't a matter of waltzing into a combat zone and doing cleanup. The medevac choppers are crewed by a pilot, copilot, two gunners, and two medics. We evacuated the wounded, usually from hot fire zones. We'd move into the zone, machine guns blazing, and the medics jumped out with the stretchers. It was my job to get us in and out. Some guys got high with excitement, but I always felt I was playing Russian roulette with a fully loaded gun. From what my friends told me, I was better off in the air than on the ground. Still, I experienced a lot of things I could have lived my life without."

He fell silent, and Sharley knew he had said more than he intended. She changed the subject. "So tell me the story of how Sam made his fortune in Boston. He didn't take a lot with him when he left."

"Sam has always been a visionary," Kenan said. "He worked hard and made his first million marketing items for inventors. He kept investing and backing new ideas and built up a group of loyal followers. People who invented regularly and were interested in him marketing their product. It was a workable relationship for everyone."

"Why did he have to go to Boston to do that?"

"Sam told me his father didn't care much for change. When he worked in the bank, his dad wasn't interested in anything but a sure bet."

"Most bankers aren't."

"Most bankers aren't Sam Samuels. Every time he approached his father with some innovative technique he was sure would make a difference, he was told, 'That's not the way we do things.' He stood it for as long as he could, and then one day he packed up his bags and left. Unfortunately it appears he left his wife and child behind."

Maybe Sam had the right idea, Sharley thought, *at least financially.* The First National Bank of Samuels had merged into a larger banking system long before she came into adulthood.

"So maybe if his dad had been more flexible, Papa Sam would have stayed in town?"

"Possibly. It's hard to imagine, though."

Sharley nodded, not realizing that Kenan couldn't see her in the dark. "What about his personal life? Did he remarry? Do I share him with other grandchildren?"

"Sam once told me he wasn't cut out to be a husband. Over the years, he escorted women here and there, but he never committed to anyone else. And while I'd love to tell you everything I know about Sam, there are things he shared in confidence that I would never be able to tell you."

Sharley smiled. "I can respect that. I've prayed a lot over this situation. As a child, I was the focal point of my parents' lives, and I couldn't understand why my grandfather Samuels treated Mom as he did. It didn't matter when Mom told me it was okay. I held a grudge. Then I grew up, and I became a Christian. Forgive and forget became part of my life. I'm being tested now. Am I the Christian I want to be? Maybe. I have to be sure I'm not being hypocritical. It's not about Papa Sam making up the past to me. It's about our making a future with the time we have now."

"Well, I can understand the hypocrite part."

The dryness in his tone caught Sharley's attention. "What do you mean?"

"Forget it."

Like a dog worrying a bone, Sharley asked, "What's on your mind, Kenan?"

"I'm just trying to reconcile this new truth about Sam with the man I thought he was. He's always going on about Jesus, and then I find out he deserted his family. That's not something a Christian does, is it?"

"It's something a confused Christian might do," Sharley pointed out. "Or something that someone might have done before he became a Christian. Our God is a forgiving God. He forgives us when we do things that are wrong."

"Well, I don't know much about that, but you should see him when he tells people about his beautiful granddaughter. Sam particularly likes to tell them you're an undertaker. Most of the staff were as shocked as I was. They had no idea. He loves to tell them you call him Papa Sam and you're as alike as two peas in a pod."

Sharley found it interesting that Kenan didn't want to discuss the matter further. "I wouldn't go that far," she said softly. "My friends have been shocked by the news. Maybe I can get him to come for a visit. There aren't a lot of his generation left, but there are probably people who remember him."

"Sam doesn't travel much, Sharley. The trips to and from the office are about the extent of his excursions."

"I see."

"You seem disappointed."

"No, just confused. Tell me, Kenan, does Sam really want me to act as his hostess, or was it an excuse?"

"Sam's talked about you all week. He's impressed by his granddaughter, but he is dealing with his pride. I don't think he's ever come to grips with what he did to his family. He justifies it by telling himself they were better off—but he missed them, too." Kenan sighed. "No, Sam didn't send me here. But he does hope you'll be his hostess."

Sharley looked thoughtfully up at the sky for a moment, and then she got to her feet. "It's getting late. We'd better call it a night. You probably want to get an early start tomorrow."

"We haven't discussed us yet, Sharley."

She turned to look at him. "Is there a future Mrs. Montgomery in Boston, Kenan?"

"I was involved with a woman until just before my vacation. We were good friends. I felt we had enough going for us to make a good marriage."

"She didn't agree?"

"Jocelyn didn't want a marriage based on friendship. She feels we deserve the fireworks."

"I see. Do you see these fireworks as part of our relationship?"

"There have already been a few explosions." He chuckled, and she found herself liking the sound.

"I'm nothing if not voluble, but my fuse isn't that short. What about our differences, Kenan? The potential problems we might face?"

"I'm not thinking about them right now."

"So I'd be a diversion?"

"I'm ready to settle down. Eager to find the right woman and start a family Why are you running for coroner?"

"It's something I want to do."

"Isn't your job gruesome enough without you being called to heaven only knows where to look at all kinds of horrible sights?"

"This is a small town, Kenan," she said, a small measure of exasperation in her tone. "We rarely have anything more involved than someone slipping away peacefully in their sleep. Granted, old age may be considered gruesome by some, but it happens to us all sooner or later."

"And how do you feel about this thing that's happened with us?"

"I'm as curious as you are, but I'm not packing to move to Boston. I'm praying about it."

Kenan sprang to his feet and paced restlessly. *And that pretty much says it all,* Sharley thought. She sighed. "As I said, it's late. Let's just sleep on this."

Sharley went into her room next to Aunt Liza's and listened to the sound of the shower and then heard his door click shut. Kenan Montgomery fascinated her. In some ways, he was everything she wanted in a man, and more—and she surely was getting impatient for a husband.

She slipped into her nightgown and picked up a brush, sweeping it through the curls. So what did she think about his readiness for commitment? She was ready to find the right man and settle down to married life and babies herself, but she had her doubts that she and Kenan could ever be right for each other. Not if his life wasn't committed to Christ.

❧

Kenan stepped from the shower and toweled dry, taking care to pick up after himself. At home he might not have bothered, but for some reason he didn't want Sharley thinking he was a total slob.

He had surprised himself with the overwhelming urge to see her again, but he had hated to admit to her that his visit had absolutely nothing to do with Sam Samuels and his birthday. It was an excuse and a sorry one at that. He should have just told Sharley he wanted to see her again and left it at that. Now he had her upset because Sam hadn't taken the time to call and invite her to the party.

Sam would probably rip into him for that one. He knew Sam and Sharley were negotiating the most complicated contract of all, and now he'd botched it up miserably. No way she'd believe now that Sam was calling because he wanted to. Not unless he made her understand.

Kenan pulled on a pair of sweats and the shirt he'd worn earlier and stepped into the hallway, searching for an indication of where Sharley's room was located. He spotted the light underneath the doorway on the other side of her aunt's room. He tapped and listened for sounds of stirring. She might have drifted off and left her light on. No, he could hear the muffled volume of the television, the nightly news.

Sharley was belting her robe when she opened the door. "Kenan, what is it? Is something wrong? Did you need something?"

Now that he had her full attention, Kenan didn't know where to start. The truth was always the best place. "First off, I need to apologize."

"Apologize?" Tiny lines of confusion crinkled her forehead.

"For not telling you why I came. I misled you into believing that Sam sent me. He doesn't even know I'm here, nor was it his intent that I invite you to the party. He told me yesterday that he planned to call and issue the invitation this weekend. I jumped the gun because I wanted an excuse to see you. I needed to see you."

"Needed to see me?"

Kenan nodded. "We might have some major differences of opinion on a variety of topics, but attraction has an agenda of its own. The heart doesn't always figure the differences into the equation. It just knows that something is right, and I can certainly tell you my heart is pretty impressed."

Her eyes were swimming, he saw. Maybe he wasn't doing such a good job here.

"Thank you, Kenan. That was so beautiful."

He reached for her hand. "I don't want you upset with Sam for something that isn't his fault. I should have told you the truth from the start. See, you're already having a good influence on me."

Sharley laughed.

"Now get some sleep," he said, leaning to kiss her forehead. "I'll see you in the morning."

❧

Long after she returned to bed, Sharley lay thinking of what he had said and wondering what hope there was for the future.

"Lord, I believe You have a plan for me that You will one day make clear. Help me be patient and receptive to Your wishes when that day comes."

Chapter 5

A week later, Sharley adjusted her body against the strings of the hammock and smiled her satisfaction at having a Saturday afternoon free to enjoy such a beautiful setting. The yard overflowed with flowers planted by generations of Montgomery women. Old-fashioned wild roses; pink, purple, and white Formosa azaleas; white baby's breath; and a pink dogwood were just a few of the bounty of blossoms.

The daffodils had already shown their sunny little faces, and Sharley looked forward to seeing her personal favorite, the irises. Gladiolus, lilies, and a multitude of others would follow. She pushed the feeling she should be working in the garden far back and felt little remorse. The sun shone brightly, the sky was a clear blue, and the air was redolent with the odor of the grass that had been cut the previous day.

The only thing she could think of to make it better was Kenan. *Kenan,* she thought dreamily. Her eyelids drifted closed with the lazy sway of her string cradle in the spring breezes, her thoughts on the man who had happened into her life.

He had left town early the previous Sunday morning. Sharley insisted he stay for breakfast and meet Aunt Liza. Her mother's best friend had come to visit for a few days, and the three of them had talked more over eggs, toast, and coffee.

Her relationship with God kept Sharley thinking that to pursue a romance now with Kenan would mean being unequally yoked together—but she couldn't help but hope that one day Kenan would find Christ and things would be different for them both.

She had no idea when she would see him again. No doubt a religious mortician gave him plenty of room for dilemma.

❧

Kenan's eyes were drawn to the tiny smile at the corner of Sharley's mouth. Her devil smile, he called it, noting its frequent appearance, particularly when she was in a playful mood.

He had meant to surprise her but instead he found himself surprised. Her business was locked up tight, and she was here, resting peacefully in her backyard. He hated to wake her, but their time together would be limited as it was.

The fragile stem of the flower snapped beneath his hand, and he moved to tease Sharley awake. A gentle brush across her nose resulted in a wrinkle and a frown. Her hand rose at the second sweep, and Kenan's lips replaced the flower with the third.

Her eyes opened wide as he locked his fingers in the mesh fabric and lifted playfully. "You're looking entirely too comfortable."

"Kenan. You're here," Sharley cried. He let go, and the hammock swayed softly.

"In the flesh." One long finger tapped the book that lay open against her chest. "Boring?"

Sharley lay back, feeling at a slight disadvantage as she looked up at him. "I didn't hear a chopper."

"It's in Boston. Sam didn't send me so I couldn't take advantage of his good nature. I caught a flight and rented a car."

"But you drove for two hours. Why didn't you call?"

"If I'd known business was so slow, I would have."

"No funerals this week."

"You mean you've had the entire weekend off?" Kenan asked. He could have flown up earlier and spent more time with her.

"Yes, but I had to stay close to home. You never know."

Deathwatch, Kenan thought grimly. He wouldn't let the thought spoil their time together. He was here, and they were going to be happy. "You never answered my question about the book."

"Definitely not boring. It's my grandmother's journal. I know more about Papa Sam's parents than I ever did. Mommy Jean lived next door to the Samuelses when she was growing up, and from what I've read, spent almost as much time at Stewart and Catherine Samuels's as she did at home."

"Sounds like quite a discovery."

"Oh, it is. Can you believe it? She's written about my great-grandparents, Papa Sam's parents."

"You seem excited."

"Well, it is another part of my life I didn't know. And a different side of my grandmother. Her mother died when she was an infant. My great-grandfather never remarried."

"Why haven't you read the journals before?"

"When Mommy Jean was alive, it seemed an invasion of her privacy. I don't think Mother ever read them."

"Have you read the part where she and Sam fell in love?"

Sharley smiled at the thought Kenan was as intrigued by Sam and Jean's romance as she was.

"For the longest time, I think she was more in love with his parents. In the part I'm reading now, she's at that age where young Sam is a real pain, but they're on the verge."

On the verge. Just where their own relationship teetered.

"I just ran across this entry. Listen. 'Sam noticed me for the first time today.

For my sixteenth birthday, his mom brought me a grown-up dress and helped me put my hair up. When I took my regular seat in the Sunday school class, he actually smiled and waved, even though he was with a bunch of his pals. It was wonderful. Then he came over and sat with me during the sermon and afterward asked if he could walk me home. I said okay since we were both going that way anyway. Mary Beth Langley didn't like it one bit. She's so sure Sam will marry her, but she need not be because one day I plan to marry him.'" Sharley reread the name, trying to place the woman. "Mrs. Hinson and Papa Sam?" she exclaimed in disbelief. She laughed outright. "I can't imagine that peppery old lady and Papa Sam together."

"Go on. Does she say how she managed it?"

"'He lingered for a while until Daddy announced it was time for lunch and told Sam he'd better get home before his father came looking for him,'" Sharley read. "'Daddy's such an old grouch at times. I don't know why he couldn't have invited Sam to stay.'"

Sharley laughed. "That's not what she said when I was sixteen and interested in a boy."

"No encouragement?"

"None whatsoever."

Kenan bent to examine the hammock. "Will this thing hold two people?"

"It's supposed to."

"Slide over. I suddenly feel the urge to be lazy."

Kenan lay beside her, keeping one foot on the ground. They hung at an angle; Sharley rolled up against him.

"Come on, Kenan. Lift your other leg. We aren't going to tip over."

He relaxed, and they rested together in the webbed enclosure.

"How's Triple S?" Sharley chuckled at his quick frown. "You're determined he and I will adore each other, aren't you?"

"I'd like to see you accept your grandfather."

"He called me last week. Wants me to come up for his birthday party."

"Will you? It could be his last birthday."

A jolt of dismay shot through Sharley at the thought. She didn't want to lose her grandfather. "Let's hope not. Besides, can you imagine what some of his guests would think? Not only a surprise granddaughter, but a mortician."

"Are you worried about what they would think?"

"Not particularly."

"Sam gets a real kick from telling his friends his granddaughter is an undertaker."

"I'd prefer mortician or funeral director." They shared a smile. "I plan to visit Sam again. Just as soon as I get my life in order."

"What about becoming coroner? You'll have even less time and more demands on the time you do have."

"I'll find a way. I always do. Does he know you're in Samuels?"

"No."

"Why? It's not his place to approve or disapprove of our getting to know each other."

"I can't say that. He's my friend. The fact that he's related to you makes it doubly hard to keep it between us."

"Why does it have to be a secret?" Sharley asked finally.

"Because I don't want to get his hopes up. I'm afraid Sam would push us if he knew."

"Maybe so." Sharley gave him a skeptical glance.

"You don't believe me?"

"Oh, I believe Sam might push you. But I was wondering if you were reluctant to talk to him about your own attraction. You have to admit you aren't exactly delighted with the way things have been happening between us," Sharley said.

They lay in total silence, each contemplating the words.

"So, how's the historical research going?" Kenan asked finally.

"Nothing new on the town, but lots of interesting reading on our family. These journals are memoirs. Mommy Jean covered every little detail. There's a lot about their childhood years. Her family were Reynoldses. They moved here when she was eight, and her father bought the local hardware store."

"You won't find anything like those journals in our family. I doubt my dad could tell you his great-grandfather's name."

"Too bad Papa Sam can't attend the celebration," Sharley said thoughtfully.

"Don't suggest it to Sam, Sharley. He'd send me as his representative." Kenan flashed her a lopsided grin.

Sharley smiled back. "So how was your week?"

"Extremely busy."

"And you jumped on a plane and came here rather than resting over the weekend? I wish you had called."

Kenan wondered about the regret in her tone. "What are your plans for the rest of the day?"

"Strictly politics. I've got to get out on the campaign trail later on to shake some hands and kiss some babies."

"Do you really do that? Kiss babies," he supplied at her questioning look.

Sharley grinned. "I can't resist most of them. If I'd known you were coming, I would have scheduled this for another time or at least gotten some volunteers to take my place."

"Sounds as if you're already too busy for me. But if you need volunteers, I'm good with a hammer and a stapler."

"Never let it be said the Montgomery Campaign for Coroner turned down a pair of willing hands."

Two hours later Kenan's feet ached and he forced a smile. He stopped thinking of Samuels as a small town at the end of the first hour. He was on intimate terms with every intersection and had a passing acquaintance with all the places a person could rest their weary body.

"Stop frowning, Kenan. You're scaring away my supporters."

He wasn't having fun. He'd walked alongside Sharley, growing more perturbed when their conversation was frequently interrupted by her stops to shake hands and distribute campaign literature.

"You don't have to do this," Sharley said at his long-suffering expression.

"I don't mind."

Her laughter trilled around them. "Like you don't mind a root canal."

Kenan caught her hand in his. "I came to see you. If this is the only way I can see you, I'll deal with it. Meanwhile, I'll help in any way possible."

"In that case, I'll let you take this future coroner out to dinner after we finish. I know just the place."

"Pretty confident, aren't we?"

"Why not? I go after the things I want. Mr. Jones," she called and moved to talk with the potential supporter.

Things she wanted, Kenan thought as he waited for her to finish her conversation. Did he fall in that category? *Obviously not.* If he had called, Sharley would have given him a million reasons why he shouldn't make the trip.

In his heart, Kenan knew the biggest reason was fear. No doubt his hot and cold behavior confused her as much as it did him. Probably explained why she constantly reminded him of the distance that separated them.

Maybe she was right. He felt like he was beating his head against a brick wall. The situation seemed pretty hopeless. Sharley's life was entrenched in Samuels. He doubted she took time from her busy campaign schedule to think about him.

She returned, and they continued to walk. "Tell me about the dinner everyone keeps mentioning," he said.

"The church holds fellowship dinners. The members invite their friends to break bread with the congregation. We don't have to go if you think you would be uncomfortable."

Before he could answer, a young woman pushing a baby stroller hailed them. Kenan smiled when the baby lifted her arms toward Sharley, indicating that she wanted to be held.

Sharley handed him the flyers. The mother nodded her okay, and Sharley leaned down to unsnap the restraining lap belt. "How's my girl?" she asked.

The toddler jabbered some nonsensical language that contained one understandable word: Sharley.

"Kenan Montgomery, this is my friend, Beth Thompson, and her daughter, Claire. Where's my other girl?"

"Welcome to Samuels," Beth said to Kenan before turning back to answer Sharley's question. "With her daddy. A group of men started practice for a T-ball league. That's where we're headed now. To see Cindy play."

A wistful smile touched Sharley's face. "Oh, I bet they're too cute for words."

"It's interesting," Beth said, grinning broadly. "Cindy and the others haven't quite grasped the concept of team sport."

"Cindy's in my Sunday school class," Sharley told Kenan. "Maybe we'll stop by after we finish."

"Cindy would love to have Ms. Sharley in the stands rooting for her. Of course, she'd probably rather sit in your lap than play ball."

"Give me some sugar, Claire?" Sharley coaxed. The baby allowed her cheek to be kissed and was all smiles when Sharley returned her to the stroller. "I'll be rooting for Cindy."

"Don't show too much enthusiasm. Dan is looking for sponsors for the team." When Sharley laughed, Beth said, "Hey, I'm serious. These guys are getting so desperate they'd take the funeral home's money in a heartbeat."

"How many of my other kids are playing?"

"At least four."

"That's enough for me. Tell Dan he's got a sponsor if he's interested."

"You don't have to, Sharley."

"Sure I do. I want my little darlings to be as well dressed as the other teams. Just tell Dan not to make the uniforms dark and let's keep the funeral home name low profile and dignified."

They waved the mother and child off, and Kenan asked, "Why did you do that?"

"It's a few dollars for a good cause. These children aren't exposed to a lot of extracurricular activities, and it doesn't hurt me any to help where I can."

"Do they all know what a generous person you are?"

"Afraid so. Let me take some of that stuff," Sharley offered.

"I'm balanced. Lead on, Ms. Montgomery." Kenan found himself shifting the items until he could take Sharley's hand in his. "I imagine the town is a far cry from the one Sam knew."

"Not really. Some things have changed. The bank doesn't have the Samuels name associated with it. The Reynolds family no longer own the hardware store. There are a few new businesses and less old ones. More cars on the street. A few less people in the population count."

When they passed a church, Sharley drew to a halt at the gate. "Here's something you might like to see."

Kenan eyed the cemetery and said, "Not particularly."

"Oh, come on. It's where Sam will be buried. My mom and grandmother are here, along with Sam's parents."

The cemetery was well kept with monuments dating back to Samuels's beginning. Sharley pointed out various ancestors.

"You don't have to go far to shake your family tree. Appears they're all right here."

"My tree is down to a branch."

"Don't worry. You'll give it new roots."

"I hope to."

"How many miles do you plan to walk today? My feet are killing me."

"Oh, you. We'd better get moving. We're losing daylight here."

Later, while dressing for dinner, the situation between Kenan and herself overwhelmed Sharley's thoughts. She cared deeply for Kenan, but if he was right with Christ, her own life was important, too. Certain things, the family business and even her political career, had been a part of her life plan for as long as she could recall. Reconciling Kenan's place in her life seemed impossible.

She thought about it often, sometimes telling herself that once he had a living relationship with God, all they would need to be happy would be for him to give up his life and move to Samuels. And then she would shake her head at herself, for that was about as realistic as Santa, the Easter bunny, and the tooth fairy all rolled into one. Kenan enjoyed his job with her grandfather. She enjoyed her life in Samuels. And the miles separating the two made it highly unlikely either of them would find common ground.

Kenan couldn't cover the distance that separated them forever. Still, she did something she'd learned to do a long time ago and put it into the Lord's hands. The doorbell rang, and she glanced in the mirror one last time. Kenan was here to take her to dinner.

"You're looking mighty handsome," she said, taking in the sight of him in jeans and a casual shirt. "There will be a gleam in several sets of mothers' and daughters' eyes tonight."

"Too bad. There's only one Samuelite I'm interested in."

Kenan drove them to the church in his rental car. Sharley led the way inside and introduced him around the room. One of the town's oldest citizens sat in her usual place of honor. "Who have you got here, Sharley?"

"Mrs. Hinson, this is Kenan Montgomery. He works with my grandfather in Boston."

The old woman's piercing eyes pinpointed Kenan. "So you work with Samuel?"

"Yes, ma'am."

"Mrs. Hinson," Sharley said, "I ran across your name in Grandmother's journal.

You never told me you dated my grandfather. You know we recently met for the first time?"

"I imagine Jean didn't say much that was good. That was many years before I met my Billy. Of course, if I had married Sam Samuels, he'd never have gone traipsing off to Boston."

"Oh, I don't know, Mrs. Hinson. I get the impression nothing would have kept him in Samuels."

"It was your grandmother's fault. She wasn't woman enough to keep her man by her side. All her highfalutin ways, thinking she was better than everybody else."

Sharley bit back her temper. "I'll be sure and tell Papa Sam I met one of his old sweethearts next time we talk."

"Don't matter one way or another to me. Never did hold much to him running off and deserting his family. God blessed me with a much better man."

Sharley almost snorted her disdain. Billy Hinson barely had two pennies to rub together all his life. He had lived off his wife's family for as long as Sharley had been alive. Of course, Mary Beth Langley had been an old maid when she met Billy Ray Hinson, and chances were she'd given up on marriage.

"Forgive me, Lord," Sharley whispered, realizing she was being judgmental. She couldn't help but think how everyone's life could have changed if her grandparents had never met. Especially hers. If Sam Samuels had chosen this woman as his wife, she would not have existed.

"It's been nice talking to you, Mrs. Hinson."

"You tell Sam I still think he did wrong."

"Persistent, isn't she?" Kenan held Sharley's hand as she pulled him through the crowd. "Is that the one we read about this morning?"

"I imagine she was more his type at sixteen. The years have a way of changing people."

"Maybe she's one of the reasons he left. I wonder how many more feel like she does?"

"Most men and women in this town don't take kindly to someone being done wrong, Kenan. But they are Christian enough to forgive and forget when someone does make a mistake. If Papa Sam came here, he'd be welcomed as befits his status as descendant of the founding father. No questions asked. Come on, let's fix ourselves a plate."

Kenan followed Sharley through the line, and they joined a table of her friends. She introduced him around and then joined the chatter. A young man stopped by the table and rested his hands on Sharley's shoulders. She looked up at him, and her face blossomed into a pleased smile.

"Pastor George, this is Kenan Montgomery. Kenan, this is our pastor, George Roberts."

"Glad to have you with us, Kenan."

"Good to be here, sir."

"Call me George. Perhaps we can talk a bit later. Enjoy yourselves."

"Isn't he a bit young to be a pastor?" Kenan whispered after the reverend had moved on to another table.

"He's the best, stomps on toes, wakes people up, and everyone still loves him. His wife's a real sweetie, too. You'd better finish that if you want seconds. The food at these dinners disappears fast."

Sharley's popularity was even more obvious as she chatted with the various people who made a point of searching her out. Kenan gave up when the team coach claimed her attention.

"Beth said you were willing to be a team sponsor."

"Don't sound so eager, or I might be tempted to put stipulations on my sponsorship."

"Sharley honey, we're so desperate that if you insisted on glow-in-the-dark skeletons and calling the team 'Dem Bones,' we'd take you up on it."

Sharley laughed in delight. "Hmm. Scare the competition away. Now that's tempting, but I think the objective is to make our little darlings look as good as the other team. It's bad enough that they have to have Montgomery-Sloan on their uniforms at all. Maybe I should just make a private contribution."

"After all you've done for this community, we'd be proud to wear your name on our uniforms."

Kenan wandered over to the dessert table. He took a serving of lemon pie and was about to take a second for Sharley when Pastor George came to stand beside him.

"Kenan, right?"

"Yes, sir."

"Please call me George."

Kenan smiled politely, but he wasn't comfortable with calling a man of the cloth by his first name.

"We have a larger group than normal tonight," the pastor said. "I'm glad you could come with Sharley. Remind me where you're from."

"Boston. I work with Sharley's grandfather."

The pastor smiled. "That certainly was a surprise. And where do you attend church?"

"I get to the Baptist church near my home occasionally."

"Easter and Christmas?"

Kenan was startled by the man's bluntness. He was embarrassed to admit the pastor was right.

"I see. So are you a Christian?"

"I believe in Christ. I suppose I haven't been all that faithful about serving Him."

"Believing is half the battle, Kenan. Serving Him is important, too. Sharley would be the first to tell you that. She's one of our best workers in the church. I've come to know her even better since we conducted several funeral services together and can honestly say she has a steadfast devotion to the Lord. And that's what really counts—a living relationship with the Person of Christ."

What was this man trying to tell him? Kenan wondered as he glanced over at the table where Sharley sat. "From what I know about Sharley, she does everything with gusto. Seems only natural she'd give her all to her church, as well."

"So true. I'd say she's given her all to God as well. It's been good talking to you. I'll remember you in my prayers."

Kenan muttered his thanks and escaped the uncomfortable ordeal, his mind spinning with the pastor's words. Was Christianity like a badge you wore for the world to see? True, he'd always been told a true believer was known by his actions, but he'd done nothing here tonight to indicate he wasn't a Christian. So why had the pastor buttonholed him this way? And yet strangely enough, these people accepted him into their group, without demand that the sinner leave their presence.

Kenan wandered back to the table, passing Sharley the pie. She told him about the team's escapades. A number of the little team players stopped by to hug Ms. Sharley and to tell her they would see her in Sunday school. *She's good with children,* Kenan thought as she pulled another one onto her lap and teased him into a big smile.

The time slipped by, and before either of them realized it, most of the food had been packed away and the cleanup process was well underway. Kenan helped Sharley pick up the few plates and cups that dotted the tabletops and tossed them in the trash.

"We'd better get you over to the B and B before they lock up for the night."

Kenan negotiated the way to Sharley's house with relative ease and caught himself thinking of how long the same trip would have taken in Boston.

"What are your plans for in the morning?" she asked him.

"Nothing really," he said. "I've got a flight out in the afternoon around four, but I'm free until then. What did you have in mind?"

"I thought you might want to go to church with me."

"I don't have suitable clothes." An excuse. Years ago when his mother had made him attend Sunday school, he learned you always wore your best. Of course he did have a pair of dress slacks and a little dressier sport shirt.

"It was just a thought. You seemed to get along well with Pastor George. I thought you might like to hear him preach."

"Do you ever miss church?"

"Rarely. My week feels incomplete when I do."

"So you wouldn't consider taking off to be with me?"

"God never takes a day off, Kenan. The least I can do is spend a couple of hours in His house. Besides, my little ones will expect their Sunday school lesson. You're welcome to come with me. No one would mind if you wore your jeans."

"I could treat you to lunch afterward."

When she didn't make a comment right away, Kenan realized Sharley was disappointed.

"I'd like that," she said at last.

The following day they lunched at the bed-and-breakfast restaurant. Sharley met him there after church, and they spent an enjoyable hour together. "This place has good food," he commented.

"Martha does know how to cook," Sharley agreed. "She could open a restaurant if she didn't like the B and B better."

He rolled his arm to look at his watch and sighed. "Time for me to hit the road if I plan to make my flight."

"I'm glad you came."

Kenan didn't respond. He picked up the check and stopped by the cashier to pay before ushering Sharley to her car. He bent and looked in the open window. "What if I asked you to give my world a try? I've come to Samuels and spent time doing the things you do. Will you do the same for me?"

Sharley stared into the dark depths of his gaze. "It's impossible. I have commitments. I can't just pack up and go running off to Boston. Besides my business, I have my Sunday school class and my campaign. May is closer than you realize."

"So, I'm not worth the effort. Everything is more important than me?"

She sighed her exasperation. "I didn't say that."

"I've put everything in my life on hold for the past two weekends. I've had work to do, places to go, people to see, but you were important enough for me to decide I should come. I guess I know where I stand."

"Don't give me that, Kenan Montgomery. If it had been really inconvenient, you wouldn't have come. You've surprised me both times, so it wasn't a planned thing. Just maybe in the back of your mind you thought, 'I'll pursue this thing with Sharley'—but it wasn't an anticipated, planned trip."

"I did anticipate seeing you again," Kenan growled. "That's what this is all about. I don't plan my life anymore. Mostly life happens—and we happened. So now, what are we going to do about it?"

"You tell me."

"You really want to know what I think?" Kenan asked, anger simmering deep in the black gaze. "No, I don't think you do. I know your entire family was so caught up in proving Sam made a mistake in leaving Samuels that you would never consider wanting a life elsewhere."

"That's not true. I have traditional values that include pride in my hometown. I would never desert Samuels."

"Finish your sentence."

"What do you mean?"

"The unspoken 'like my grandfather deserted his town.' You claim you don't harbor any resentment, but deep inside you do. You've taken on your heritage like a burden. This is a community, not a dictatorship. You're not mayor or a member of the city council. You're just a prominent businesswoman in the community. I think you're running for coroner to get a political in."

"That's not why."

"Then why?"

"Because I'm qualified. My sense of civic duty is strong. I want to be important to Samuels."

"You want to be recorded in the annals of history?"

"I want my kids to have a sense of belonging."

Her words hit Kenan with all the force of a kick in the stomach. "A sense of belonging," he repeated slowly. He could understand that.

His father had been in the military, and as a child, he had moved frequently until his father left the military and used the land his parents left him to open a flight school. Kenan was ten, and the idea of staying in one place forever excited him. No more transient friends. He loved everything about Texas and flying. It was as close to perfect as he thought life could get. And then Vietnam destroyed all that. By the time he returned home, his world was too out of whack for him to live there.

Kenan stared at her for a minute longer before he said, "I've got a plane to catch."

Chapter 6

T his is too unreal," Sharley whispered, looking out the window as the plane circled Logan International.

"Did you say something?"

She glanced at the man who had traveled from North Carolina in the seat next to hers and shook her head. "Just thinking out loud."

Sharley couldn't believe she was doing this. Sam and Kenan had no idea she was coming to the party. She had just decided herself this morning after the two huge flower arrangements arrived, one from Sam, the other from Kenan. She wasn't looking for excuses, but she had to acknowledge that this was one of the few remaining birthdays she would share with her grandfather.

Her attempts at resuming life as normal failed miserably. She filled every waking hour with Montgomery-Sloan, politicking, church activities, and any social event she could cram in, but the unfinished business with Kenan and Papa Sam lingered, refusing to allow her to forget.

Every time she considered their conversations, she told herself that she was better off without either of them—but her emotions were telling her the complete opposite. Kenan had made an impact on her in more ways than she wanted to consider.

She read the journals and contemplated how it must have been for her grandparents when they were in love. The truth that she, too, wanted to be in love weighed even heavier. Sharley sensed her emotions could easily grow, but she refused to give consideration to Kenan's terms. And anyway, until he drew closer to the Lord, she couldn't even consider pursuing their relationship.

For her birthday, the guys had taken her out to breakfast and presented her with a beautiful cake. *Too beautiful*. She insisted they have a slice, and the moment the knife touched the luscious frosting, it exploded in a boom of confetti and frosting.

Jack and Devlin had all but rolled on the floor laughing. The lack of business gave them more opportunity to laugh and gloat, and finally Sharley left them to their merriment and went to her office.

She picked up the fax from the machine to find it was from Sam. It was a birthday greeting of sorts, filled with wishes for a wonderful day. He had penned a note reminding her the scheduled date of the party was that night and he'd love to have her there.

And since no business commitments stood in her way, she packed her bag and made her reservations. Jack and Devlin thought it was a great idea. Jack volunteered to drive her to the airport, and Devlin ran by the dry cleaners to pick up her dress. Sharley knew subconsciously she must have all along wanted to attend because she had taken her best evening gown to the cleaners on Monday.

Kenan's most recent visit was all the impetus she needed. She was drawn to him and though she prayed constantly for God's guidance in the matter, she understood exactly where Kenan was coming from when he spoke of the heart being involved. In a very short time, she had grown exceedingly fond of him. Actually she knew her feelings had gone far beyond fondness, and while they might not be full-fledged love, they were something very close.

"Do you think I'm doing the right thing, Jack?" she asked, just minutes before leaving for the airport.

"I think that if you don't go and see what it is you're missing, one day you'll be sorry."

"Hey, boss, got your dress here," Devlin yelled. "Jim put it in the garment bag and stuffed it with tissue to keep it from wrinkling. Better get a move on if you want to catch that plane. This dress is going to impress your new boyfriend."

"Kenan's not my boyfriend."

"Sure he's not," Devlin said.

"Haven't seen anyone so moony-eyed since Devlin's lady said yes to his proposal," Jack teased.

They weren't far off with their teasing. "You guys are crazy."

"Crazy like a fox. You can't fool us. Your grandfather may be in Boston, but someone else is there, too."

She couldn't lie. Not even the anger she had felt after Kenan's accusation changed her feelings. They hadn't talked since he'd left Samuels, but she hoped to discuss the matter while she was in Boston. He deserved the same chances he'd given her.

The plane touched down, and Sharley retrieved her carry-on bag and the garment bag holding her dress. Outside the airport, she hailed a cab and directed the driver to take her to the hotel. She needed to call Kenan and ask if he would mind giving her a lift to the party.

Would Sam be surprised? Sharley thought so, despite his persistence. The note had been only one of the reminders he'd sent; most of them had been closer to demands that Sharley act as his hostess. She had refused repeatedly before he finally accepted her decision. Last time they spoke on the phone, he said he understood. They chatted for a few minutes longer, and he suggested they get together soon. Sharley promised to make every effort to schedule another trip to Boston.

After checking in, Sharley went directly to the phone and called the number on the card Kenan had given her. His instructions had been to call anytime she needed to get in touch with him. *Now would be one of those times,* she thought as she waited for his secretary to answer. What was Kenan going to think about her change of plans? She gave her name, and the secretary transferred her without hesitation.

"Sharley? Is something wrong?"

"Everything's fine. I'm here in Boston. At a hotel. I decided to surprise Papa Sam."

"He'll be delighted, but why didn't you go to the house?"

"Surprises are generally more effective when the person being surprised doesn't know he's being surprised," Sharley pointed out.

"Fine. Sam will be happy. He was disappointed that you couldn't come."

"I need your help."

"How so?"

"I couldn't find Sam's house if you offered me a million dollars, and I suspect it's a steep fare for a taxi."

"Why don't you call and have Jamie pick you up?"

"I could do that," she agreed, trying not to show the disappointment she felt at his words. "I just thought you might like to take me to the party. Sorry to have bothered you. I'll see you later."

What had happened? The chill in his voice was enough to give her frostbite. Maybe he was still angry because she hadn't agreed right away when he asked her to come to the party.

She started to say good-bye, but he interrupted her. "Sharley, wait. I'd love to be your escort. Can you be ready by six?"

"Are you sure, Kenan?"

"Positive."

"Then I'll be ready and waiting."

"See you shortly."

Sharley hung up the phone and glanced at her watch. There was time to grab a bite to eat before she dressed. She went downstairs to the restaurant.

Five-star certainly didn't have anything to do with their restaurant service, Sharley decided almost forty-five minutes later when her meal arrived. Her plenty of time had been cut by almost an hour. She'd be doing good to have showered by the time Kenan arrived. He was going to be upset. Oh well, she could always tell him to go on and call Jamie as he'd suggested.

❧

Kenan hesitated outside Sharley's room door and listened to the sounds coming from inside. *Why is she laughing?* he wondered as Sharley's uproarious laughter drifted out into the hallway. He knocked loudly enough to be heard.

The door opened, and he stopped short at the sight of her in a long satin gown, holding what looked like a formal red dress.

"What's so funny?"

"Those guys are a riot. Read this."

Kenan didn't have to ask which guys. What had they done now? He took the paper and read aloud, " 'Thought you might like a new dress for this formal occasion.' "

"I had Devlin pick up my dry cleaning because I was running late," she explained.

"I must be missing something here."

"Look," Sharley said, flipping the beautifully beaded red gown. "They've given new meaning to the term backless."

Puzzlement creased Kenan's face as he fingered the fine fabric of the dress.

"It's a shroud, Kenan. Funeral clothing. They must have switched it after he picked up my dress."

He dropped the fabric as though it were red-hot.

"Wonder what Triple S would think if I showed up in that?"

"What were they thinking?" Kenan exploded. "Doesn't it bother you in the least that these guys have pretty much stopped you from attending the party? You can't go with your entire back exposed."

"It's no big deal, Kenan. I can probably pick up something in one of the shops downstairs."

"Sam's guests will expect to find his granddaughter attired for the occasion."

"Haute couture? Well, then they would have known the gown I intended to wear was off the rack, wouldn't they? So, tell me, what do I wear to Sam's party?"

"You should fire those guys."

"I know beyond a shadow of a doubt that something backfired. They wouldn't have intentionally left me without a dress. Besides, how can I fire them for something I started? Our jokes bring fun into the back rooms, and no one gets hurt."

Kenan felt his cheeks redden as he recalled his reaction at their first meeting.

"Well, not usually," Sharley said. "That time with you was the exception." She touched his face. "There's no reason to be ashamed. We did agree no customers in the future. I was afraid you would sue me."

"I suppose we could call a few shops and see what we can find. Or. . ." Kenan began, breaking off as he realized Sharley probably wouldn't care for the idea.

"Or what?"

"There's a woman I know. She's about your size. Has a lot of formal clothing."

"How do you know what's in her closet?" Sharley asked.

Kenan refused to meet her gaze. "We, ah. . .we. . ."

"Spit it out."

"It's the woman I used to date. Jocelyn."

"And it doesn't bother you to ask a favor of her?"

"Well. . .no," he admitted. "We had an amicable enough parting. You need a dress, and she has enough gowns to outfit her own shop. I'm sure she has something more appropriate than we can find on such short notice."

"Don't just stand there. Call her."

Sharley watched Kenan walk across the room. The sight of him in the black tuxedo took her breath away. She'd never known a man who could look so at home in a monkey suit, as her dad called a tuxedo. As he spoke on the phone with the other woman, one part of her wanted to be jealous that there had been someone in his life, but another part knew she had no right to feel anything.

"She'll wait for us," he said as he hung up the phone.

"Wait? Kenan, are we interrupting her plans?"

"She has a function. All the more reason for you to throw on something, and let's drive over right now. She lives in my building."

"I'll get dressed."

Minutes later, Kenan was tapping on an elegant door in an expensive high-rise condominium. The doorman had cast a doubtful look at her when she entered with Kenan. No doubt he found her wanting when it came to Kenan's usual companions. She had to admit she did look like she couldn't make up her mind: Her denim jumper was a bad match for the hair, makeup, and silver pumps.

The door opened, and Kenan said, "Jocelyn Kennedy, this is Charlotte Montgomery, Sam's granddaughter."

"Ms. Montgomery, I'm so pleased to meet you."

"Sharley, please. I can't tell you how thankful I am for your help."

Jocelyn Kennedy was dressed in a gown that made Sharley's original choice look like a bargain basement treasure. Her dress matched the beautifully deco-rated home, and yet Sharley felt comfortable with this woman who was certainly upwardly mobile career-wise to have achieved so much in her life. Or maybe she came from a wealthy family as well.

"I nearly died when I found that dress," Sharley said, launching into a descrip-tion that soon had the other woman fighting tears of laughter.

"That's priceless," Jocelyn whispered, wiping her eyes. "Let's go take a look in my closet. Actually I should let you see if you can wear this one." She waved at the dress she had on. "It's new and none of the guests will have seen it before."

"Absolutely not," Sharley said. "I'm sure you have something that will suit me just fine without taking the clothes off your back."

Jocelyn looked doubtful. "But everyone will expect Sam's granddaughter to. . ." She trailed off.

Sharley laughed. "Kenan and I just had this conversation. The first thing people will have to learn about Sam's granddaughter is not to expect the expected. I'm certain any gown you loan me will be more appropriate than the one I left in my hotel room."

They left Kenan in the living room, and Sharley followed Jocelyn through her beautifully decorated bedroom into a dressing room the size of her bedroom at home. One entire section was devoted to evening gowns. "Let me think for a second. Some of these wouldn't suit your coloring." Jocelyn sorted through them quickly before pulling one out. "Try this. I have no idea why I let myself be talked into buying it in the first place. It really doesn't suit me."

"Obviously so you could loan it to me," Sharley said as she quickly slipped her jumper off and reached for the emerald green satin dress. It was the most beautiful thing she had ever seen, exactly the type of dress she would have chosen.

She stepped into the gown and pulled it in place. It was a perfect fit. "I think we've found the dress."

"You're easy to please," Jocelyn said, smiling as she zipped the dress. "But I must admit it never looked that good on me."

Sharley glanced over her shoulder into the mirror. "I know better than that. You've saved the day, Jocelyn. I hope we haven't ruined your plans for the evening."

"Don't worry. I canceled."

Sharley's groan of dismay sounded throughout the room.

"Really, it's not a problem. It was more of an obligation than anything else, and I told the hostess an emergency had arisen. You'd better go before you're late. Kenan's probably wearing a hole in my carpet. I've never seen him so overwrought."

Sharley looked into the mirror and reached to tuck a loose strand into the neat upswept hair style. "Do you see a lot of each other?"

"Are you asking if we're involved?"

Sharley nodded.

"He's a friend. Kenan helped me through a rough period of my life." Jocelyn reached for a tissue. "I was jilted. He let me borrow a shoulder. He wasn't dating anyone then either."

"I wouldn't blame you if you had feelings for him," Sharley said, watching Jocelyn in the mirror. "He's quite something."

"He's a wonderful man, but there's nothing there for us. Now, let's get you to the party."

Sharley did a whirl as she stepped into the living room. "So, what do you think? Isn't this better than a shroud?"

He gave her a once-over. "Much better."

"You're an absolute lifesaver, Jocelyn," Sharley repeated.

"Glad I could help. What about your guys and the dress?"

"Could I borrow your phone?" Sharley dialed Jack's home number. "Hello, Jack. Thought I'd check in and see if you and Devlin were running my business into the ground?"

She caught Kenan's grimace out of the corner of her eye and winked at Jocelyn when she giggled. Sharley placed a hand over the receiver and whispered, "Kenan hates our funeral home jokes."

"It's quieter than a tomb around here," Jack said. "How are things in Boston?"

"Not good. The backless dress you and Devlin slipped in on me isn't going to go over well with my grandfather."

Silence greeted her words. "Didn't you get the other one? Devlin sent it special delivery."

"Where?"

"To your grandfather's."

"Since he doesn't know I'm in town, I bet he wonders why my dress is over there."

"Sharley, I'm sorry."

"That and a dollar will get me a cup of coffee, Jack. I owe you big-time for this one."

"Retribution doesn't become you, boss."

"Oh, I'm not harboring a grudge, but I will get even. You'd do well to remember that warning. Kenan thinks I should fire you both, but I think I'll keep you around to torment."

"You could change once you get there," Jack suggested.

"Maybe. Meanwhile I suggest you let Devlin know I said no more tricks with my wardrobe. You've caused a lot of trouble. Good night." Sharley replaced the receiver and grinned at Kenan and Jocelyn. "He's dialing Devlin's number right now."

"This is pretty bad," Kenan said.

"Not as bad as the time they had a mock paper made up with my obituary. I did a double take at breakfast that morning."

"What other kinds of jokes have they pulled?" Jocelyn asked.

"There was the time they set up my entire office under a tent in the parking lot. I just sat there until they tired of that one. Then there was the time they left a note for me to call Mr. Fox, and when I called, I got the zoo. They wrapped my favorite coffee mug in cellophane, and I poured coffee all over the table without getting a drop in the cup. The list goes on and on. Oh, we're going to be late. Jocelyn, since we ruined your plans, why don't you come with us? It's a dinner buffet so one more won't hurt. Besides, you're already dressed for a party."

"I couldn't. It wouldn't look right," Jocelyn said quickly.

"It's better if she doesn't," Kenan agreed.

"Sure you can. You know everybody." Sharley watched as Kenan and Jocelyn shared looks of surprise. "You're afraid it might be uncomfortable?"

"Well, yes. Kenan and I did see each other for some time."

"Which means my grandfather is well acquainted with you, and I'm certain he would love to have you attend. Besides, I'm indebted to you, and if you don't come, I won't enjoy my evening. Not to mention, there are bound to be eligible men at this party, and no beautiful woman should ever pass up the opportunity to meet handsome, wealthy men."

"Sharley." Kenan's voice held a note of warning.

She flashed Kenan a stubborn look. "Well, she is available. Can't you introduce her to some nice men?"

"Deliver me from matchmakers," Kenan all but shouted.

"It's okay," Jocelyn said softly. "Sharley's right. I'd like to find the same thing you've found."

Sharley looked at Kenan. "No, it's not like that," she said. Kenan echoed her words.

"If you say so. Mr. Right could be at that party tonight, and not only would I miss him, but I'd also spoil your evening."

"Exactly. Now grab your coat, and let's surprise Papa Sam."

❧

The party was everything Sharley imagined, and more. Her grandfather appeared both pleased and surprised by her arrival and insisted that she join him in the receiving line. The next hour became a whirlwind of new names and faces. She hoped there wasn't a test later, for she couldn't recall any of them.

Just when Sharley wasn't sure whether her feet or legs would give out first, the line diminished. Papa Sam led the way to a grouping of comfortable chairs. "A concession for my old age," he said as he settled in one and indicated Sharley should do the same. "Now, when did you arrive? Where is your luggage?"

She named the hotel. "I got in this afternoon. I wanted to surprise you, so I called Kenan and invited myself along."

"You should have called me. I suppose I should be grateful that you're not staying with him."

"What do you mean by that? Kenan doesn't deserve that. He's been nothing less than a gentleman."

"Maybe not, but I'm not a blind old man either. I know mutual attraction when I see it. He's a striking young man. Perhaps you're flattered by his interest?"

"And if I were?"

"I don't want you making a mistake."

"And would Kenan be a mistake?"

"You deserve someone who is as close to the Lord as you are. And I can't help but think of my own marriage. My problems with Jean weren't about love. They had to do with our lifestyle. She refused to bend. She wanted to live and die in a small town. I didn't. If either of us had been willing to change, chances are we would have stayed together."

Like herself and Kenan: They couldn't agree on lifestyles either. He would never be content to live in what he called a one-horse town, and she was too steeped in tradition to give it up. Was Sam trying to warn her?

"Kenan's a lot like me," the old man said. "I pray every day that he'll come straight with God—but even when he does, he likes it here. He has a future with the company. I don't see him giving it up. Now on the other hand, if you came to Boston. . ."

"It's not going to happen," she said softly. "Kenan knows my reasons. He's been to Samuels a couple of times. I know he considers you a friend and is afraid you'll disapprove of our relationship."

"There's nothing I'd like better than to see the two of you together. That is, if you were more evenly matched."

Sharley was beginning to hate that phrase. "You're right about the attraction. Kenan asked me to come to Boston. Your birthday party was an excellent excuse, but he's the main reason I'm here. I know I must wait until God shows me the man He wants in my life, but I'm drawn to Kenan like a moth to flame. I just need to make sure I don't get singed."

Sam laughed. "We all get a little crisp around the edges in our search for God's companion for us. Heaven knows I've tried, but for reasons known only to him, Kenan has refused to open himself to God. I play on his good nature all the time, asking him to accompany me to church. I can tell he sometimes wants to refuse, but my frailty has served as an excuse many times over."

Sharley's wry smile was indication of her own guilt. "I took him to a church social last Saturday night. But I don't think force-feeding him religion is going to do the trick."

"Perhaps not, but I think maybe you're the person who can help him understand God's plan for him."

"Kenan and I are dealing with an attraction right now, but I seriously doubt it will ever get to the point where our differences will be an issue."

"Never underestimate the power of love, Sharley."

"I exercise a great deal of caution in terms of my physical needs."

"Sharley! That wasn't what I meant."

"Yes, it was. And don't sound so shocked. God gave me those desires, and He will lead me to the man He wants to share my life and father my children. That's just one of the areas I place in His hands. I refuse to attempt to second-guess Him."

"Then perhaps Kenan Montgomery isn't that man. So stay away from the fire."

"How can you be so sure, Papa Sam? God brought me to you. Maybe God sent Kenan to me."

"Think, Sharley. You're here tonight with one of his old flames. Get to know him first."

"If it weren't for that old flame, I'd either not be present or woefully underdressed for this crowd." She told him the story of the practical joke that had gone awry.

Her grandfather shook his head. "If you'd called, I could have had a selection of gowns here in a matter of minutes."

Sharley didn't tell him her gown was probably somewhere in the house. She just shook her head. "I think you're missing the point. It's because of Jocelyn that I'm here dressed as I am, and because of me, she's here. She had other plans, which she canceled to help me out. I'm in her debt."

"Then I'm indebted as well."

"As you should be." Sharley slipped her shoes off and massaged her aching toes. "I think I'll visit the buffet. Can I get you anything?" She stood, wiggling her toes in the deep pile of the Oriental rug.

"Sharley, put your shoes back on immediately."

"You aren't ashamed of your country bumpkin granddaughter, are you?"

Sam leaned his head back against the chair and stared at her. "No, my dear, tonight you're a very beautiful reminisce of the wonderful times I had with Jean. You look very like her, as did your mother in those photographs you shared. Thank you for taking the time to send them to me."

"You're welcome. Mommy Jean and Mother were class acts."

"She would have fitted in well here," Sam said softly. "If only she had been willing to try."

He seemed miles away, and Sharley offered no response. She could only agree that her grandmother would have been an asset to Sam's world. A class act from the top of her elegant head to the bottoms of her well-shod feet, Jean Samuels always knew the right things to say and do, a trait Sharley wished she had inherited.

"So tell me, did you bring your old grandfather a gift?"

"I'm not gift enough?" she countered.

"You're a wonderful surprise."

Sharley reached for the small bag that matched her shoes and retrieved an envelope. "Sorry it's not gift wrapped."

Sam slit the seal on the back. He scanned the greeting card and then the enclosed document. A huge grin split his face wide open. The grin was soon followed by guffaws of laughter.

Sharley looked up to find Kenan quickly approaching.

"Kenan," Sam gasped, laughter punctuating his words, "she gave me a funeral for my birthday."

Heads turned all around the room, focusing on Sam as he laughed with abandon.

"Well, it is something I knew you wanted."

"Sharley darling, you're a treasure. Don't ever change," Sam instructed. He gestured for Kenan to come closer and whispered a few words. Kenan disappeared from the room and returned with a small package. Sam placed the box in Sharley's hand, closing her fingers about it. "I want you to have these. They belonged to my mother. There are other pieces I plan to give you as well. Jean insisted I take them when I left. Wouldn't even keep them for Glory."

Sharley snapped the hinged lid open. "They're stunning." Her fingers trembled as she removed the antique pearl earrings from their velvet bed.

Jocelyn moved quickly, resting one hand on Sharley's shoulder. "Why don't we visit the powder room? You can put them on. They'll look wonderful with your dress."

Sharley appreciated the woman's effort to help as a flood of emotion overwhelmed her. "Excellent idea. If you gentlemen will excuse us." As they moved through the guests, Sharley whispered, "Thank you for understanding, Jocelyn."

Jocelyn nodded politely to someone she recognized and flashed Sharley a sympathetic smile. "I remember how I felt when I was given something that belonged to my grandmother."

The ladies' room was almost empty, and Sharley was glad. "It's just that I never had a chance to know her. Now I have something that belonged to her."

Jocelyn hugged her. "Thank you for insisting I come. Kenan didn't think it was a good idea because he was afraid of the gossip, but I don't think he argued the point because it was something you wanted."

"An argument would have been senseless. Thanks to you, I'm here tonight. I'm going to strangle my employees when I get home."

Jocelyn chuckled. "Don't. I can't wait to hear how you get retribution."

"One of them is getting married in a couple of months. What do you think? A backless tux or something really original on the soles of his shoes?"

"Provide the limo and substitute the hearse."

Sharley broke into laughter. "That's priceless. If I didn't care so much about ruining his bride's day, I would."

"Bring her in on it. Just park the limo around the corner." Jocelyn smiled.

They stepped around the corner, just in time to overhear two women talking.

"What do you think about this granddaughter? Isn't she cute in Jocelyn's castoffs?"

"With more than one of her castoffs." The catty remark launched them into sniggers of laughter.

Jocelyn looked horrified, and Sharley dropped one eyelid in a wink and lifted her head higher. She wrapped one arm about Jocelyn's and pulled her forward.

"Grandfather is eternally in your debt for loaning me this dress after that fiasco with my gown. He asked about repayment, and I suggested a large donation to your favorite charity. You should be hearing from his office any day now."

Jocelyn almost laughed at the women's gasps. "There's really no need, Sharley."

"Of course there is. Goodness should be rewarded. So, are there any keepers out there tonight?"

Jocelyn caught on quickly. "One guy asked if he could take me out after he got rid of his date. Said she was in the ladies' room and he could be rid of her in under thirty minutes."

Sharley winked and gave Jocelyn a thumbs-up when the women all but ran back from the room. "That was bad. My mom always told me God doesn't like ugly."

"It wasn't a lie," Jocelyn defended. "One of their dates did ask—and those women weren't being particularly nice."

"True, but I call myself a Christian. Following God does not mean that He doesn't want us to laugh and enjoy life, but I was pushing things pretty far just now."

Jocelyn looked at her thoughtfully, but all she said was, "I see."

Sharley wasn't sure that she did, and she offered up a quick prayer that Jocelyn would find all she herself had found in service to the Lord. She replaced her earrings with her grandmother's and tilted her head from side to side. "What do you think?"

"They're beautiful. Why don't you sit here and admire them for a few minutes? I'll let the men know you'll be back shortly."

Sharley smiled and reached to squeeze Jocelyn's hand. "Thanks."

After Jocelyn left, Sharley reached to touch the earrings that dangled from her lobes. They were valuable, but they were more precious because of their connection to her great-grandmother. Even if he'd used all his considerable funds, Papa Sam couldn't have given her a more priceless gift.

She stood and lifted her purse from the vanity, taking one more look at herself in the designer gown. It wasn't a look she was familiar with. While her clothing wasn't cheap, it was a far cry from this elegant creation. She shrugged. It wasn't something she planned to get used to. There weren't many occasions in Montgomery that warranted the formal wear she already owned, and certainly none where people expected her to wear designer originals.

Sharley rounded the corner and glanced at the small groups that dotted the room. Papa Sam was holding court from his chair. Sharley decided it was a good time to find Kenan, but she didn't see him anywhere. She stepped through the open door onto the terraced patio and looked around. There he was, with Jocelyn. She took a couple of steps and found herself stopping when Jocelyn mentioned her name.

"You've really found a jewel in Sharley."

"Yes, she's wonderful." Kenan's grim acceptance seemed to surprise Jocelyn.

"What's wrong, Kenan?"

"I now know what you meant by fireworks, but our situation is far from perfect."

"Why on earth would you feel that way?"

"Her life is thousands of miles away," Kenan said, sounding discouraged. "Our opportunities to be together are so limited."

"But surely now that she's found her grandfather, she'll consider coming here."

Kenan shook his head. "Sharley and Sam don't know each other well enough for her to take that step. Besides, she's developed roots to that place that go all the way to China. Her business has passed through generations of Montgomerys to her. She won't let anyone else have control."

"Still, if the flames burn high enough, you'll change for each other. Nothing stands in the way of people who truly love each other."

"You'd be surprised at the walls between Sharley and myself."

Sharley felt a childish urge to stamp her foot and demand they stop discussing her. Why couldn't Kenan understand there was no one else to take over Montgomery-Sloan? She was it, the end of the line, all there was. Perhaps if she'd had other siblings the situation would have been different. She might have been free to leave her life in Samuels—but she wasn't. She couldn't even think of a way to communicate the importance of what she had to do to Kenan.

Sharley charged forward. "Enjoying yourselves?"

Jocelyn turned and smiled. "I've never had so much fun at one of Sam's parties."

"It's quite an affair," Sharley agreed. "Of course, you could fit most of the population of Samuels in this house. The crowd literally leaves me breathless. I need to walk in the garden. A breath of fresh air and some time to enjoy this glorious moonlight might just revive me."

"I'll go with you," Kenan said.

"Are you sure you should?" Sharley asked, glad he couldn't see her face in the dimly lit area. "Morticians are used to darkness. They deal with it more than other mortals."

"Aren't morticians normal mortals?" he asked.

"I like to think we're as human as the rest, but a lot of people seem to think we're not quite normal." Even as the words left her lips, Sharley knew the best way to handle things was to get through this party and go home to Samuels. Back to the people who understood her.

"Everything okay?" Jocelyn asked.

"The emotions are under control," she said, forced cheerfulness in her tone. "I do love these earrings."

"Sam has a portrait of your great-grandmother wearing them."

"Oh, I saw it before," Sharley said, realization dawning. "I didn't know who she was. I'll have to take another look."

"Why don't we do it now?" Kenan suggested, taking her hand in his.

"No, you two go ahead with your conversation," Sharley insisted. "I can go alone."

"I want to show you," Kenan insisted. "Coming, Jocelyn?"

"Thanks, but I've seen it."

Kenan led the way up a wide staircase that would have done the most majestic Southern mansion proud. Once more Sharley was struck by the fact that this place was literally a palace. The gallery was an extra-wide hallway showcasing Sam's art collection. Numerous artistic renderings by famous and not-so-famous names lined both sides of the wall.

"Sam's gallery reflects his personal tastes and not what some gallery owner says it should," Kenan pointed out.

Sharley turned on her heel in a complete circle and nodded. "I like most of what I see here."

"There's the painting."

She stood before the picture of the woman who had given birth to her grandfather. "She's beautiful."

Kenan nodded. "From what I can understand, this is another of the items Sam brought from Samuels. Your great-grandfather gave her the pearls for their twenty-fifth anniversary and had the painting done."

For a moment, Sharley was almost angry that Mommy Jean had so effectively cut her off from the Samuels side of her family. She could have kept the painting and the jewelry for her mother and herself, as a memento of Papa Sam.

"Are you glad you came?" Kenan asked as Sharley moved slowly along the area.

She stopped and turned to face him. "Not particularly. Tonight has certainly been eye-opening. I overheard your conversation with Jocelyn just now."

"Does it bother you that I was in the garden with her?"

"Not as much as it does that you'd discuss things with her that you haven't shared with me."

"We're old friends. Tell me what's upsetting you."

"There's nothing bothering me beyond the fact that I didn't use the sense of a gnat before making the decision to fly here. It's not exactly been ideal, has it? You weren't pleased by my surprise appearance. Then there was the debacle with the dress. And my insisting that Jocelyn accompany us even though you both felt it would be uncomfortable. Tonight has been reinforcement after reinforcement that we're not right for each other. I already knew, but then I met Jocelyn and got a good look at the kind of woman who interests you. I like her very much, but I could never be like her, Kenan."

"I wouldn't want you to be."

"Papa Sam pointed out that you and I don't really know each other. We both know it would never work. I've even heard the words from your own lips. Don't deny it. I arrived in time to hear you voice your doubts to Jocelyn."

"I'm sorry, Sharley. She's a good friend. I've always been able to talk to her about anything." He shoved his fingers through his hair and gave her a sideways glance. "So, what do we do?"

"We concentrate on a friendship rather than a relationship. When you call now and then because Papa Sam asks you to, I'll greet you politely and ask how things are. You find the woman who's right for your world, and I wait for the man God intends to share mine."

"God can't intend you to have another man," Kenan growled. "Why would He put us together and allow these feelings to grow if it weren't His intention that we share something?"

"Perhaps we should give the devil his due. Maybe he's tempting us. Probably he wants to confuse you even more about God."

Kenan gave her a skeptical glance. "So what's the devil trying to do to you?"

"He's testing my commitment to the Lord."

"Is that all we are? A temptation to each other?" Kenan moved forward and slipped his arms about her. His face loomed closer, and his warm lips touched hers. The kiss went on until finally Sharley wriggled from his hold.

They stood silently for a moment while their breathing slowly returned to normal. "I'm sorry, but my feelings run more deeply than that," Kenan snapped. "I'm tempted, okay. Tempted to see if I can stomach life in a little one-horse town to be closer to the woman I love."

The consequences of her actions hit Sharley hard. She'd been claiming God was in control, but in her usual controlling manner she was prompting Him with answers to her own questions. And just as surely as she drew her next breath she was in love with Kenan Montgomery. A deep, irrevocable love that would serve no purpose beyond the heartbreak of them both.

"Well, don't just stand there," Kenan complained. "Say something."

"It's exactly as you said," Sharley managed finally. "We care about each other, but the obstacles are insurmountable. There's no way you can understand where I'm coming from on the matter of Samuels."

"Why couldn't you come to Boston? Sam's here. And me." *And I love you,* Kenan admitted to himself. Since the day he had first laid eyes on Sharley Montgomery, his heart had been trying to tell him something.

"It's not that easy, Kenan. You just can't understand how anyone can claim to love somebody and just walk away, can you?"

"Can you?" he demanded, taking a step forward. "If I remember correctly, you never claimed to understand Sam's reasons for leaving your grandmother and mother. Why would you want to do the same all these years later?" Kenan's face was serious. "Think about it, Sharley. You say there's only a blood bond between you and Sam, but no real emotional tie. Both of you want a relationship but don't really pursue one. Sam, probably because of guilt," he guessed, shrugging his shoulders. "Your reasons go a little deeper. Maybe fear of being hurt—but then there's loyalty to your mother and grandmother. And yes, I know you're a Christian, but that doesn't mean you're any less likely to be hurt if things don't work out. I think you've been guarding your heart."

"You think you have me figured out, don't you?"

"Close enough."

"I'd say it's possible you missed your calling. You're right about most of that—but there's still the fact that though Sam and I may be related we're still strangers."

"Nonsense."

"Why are you trying to turn this around on me? I wasn't even born when Triple S made his decision."

"But your mother was, and I can imagine your grandmother told the story often."

"You don't know anything about my family," she protested. "Maybe I am too committed to Samuels. I know and love those people. Every year I see the population shrinking when young people go off to better-paying jobs while Sam Samuels runs a multimillion-dollar corporation in a city hundreds of miles away. Think what that business would have done for Samuels. He could have turned the town into a thriving metropolis."

"It wouldn't be the same place, Sharley. More people, more crime. More of the undesirable elements than you can imagine."

"I could accept that more easily than I can its turning into a ghost town."

"Why don't you just say it?"

"Say what?" Sharley demanded, exasperated by the way he had turned this situation on her.

"That you could never love me as much as you love Samuels?"

What had she done? Things were totally out of control. One moment Kenan was telling her he loved her, and the next moment they were attacking each other. She took a deep breath and said coolly, "Since you're so intent that Papa Sam and I bond, I'm going back to the party. He'll wonder what happened to me."

She walked slowly toward the stairs, her feet dragging as she wondered if each movement took her away from Kenan for the last time.

"Sharley, don't do this. Please, not now."

She glanced over her shoulder. His agony impacted her as nothing ever had before. She couldn't run fast or far enough to escape the gut-wrenching pain that filled her. "Good-bye, Kenan."

"Sharley."

Don't look back. She repeated the words like a silent litany, trying to convince herself it was for the best. Tears welled in her eyes, and she knew her mascara wouldn't survive the trip downstairs.

Back in her grandfather's presence, Sharley was drawn into a conversation with the group of people who now surrounded him. She had no idea how much time had passed and only spoke when her grandfather prompted her with a question.

Once, as though he knew what she was feeling, Papa Sam reached for her hand and patted it gently.

He spoke softly, and she leaned down to catch his words. "Will you stay here for the rest of your visit?"

Sharley nodded, certain she couldn't get words past the lump in her throat.

"I'll send Jamie to pick up your bags."

"Perhaps I should go with him. I left the room in rather a mess, and I need to settle the account."

"I'll send someone to help him, and he can take care of the account."

"Okay," Sharley agreed simply. There was no fight left in her. "I need to tell Kenan."

Sam handled things quickly, and the conversation promptly picked back up. Sharley noted Kenan standing with Jocelyn on the fringes of the crowd that had gathered about them and refused to meet his eyes. She couldn't make herself tell him of her change in plans. Not yet.

It was almost midnight when he approached her. "We should be going."

"I think it best if I stay here with Papa Sam for the next couple of days. He's already sent someone to pick up my things so I won't trouble you again."

He looked like he wanted to say something but didn't.

"Thank Jocelyn for me, please."

"Thank her yourself," he snapped before turning away.

Sharley bowed her head and whispered a small prayer for Kenan's comfort.

⁂

How could she do this to them, to him? Kenan wondered. And for what? A business and a town? A sense of belonging? He had never felt this way until Sharley had walked into his life. For the first time, he was truly in love.

His life had been in turmoil since Vietnam. He'd made some strides over the years, buying the condo, his first real home; deciding he was ready for marriage and a family was another step in the right direction, even though Jocelyn refused him.

Thank God for that, he thought now. He would have been miserable with her after meeting Sharley. But why had the Lord put Sharley in his life only to tear them apart? She could pretend there was nothing between them, but in his heart, Kenan knew his feelings for her had moved beyond friendship.

"Sharley's not coming with us?" Jocelyn asked.

He looked at her and sighed. "No, she's staying here with Sam and her God."

"Kenan?"

He shook his head sadly, unable to look her in the eye. "I'm sorry. That was uncalled for."

She touched his arm. "It'll be okay."

"I'm glad you think so because I'm not so sure."

"She loves you, and believe it or not, Charlotte Montgomery is going to be worth everything you have to do to bring her into your life."

"She wants my soul."

"No, Kenan," Jocelyn corrected. "She wants you to give that to God. Maybe it's time we both considered taking that step. For the first time in my life, I'm thinking I'd like to have Him in my corner. Sharley and Sam don't appear to be doing too badly."

Kenan just shrugged. "Let's call it a night. I'd say the party's over. Wouldn't you?"

Chapter 7

After her return home, Sharley prayed for answers, read and reread every relevant verse in the Bible, and did everything in her power to convince herself she was better off without Kenan Montgomery. Nothing worked. Loving and trusting the Lord was the only thing that made the disappointment and heartbreak easier to bear. Sharley believed with all her heart that He wouldn't put more on her than she could endure.

She scowled at the piles of work on her desk. The lack of desire to work ranked right in there with her lack of desire to eat, sleep, and campaign. While dressing for work that morning, Sharley had assembled a mental to-do list. The list was long, work to be caught up and a campaign to be won. And she felt no excitement about any of it.

Determined to shake her lethargy, she pulled the center desk drawer open. It was packed tight with shredded bits of paper. She tried another and found it to be the same. A tug on the last drawer handle resulted in a booby trap popping out and bouncing off her chest. She gasped and rammed her chair back into the credenza. "Devlin! Jack! Get in here!" Sharley screamed.

The two men could hardly walk for laughing.

"What's up, boss?" Devlin asked.

"You just made a couple of hours' work for yourself. That's what. I want all this paper out of here. *Now*," she stressed angrily.

Devlin looked at Jack and back at Sharley. "It's a joke."

"Well, I'm not in the mood for your jokes. In fact, let's just discontinue the pranks as of this moment."

"Sure." Jack shrugged his shoulders, a frown touching his face. "We'll get some garbage bags and take care of the desk drawers. We didn't mean to upset you."

They quickly disappeared from the room, and Sharley felt a twinge of remorse. It wasn't their fault that the joy had gone out of her life. Her concern grew as she caught their conversation in the hallway.

"You think it was the dress?" Devlin asked.

"She's been like this ever since she came home from that party. I don't know who that woman is, but she's not our Sharley."

A grim smile touched her lips. Never had truer words been spoken. She owed them both an apology. "Devlin. Jack. Come back in here, please."

"Rats, I forgot she's got hearing like old lady Jenkins with them hearing aids on high."

Sharley smiled at that. Mrs. Jenkins was renowned for her ability to pretend she couldn't hear when she wanted to ignore people. In truth, with her hearing aids she could hear a car turn the corner half a mile from her house. They stepped into the doorway. "Guys, come in and sit down. I promise to keep the dragon lady under control."

Sharley forgave them their wary expressions as they settled before her desk. "First, I want to apologize for my bad mood. It's nothing you did. And you're right about the old Sharley. She's not here right now. Hopefully she'll be back soon, but if she never comes back, I hope you can come to love the new Sharley."

"What happened?" Devlin asked.

The sting of tears burned her eyelids, and overwhelming sadness made itself felt. "It's not something I can talk about. Let's just say God is working some changes in my life, and I need you to pray that I'll be able to accept them."

"Sure," Devlin agreed.

"If we can help, let us know," Jack added.

"Thanks, guys," Sharley said, flashing them a smile. "Right now I need you to be patient with me, and to get this paper out of my desk drawer. Where did you get it from anyway?"

"Melanie's got one of those new crosscut shredders at her office," Devlin explained. "When she told me about it, I had her bring me a bag."

"I can live with the paper, but that snake thing nearly put me in my grave," Sharley said, rising to her feet. "I'll be in the display room. Let me know when you finish. There are some papers in that center desk drawer I need this morning." She didn't mention that the papers she was eager to find were her grandmother's journal.

They took an hour to remove all the shredded bits. By the time they finished, Sharley had reprioritized her list, and all the important to-do things were going to have to wait another day. She swiveled her chair back toward the door, not quite sure why she felt the need to hide her nonwork activity as she opened the journal to the ribbon bookmark where she had left off before flying to Boston.

Just what I needed, Sharley thought, as she began to read her grandparents' love story. "I have found the man I intend to marry," Jean Reynolds wrote in her elegant flowing script. "The boy next door. Who would have believed I could love Sam so much? He is the perfect man for me. So sweet and caring."

The next few pages covered the halcyon days of her grandparents' courtship. "Sam came over today, and for the first time we were allowed to sit alone in the living room. Daddy asked me to fix lemonade, and afterward Sam seemed a little quiet. I wonder what Daddy said to him. Hopefully nothing to make him stop seeing me.

"Mary Beth taunted me today about Sam. She doesn't fool me. She thinks she can make me doubt my Sam, but it's not possible. I know he's beginning to care as deeply for me as I do for him. He's always so gentlemanly. I feel quite the lady in his company. Still, I remember the fun times we had as children and now realize that Sam looked out for me even then. I'm glad he no longer thinks of me as a little girl."

Sharley read numerous accounts of church functions attended by her grandparents. Every entry started out Sam this or Sam that, and for the first time Sharley felt the depth of her grandparents' love for each other. As Papa Sam said, probably no less than stubborn pride had been their downfall. One thought underscored her earlier doubts: Back then they had shared their faith, and yet being equally yoked had not solved their problems.

Once Papa Sam had recognized that Jean Reynolds was no longer a child, he had been persistent in his courtship. One entry had to do with his objections to her desire to bob her hair. He wanted nothing done to the glorious curly red locks. So bothersome, her grandmother lamented, but she was still pleased Sam liked her hair.

"Sam talks of going off to college, and the thought scares me so. Will he come back? Sometimes he seems so restless when he comes to visit after working all afternoon for his father. He talks constantly of the future, and I don't think he sees his future in Samuels."

"Sam came for dinner today. We had all his favorites. Daddy was his usual strict self, but Sam didn't seem troubled. Then he's probably used to it because his dad acts the same when I'm over at their house. Sam cleaned his plate and took seconds when Daddy offered.

"He winked at me when Daddy wasn't looking. That smile of his just melts my heart. I love the little dimple beside his mouth." Sharley smiled and traced a finger along her own dimple. "Sam kissed me for the first time today. I have no comparison, but surely no one could ever kiss better."

Sharley skimmed the pages of their continued courtship and then read of the wedding plans. From the description, she knew it was the event of the year in Samuels. Ben Reynolds spared no expense when it came to the marriage of his only child. There had been bridal showers and parties galore.

She read on until she reached her grandmother's entry on the first morning of her marriage: "For the first time I completely understand the importance of waiting until marriage to share our love. Our vows were the outward sign of our love, but the union was that of our body and soul. To have one without the other would have been wrong. We are one now, husband and wife forever."

Forever. Sharley reread the word. What a rude awakening life often threw into the path of unsuspecting lovers.

Already Kenan played a tremendous role in her thoughts. Sharley knew she cared more than she should. She felt a greater attraction to him than to any man she had known in the past. In truth, all others paled in significance to him.

Oh, why must there be thorns in life's garden? Perhaps to remind her of Christ's precious love. No amount of temptation had brought Jesus down from that cross, and no amount of temptation should make her regret her allegiance to her Father in heaven. Her life was His, to do with as He would, and Sharley knew He would never give her anything but the best.

Stop thinking about it, she cautioned, forcing her gaze back to the journal. "Sam is so tired of the Depression. Even though they claim we're recovering, he knows there is little likelihood his father would ever take any great risk after surviving when so many did not. Not that I would tell Sam, but I agree with Mr. Samuels. I'm sorry Sam is unhappy, but there are more important things to consider now that we have a baby on the way. Sam needs to accept that a good job and home are more important than taking chances. The one thing I want most for our unborn child is a happy home. I am most hopeful Sam will soon accept his role as businessman, husband, and father."

Her grandmother wrote of Sam's exploits: his daredevil behavior, as she called it. One way Mommy Jean seemed to deal with it was tears. Sharley frowned. Based on the recount of her tearful remonstrations to Sam Samuels, her grandmother should have owned stock in a tissue company.

Sharley shook her head. She hated manipulation. She had reacted strongly to Kenan's efforts for that very reason. Even when the manipulator was victorious, they lost because of the resentment felt by the person being controlled.

But hadn't she made the same attempt? She'd been trying to manipulate God into finding a way for her and Kenan to be together. God didn't need her input. He didn't need her to show Him what He wanted in her life. He would show her the way, and until He did, it was back to the things that were a constant in her life: God, the church, her work, her campaign, and the centennial celebration.

She had been firm with Kenan about their relationship. Now she just needed to get firm with herself and get on with her life. Sharley sighed and murmured, "The Lord's been trying to teach me patience for years. I must be a slow learner."

The phone rang, and Sharley reached for the receiver.

"I can't believe you left without talking to me," Kenan said without prelude.

"We talked. Don't you remember? It was the conversation where we decided it wouldn't work."

"Is this because I voiced my concerns to Jocelyn and not you?"

Sharley frowned. Though she didn't much care for the fact that he would admit his feelings to another woman first, that was not her concern. "No, it has more to do with the fact that you have those concerns in the first place."

"Not about you," he defended. "About the miles that separate us."

"It's more than that, and you know it. We're already hurting, Kenan. Don't make this worse on either of us."

"I'm coming to Samuels. We're going to discuss this like two rational adults."

"Stay in Boston where you belong, Kenan."

"That's just it, Sharley. I don't feel like I belong here anymore. My heart tells me I belong wherever you are. I'll be there as soon as I can catch a flight."

"Kenan, don't. . ." It was too late. He'd hung up the phone. Sharley replaced the receiver and used a tissue to dab the moisture from her eyes. He was coming. What was she going to do?

"She says she's too busy. Sorry."

Kenan hesitated outside the door as Devlin went back inside. If Sharley thought she was going to avoid the situation, she had another think coming. He drew a deep breath and reached for the doorknob.

Sharley gave him the briefest of glances before she continued her task. "Visitors aren't allowed in here."

"If the mountain. . ."

"The mountain doesn't need to see Kenan Montgomery. I think we've pretty much covered everything."

Kenan noted Devlin was having difficulty with his attempts to focus his attention elsewhere. Well, if she wanted to discuss the matter in front of her employee, he would.

Before he could mutter a word, Sharley continued manipulating the face of the man on the table. Kenan tried to maintain his control, but the nausea crept over him. Sharley's gentle touch as she stroked his face and called his name woke him a few minutes later.

"I told you not to come in. It's not a corpse. Jack splashed some cleaning chemical in his eye. I was just washing it out for him."

There was a bottle of eyewash at his side, and she sounded exasperated. Kenan reached to rub the throbbing spot at the back of his head, finding he had a goose egg where he had made contact with the tiled floor. Not even the fact that his head rested in Sharley's soft lap eased the ache.

"I had to come in. This is important to me. I love you, Sharley. I don't want to lose you."

"Kenan." His name came out sounding like a sigh. "We've been through this. We're at an impasse here."

"Obviously this business means more to you than I do."

His disgruntled words only served to make Sharley push him away and get to her feet. "I won't be made to feel guilty because I have certain needs that are important to me. Montgomerys have filled important roles in this town for centuries. I won't be the first to break tradition. I'm sorry."

His movements were unsteady as he got to his feet. "And I was foolish enough to think people did all sorts of things for love."

"That's right," Sharley agreed with a steady stare. "They do."

Kenan felt almost impaled by the barbed words. "You think I only expect you to make sacrifices? That I'm not willing to make any of my own?"

She raised her eyebrows. "I'd be giving up my business, my home, my town, my dreams, my friends, my lifestyle. What sacrifices are you willing to make? Your freedom for a ring on my finger? Pardon me if I find that a bit unequal."

Maybe she was right. It was old-fashioned to expect a woman to mold herself to the man's life. Deep down, though, Kenan knew there was more to their problem than that.

"Your fear of death is playing a bigger role in this than you realize," Sharley said softly. "You think that if I move to Boston and give up my career, we could live happily ever after."

"I don't. . ." Even as he uttered the denial, Kenan had a gut feeling she'd neatly pegged his subconscious thoughts.

"I love you, Kenan, but I have roots here. It's more than the business. I like knowing my neighbors. Hey, I even like them when they meddle in my life because I know it means they care. The need to escape is not something I share with my grandfather. In fact, I believe he could have come to love the town if he'd really given it a chance. If he'd opened his mind and become involved, he could have built a business here that would have benefited the community and kept him with his family."

She sighed. "This is what I do. It's not some little job to keep me busy until I find a husband. It's my heritage and will be my children's heritage."

"My kids aren't going to be morticians."

Sharley moved closer, almost face-to-face. "Then it's a good thing we're not getting married. Now, if you'll excuse me, I do have a body to prepare. I think you know the way out."

"Right back to impasse. Why do you insist on doing this to us both?" Kenan demanded when she turned away from him. "I'll leave, Sharley. I'll get out of your life. But fate has already dabbled in both our lives. Or maybe I should say that God has—the same God who you're always claiming to serve. I suspect we'll see each other again."

"Can't we simply be friends?"

"Friendship is a pretty pale comparison to all we could have."

"It's in God's hands, Kenan. Papa Sam reminded me that loving each other is not enough. I depend on God to light my path."

"Do you really, Sharley?" Kenan shrugged. "Maybe so. Or it could be you're so blinded by the floodlights surrounding us that you can't see the path."

Chapter 8

A few weeks later, the phone rang as she stepped into the office. Sharley rolled her eyes, positive she knew who was on the other end. The same person who tied up her fax machine all morning with his one question in giant letters: "How can we work this out if you won't talk to me?"

He was inventive, she'd give him that. She was sure the local florist loved him. The delivery truck arrived with a lead-crystal bud holder, and each day they delivered a fresh rose. Then the e-mail messages began to arrive. Sharley knew she shouldn't read them, but each one told her he hurt as badly as she did. His friends had gotten into the act, sending her references and e-mail messages, saying how miserable he was and vouching for his character. Then last night—well, the virtual flowers and cards accompanied by sentimental greetings made her want to run to Boston.

The same fax rolled out of the machine every fifteen minutes, generally followed by the ringing of the phone. Like now. She could set her clock by this man's schedule. She restrained herself from tossing the phone out the window.

She couldn't talk to Kenan right now. Her resolve wasn't strong enough. The way she felt, Sharley knew she was likely to forget all responsibilities, and she couldn't do that. Reluctantly she lifted the receiver. "Montgomery-Sloan."

"May I speak to Charlotte Montgomery?"

Relief surged through her as she realized it wasn't Kenan. She listened as a student from the high school outlined the plan to sponsor a candidate forum. "It's scheduled for the Thursday night prior to the election."

"I'll be there." She thanked him and hung up the phone.

Election day was less than three weeks away. If she hoped to find herself successful in her bid for coroner, she had to get busy. She had to make herself visible. If she marshaled her volunteer forces and made sure her personalized campaign literature was in every registered voter's hands, her chances for success would be much greater.

The fax machine went off again. "There's no time to play, Kenan," she said determinedly. "I've got a campaign to win."

❧

"You're doing what?"

"I'm going to Samuels. To visit Sharley."

Kenan stared at his employer, dumbfounded by the words he uttered. "Let me see if I have this right. Sam Samuels, the man who wasn't up to a trip to Samuels a few weeks ago, is going to visit his granddaughter?"

Sam nodded. "That's right. Plan to surprise her, too."

"Surprise?" Kenan sputtered. "Sam, are you sure you've given this enough thought? It's a long trip. Sure, you've got the company jet, but it's a two-hour drive from the nearest airport to Samuels."

"Cynthia's checking on a helicopter now."

Sam didn't do things in half measures. The plan was already well on its way to completion.

"What changed your mind?"

"I owe it to her."

A frown bracketed Kenan's face.

"I need to see her in her natural environment," Sam explained. "See the place where she lives, her business, meet her friends. I can't do that on the phone."

"I suppose you want me to go with you?"

Sam appeared to be deep in thought. "Not necessarily. Sharley hasn't said much, but I got the impression something happened when she was here for my party. She might not want to see you again."

The words struck dread in Kenan's heart. She probably didn't. He wondered if absence really made the heart grow fonder. He missed her—a lot, but he couldn't change that stubborn woman's mind. He might as well keep things going at home while Sam was away.

"We talked last night. She told me about Jean's journals," Sam was saying.

"There's a stack of them," Kenan said absently.

Sam's eyebrows shifted, and Kenan realized he'd given himself away. "Sharley told me a little of what she's read."

"When was that? I was under the impression that she started reading after you went to Samuels for me."

"I've visited her there. Twice."

"She told me. I've been wondering why you were so secretive."

"I didn't know how you would react to my visiting your granddaughter."

Sam shrugged. "You're a pretty decent sort of fellow. I wouldn't mind if she doesn't."

"Well, she does. Now you know. Let's leave it at that."

"Can't I at least ask what her objections to you are?"

"It's our concern." The situation between them was killing him. Kenan hadn't felt this degree of desolation in years. It was like coming home from war again, not knowing what to do, how to disconnect himself from the feelings of loss.

"Must be pretty bad for you to take on like that."

"Do you want me to accompany you to Samuels? I need to rearrange my schedule if you do."

"Marie's rescheduled your appointments for the rest of the week. Go home and pack your bag. We leave after lunch." Sam chuckled heartily at Kenan's expression, a mixture of doubt and relief.

"A surprise visit probably isn't a good idea," Kenan protested halfheartedly. "That town only has a small bed-and-breakfast."

"We'll stay with Sharley." He looked at the younger man from under his eyebrows. "I think I'm still functioning as an adequate chaperone for my granddaughter."

The trepidation Kenan felt surrendered to his joy at the thought of seeing her again.

As with everything Sam Samuels did, each plan was quickly brought to completion.

"We'll be picked up at the airport and driven to Samuels. Sharley's going to be surprised."

"No doubt," Kenan mumbled, half listening to Sam as the plane sped down the runway. *In more ways than one,* he thought. His coming along was probably not the best idea, but he realized he truly did have a legitimate reason to be there. If Sam insisted on traveling to Samuels, Kenan planned to help him bear the stress of the journey. He couldn't help it if, besides the practical reason, he simply needed to see Sharley.

He hadn't felt such hopelessness in years. Sharley's refusal to respond to him hurt. A time or two he'd found himself praying for God to guide him through this troubling time. He loved her—nothing would change that. If only she would hear him out.

He'd been truthful about his doubts, but that didn't mean he believed they couldn't find solutions to the differences between them. Why was she so certain their problems were insurmountable? They didn't have to be—not if they both gave a little.

"The last time I talked with her on the phone," Sam was saying, "she was busy with the town celebration plans and was asking me what I remembered. She has so many unanswered questions. It occurs to me that it's my responsibility."

"Responsibility?"

"Sharley deserves to know about the past. Father and I often butted heads, but we loved each other. This planning committee stuff is in Sharley's blood. Her mother, grandmother, great-grandmother were all civic leaders in their time. Sharley's carrying on tradition."

"She's certainly civic-minded." Kenan noted the way Sam's gaze lingered on him, and he explained, "She took me politicking and to a church social."

Sam's grin turned into full-blown laughter.

"Don't laugh, Sam. One of your old flames gave Sharley a message for you."

"Warm regards?"

"Not exactly. Are you sure you don't want to turn around and head back to Boston?"

Sam laid his head against the seat back and stared ahead. "No, Kenan. It's time to prove you can go home again."

Kenan thought of his family, people he hadn't seen in years. Could he prove the same thing?

They arrived in Samuels just after five. In the end they had decided to drive down from the airport in a rented limo. The ride would take a little longer, but it would be smoother and more relaxing than the chopper. "Knowing Sharley, she's still at the office," Kenan said as they entered town.

But Montgomery-Sloan was locked up, and Jack was climbing in his pickup. "Kenan? Didn't think we'd see you around here again."

"I came with Sharley's grandfather."

Jack's brows lifted. "Old Sam Samuels? You're kidding?"

Kenan gestured with his head. "He's in the car. Has Sharley gone home?"

"She's over at the high school. Tonight's the meet-the-candidates forum."

Kenan frowned.

"I think Sharley would appreciate the support of her family," Jack prompted. "That's where I'm headed."

"Would you like to ride with us?" Sam called through the open window.

"Yes, sir. I'd be honored."

Jack climbed in front with the driver, and Sam lowered the dividing glass. "You say tonight's the candidate forum?"

Jack nodded. "Yes, sir. The election's next week. This is Sharley's last chance to convince people she's right for the job."

"You believe she is?"

"I sure do. That other guy ain't qualified to wipe her shoes."

"This should be interesting."

"Mr. Samuels, sir. . ."

Kenan quickly corrected his oversight and introduced the two men. "Sam Samuels, Jack Jennings. Jack's Sharley's right-hand man."

"Call me Sam."

"Well, sir, Sharley didn't know you were coming, did she?"

"I planned to surprise her."

"You're definitely going to do that. Turn right here," he instructed the driver. "You can let us out up by the door and park in the lot. Might want to keep an eye on your car. Don't too many people see a full-fledged limo sitting around in this town. Besides the one at the funeral home, that is."

Already a crowd filled the room. Jack led the way, and Kenan followed Sam. "There she is," Jack called over his shoulder. "Sharley, look who's here."

⁂

Sharley glanced around at the sound of Jack's voice. Every drop of nervousness she had felt about the forum disappeared with the shock of seeing Kenan and

Papa Sam standing there.

"Please excuse me," Sharley said to the reporter. "Papa Sam?" She leaned to kiss her grandfather's cheek. "What are you doing here?"

"We'll wait over there while you finish your interview."

"I think I have all I need," the female reporter said, her eyes moving to Kenan.

"Renee Hodson, this is my grandfather, Samuel Samuels, and a friend of the family, Kenan Montgomery."

"My pleasure. Wait, you're the Samuels who moved away, aren't you?"

"I've made my home in Boston these past years," Sam said.

The woman brightened. "I don't suppose you'd be interested in doing an interview—you know, something along the lines of local boy makes good?"

Sharley felt almost embarrassed for her. Sam's story had appeared in more publications than he could name.

"I doubt there's much about me that would interest the people of Samuels, but I thank you for asking."

"Too bad. I'd better get on over there and get a few words from Miss Montgomery's opponent. Nice meeting you both."

"So, what are you doing here?" Sharley refused to meet Kenan's eyes. She didn't need this right now. Her plate was full enough without having to deal with Kenan and their situation.

"Can't a grandfather surprise his granddaughter?"

Sharley's answer was drowned out by an overeager youth on the loudspeaker. "Ladies, gentlemen, we need to get started. Please take your seats. Can we please have all candidates on stage?"

She smiled and squeezed Papa Sam's hand. "Yes, you can surprise me."

"Go get 'em, Sharley girl," Sam whispered.

❦

"Good luck," Kenan called, feeling inordinately happy when she stopped and smiled back at him.

The three men found seats close to the front and settled in. Kenan found himself enjoying Jack's play-by-play as the various candidates were allowed to speak. Sharley proved to be eloquent, entertaining the audience with her mixture of humor and serious repartee. Her opponent lacked her vitality, and Kenan considered him more suitable for this job of death.

Another thought occurred to him as well. The more he visited, the more he liked the town of Samuels and its inhabitants. Jack was a good person, as were the others he had met. Maybe if he gave the town more of a chance. . .

The master of ceremonies approached the microphone and announced the question-and-answer period. An old woman got to her feet. Kenan sat up even straighter when he recognized the elderly woman from the church dinner. She stood with the help of her cane, her voice carrying in the big room. "Charlotte Montgomery, will you stick around if you get this job? Now that you have Boston connections. . . Well, we know your family history."

"It's your old flame," Kenan whispered to Sam.

Sam assessed the situation. "Mary Beth Langley. Wonder what she has to do with the other candidate?"

Kenan glanced at the flyer that had been distributed. He pointed to a name. "Sharley's opponent must be her son-in-law."

He had never seen Sam move so quickly as he jumped to his feet. Kenan frowned as Sam fired back a response to Mrs. Hinson. "What I did with my personal life has no reflection on Charlotte."

"She's got your blood in her veins, Sam Samuels. Who's to say she won't up and do the same thing you did?"

"I account to no one but God above for my actions, Mary Beth, and He forgave me."

"Still cocky as ever," she mumbled. "She'll probably run off and marry that man who's been courting her."

Jack leaned over and spoke, not bothering to lower his voice. "Sharley ain't gonna have no competition if old lady Hinson don't shut up. Look how red Ray's face is. He looks like he's about to have an attack."

Kenan glanced at Sharley, noting that her cheeks were also pink. "Grandfather, Mrs. Hinson," she said, "please. The students worked hard to make this a credible event."

The voice of reason, Kenan thought as he watched the elderly adversaries settle in their seats.

"First," Sharley continued, "let me say my background speaks for itself, both professionally and personally." She stood tall, her voice clear and strong. "As for the family history, my grandfather understands that I plan to stay right here in Samuels. Some dreams are too big for small towns like Samuels. Grandfather did what he had to do. The scope of my vision is limited to this county and my life here. As for the matter of courtship, Mr. Montgomery is a friend of the family. I have no plans to marry and run away from my responsibility."

"I'd marry him in a flash," said a feminine voice, followed by a chorus of giggles.

Kenan didn't look to see where the words came from. This was turning into a fiasco.

Sharley surprised them all by laughing. "Excuse me, please. These issues have nothing to do with my qualifications for the job. I can promise you that I am dedicated to the task I've set forth for myself. Be sure to vote, and God bless you all. Thank you." She stepped away from the lectern, shook her opponent's hand, and came down the steps.

The three men rose and followed her from the gym. "Ready to run us out of town?" Sam inquired as the doors closed behind them.

"I'm sure I'll make the paper tomorrow." She fixed her eyes on her grandfather. "Was it necessary to get into a mudslinging match with Mrs. Hinson?"

"I was defending your honor. Just as you defended mine."

Sharley hesitated, surprise showing in her facial expression. "I did, didn't I? Well, she had no right making such allegations. I certainly wouldn't be running for coroner if I planned to up and move to Boston." She slipped her hand around his arm.

Sam seemed to stand a bit taller. "Kenan and I could use a room for the night."

"You'll stay with me."

Jack held out his hand. "Give me your keys so you can ride with your grandfather. I'll drop your car by the house and walk over to pick up my truck."

"Nonsense," Sam said. "You drop her car off, and the driver can take you to pick up your vehicle. You've been very helpful, Mr. Jennings. It warms my heart to know Sharley has someone like you taking care of her."

"Call me Jack."

Kenan waited for Sam to shake Jack's hand and then stood by as he climbed into the limo, followed by Sharley.

Inside the car, she turned to him. "When did you arrive?"

"Just before the candidate's forum," Kenan answered. He glanced at Sam to make sure the elderly man was doing okay.

Sharley looked from one to the other. "It's good to see you both."

Chapter 9

Sharley threw back the cover and crawled off the bed. No sense tossing and turning the rest of the night. Sleep became an impossibility from the moment she ran into Kenan in the upstairs hallway just before bed.

"Sharley, please," he had said.

Two words and one look that spoke volumes. "Kenan, I can't talk to you," she cried out, running from him. She should have insisted he go to the bed-and-breakfast.

Sharley tiptoed down the stairs and into the kitchen, astonished at the sight of Papa Sam sitting at the kitchen table, reading his wife's journal, a cup of coffee at his elbow.

"You should be in bed."

He flashed her a shrewd look. "Old people don't need as much sleep. What's your excuse?"

"As if you didn't know." Sharley filled a cup with coffee and sat down. She cupped it in both hands and took a sip.

Her grandfather smiled. "I asked Kenan what your objections to him were. He said they were personal."

"They are."

"And history repeats itself."

Sharley's finger ceased tracing the cup rim, and her head flew up. "I'm sorry. I love him, but I can't be with him."

"These journals are a pretty true representation of our lives. I've learned all sorts of things about Jean that I didn't know. A man should be smart enough to know his pregnant wife was feeling insecure. I can't believe she ever thought I'd fall out of love with her. As for Mary Beth Langley, well, Mary Beth was the one to be pitied. I tried to take care of Jean. As far as I was concerned, she had never been prettier. Why would she think I was unhappy?"

"Weren't you?"

Sam laid the journal on the table. "Not with her. But I felt trapped. We were kids. I was barely eighteen when Glory was born. Jean had her doubts, too. What was it she said?" Sam thumbed back in the journal and read, " 'Not so young but not so old considering the monumental step of bringing a child into the world.' So true. She was so sure a boy would make me happy."

"I was surprised to learn Great-Grandfather Reynolds died the night before

Mother was born. Mommy Jean was sure the baby would lift his spirits."

"Her grief brought on the labor. I prayed nothing would happen to either of them. She's right about Glory being a beautiful baby. All pink and rosy, with my dark hair and Jean's green eyes." The love was there in his eyes for anyone who looked to see.

"Were you upset because she named Mom Gloria?"

"I hated that name," Sam said. "Still do. I thought Charlotte was a much prettier name. I had no idea she made a vow to her father to name the child after her mother. I wouldn't have objected if I'd known."

"She says you were a good father," Sharley pointed out. "I liked the parts where she described how Mother was all smiles when she was with you."

"I did love your mother, Sharley. My wife and daughter were the only bright spots in my life. I'd go to work, and Father refused to allow any newfangled ideas in his business. I resented him, and the discontent spilled over into my personal life as well. My mother died, and I was devastated. I loved her so much. Father became even more rigid. Mother had a way of convincing him to at least think about things."

"What about the hardware store?"

"Jean was busy at home, and I was at the bank, so I hired a manager. When Glory grew older, Jean started taking over. The business did well, and she was so excited about her success."

"Why didn't you help her?" Sharley asked.

"Jean was an old-fashioned wife. If I had shown an interest in the hardware business, she would have turned over the reins to me. I couldn't take that away from her. I never knew exactly how bad I hurt her," Papa Sam said brokenly. "Listen to this. 'Sam left me today,'" he read. "'He will always be the love of my life, but I'm not ready to traipse around the world and drag our daughter away from the only home she has ever known. I've lived that life, and it is not what I want for my child. For the first time in my life, I feel I am where I should be, and my only wish is that Sam shared that sentiment.'"

The heartbreak in Mommy Jean's written words brought tears to Sharley's eyes. She nodded slowly. "There are other journals where she describes her childhood, how she missed her mother, how hard her father was on her. She found contentment in Samuels. It was her first settled home."

"One parent for her child in a secure setting, or two in an unsettled environment. What a choice," Sam said with a shake of his head. "I remember the day like it was yesterday. Jean described me as distraught. No doubt I was. I wanted to make a loan to an inventor, and my father called me an idiot and ordered me to stop this foolishness. He embarrassed me in front of everyone. I walked out, came home, and ordered Jean to pack our bags. Glory was six, and Jean kept on and on about our wonderful life here in Samuels and Glory's school and friends. She insisted we could work it out. That night, after Jean went to bed, the scene kept playing in my head. I got angry. If she didn't trust me to provide for her and our child, I decided she should stay in Samuels with my father. I wrote her a note and ran like a thief in the night."

He shook his head. "She was right about my pride. Father was sure I would come back, but I was determined to prove him wrong. Like she said, I would have lived on the streets before asking my father for a job."

"But why did you let it go for so long? How could the two of you not communicate when you obviously loved each other?"

"Like you and Kenan?"

"Yes," Sharley snapped. She sighed. "It's different. He's not my husband. And even if things were different, I couldn't marry him. He doesn't have the same commitment to God that I have, after all. In the meantime, I can't talk to him—he tempts me too much."

Sam patted her arm. "Makes you want to throw off the ties and take off for Boston, does he?"

"Not particularly Boston. Just wherever he is."

"Now we're getting somewhere."

Sharley hated his happy grin. "No, we aren't. There's too much at stake. I'm committed to God, yes, but I'm also committed to my life here."

"Try telling your heart that. And make sure you're really listening to God and not putting words in His mouth."

She settled the cup back onto the table. "I have done nothing but pray about this, Papa Sam. I just go around in circles."

"I have good feelings about the two of you."

"You do? Why? I thought you were bothered because he's not a Christian."

"Maybe not yet, but the Lord is using you to work miracles in Kenan's life. I just know it."

"I don't," Sharley said, feeling even more skeptical than before.

He smiled at her sadly. "Even if I wanted to, I can't go back and change my life, Sharley. I distanced myself from everyone who loved me because I thought it was what I had to do. I didn't ask Jean how she felt, and now all these years later, I read how I hurt her. I didn't ask God what He intended either. Obviously part of my plans were good. I've been successful in business, able to help a great number of people get their start—but at what cost to myself? Maybe if I had waited on the Lord, instead of rushing off under my own steam, eventually He would have worked out all our lives so that we could all have been happy. Instead, I nearly lost everything that was important to me."

"Nearly?"

"You haven't finished reading this journal, have you?"

Sharley shook her head.

"Can I ask why you left me this one to read?"

She hesitated, searching for the truth. "So you could see what your leaving did to Mommy Jean and Mother," she said at last.

"I thought so," Sam said softly. "Thank you for the truth. What you haven't read yet will probably shock you. Jean and I shared some wonderful times after I left."

His words confused Sharley. "I don't understand."

"A year passed, and Jean came to see me. She refused to accept that our love had died. She was like a child, guilty one moment, excited the next, but we spent two weeks together. She told her family she was in New York." Sam chuckled heartily. "She made me take her clothes shopping before she left."

No one had ever known that Mommy Jean had visited Boston with Papa Sam. Sharley stared at her grandfather.

"Those visits rejuvenated us both," Sam said. "She took about four long vacations a year. Not just to Boston. We traveled extensively. It wasn't a normal marriage—but it was still a marriage."

"So you didn't need pictures to know how Mommy Jean and Mother looked. I'm sure she kept you current."

"Until her death."

"So you knew about me?"

He nodded. "I knew when your mother married, and I knew she had a baby girl. I had no idea what happened to you after your grandmother's death."

"And you were never tempted to find out?"

"I did find out. When Kenan came to Samuels."

"I don't know what to say," Sharley said. "I told myself I didn't hold it against you, but obviously I did."

"I can only ask you to pray about the situation, Sharley. To try and find it in your heart to forgive an old man who made a bunch of mistakes."

Both of them looked up as Kenan stepped into the kitchen. "What are you two doing up so early?"

They stared at each other. Only then did they realize they had talked the night away.

Chapter 10

Sam and Kenan left on Monday morning, and Sharley found herself tearful as she hugged Sam. "I'm glad you came."

"Me, too, Sharley girl."

"Now that my eyes have been opened, I know that God can use everything that's happened to us. The Bible says that all things work together for good for those who are called according to His purposes, and I see that now. And I thank God for bringing you back to me."

Tears misted the old eyes. "I love you."

She hugged him close. "I love you, too. We're going to spend more time together. I promise."

"I look forward to it."

Sam climbed into the back of the car, and Kenan stood, waiting and watching. "Good-bye, Kenan," Sharley said softly. "It was good seeing you."

"I'm glad you and Sam were able to work things out. Do you think we'll ever be able to do the same?"

"I honestly don't know, Kenan," she admitted. Tears trailed along her cheeks as she forced a watery smile. "I haven't been fair to you, but truth is, I'm afraid of what I'd say or do if we talked. I love you, but I can't go to Boston. In the interest of fairness, I can't ask you to give up your life there to come here."

"What if I said I would?"

"I'd say give yourself some time to think about it. Pray about it. Don't make a decision you'll come to regret later in life. I refuse to be the Sam and Jean of our generation."

"Can I kiss you good-bye?"

She stepped forward and lost herself in his tender embrace. Neither wanted to let go. Sharley felt regret for the lost weekend, time she could have shared with him.

"If I call, will you talk to me?"

"Not until I get everything straight in my head. You'd better go. I think Papa Sam's eager to get home."

"Good luck with the election. I think you'll make a fine coroner."

She pushed back her surprise and squeezed his hand. "I'll do my best. Good-bye." After she broke away, she stood and waved as they drove away.

In her office, Sharley sat and thought about the visit. They had visited the ld home place, Papa Sam saying he understood why she preferred her house to hat one. He teased her about nothing in the town being any different than he remembered from his youth. On Sunday morning, he and Kenan accompanied her o church. In the classroom, Sharley got her first glimpse of the type of father Papa am would have been, the great-grandfather he still could be, as he entertained the nall children with Bible stories.

Pastor George's sermon stomped on their toes as he preached on forgiving and orgetting. One verse opened her eyes, 1 John 4:20, "If anyone says, 'I love God,' yet ates his brother, he is a liar. For anyone who does not love his brother, whom he as seen, cannot love God, whom he has not seen."

Hate seemed a strong word, but Sharley knew she had lied to herself for o many years, pretending her grandfather's abandonment didn't matter. Her method of dealing with it had been to ignore, not forget and forgive. Sharley sked Sam to join her at the altar, and together they prayed that God would ouch their hearts and help them to share the rest of their lives in a spirit of love nd family.

Now Jack stepped into the office. "Hi, Sharley. Mr. Sam get off okay?" At her od, he asked, "How did it go? You two enjoy your visit?"

"You were right, Jack. Family is important. Once you get beyond the petty stuff, ou realize that even more."

"Mr. Sam seems to be a good man, but then I already knew that. I've had e pleasure of knowing his daughter and granddaughter, and they do any man oud."

"Thanks, Jack."

❧

he rest of the week was hectic. Sharley was still intent on her campaigning, spend-g days and evenings contacting the county residents.

One morning before work she found the time to finish reading the journal and t even more amazed that her grandparents had carried on a secret relationship for many years. She didn't pretend to understand why they chose to keep it secret. arley doubted Sam could tell her the reason. In her heart, she felt certain the two them had been in love but unsure how to handle the situation. Together they had it go on until too late. Because Mommy Jean never confided the truth to her ughter, her mother had never bonded with her father.

Sharley shook her head at the thought. *Such a loss. In life, no one is more impor-t than family.* Even as she thought the words, Sharley felt a sense of something ne wrong, but the feeling soon passed.

The phone rang, and she reluctantly marked her place and closed the jour- before lifting the cordless to her ear. "Sorry to bother you, Sharley, but the mmonses and Williamsons are here to make arrangements."

"John and Leslie? Jim and Allison? What arrangements?"

"Their boys. You didn't hear?"

"Hear what?" She hadn't read the paper or turned on the television for days.

"The boys went joyriding last night. There was an accident involving drinkin and a high-speed chase. Jeff and Lynn were killed."

Sharley found herself at a total loss for words. "I'll be right there."

As she dressed, she prayed God would give her the right words of reassur ance for these parents deprived of their loved ones by such senseless acts of utte stupidity.

She arrived at her office to find two teary mothers and two fathers who we: intent on being strong for their wives. They went through the process on automati making decisions none of them had ever expected to make in their lifetimes. Bot boys were football stars, and the high school had offered the use of the auditoriu. The joint funerals were scheduled for Wednesday at one in the afternoon.

Sharley hugged Allison and then Leslie, and said, "I'm so sorry. If we can be . service to you in any way, please let me know."

Leslie Timmons dug in her purse and pulled out a photo. "This was my beaut ful boy," she sobbed as she placed it in Sharley's hand. "Please give him back to n for the funeral." Tears streamed down her face. "I don't think I could stand it if l didn't look like himself."

The grief-filled words presented a daunting challenge. From what Devl had told her when she arrived, Sharley knew this young man had been throw from the vehicle upon impact. She breathed a prayer and nodded. "I'll do ever thing possible."

The woman gave a feeble smile and said, "You'll do a good job. You always dc

"My husband is going to talk to the coach about his team members servi: as pallbearers," Allison said softly. "We'll drop off his letter jacket later today.'

After they left, Sharley went into the back and started her job. Tears stream down Sharley's face as she worked. The waste of such young lives tore at h heart. Temptation stronger than they could defeat had been their downfall.

"You okay, Sharley?" Jack asked.

"No. I need a few minutes to pull myself together."

"Go ahead. I'll take care of this."

In the employee bathroom, Sharley allowed the tears to fall freely. "They're Your hands, God. Keep them and be with those they left behind."

Left behind. How apt a description for those left to face the loss. Sharley wo dered how big a part her own desolation played in her grief for these two childr She felt abandoned, left behind because she couldn't be the woman Kenan wan her to be and he couldn't be the man she needed him to be.

Chapter 11

What's wrong with you? You've been moping around this office for days."
Kenan looked up at his boss, wondering why Marie hadn't warned
him of Sam's arrival. Probably because she hadn't had time. Sam had a
way of popping up when he was least expected. And right now Kenan wasn't too
sure he wanted to answer any questions. He wasn't sure he could for that matter.

"I'm not moping."

"Hmmph." Sam rolled his eyes and settled into a chair before the desk. "You
might as well get it off your chest."

Kenan glared at him. "Your granddaughter is a royal pain."

"Tell me something I don't already know. I talked with her yesterday. I'd say
she's suffering from the same malady as you."

"She's miserable, too?" He leaned forward, eager to hear what Sam had to say.

"Not that she'd admit it, but it sure sounded that way to me."

"This mess is all your fault," Kenan complained. "If you hadn't sent me to
handle your business, I'd never have met up with Sharley Montgomery and my life
would have been a lot simpler."

"Oh, you'd have met her sooner or later. I think God had a plan all along for
you to meet."

Kenan thought about that for a moment, then shrugged. "I don't know what
else I can do. She's made up her mind and says it's in God's hands. What kind of
answer is that?"

"A Christian's life is always in the Father's hands, Kenan. If you can't understand that much, you don't deserve Sharley."

"Oh, I understand, and I'm not saying there's anything wrong with her beliefs.
I just don't understand this stuff about harnesses or whatever it is. Did I tell you her
pastor cornered me at the dessert table at the church social? I think he was trying
to feel me out."

Sam guffawed with laughter. "It's yokes, Kenan, not harnesses. Tell me, how
would you deal with Charlotte's religion if you were her husband?"

"Things haven't advanced that far," Kenan protested uncomfortably.

"Do you love her? Are you considering you might like to have her in your life?"
Kenan's reluctant nod, he added, "Then you're contemplating marriage. And I
don't have you playing fast and loose with my granddaughter."

"This is between Sharley and me, Sam," Kenan said, a hint of warning in his

347

voice. "We discussed your role in the matter when I first traveled to Samuels, an
Sharley says you have nothing to do with our decisions. I have to agree."

"I have the right of an old man who loves both of you."

"I'll concede to that." Kenan rubbed his eyes. They were on fire from lack c
sleep. Every night he went to bed, hoping he'd exhausted himself with a strenuou
workout, and every night he spent half the night thinking about the situation wit
Sharley and wondering what he could do to make things right. "I would accept he
religion," he admitted with a sigh. "In fact, whatever happens between her and m
I think I already have accepted her religion."

The old man gave him a keen-eyed glance. "What do you mean by that?"

"I—" Kenan hesitated. "Well, there's nothing wrong with going to church.
she and I were together, I'd go to church with her and see to it that our childre
were in church as well."

"You wouldn't send them like your mother sent you?"

He shook his head. "I wouldn't expect them to have a faith I didn't sha
Maybe that's why my belief in Christ never amounted to much, because I w
too influenced by my parents' example. I did go to church as a child and even son
as a teen, but they never went with me. I sort of dropped out of church after I g
back from Nam. Christ didn't seem very real to me."

"You stopped seeking the Lord when you needed Him the most," Sam pr
nounced sadly. "He could have provided you with answers if you'd been willir
to open your heart and listen."

"I did listen, and I didn't like the answers I was getting. It was all so sensele
I hated that part of my life. I only wanted to be left alone."

"I don't believe you did. I think you wanted to understand the senseless killir
And you felt a little guilty that you didn't die with the others."

Kenan had a sinking feeling Sam was right on target. He had certainly be
unable to settle in any one place for a number of years. Then the nightmares h
begun to recede slightly, and he was able to get on with his life. But an emotic
wound had been left behind, always there no matter how well he hid it.

"What does it matter?" He sighed. "Even if we could work out the religi
thing, I'd have to move to Samuels. Heaven only knows what's there for me
terms of work."

"I hope you're planning to give me sufficient notice?" The old man gave h
a roguish grin.

"For what?" Exasperated, Kenan rolled his eyes. "That stubborn Sharley wc
give me the time of day. She wants to be friends. Friends," he spat. "What m
wants to be friends with the woman he loves?"

"Oh, I don't know. Seems to me not so long ago you were offering Jocelyn m
riage based on friendship. At least she had the good sense to refuse you. Let me
you something you don't know, Kenan. There are two things you'll find in any gr

marriage—one is God in the home, and the other is friendship. Love grows from friendship. Many a man and woman have married their best friend."

"So you think I should be Sharley's friend?"

"I think you should get your life in order. You have to get right with Jesus Christ. And then you have to decide if you're willing to give up Boston. If you can't, don't tease her with the possibility of a future. It's not fair to either of you."

Kenan lifted his shoulders. "No. You probably noticed how she wouldn't give me the time of day when we were in Samuels. I haven't felt so desolate since I was in Nam. I don't know what to do."

"Have you considered prayer? For the right reasons, I mean? Not because you want to be with Sharley but because you believe God died for your sins and because you want to know His master plan for you?"

"I have been praying, Sam." He looked embarrassed, and the gray eyebrows across the desk shifted a degree higher. "I've been praying pretty much along the lines you just said. Whatever happens with Sharley, I know now that I need God in my life. I need Him to be more than an idea that I think about now and then. I want the kind of living relationship with Him that I see in you and Sharley." He shoved his fingers through his hair. "Oh, I know neither one of you is perfect, and you both make mistakes. But you have something with God that I now know I need." He sighed. "I guess I might as well confess what I've been thinking lately. I am a Christian, Sam."

Sam's eyebrows shot higher than Kenan had ever seen them. "Why didn't you tell Sharley? Me?"

"Because I guess I've been embarrassed. I'm not sure I can ever be the Christian either of you are. I feel as though I don't deserve to claim my salvation."

"Few of us do," Sam pointed out. "But you believe. That's a first step."

Kenan could sense the man's excitement. "I'd have told you before if I knew it meant that much to you."

"I've been after you for years. I can't believe you didn't say anything before."

Kenan shrugged. "I've turned my back on God for so long I'm not even sure He's willing to let me back into the flock."

"Remember the parable of the good shepherd? To Christ you are more precious than anything else. You know, I think I'll rest easier tonight now that you've shared this." He leaned forward and met Kenan's eyes. "Get your life straight, Kenan. When I go to heaven, I want to do so knowing I'll see you again."

Kenan smiled at that. "I'd hate to think I'd never see you again either," he whispered after Sam had gone.

Sam's words played around in Kenan's head, pulling his concentration away from the piles of work on his desktop. Finally he gave up and began to pray.

Sharley had remained firm in her resolve to keep her distance from him. What an effective witness she was. So many people would put their own needs and desires before service to God. Not his Sharley. She was right. Their relationship was in the Lord's hands. Just as it should be.

Repent. Well, he'd already done that. Now he bowed his head, and at last he felt the acceptance of Jesus' loving arms. Then he reached for the phone. He wanted to make an appointment with the pastor to discuss this new commitment to God that he'd made.

Before he could place the call, the door was flung open and a hysterical Marie cried, "It's Sam. He's in trouble."

He sprang to his feet and raced across the hallway. "Sam?"

The man was obviously in agony. Kenan began loosening Sam's tie. "Sam, what's happening? Is it your heart? Where's your medicine?"

Kenan patted Sam's pockets in search of his nitro. How many times had he warned him? "Call 911. Get his nitroglycerin. In the desk drawer." Kenan had never seen Sam's efficient secretary so flustered. She seemed incapable of movement. "Now!" he yelled.

Sam's grasp on his arm was feeble as he said. "It's too late, Kenan," he gasped. "Remember what I said. I love you, son. Tell Sharley I love her too. And tell her what you just told me."

"Sam. Noo!"

❧

"Sharley?" Devlin called her name softly as he tapped on the door. "You have a call. I tried to take a message, but he says it's extremely urgent."

She grabbed a fresh tissue and dabbed at her eyes. It was probably one of the boys' fathers calling with another request. "Tell him I'll be right there." She went to her office and picked up the phone.

"Sharley?"

"Kenan," she groaned upon recognizing his voice. "I can't do this right now."

"Sharley, are you okay? Have you been crying?"

"No, I'm not okay. My life is miserable, and I think we both know why."

"And I'm about to add to that," he muttered.

"What? If you have something to say, just say it."

Still he hesitated, and Sharley felt tempted to thrust the receiver back into the cradle and run until she couldn't run anymore. Quickly she offered up a prayer for strength.

"Sharley," he said at last, his voice gentle, "Sam died about thirty minutes ago."

She froze. Sam couldn't be dead. She hadn't had a chance to visit him again, to share her life with him. "No," she gasped.

"Sharley?" The frightened tone of his voice told her how much he cared for her. "Sharley, honey, are you okay? Say something. Please."

"How?" The question was the only word she could croak past the growing lump in her throat.

"Heart attack. He had just left my office. Sam was gone before the ambulance arrived. I was with him when he died."

She felt herself wavering on her emotional tightrope. "I'm glad he wasn't alone." Silence stretched between them. The tears returned, chasing each other down her cheeks.

"If I'd just been able to get him his medicine sooner," Kenan murmured.

His distress was so obvious, his words choked. The need to comfort him overwhelmed Sharley. She knew he loved Sam, and his connection to the old man was stronger than hers. "Don't blame yourself. You did all you could."

"He had just finished telling me he wanted to see me again in heaven."

Sharley managed a teary smile. "So do I."

"You will."

Had she imagined the words? "Kenan, are you okay?"

"What can I do to help?" he asked, ignoring her question. "Would you like for me to arrange for extra cars for the procession?"

"I'm sorry. What?"

"Extra cars. There's going to be a number of people flying in for the funeral. They'll need transportation from the airport."

"Of course," she said, recalling the job she had to do. "What about services? Papa Sam requested a memorial service in Boston. He gave me a list of the people he wanted at the graveside services here."

"It's all being kept very private. The office is not releasing any information to the press."

"I'll caution my guys to keep it quiet as well. And I'll arrange for limos to pick everyone up at the airport."

"Sharley, will you come to Boston for the memorial service?"

"When is it?"

"Thursday morning."

"I've got two funerals on Wednesday. I'll get a flight out just as soon as possible."

"I can send the company jet."

Sharley almost refused and then realized she didn't want to. "That'll be fine. I'll let your secretary know the exact time just as soon as everything is finalized."

"There's the matter of the business. I'm going to have my hands full."

"The suddenness must have. . ." Sharley felt choked by the words.

"Sam had set certain safeguards in place to assure nothing interfered with business."

They both fell silent, as grief washed over them in a deep tide. Then Sharley said, "I'm going to bury him beside Mommy Jean. I'll have a new grave marker cut."

"Nice thing to do for old Triple S."

A weak smile touched her lips. "Did he tell you that he and Mommy Jean saw each other regularly after he left Samuels?"

"You're kidding."

"According to her journals, they stayed in touch by letter and then got together several times a year for vacations. She loved him, you know. I hope he knew I loved him, too."

"He does. The last thing he said was to tell you he loved you. I like to think he's reunited in heaven with your grandmother and mom and all the people from Samuels."

"You think maybe they finally found a place where they can live happily ever after?" she asked, a wistfulness filling her voice.

"I'm sure of it. Sharley, will you call me if you need me?"

The silence stretched over the distance, and she knew that he waited for an answer. Now was a time for leaning if ever there was one, and God would want her to share her grief with this man Sam had loved.

"I need you now," she admitted. "Talk to me, Kenan."

"Sharley, honey, I'm so sorry. I don't know what to say."

"You don't have to say anything in particular. I know you loved Sam and he loved you. I talked to him yesterday, and he voiced his concern about our unhappiness."

The conversation stretched on and on, neither wanting to say good-bye. There was consolation in sharing.

"I've got to go," Sharley said finally. "There's a lot to be done before I can get there on Thursday. I'll contact a funeral home there in Boston to handle the embalming for me. If you don't mind, how about contacting his pastor and making arrangements for the memorial service? Did he leave any last-minute requests?"

"Nothing other than he be buried in Samuels in the family plot."

Tears flooded down her face. "Oh, Kenan, he wanted to come home."

Chapter 12

Kenan found himself watching everything Sharley did and feeling impressed and proud of the way she carried out every detail of Sam's burial. Now, though, the graveside service was over, and her professionalism was beginning to crack around the edges. His heart broke as he watched her dabbing her eyes with a handkerchief. If only she would allow him to hold her, to comfort her.

"I'm sorry, Sharley."

"Me, too." She sniffed and turned to make her way to the family car.

"Sharley, please," Kenan said, catching her arm. "I know I said a lot of things the last time we were together. But so much has changed. I've missed you."

"I know, Kenan. Can we discuss this later?"

"Okay, so I was stubborn."

"You were waiting for me to throw in the towel and come running to you. I thought about it a time or two, but nothing has changed. I still have my business, and I'm still running for coroner."

"Good. How's the election looking?" The uncertainty in her expression proved he had garnered her attention.

"Pretty good, I think."

"I'm sure you'll be victorious. I'm sorry this had to happen right now. I know it's not a good time."

"There's never a good time to lose someone you love, is there, Kenan?"

"No. Sharley, I have to fly Sam's friends back to Boston. We'll be leaving in an hour."

She nodded. "I'm serving refreshments at the house if you'd care to stop by. I've invited the others already."

"That was nice of you."

She shrugged. "I figured somebody should do something. He was my grandfather. I'll miss him."

"I'm sorry the two of you didn't get an opportunity to meet earlier," Kenan said.

"Me, too."

"Sounds as though you've forgiven him."

She nodded and blinked away her tears. "I'm so glad God gave us the chance to work things through the last time I saw him."

"You know he left a will. His attorney wants a few words with us."

She sighed. "I hope you're his beneficiary. I've got just about everything I need right here."

"Everything?" Kenan asked softly. *Tell me*, his heart cried. *Tell me I mean as much to you as you do to me.*

She looked away. "I've got to finish things here and get over to the house, Kenan."

She had invited the entire town, Kenan realized as he recognized a few faces from his time spent in Samuels. He was amazed that they remembered him, and all took time to thank him for being there in Sharley's time of need.

"Good to see you again, Kenan," Pastor George said as he took the seat beside him.

"You, too, Pastor."

"Sharley seems to be holding up well."

Kenan glanced at him. "I'm afraid she's more upset than she's letting on. She won't let me help."

"What happened between the two of you?"

The need to confide in the man was suddenly overwhelming. "Is there somewhere private we can talk?"

"I'm sure Sharley wouldn't mind if we went out on the patio."

Kenan found that once he opened up, the words poured freely. He told Pastor George about his time in Vietnam and about his recent commitment to Christ. The man said very little, only nodded his head now and then.

"Would you like me to pray with you, Kenan?"

"I'd be honored, Pastor George."

"I have one other question I need answered first. Are you making your commitment to Jesus because of Sharley and Sam?"

Kenan knew there was only one honest answer. "Probably, but not for the reason you think. I love them both, and I do want to be with them in heaven—but because of what I saw in their lives, I finally understand I need God in my own life, now more than ever. I've been lost for a long time. There are longings inside me that places and people can't fill. When I was a child we sang of the friend we have in Jesus. I want that friendship now. More than ever."

Pastor George grasped Kenan's hand in his. "Then let's pray."

All the burdens seemed to lift up and drift away as Kenan listened to the man's words.

Sharley wondered where Kenan had gotten to. Papa Sam's attorney had approached her a few minutes before and requested a private meeting before they left for Boston. She told him she would find Kenan.

She stepped out onto the patio and hesitated. Kenan and Pastor George were in prayer. Hopes that had been dashed suddenly seemed to skyrocket joyously.

Sharley forced them back for fear that she was wrong.

Pastor George was the first to spot her and glanced at Kenan. Kenan nodded his head, and the pastor summoned her into their little group.

"I thought you might like to know Kenan has recently made a commitment to God."

She flung her arms about Kenan's neck, happy that he enfolded her in his tender arms and held her near. "Oh, Kenan, this is so wonderful."

Neither of them were aware when Pastor George quietly went inside the house. "You might want to give them a few minutes," he told Sam's lawyer when the man came to stand in the doorway.

The lawyer pulled two letters from inside his coat. "I'll just give them these, and we can talk later."

Sharley and Kenan looked up at the man. "I'm sorry to disturb you, but Sam asked that you read these carefully and consider what he has to say."

"Thank you, Mr. Glenn. We'll be in to see you shortly. Read your letter, Kenan. Let's see what Papa Sam has to say."

They settled into the glider, each intent on this last communication from the man they had loved.

Kenan,

You're the son I never had. It's been a true pleasure teaching you the ropes and watching you grow from the shell of a man who first came into my company. Now, only because I don't want that shell to return, I make this suggestion to you. Open a second branch of the business in Samuels. You've been at odds with the situation between you and Sharley for a while now, and the time has come to pursue your happiness. If you can't get the girl out of Samuels, turn the town into a place where you'd want to live and stay there with her. She's worth the battle. It's about time I did something decent for the town and my family. I'd like to think I could do that through you—but most importantly of all, I want you to do something for yourself. God can give you the peace you need, if you will only open your heart and let Him in. I'm hoping to see you again in heaven.

Kenan blinked furiously and reached for Sharley's hand. She squeezed it and picked up her own letter.

Well, Sharley, it's happened. A force much greater than the two of us has separated us again. Like you, death carries no worries for me. As the years passed and the body weakened, so has my desire to remain on this earth. I've looked forward to my heavenly journey for so long. You have been a bright shining star in these last days, and I can say I've been wonderfully rewarded to leave someone like you behind to carry on. You made me realize what I gave up by leaving Glory behind, and though I know I have God's forgiveness in the matter, I pray that one day you, too, can forgive an old man for his stubborn pride.

Tears streamed unchecked down her face for several minutes, and Kenan placed an arm about her shoulder to comfort her. She wiped her eyes and picked up the letter again.

I know Samuels is the home of your heart, and I will not ask you to relocate to Boston. The business there pretty much runs itself these days, but if you prefer, you may sell your inheritance and invest the proceeds in Samuels. I'm leaving this to your discretion. Kenan and I have discussed your concerns for the town, and hopefully it's not too late to revitalize and renew.

As for Kenan, I don't know if the two of you can leap beyond the differences, but the world will be richer for your love if you do. You've helped him remember that while death may be an ending here on earth, it's a beginning in heaven. Whatever you decide, live in joy and peace and know that you've always been much loved by the one you called Papa Sam.

Sharley dropped the pages into her lap. "Oh, Kenan." She turned to face him, amazement in her eyes.

He smiled. "I've got a long way to go before I'll be the man I want to be for you, but now that Sam's prodding," he said, waving the letter, "has boosted my courage, I want to ask if you would consider marrying me one day. You don't have to answer now."

Her eyes shone. "Yes, I do. The Lord has opened my eyes to a lot of things here today. He's shown me that you are indeed the man He chose for me, and He's taught me about forgiveness, particularly for those you love. Papa Sam may never know how much I love him, but it's my intention to make you very aware of how much you're loved. And Kenan, there's something else. I won't insist that we live in Samuels. I may have to travel back and forth frequently, but I'll go to Boston with you."

Kenan hugged her close. "Oh, Sharley darling, thank you for loving me. I've never been so miserable as I was when you sent me away."

She smiled at him. "But you didn't give up. The faxes and the e-mail references were pretty good."

"Liked those, did you?"

"I'm sorry I led you on and then ran away when things weren't going exactly like I thought they should. I should have trusted God to make them right."

He brushed her face with his fingers. "I won't ask you to leave Samuels. There's nothing in Boston for me, now that I've learned belonging with someone takes precedence over a lot of things."

"Belonging?"

"Wanting to be in a place because all the ties in the world make it the most important place in the world for you to be."

Sharley nodded. "Oh, Kenan, I can't wait to marry you. And you know what the best thing of all is?"

"Um, what?" Kenan asked after kissing her.

"We won't have to argue over whether I take your name. I'll already have it."

"But you would agree to take it formally?"

"I won't go through the rest of my life as Charlotte Montgomery Montgomery, if that's what you mean. As far as the world is concerned, I'll be your wife and the mother of the children who also bear your name. But you allowing me to be myself, well, that's the most precious gift you're giving me. Are you sure you'll be able to give up the big city for this?"

"All the excitement in the world doesn't compare to the joy of being here with you. Besides, Boston wouldn't be the same without Sam."

They fell silent for a few moments as both considered their loss. Sharley's time with the elderly man she had come to love had been too short. Kenan owed him his life, for it had been Sam who helped him fight off the nightmare of Vietnam. And it had been Sam who had led him to find the true love of his life.

"I think maybe he knew his days were numbered," Kenan mused. "Sam kept asking when I was going to get my head screwed on right. Said he wanted to see me again in heaven and that you were too much of a woman to lose because of some old fears. I was holding his hand when he died. And you know, for the first time, death didn't seem like such a frightening, terrible thing."

She met his eyes. "I know how much my business has freaked you out. Are you really going to be able to handle that?"

He nodded, his gaze filled with love. "Even knowing you'll always have the business doesn't make me want to run the other way."

"And if you get caught in the backlash of some of our jokes?"

He grinned. "I'll have a few of my own."

Sharley smiled as Kenan wrapped her in his loving embrace. Their lips met, sealing the commitment of forever. Not even the darkness of her career could dim their bright future.

Epilogue

H appy anniversary, my love."

Sharley twisted in the hammock and looked at her husband's face. "Nineteen years. Who would have thought it?"

"God," Kenan supplied with a broad grin. "He certainly knew me better than I knew myself. He knew I needed you to lead me back to Him. I'm so glad you came into my life."

The intervening years had been good to them. God had seen fit to make them the parents of two beautiful children—one not-so-somber daughter and a son who had inherited his father's love of flying.

"So how do you feel about Samantha's career choice?"

Kenan knew she was thinking of the vow he'd uttered so many years ago, before he understood he needed her in his life; he would never have suspected that one day he might accept the fact that his daughter wanted to be a funeral director. He smiled. "I think if it's what she wants, it's what she should do."

Sharley grimaced in good humor. "That certainly ranks up there with every evasive answer you've ever given me."

He laughed. "Sharley darling, you know I was never certain I wanted my children to take over your business."

"But dealing with me and my business has become easier over the years, hasn't it?"

"You've made it easy," Kenan said. The hammock rocked with the breezes of late spring that stirred the sweet scent of flowers about them. "You've even made death come alive for me." Sharley looked puzzled by his strange comment. "Your love has shown me that morticians are people to be admired. Your caring has helped relieve the suffering of so many people over the years. I've seen the faces of the bereaved, and now I understand their pleasure at doing this one last right thing for their loved ones. You've helped me understand that death is just a part of life. In fact, I see now that it's the door that leads from this life into a fuller, richer life. And when the day comes that God sees fit to separate us, I'll know my life has been enriched by having you in it. Our children will carry on what we are and for that I'm eternally grateful."

"Mom? Dad?"

Kenan called an answer to their daughter. He looked at her with pride as she crossed the lawn. She was the young version of Sharley all over again, beautiful, full of life.

Sammy was waving a letter. "It came. I've been accepted."

Sharley almost tumbled them out of the hammock as she sat up. She glanced back at Kenan, and he winked, his lined face curving into a deep smile.

"Oh no, not another gravedigger," he teased.

"Ah, Daddy," Sammy groaned, and their laughter filled the air.

A Letter to Our Readers

Dear Readers:

In order that we might better contribute to your reading enjoyment, we would appreciate your taking a few minutes to respond to the following questions. When completed, please return to the following: Fiction Editor, Barbour Publishing, Inc., P.O. Box 719, Uhrichsville, OH 44683.

1. Did you enjoy reading *North Carolina* by Terry Fowler?
   ❏ Very much—I would like to see more books like this.
   ❏ Moderately—I would have enjoyed it more if _____
   _____
   _____

2. What influenced your decision to purchase this book?
   (Check those that apply.)
   ❏ Cover   ❏ Back cover copy   ❏ Title   ❏ Price
   ❏ Friends   ❏ Publicity   ❏ Other

3. Which story was your favorite?
   ❏ *Carolina Pride*   ❏ *A Sense of Belonging*
   ❏ *Look to the Heart*

4. Please check your age range:
   ❏ Under 18   ❏ 18–24   ❏ 25–34
   ❏ 35–45   ❏ 46–55   ❏ Over 55

5. How many hours per week do you read? _____

Name _____

Occupation _____

Address _____

City_____ State_____ Zip_____

E-mail_____

If you enjoyed

North Carolina

then read:

MISSOURI

Variety Is the Spice of
Four Romances in the
Show-Me State

A Living Soul by Hannah Alexander
Timing Is Everything by Tracey V. Bateman
Faith Came Late by Freda Chrisman
Ice Castle by Joyce Livingston

If you enjoyed
North Carolina
then read:

WASHINGTON

Small Town Romance

in Four Distinct Novels

The Neighborly Thing by Wanda E. Brunstetter
Talking for Two by Wanda E. Brunstetter
Race for the Roses by Lauraine Snelling
Song of Laughter by Lauraine Snelling